playing LADY GAGA
being NAN PAU

playing LADY GAGA

being NAN PAU

STEVE TOLBERT

[Lacuna]
2017

Published in 2017 by Lacuna in Armidale, New South Wales, Australia
http://www.lacunapublishing.com

Lacuna is an imprint of Golden Orb Creative
PO Box 428, Armidale, NSW 2350, Australia
http://www.goldenorbcreative.com

Cover design by Golden Orb Creative
Cover photograph © Warrengoldswain | Dreamstime.com

Text design and production by Golden Orb Creative
Typeset in 11.5/14.5pt Minion Pro

National Library of Australia Cataloguing-in-Publication entry:

Tolbert, Steve, author.

Playing Lady Gaga, being Nan Pau / Steve Tolbert.

ISBN: 9781922198280 (paperback)
ISBN: 9781922198297 (ebook)

Subjects: Rangoon (Burma)—Politics and government—Fiction.
Rangoon (Burma)—Fiction. Thailand—Fiction.

For Sue and Elise

The Burmese say if a man has no education he becomes a soldier. If he has no brains he joins the police. If he has no luck he goes into a monastery ... There are many monks in Burma.

from Rory Maclean's *Under the Dragon* (HarperCollins, London, 1998), page 218.

Prologue

Back from a distant place in her mind, full of family and friends. The prattle of motor scooters outside, Pink's 'Bad Bad Day' coming up through the floorboards, on the end of her bed the dark figure of a man preparing to leave.

'Try each day to smile. It is good medicine.' If you saw me now, dear abbot, you'd understand how difficult that is.

She looked across the room at her low table, its candlelight glow. White lotus flowers in a small vase on one side of her small Buddha, burning incense sticks on the other. The incense was strong, stronger than the man's alcohol breath. She inhaled the incense deeply through her nostrils while staring at the flowers, until the man left, leaving her with twenty-five minutes to do what she pleased. 'Thank you,' she muttered. She meant it. At this hour of night, time alone was a gift.

She got out her English dictionary, a pen and writing pad from under the bed and set about composing a haiku, adapting something the big-nose westerner had shouted out as they came up the stairs together. She wrote:

> The best of Thai life –
> A monastery by day,
> The Snake Skin by night.

Had he stayed she would have asked him which monastery he'd visited that day because she suspected he hadn't visited any. She stood, put on her lilac robe and went out along the corridor to the bathroom.

Ten minutes later she returned showered and dried and perfumed, mascara brushed through her eyelashes, her blue body-paint tears and lightning bolt, silver eyeshadow and gash-red lipstick all back in place, her white wig brushed free of tangles. She lay back down on her bed listening to Pink's 'Sober', then to laughter and screeching from the room above, soon drowned out by the rumble and roar of a passing truck.

The nightmare of her recent past, not a good place to revisit. Despite the noise – as familiar as her own heartbeat – her mind went back there anyway. The same faces as always formed, their voices rising and falling: her own, Thant's, the old nun's, the abbot's, Mister MI's and others' from that day, and every day and night since.

Part One

_____

I

A YEAR EARLIER. YANGON, MYANMAR.

Mya Paw Wah and her brother – Thant first of course – stepped off the bus and looked down the road, black exhaust sticking like cobwebs to their skin. The slap of bare feet on the pavement turned their heads. Four monks passed carrying their begging bowls upside down. One limped, wore an eye patch and had a jagged scar running across his nose and cheek. He looked over at Thant and smiled, baring broken and missing teeth.

Damn, thought Mya. Why did monk whoever-he-was have to hobble past now? And if he had no choice, why couldn't he at least have kept his face turned away?

'Khoo Tone,' Thant said in a low voice. 'We used to play football together. Two years ago he scored three goals for us in our regional final, the winning one in the final minute.'

Mya glared at Thant, knowing exactly what he was thinking. 'What happened, did he run into a goal post?'

He ignored her, continuing to watch the monks. 'Do you know why they're carrying their bowls that way?'

The topic of troubled monks was *not* what Mya wanted to talk about, especially now. 'They're not hungry, I guess. Come on, let's go or I'll be late for school.'

Thant stayed put, irked by his sister's indifference. 'To show they'll accept nothing from the police or military. Khoo Tone didn't get his face broken on the football pitch. It happened in a police interrogation cell. If monks aren't safe in Myanmar, what chance do the rest of us have for better lives?'

There was another way to end this. 'So was he in last year's protest march too?'

Thant eyed the broken footpath like hearing her words was painful. 'Go to school, Mya. You know you love it there.' He strode off past fortune-teller stands and umbrella-shaded fry stalls towards the great mass of red-robed monks and their supporters gathering outside Sule Pagoda, from today the most dangerous place in Myanmar to be. Police trucks had come in the night, their mounted megaphones screeching out warnings about defying curfew restrictions, about joining the recent outbreak of protest marches. And just half an hour earlier their mother had repeated those warnings before waving them off to school and work.

Well Mya wasn't going to school. Not until Thant was inside the Trader Hotel donning his doorman clothes. She chased after him, seized his arm and pulled him around. 'Don't be so stupid, Thant! If what happened to Khoo Tone and our own father aren't enough to keep you from joining the protest, think of Hla Hla Win. Remember her? Sentenced to twenty years in prison just for interviewing pro-testing monks. And you're planning to march with them. You know what'll happen. You know, you know, you know!'

'There are times,' he replied, his voice dripping with insincerity, 'when your perfect face takes on the serene beauty of a temple paint-ing, and other times, like now, when it resembles the face of a naga serpent about to attack.' His fake smile was meant to soothe her, his words to make her laugh.

No chance. She wasn't his slavish little sister any more, auditioning for his approval, responding all wide-eyed and expectant to his every wish, believing every word he said. She knew his tactics now, how manipulative he could be. 'Look at me, Thant.' Mya spoke very slowly. 'My face has nothing to do with what we're talking about. This does. Only when you go to work do I go to school. Understand?'

He prised her hand from his arm without commenting on her long, delicate fingers. 'I want to meet a friend at Sule Pagoda. It won't take long.'

Finally, a straight answer out of him. She shook her head. 'If you go down there you'll get caught up in the protest march and probably be thrown in prison and we'll never see you again.'

He glanced up the footpath. His eyes sharpened. 'MI coming,' he muttered, his face suddenly tense. 'Talk to the footpath.' He raised his voice to performance level. 'You know what we forgot to buy at the market?'

Mya looked around. True, a Military Intelligence agent *was* coming, his mirror sunglasses turned their way. 'What?'

'Cooking oil.'

Mister MI slowed, lingering. Despite his closeness, this was better, the two of them working together instead of bickering.

'You're right. How could we have forgotten that?' Mya considered putting on one of Thant's fake smiles and waving to Mister MI, maybe even saying 'Hello' just to show she wasn't intimidated by him, though she was. But when she turned his way he was staring down the road in the other direction.

'So do we go back and get it?'

'I think we'll have to.'

As Mister MI moved on, Thant's mood darkened. 'Life's good when you're them.'

They watched Mister MI quicken his pace then slow again behind Khoo Tone and his monk friends, one with a mobile phone pressed to his ear.

'Did I mention the words "cooking oil"?' Thant asked.

Mya sighed, knowing what was coming next.

'Not unless we steal it. "Welcome to Myanmar, the Golden Land" is how that big billboard near the airport greets international tourists. It's easier to buy drugs in this golden land of ours than the essentials we need.'

He looked around for more agents before his eyes settled back on Mya. 'Though it's a golden land for our generals. What happens to people when they put on officers' uniforms, self-awarded medals covering their puffed-out chests? What part of themselves do they turn off while the rest of the population goes hungry? So the question is, Mya, how much injustice are we, the other ninety per cent of the population, prepared to live with?'

'Just go to work, Thant – please.'

'Soon we won't need to take bags to the market. Our pockets will be enough to carry what we have the money to buy. Sawdust and fish paste. "Believe nothing unless you hear it from us." That's what the generals tell the people, as if we're too stupid to think for ourselves. Myanmar's a prison, Mya, the police and military our guards.'

She glanced up the footpath, fearful of people listening. 'Ssshhh.'

'Yes, exactly. Ssshhh.' He didn't bother to lower his voice. 'Ssshhh. Everyone is listening. Ssshhh. We're all so dead-scared of going to prison we see informers and spies everywhere. Ssshhh. Like "In the Quiet Land of Burma".'

'I know you like to recite that poem as passionately as our father once did,' Mya said, 'but you always forget the lines about the soldiers coming. And the soldiers did come, didn't they, Thant? And they did carry our father away. Why – why do you think that happened?'

Instead of answering, Thant turned in the direction of the pagoda. 'Look at them down there. The city's monks and students on strike, Khoo Tone included. They're our courage. They're our hope. All of Myanmar should follow their lead. Anger solves nothing on its own. It's got to be channelled into mass protests that give us a voice – a voice that tells the world we're still here; the generals are still raping the country. And the bigger the protests, the likelier the outside world will listen and the likelier things will improve.' His voice quickened. 'The power of the powerless, Mya: people realising they can change things simply by working together. Besides, I'm my father's son. Given the choice, you know where he would be right now.'

And for a few moments, there she was – a little girl in the market place being hoisted up on her father's shoulders, so high, so look-where-I-am-everybody excited, leaning forward, locking her arms around his face, using his eye sockets as finger-holds.

'If he was out of prison, or a labour camp, or still alive, but we don't know, do we? Not since you two last marched for the good of Myanmar. And we'll probably never know what's happened to him, unless one day he suddenly appears at the door, a toothless, stooped-over sack of bones. Can't you see, Thant? We need you at home more than ever, and we always will.'

He kept his eyes on the pagoda, its golden spires gleaming in the morning sun. 'Remember what he'd say to us whenever we got depressed about something? "Don't let it defeat you, be strong, find a way to rise above it." Doing that is what the march is all about.'

'There are enough protestors down there to make the whole world take notice without you getting involved. If mother knew you were joining the march, she'd go crazy. You know that. Our first concern must be her. She's suffered enough.'

'I don't have to be reminded of that.'

More students passed, chanting slogans and waving banners, like they were on their way to a football match.

'Watching is not joining,' Thant said. 'I'll just walk along on the edge of the march until it gets to here, then I'll go to work. Promise.' He turned and, before she could say anything, sprinted after the students.

'Remember, I'm not going to school until you go to work!' she shouted, her scowl meant to penetrate the back of his head. 'I'm not! I'll be waiting for you right here, Thant! Right here!'

A storm approached, wind stirring the trees, thunder rumbling, lightning cracking the sky. She could smell the rain before the first heavy drops sent her scurrying under a tarpaulin where child construction workers squatted and chewed betel or smoked cheroots, their faces turned towards the Sule Pagoda.

And there she stood fretting and waiting, the rain pouring down as though from a hole in the sky.

Minutes later the march came up the road, monks' shaved heads bobbing above their red robes, their student supporters encircling them and everyone chanting:

'Improve the lives of the people.
Our cause, our cause.
Reconciliation now.
Our cause, our cause.
We demand a dialogue.
Our cause, our cause.
Free all political prisoners.
Our cause, our cause. ...'

Onlookers jammed the footpath, were up in trees, hung out of windows or perched on the rooftops. Some took up the chant or offered umbrellas, snacks and bottles of water to the older monks and nuns.

The rain eased.

The protestors passed and kept on passing, far too many to examine closely. But still Mya searched for Thant, glancing around occasionally for the well-fed faces of MI agents with their biros, notepads and camcorders, fearful she'd be recorded and later taken away, interrogated, jailed.

By the time the last protesters straggled by, she'd grown frantic. She dashed across the road and caught up with the march just as it slowed and stopped.

Monks squatted on their haunches, pressed their palms together and began to pray in deep, murmuring chants, their wet heads and student-held umbrellas dripping little rivulets, the potholes filling with rain.

Finally she spotted Thant next to a girl with long braided hair. They were wrapping the feet of an old nun. Mya recognised the girl. Thant had introduced them the previous day at the market and talked to the girl the entire time they toured the food stalls. She was the friend Thant had mentioned earlier. He hadn't lied after all.

With the marchers sitting or kneeling down, Mya now had a clear view of the intersection clogged with barbed-wire barricades, dark-green cage trucks, an armoured truck with a water cannon mounted on top, and rows of policemen in helmets and gas masks. Those in the first two rows held riot shields and truncheons. The others gripped rifles across their chests.

A megaphone blared, the words loud one moment, static-filled the next. 'Residents of Yangon, gatherings of more than five people are prohibited. Disband now or you will be arrested.' As if giving force to the words, thunder rumbled, lightning snapped in an arc over the city.

Many protestors lit candles, their faces luminous in the candle flames, while others joined in chanting prayers.

Dread filled Mya's chest, took hold. A year earlier her father had chanted prayers here too.

A monk in the front row stood up, turned and shouted, 'If you're not afraid to die then come to the front!'

Dozens got to their feet, made their way up and locked arms to form a human chain.

Mya moved quickly. 'This place is going to turn into a battle-ground,' she called out as she neared her brother, still with the girl and the nun. 'Come with me, Thant – now, please!'

Three sets of eyes met hers. The girl's broke contact first, then Thant's. But as Mya stood over her, the old nun continued to gaze up at Mya, her eyes milky with cataracts. 'Is he your brother?' she asked in a croaky voice.

Mya's shouting had turned heads. 'He is, but there are times I wish I didn't know him, like now!'

'I should tell you, dear,' the old nun said, slipping flip-flops on her bandaged feet, 'I could not have got this far without your brother's help.'

The praying ended.

A hush fell over the road.

The old nun found her walking stick and, with Thant's help, rose to her feet and took a few practice steps.

The other marchers rose too. Banners and flags went back up. Prompted by the front row monk, the chanting resumed:

> 'May all living beings
> Be free, be free.
> May all living beings
> Be free from harm.
> May all living beings
> Be free from poverty. ...'

The megaphone blared, that same threatening voice having to scream to be heard, 'Disband now!'

A voice at the front shouted back, 'No! You disband! It's time for the people to stop being afraid!'

The crowd surged forward, pushing the four of them along.

> 'May all living beings
> Be free, be free ...'

The armoured truck shot forward, its water cannon sweeping back and forth, shooting out torrents of water, knocking protestors off their feet.

Tear gas canisters lobbed into the air, landed and skidded along the ground, turning the air ghostly white.

Policemen attacked, wielding truncheons, kicking, grabbing and dragging screaming protestors toward the cage trucks.

Gunshots smacked the air. *Pop-pop-pop-pop-pop.*

'This way!' Thant's friend shouted, fleeing.

Pop-pop-pop-pop-pop.

Thant reached out for the old nun. *Pop-pop-pop-pop.* He staggered, blood spurting. He opened his mouth as if to scream, grabbed his neck and collapsed.

'Thant?' For seconds a sick silence, before a cry rose from Mya's throat. 'Thant!' She dropped to her knees, lifted his head into her arms. 'Look at me, look at me, please!' He did, twitching and gurgling, his eyes going from shock to acceptance to glassy stillness. 'NO!' She wrapped herself around him, feeling her heart pounding, willing it to be Thant's.

Two, five, ten minutes maybe, before Mya let go and leaned back; this the first time she had looked at death. She could never have imagined him so still. Never.

A strap hung loose from over her shoulder. How was it she was still carrying her school bag?

She raised her eyes to the fighting swirling in and out of focus through the gauzy, eye-stinging air.

A man ran past screaming. Others followed: the slap of flip-flops, sandals.

Pop-pop-pop-pop-pop. A monk in front of Mya, the old nun by his side, toppled to the ground, blood spreading through their robes. Before she could go to them, a voice cried out. A construction worker collapsed at her feet, a policeman beating him with a truncheon. In seconds blood streamed from the worker's nose, down his lips and chin.

Still on her knees, blood pooling around Mya like the road itself was bleeding, she stretched forward, put her weight on her hands and vomited.

And still the policeman beat the worker.

Pop-pop-pop-pop.

Mya thought: *If by chance you survive, remember all this. Remember every detail.*

She took off her bag, rage filling every cell of her body, turning her into someone beyond her control. She stood, curling her hands into fists.

Just metres away lay a stack of bricks. Mya collected one and returned, preparing to die. But first, how hard was it to crush a policeman's skull? She gripped the brick with both hands. 'This is for Thant!' she screamed, belting the policeman below the ear. His head snapped sideways. He fell onto the worker, his helmet, truncheon and shield hitting the ground, his gas mask askew. He looked up, stunned and groggy.

'And this is for the monk and old nun!' Mya hit him square across the face, his spittle and blood spattering.

He tried to crawl away, tried to get up, but she hit him again and again before someone with thick arms lifted Mya from behind, knocked the brick from her hands and carried her towards a gap between two buildings, her toes dragging along the ground.

Their pace slowed; her abductor was breathing hard. Mya saw Thant's friend with the long braided hair and two men lying sprawled across the gap, their backs bleeding bullet wounds.

'I'm about to join you,' Mya muttered to the girl. Death and rebirth; death and no rebirth – it didn't matter. Nothing did.

2

Mya sat on stacked bags of cement, dazed, trembling, her school uniform – green skirt, white blouse – dripping blood and rain into a watercolour on the floor. Hair, then soapy stubble, followed. That it was her hair and stubble barely penetrated her mind. 'Sule Pagoda?' she asked finally.

'Below it, yes. As an abbot I have keys to its locked doors.'

She grew aware of his robe dripping, of a bitter taste in her mouth. 'Is there water?'

The abbot flicked the razor to clear it of stubble and put it down.

He passed Mya a bottle of water. She drank, passed it back, and he continued shaving.

'Monks are prohibited from touching women, and still you carried me here and … touch my skull … cut off my hair, shave my head.'

'Under the circumstances the *sangha** will understand.'

He finished, used a cloth to dab at shaving nicks, then started sweeping up.

'Widows' heads are shaved,' Mya said, her own shaved head feeling as shrunken as the rest of her.

'As a sign of having left family life behind, yes.'

She pictured political prisoners – her father even – sitting on stools under this sort of low light. Shouting voices demanding answers. Fists, boots and belts lashing out, their bodies soon aching, as hers would be after she was discovered and taken away.

Fast, hard footsteps came down the wooden stairs.

Mya's eyes shot to the door.

A padlock scraped, clicked. The door burst open and in came a boy monk, his shoulder bag bulging. 'Many police are on the streets,' he said, acknowledging Mya with a nod before diverting his eyes to the abbot. 'I got to Botataung District, though, and to the unit. No police were there.' He stretched a hand Mya's way. 'But this girl's mother was, and … she knew, she knew.'

The abbot mumbled something before leaning the broom against the wall and eyeing Mya.

'I gave her your message and package,' the boy monk continued. 'Then I went to the monastery and nunnery. No police at those places, yet.' From his shoulder bag he took out a mobile phone, a camera, a brown umbrella, two books, a wash cloth, a pink robe, an orange under-dress, a brown sash, a sling shoulder bag, a pair of sandals and a small roll of money, and placed them on a shelf next to Mya. He grabbed a bucket and took off again, closing and locking the door.

Once the staircase went quiet again, Mya reached up, touched her shorn head then moved a hand over the clothes. 'So what happens now?' she asked, though she'd worked out at least part of the answer:

* Community of monks and nuns.

this was the garb of a novice nun.

The abbot sat on a stool. 'You'll need to stay here a while.'

'And if I go home?'

'You will be arrested.'

'Along with my mother?'

'Standard government policy: punish the womb that gave birth to the protestor. It's not just the single person who can go to prison, but the person's entire family.' He kept his eyes on her. 'Your mother is Karen,[*] I believe.'

'Partly.'

'As you heard, she's been contacted. She knows what's happened, as everyone in Yangon must know by now. She knows you're in hiding. She knows once your brother's body has been identified it will be cremated, along with the others killed, and their relatives will be arrested. So she is leaving Yangon now in disguise and getting as far away as possible.'

'How far away?'

'If you know the answer to that and you are caught, resistance will be ripped out of you and you will tell the interrogators everything they want to know.'

'I read once about a group in Sri Lanka called the Tamil Tigers. When they were at war against the government, each one of them wore an amulet around their neck containing cyanide tablets. When they were about to be captured, they swallowed the tablets. Every market in Yangon sells rat poison.' Her eyes lingered on his. 'So where do I go to find her?'

'Have you been to Karen State?'

'No, but I have an uncle there. And I've heard stories about it. I know that Karen people consider Karen State their homeland and that their bloodthirsty army are fighting the country's military there. I've read about Karen cannibals, about Karen with horns growing out of their skulls, about Karen who kill just to cut off and bury their victims' heads under bridges for good luck.'

---

[*] One of the many ethnic minorities in Myanmar's east along the border with Thailand.

'Stories the government features in its newspapers, its agents spread in the market places, its generals tell their soldiers. But the Karen people are no more monsters than you or I. If you go into Karen State, yes, you'll be amongst the government's bitterest enemies. But you understand that already.'

Mya gazed at the floor, an ache gripping her throat. She took a deep breath, clenched her teeth and told herself if she did not move she would not cry. Her mouth tightened and she burst out in loud hiccupping sobs, like a three-year-old. 'I start the day with my mother and I end up ... here with no family at all; this storeroom, or a prison cell, or ... or escape to a war zone my only options in life.' She bent over, covered her face with her hands. 'I hate Myanmar, its pig government, its police and soldiers who torture and kill people who want to make the country a better place. If I had a gun I'd go out on the street right now and willingly spend my next ten lives in the darkest pit of hell for the chance to shoot every policeman I saw. I've never felt so much hatred – and when I leave here, I'm supposed to be a nun?'

'A novice nun.'

'A novice nun then.' She shook her head at the lunacy of the idea.

'A novice nun who must learn quickly to control her emotions.' The abbot paused, giving Mya time to settle down. 'If MI discovers anyone mourning over the death of a protestor, that person will be arrested.' He stood up to move the broom and dustpan to the corner then sat back down on the stool and watched her. 'The fact is the protest march was recorded. Soon MI will be looking for you and everyone else involved in the violence, if they're not already doing so. They'll know your face. They'll know your family. Disguised as a novice nun, you have some chance of getting into Karen State and joining your mother.'

'Whereabouts in Karen State?'

He shook his head. 'This is what I suggest. You travel to Karen State as your mother has. Trusted people will contact you. You'll know who they are when they use the words, "Myanmar is beautiful this time of year. Don't you think so?" Don't open yourself up to anyone else. Memorise whatever information you're given. Don't write anything down. Be accepting. Be patient. You can no more hurry life than hurry the phases of the moon.'

He paused, a smile on his face, as if he were modelling it. 'Try each day to smile. It is good medicine. Learn to avert your eyes, to make a mask of your face, to disappear into yourself. Feel yourself grow invisible in your stillness. Remember, as a novice nun you're learning to live more in the spiritual world than the temporal one, so it is expected you'll use words sparingly, or not at all, and that you'll simply nod to acknowledge things said to you.'

He pinched his right ear. 'And remember, walls have these.' He pointed to his eyes. 'And trees have these. So don't linger next to them … Of course, there is a chance you'll be caught. So getting there will depend on good fortune and how convincing you are as a novice nun.'

He pointed to one of the two books among the pile of clothes. 'A condensed version of the Buddha's teachings: the Tripitaka. Try to read some of it. It will help you. The money is from your mother and the monastery.'

'You could be in great danger by helping me.'

'The mere act of living and thinking differently in Myanmar can be dangerous. Fortunately our religion teaches us to deal with that.'

To show her gratitude, Mya said, 'The old nun will serve as my model. Every minute I'm wearing that robe I'll be carrying her image inside me.'

'A younger version of that image, I hope, with hardier legs and better eyesight. Her nephew is a monk and a close friend of mine. Her name was Nan Pau and her karma was good … Yours can be too.'

'Did I kill him – the policeman?'

'And was that policeman killing the construction worker he was attacking before you intervened? It is how wars start. I doubt you did; but whether you did or not, the law is simple. There is only one crime – an act against the government. It covers all offences and punishment is the same, whether for speaking out freely or beating someone to death.'

'Or hiding people who've done those things. I shouldn't be here.'

'You can leave whenever you want, but if you stay two or three days, the authorities will have completed their house-to-house searches. Their interrogation cells will be full. As well, you can prepare yourself by studying the Tripitaka. Waiting will also give me time to organise your escape and find you something more effective than rat poison should your escape end unexpectedly.'

Mya stared at him in disbelief.

He went on. 'The first Sacred Truth – life is sorrow and suffering, true. But the suffering that comes from interrogation and torture goes beyond the teachings. And when Buddhist principles clash, compassion takes priority.' He stood up. 'So absorb who you are: a novice nun whose only desire in life is to worship and serve … and just quietly, to find her mother.'

Footsteps sounded on the staircase again. The door opened and the boy monk came in with a bucket of water. He set it down next to her and rushed out again.

The abbot picked up the camera from the stack of tiles, explaining, 'Your new identity starts with a photo.' He then handed Mya the robe, under-dress and sash, asking her to put them around her shoulders. When she had done so, he looked through the viewfinder and took her photo using the flash. 'I'm leaving for a little while. While I'm gone you can clean up, put on your novice clothes and rest.' He nodded towards a cot next to the nearest wall.

'If something happens and I'm not back in an hour …' He raised his eyes and pointed to a square on the ceiling that had been cut away and replaced with a panel of dark wood. 'A prayer hall is above us. It has an elevated floor. You can hoist yourself up through the panel then follow the light and crawl out.' He turned and left.

Mya washed and put on the novice clothes, then lay down on the cot. Nothing to do but mourn, feel numb, like her insides had been cut out. She picked up the Tripitaka and tried to read, but couldn't. An hour, maybe more, before the sounds of scampering feet and thumping boots on the floor above startled her. Someone shouted, 'OUT-SIDE, OUTSIDE, NOW, NOW, NOW!' There came a thud, like a bag of cement hitting the floor. Boots banged down the staircase. The padlock clattered; someone tried to wrench it off the latch. Then the boots went back up the stairs and moments later everything went still again.

She waited. Maybe a quarter of an hour passed without another sound before she climbed awkwardly onto the cement bags and lifted the panel high enough to peer out between the false ceiling and raised floor above, a rectangle of grey light to her right. She grabbed her things, shoved them in her shoulder bag and lifted herself up.

On her belly and forearms, Mya wriggled towards the light, emerging behind a large, glass-encased Buddha. She stood and peered around it. No one about, just the shrine-covered walls, and on the other side of the polished hall an altar laden with platters of hibiscus, jasmine and marigolds, smoking incense and dozens of flickering candles. Above the altar, a mammoth golden Buddha. On a cross beam above the Buddha, a swallows' nest. Daytime still and Sule Pagoda was abandoned. Just something else she could never have imagined.

She walked out into the hall and sat in front of the Buddha, curling her legs behind her and gazing up at him. She explained how much she ached, how much she feared leaving Yangon. A thought came: maybe she could just hide in the storeroom, somehow arrange to have food brought in until … until when? She was eventually discovered?

The slap of flip-flops entered the hall. She jumped up, alarmed, about to run. 'Police came and took the abbot away.' The boy monk again, moving towards her. 'I saw them from across the road.'

Mya recalled the abbott's warning about what would happen on being caught by the authorities: '… *resistance will be ripped out of you and you will tell the interrogators everything they want to know.*'

The boy monk's eyes were watery, his voice soft. 'But there are no police now, so it is as safe as it will ever be for you to go.'

Her choice: either she got herself to the train station or walked out to the pagoda steps and sat and mourned until the police came and took her away.

The boy monk turned his back to Mya, bent over and lifted his robe. There came the sound of tape being ripped from flesh. He faced her again, a small, tattered book in his hand. 'The abbot thought it would be better if I carried this, not him.' He approached and handed Mya a guide book for English-speaking tourists.

She took it and the book sprung open to a page with an identity card fixed in the binding. She stared at the photo of herself – hairless, in a pink robe, brown sash over her left shoulder, and below her photo, a name – Nan Pau. She took out the ID card and flipped through the book's pages filled with bus and train schedules, colourful photos and descriptions of famous places.

'The night train to Moulmein leaves in two hours,' the boy monk said.

Mya thanked him, knowing that in normal circumstances he wouldn't have spoken to her, and her thoughts turned to the abbot. How long would he be able to hold out before telling his interrogators everything? 'I must go now,' Mya said, as much to herself as the boy. She dropped the book in her bag, left the hall and scampered down the steps, intent on getting to the train station as quickly as possible.

Outside the rain had stopped and the sun was beating down, drawing vapour from the wet pavement. Sule Pagoda Road was close to deserted, shops and stalls looking as abandoned as the pagoda. Only a few people on bicycles, an occasional motorbike taxi or car moving slowly up the road as if a truck-load of vipers lay tipped over up ahead.

The eerie quiet and lack of traffic weren't all that surprised her. She thought she'd remain numb with grief, indifferent to being caught, and at first that was exactly how she felt. But as she walked, thoughts of her mother filled Mya's mind. She needed Mya as much as Mya needed her. Mya's feelings changed. She grew wary, conscious that Yangon was enemy territory now, that informers could be watching her from across the road, from windows and partially-hidden vehicles.

As she quickened her pace, her vigilance grew. She doubted she'd ever been more aware of herself, her surroundings and the exact distance between her and her destination. Alert to every movement and sound, she studied the road, footpath, cross streets, laneways and dead ends. And what struck her was how clean and tidy everything was: nothing at all to indicate a peaceful march for democracy, followed by a massacre, had ever taken place. Not a single blood stain or bullet casing; no bits of banner, flag or clothing – not even any plastic bag rubbish. It was like the entire area had been soaped down and swept clean by a massive broom, or most likely dozens of smaller ones.

She was approaching a boy and girl in school uniforms sitting on the low-walled border of a banyan tree, the boy eyeing its branches, his mouth pinched; the girl teary, slow to look away and keep her sorrow private. Mya recognised the girl from school, so lowered her eyes and faced the road as she passed them, half expecting her name to be called out at any moment. But the girl said nothing, and soon she and the boy rode past Mya on a bicycle, the girl side-on, head tilted into the boy's back, her arms around his waist like he was all she had left in life. Mya watched them until they turned into a laneway and disappeared.

Remaining unrecognised boosted Mya's confidence. Her determination strengthened; so too her anger. Images of her namesake – marble eyes, protruding bones – took over her thoughts. She recalled the nun's words: *'I should tell you, dear, I could not have got this far without your brother's help.' And just how far did Thant get you, old nun? Let me tell you: as far as the wall of police murderers who must have enjoyed their day. Think of the satisfaction they got. Like shooting birds out of trees. Using a hammer to crush a flea. And supposedly they're Buddhists. Doesn't that make you want to change your religion, old nun? It does me, even as I wear this robe to escape imprisonment. Buddhists arrested, beaten and killed by other supposed Buddhists. Myanmar's in hell, old nun, and with the generals as our masters, it always will be.*

She lost concentration and scolded herself, thinking: *Nothing matters but getting out of Yangon, so get back to who you are – Nan Pau: positive, compassionate, self-disciplined; forever walking in the Buddha's footsteps.* And if she couldn't be her, she might as well stop this farce right now and make up a banner saying something like, THE POLICE KILLED MY BROTHER. MAY THOSE RESPONSIBLE BECOME DOGS IN THEIR NEXT LIVES AND EAT CRAP. Then walk down the road with it, shouting and waving it in the air. How far? As far as her namesake got? Unlikely. A satisfying experience though; the rest of her pain-free life squeezed into a few minutes of revenge. And when the police came to arrest her, how long would it take for a bottle of rat poison to take effect? She looked down at her robe and shook her head. Had there ever been a more unlikely person to walk along this road in a novice's robe?

Rat poison diverted her thoughts and caused her to revise her route. She needed to buy some before going to the train station.

On the next corner, a man in a red pin-striped longyi,[*] white shirt

---

[*] A skirt-like garment worn by both males and females.

and mirror sunglasses sat under a banyan tree. As Mya neared him, her heart beat harder, her stomach tightened. He might just as well have had his job description written across his chest, for although he wore different clothes now, Mya recognised him. She wanted to stop, to cross the road, to run.

Mister MI turned and saw her.

Mya lowered her eyes and passed him, her pulse in her throat. Seconds later hard-soled sandals, in time with her own, clapped the footpath behind her.

A trishaw driver pedalled past, his arms and shoulders shiny with sweat, his passenger seat empty. 'Yes, please,' Mya shouted, in a voice more resembling a market seller's than a nun's. 'I want to go …' The words 'Chinese Market' froze on her lips, the disinterested driver well down the road by the time she finished her sentence. She continued on, listening for those sandals but no longer hearing them. She slowed, stopped, looked around. Relief was instant. No one was behind her. On she went, past vacant vendor and fortune-teller stalls, the Sakura Tower and Trader Hotel, until she spotted the railroad overpass up ahead.

One more intersection: the massacre site, where policemen were stopping vehicles, checking ID cards and possessions, pulling people out and questioning them. Mya watched as two men were shoved into the back of a cage truck and driven away.

Fear nudged her back into the shade of a tamarind tree. Her eyes darted about. She recalled a shop that sold traps and poisons across the road and down a nearby side street. How to get there without crossing that intersection? She stepped out of the shade, turned and looked straight into the face of Mister MI, his mirror sunglasses boring into her. Only his lips moved. 'You're looking confused,' he said. 'Why? Does this road, that intersection, bring back recent memories for you?'

She, novice imposter, was about to be arrested. Her eyes found the footpath. Face hot, throat constricted, she tried to speak, but couldn't. She forced a smile, gazed at cracks in the footpath and waited for what came next.

'Your ID card.'

Mya took it out and handed it to him.

'You're trembling.'

It took all her concentration to reply, 'A little. The city feels very tense.'

His eyes jumped from Mya to the card – once, twice. He returned it. 'Have you come from the Sanchaung Nunnery?'

Stupid man. Where else would a novice nun walking in this area come from? Importantly, he didn't grab her or appear to recognise her. She answered him in her quietest voice, 'Yes, I have.'

'A good distance away from there, aren't you? Have you walked or taken transport?'

Mya looked out at the road, a sponge for so much blood just hours earlier. 'I got transport,' she lied, hating him. 'I'm going to visit friends nearby.' *May you choke on a fish bone and die in agony.* Holding her body very still, she forced another smile.

'I trust they avoided the protest march here and are well.'

'Very well, thank you.' With every lying word she spoke, she sounded more and more pathetic to herself. In another life she'd have told him whose backside to crawl up. Though, like now, maybe only in her thoughts. 'I want to buy a few things at the Chinese Market before going to my friends' place.'

He studied her before flicking the back of his hand as if shooing her away. 'Go then. You need only buy food for yourself for a day, maybe two, I should think.'

She had no idea what he meant by that.

'Go on, off you go.'

Mya turned and crossed Sule Pagoda Road; she thought for the last time ever.

3

Once, when she and Thant were little, their parents took them on a day train to visit friends in Bago. Mya was really excited about the visit, as she was about anything out of the ordinary.

It was good to leave Yangon station and pass through places where children played and goats fed along the grassy track, and Mya and her brother – competing to see who could stretch furthest out the open window – waved to people and animals, then to each other, then giggled and made faces, until the train sped up and their father dragged them back inside. The two of them were too excited to nap like their parents and others did. So they snuck off again, visited other train carriages, played hide and seek, until their frowning father found them and took them back to their seats and told them not to leave again. Their window stayed open though, so Mya and Thant could poke their heads out and watch the landscape and people passing by and wave to them.

Thant suggested a game: a point for every golden stupa* or bullock cart they saw and two points for every villager they waved to who waved back. Thant won. He always won. Like all the other older brothers in their neighbourhood, he'd often change the rules to win. But on that train it didn't matter. There was always a new game to play, and so much to see outside the window that was so different from Yangon, even though Thant, typically, had to brag about how observant he was, how blind Mya was, once the train got to Bago. But this did nothing to spoil the trip. Mya loved being on the train that day. It was one of her best experiences ever.

What a fun world she thought she lived in then.

Now Mya tried to hold on to that memory, but too soon it was gone, replaced by close-up strangers, their stupid laughter, the trivial things they were talking about: soccer scores, whether they should buy food and drinks, where their children should sit. Nothing at all about the massive protest march for the good of the country, and the massacre that followed, now only nine hours old.

Then anxiety replaced irritation as Mya tried to make sense of a future without her family. She was the only one in the carriage without someone, and had never felt so alone. Besides that one day in Bago, she'd spent every other day of her life in Yangon. And she'd never gone through a night without her family or a girlfriend's family in the next room.

* A dome or bell-shaped monument up to 127 metres high that contains the cremated remains of Buddhist monks or nuns and is used as a place of meditation.

A lump formed in her throat. She shook her head to stop the tears. She placed her hands on her lap – one over the other – and took deep breaths and tried to talk herself into a calmer state. Second time at the station now, wasn't it? The same sights and sounds as before: ear-ringing platform announcements; vendor and fry stalls; people squatting and chatting, smoking cheroots, sucking on grilled chicken feet and rooster heads, or sleeping in hammocks or under tarpaulins. Inside the carriage people arriving, dropping their bundles, sitting on them or the wooden bench seats. All the while vendors – trays of trinkets and snacks and drinks balanced on their heads – roamed from window to cracked window calling out items for sale.

'*Disappear into yourself.*' Abbot-advice about as useful as a pocket on her underwear. Just how was she supposed to do that? Roll up into a ball, close her eyes and cover her ears, like in a game of hide and seek – her robe providing her hiding place? Of course not, but through deep concentration and meditation that she knew absolutely nothing about. Not something she and her girlfriends practised in between gossip and Facebook sessions, perfect boyfriend appraisals, and listening to their MP3 players.

So here she was trying to impersonate a novice nun and she couldn't even do the most basic Buddhist things. Though she did get past Mister MI on Sule Pagoda Road, didn't she? Maybe, just maybe, without realising it, she was doing some novice things right.

That last thought bolstered her and she glanced around again at the people nearby: backs of heads, conversations half heard. Just families: fathers already curling into sleeping positions, mothers looking after the children. She could be in far worse places. At least no one in the carriage was likely to attract informers.

The train jerked forward finally, slowly picking up speed and rolling side to side.

Outside three boys raced the train, shouting, laughing and waving their arms about before they tired and slowed. Mya sensed the fire in their lungs, their leaden legs, and envied them their silliness and laughter, doing fun things together, being able to stay in Yangon.

She thought how quickly lives could change, be lost; that she was leaving behind everything she'd ever known, her routine, the certainty of it all. She had no idea what was to come, or even what she'd see out the window in the morning. Though one thing was certain: nothing, no one, would be familiar to her, until finally she found her mother – and she would, surely she would.

Mya leaned her head against the half-closed window and continued to look out at Yangon slipping past, buildings getting further and further apart, night coming on. As a distraction, to keep up her English writing even as her life was collapsing, she took out her English dictionary, pen and pad as though her English teacher – a former monk and lover of haikus, tankas and short poetry – had just assigned her a writing task. She listened to the train noise, wrote, deleted and wrote more:

> Vibrating metal,
> Thumping of wheels on the track.
> Darkness thickening.

She liked words, especially English ones. Liked filling up writing pads and diaries with them. She thought of writing about the massacre, but how ridiculous was that? There weren't the words available – in Burmese, in English – to convey what had happened. Never would be. Her mind skipped to the abbot – what he said, how he was arrested. *'Feel yourself grow invisible in your stillness.'* She shook her head: incomprehensible. Yet over the next few hours, it surprised Mya how still she could sit just thinking, and how upright she could sleep; how coughing, snoring and a mother's head dropping on her shoulder didn't upset her, or at least not as much as they would have in the past. Now, strangely, she welcomed the sounds, closeness and touch.

Mya slept; woke to a baby crying. Outside, a wall of blackness until a light or two showed, and passed.

An idea came. Maybe, out of habit and yearning, an imposter could absorb the person they were pretending to be. Start by acting, end up becoming. From the Tripitaka: 'What we think, we become.' Hard to explain exactly, especially with how muddled her brain felt. But all she knew was that in the time it had taken to get from the Sule Pagoda Road to the Chinese Market and onto this train, she'd become aware of the people who nodded, smiled and pressed their palms together to greet her. And what surprised her most was how easy it was for Nan Pau to return those greetings. She'd like to talk to somebody:

an abbot, abbess, a teacher maybe; someone with ideas who might be around for her in the morning. She scanned the carriage.

Stupid girl, dreaming with her eyes open. No one was around for her: zero. Just poor families challenged enough by trying to get to their destinations. She was on her own. Maybe forever. So get used to it, Mya Paw Wah, fugitive from the law.

Her quick mood swings, feeling hope one minute, devastation the next, were not helped by stomach cramps signalling the onset of her period. As Nan Pau, or any other celibate novice or nun married to the Buddha, what purpose did periods serve?

Absolutely none: zero. That word again: the one that best summed up her prospects for the future. She'd give up ever being able to have children right now, this very instant, if she could just stop having useless, maddening periods.

No sobs like before; just silent tears. She pressed her fists into her cheeks, knuckle-dried her eyes, as those train wheels thump-thump-thumped a rhythmic chant. She put words to the rhythm – *I'll be with you soon. I'll be with you soon. I'll be with you soon* – imagining she was capable of sending brainwaves to her mother.

The train rocked and rattled, the wheels thumped on and on.

At some point she slept again and woke to a brand new landscape. To her Yangon eyes it was a different country out there. Stilted huts perched like giant crabs. Groves of bamboo, mango trees and sugar palms, and vines and rice paddies, their shoots poking out of brown water. Beyond the villages hills rose up, their brows and ridges capped in stupas and golden spires shaped like the fingers of classical dancers. A dirt road came into view, running parallel with the track. Ox carts moved over it and work gangs of women and children with baskets of stones and dirt on their heads walked along its edges in trance-like slowness.

The carriage lurched, tossing sleepers sideways, and soon they started to stir and stretch and greet one another.

To avoid conversation, Mya pretended to read, keeping her Tripitaka close to her face until the carriage lurched again, veering left then slowing. Up ahead, above a wide, brown river that emptied into the sea, stretched a massive bridge, dark against a cloudless sky.

'The longest bridge in all of Myanmar,' a voice croaked next to her ear.

She swung around.

An ancient nun stood gripping Mya's seat, her hands claw-like, her face a dried-up mango. 'Myanmar is beautiful this time of year,' she said. 'Don't you think so?'

* * *

The motorbike taxi slowed as it neared the end of a bustling alleyway full of conjoined double-storey houses, a tea shack and street dogs stretched out in the shade. The old nun muttered, 'You wear a mask and your face changes to fit it.'

It was as though she'd read Mya's thoughts. 'Or wear a novice nun's robe?' she asked.

'Or wear a novice nun's robe.'

'Does your brain change too?'

'If it must, daughter. If it must.'

The taxi stopped. Mya got out.

'Take this,' the old nun said, handing Mya a key. She nodded at the tea shack. 'You'll find the owner behind the counter. He knows a novice nun is coming. Register your name with him then use the pathway at the side. Your room is at the back with a postcard of the Shwedagon Pagoda on the door. Remember to keep the door locked. Don't go far. You will be contacted.'

'When?'

'Soon … Be patient.'

Mya reached into her bag for money.

The old nun touched Mya's shoulder, shook her head. The motorbike taxi turned around.

'And I will light a candle for you tonight,' the nun said, going past.

A second motorbike taxi pulled out heading in the same direction.

* * *

Small room. White tiled floor. Wooden bed with a sleeping mat. A ceiling fan and a light bulb hanging from a cord.

Mya dropped her shoulder bag and pressed her forehead to the window that might as well have been metal bars. The ache for her brother, of being alone – a stranger to everyone – rose up again like a sickness. Her eyes filled and she wiped them and they filled again. Before the massacre she'd felt shame if she cried. No longer.

Nothing to see out there but the thick trunk of a banyan tree and a dirt path that led to the toilet, wash basin and tea shack. Mya went and lay down on the bed, looked up at the ceiling where green geckos – the story-book bad-dream catchers of her childhood – moved in bursts, froze. 'How long will we be sharing this room?' she asked them. Hours only, she vowed. Twenty-four at the most, then she was leaving, no matter what.

'Be accepting. Be patient. You can no more ...'

Yes, yes. Mya went outside to the basin and washed, then went to the toilet before returning, her maddening monthly with her, accepted and no longer so maddening or painful. She watched the fan circle and listened to every sound: the hum of a generator, tea shack noise, the bell of a bike rickshaw, flip-flops passing the door. When she was little, she avoided ceiling fans, afraid they might crash down and slice her into pieces. Thant had told her they would.

A vision of his last moments tracked through her mind over and over, until tiredness weighed her down, her eyelids refusing to stay open. She slept until chanting and gunshots invaded her dream, jolting her awake.

Darkness. Street dogs barking a duet. She located herself and stood and turned on the light. A scrap of paper was under the door. She picked it up and read: *Your room includes free meals.*

Reminded of her hunger, she took her bag and walked around to the tea shack. Tables lined two walls, while giant woks heaped in rice, noodles, skewered chicken parts and large pots of tea and soup simmered away along the wall to her left.

He'd pinched his ear. *'Remember, walls have these.'*

But there was nowhere away from walls to sit. A stool and small table tucked away in a back corner looked the best option. Mya went there and sat down, checking for wires, tiny speakers inside tabletop shrines or under the table itself. A serving boy came and placed a bowl of fish-head soup, a slice of Indian bread and a glass of tea in front of her. He smiled and greeted Mya as though she were a regular customer. That relaxed her, as did the aroma of her first meal since leaving Yangon.

Mya ate, devouring the bread between spoonfuls of soup until the scrape of a stool made her pause. She turned and looked into the smile of a thick-set man in a dark longyi and white singlet, his arms covered in blue-black tattoos.

Her pulse quickened. Dignity, serenity, she reminded herself. She re-arranged her robe around her shoulders and ankles and took five deep breaths, concentrating on each one.

The man sat down just as the generator quit, lights flickering then dying, the place suddenly as black as the outdoors. In seconds, torch-light beamed in the kitchen. Candles were lit.

The serving boy brought one over and the man next to her emerged again, his fishy eyes wandering over Mya. She was struck by how quickly she could dislike someone trying to befriend her.

He seemed to like what he saw. He leaned closer, still smiling, before his food came and moments later a glass of whiskey. He pointed to it. 'Would you like one?'

Breath that could melt plastic. Blind to her robe, shaved brows and head. Or maybe he was just mocking her. Mya did her best to smile, serenely, saying with all the self-control she could muster, 'No, thank you,' before she continued to eat.

'Inside or outside the gut, it's the best disinfectant in all of Myanmar. You're still a bit young for it, maybe. Or maybe you're so close to the Buddha you don't need disinfecting.' He chuckled then gulped down his whiskey like it was cold tea. He wiped his mouth with the back of his hand and nodded to the serving boy. Another whiskey came. 'So which reason is it?' he asked.

'I prefer water or tea.'

'And you have a tongue and you speak as well as pray, eat soup and bread, and dress in robes.'

Mocking her and enjoying it, the pig. May he choke to death in his sleep and never be discovered, Mya thought as she forced another smile, rubbing a hand over the hem of her robe to reinforce who she was trying to be. She looked down. A section of the hem had come away and needed re-sewing. She lifted the hem to the candlelight. Another section had a small tear. If she wasn't contacted by morning, she'd find a shop, buy a needle and some thread, and mend it.

The man slurped his soup, sucking on the eyes and small bones before murmuring his approval. 'Brains and eyeballs are the best part,' he said, 'Don't you agree?'

'Yes.' She'd say nothing to contradict him. She should leave. But she was still hungry. She ate quicker, concentrating on remaining blind to his stares.

The generator sounded and moments later the lights came back on. A mosquito was on Mya's wrist. She slapped it: then came the shock of what she'd done.

The man stared, a slow smile forming on his lips. 'You'll return as a dog in your next life.'

'A mistake.' She picked the remnants from her wrist and placed them carefully on the table. 'Much regretted.'

'The excuse being you're just a novice prone to such mistakes.'

If he happened to fall off his stool in the next minute, she'd kick him in the head, also by mistake and with deep apologies. 'Perhaps.'

A black cat entered the tea shack, examined the place and disappeared.

'So which nunnery are you from?'

As Mya, she would have been on her way to another table by now. 'What?' She'd heard, but she needed time to think of the name of the nunnery she'd passed earlier in the motorbike taxi.

He repeated the question.

Mya couldn't remember. She only knew the name of one nunnery, and that was in Yangon. 'Sanchaung.'

'Ahhh,' he uttered, as though some great secret had been revealed. 'Far away from home, aren't you?' He stared at his whiskey before draining the glass and raising it in the air for another one.

Mya finished her soup and stood up in one motion.

'Leaving so early?'

A quick nod and, without looking back, she left.

Back in her room she felt panicky, trapped. She couldn't read or settle. She listened for footsteps, a knock, the door handle turning.

She wanted to find another room. Somewhere close by. So what about this? Go for a walk, find a room, return and tell the proprietor she'd met a girl she knew who lived with her family down the road. The girl had asked her to stay the night with them. She'd return in the morning.

Mya grabbed her bag, opened the door and jumped back.

In the doorway, the silhouette of a man. 'Myanmar is beautiful this time of year,' he said. 'Don't you think so?'

The whiskey drinker? But he looked to be wearing trousers and seemed smaller. A hand reached out like it was about to grab her.

'For you.'

Another note, intercepted before it could be slipped under the door. Wary of that hand, Mya snatched the note quickly and stepped back into the light.

Tomorrow Karen State. First bus for Hpa-an leaves at six am.

'Who are you?' she asked, looking up. He was gone. Mya dashed down the path to the road. No one: just sleeping dogs. She entered the tea shack. Two tables were occupied. She glanced at the faces. The whiskey drinker's wasn't among them.

Back in her room she lay on the bed, watched shadows waver on the walls, listened to bats flitter about outside. At times she confused them for people about to knock or slide another note under the door. The bat noise ended. She dozed: Mister MI's and the whiskey drinker's claw-like hands gripped prison bars, eyes staring, mouths agape.

Tiny cell, hot. Smell of mould. Stench from a toilet bucket. Biting bedbugs, mosquitoes. She curled into a ball, itching and bleeding from continual scratching.

Huge rats, one by one, came up through a broken grate. They squealed, fought and mated, then raised their noses in the air, faces twitching, and watched her.

She heard clicking sounds. Giant beetles appeared on the ceiling, antennae waving. They slid down the walls, climbed over each other in their rush to get to her.

She tried to stand, but it was like she was nailed to the floor, she couldn't move. She screamed, 'Mother! Help me!'

No one came and the squealing and clicking got louder as the rats – teeth bared – and dung beetles – emerging from piles of crap – mounted her legs and arms, intent on penetrating her, sucking on her brain. A rat scrambled to her chin, went for her mouth. She screamed.

Mister MI and the whiskey drinker – the only ones to take any notice – grinned approvingly through the bars.

Mya screamed again and snapped awake, fighting for air, heart thumping against her chest. Light still on, the roof fan circling, three useless bad-dream catchers splayed against the opposite wall. The longer she stared at them, the more the room seemed to compress, the image of those long-toothed rats and crap-covered beetles swarming over her, gnawing away at her chin, lips and tongue.

She leapt up, threw on her under-dress and dashed out to the road.

No one about. Dogs – homeless like her – still curled up asleep, one of them growling in its dreams. Over her a half moon and bright stars. She stopped, thankful for the memory they brought: her father's voice, clear; the feel of his arms around her. Like she'd been lifted up and transported back.

Sitting together on river bank rocks. The smell of mud. Thant, closest to the water, skimming stones across its dark surface. She on her father's lap, leaning into his embrace, feeling all snug and safe. 'Six thousand stars up there visible to the naked eye,' he said, looking up. 'And a hundred thousand million more that are not. Count in English the ones you see, Mya.'

'Too many,' she squealed, burrowing into him.

'Okay, twenty then. Point to them as you count.'

The older Mya finished counting, then spotted a stool and sat down on it, recalling when she was a pre-schooler thinking darkness was like paint. Go outside for too long at night and she'd come back black.

Across the road light flared between the second-floor shutters of a house. Inside a family chattered away, before the voice of a young girl rang out. And such a voice it was. Like she was seated right next to Mya as she protested about having to go to bed. Typically, the mother bribed her with a story, which was obviously what the girl wanted, as her 'Okay' was instant and expectant.

Mya recalled when she was that little girl, not getting a story read to her the greatest disappointment of her day. Recalled also her mother squatting down in front of her, gripping her hands and instructing, *'Gentle hands, walking feet, kind words and a quiet voice – yes?'* She'd given up doing that with Thant.

Mya listened, and when the story finished and 'Good nights' were said and upstairs went dark, she walked back to her room, glimpsing a figure standing under the moon shadow of a nearby building, the smoke from his cheroot rising in the air.

* * *

The first hint of dawn appeared in the sky as passengers started boarding the bus. Mya was last on and sat at the front, a woman and her toddler next to her, the driver across from them bent over the wheel yawning. The bus coughed to life, roared, steadied. Jerked into gear it took off, bouncing and swerving out of the depot.

Along the traffic-less road they went, past plaster-walled buildings splotched with mildew, people wrapped in shawls and monks carrying their begging bowls the right way up. Scrawled in red paint on the side of one building was: *Worship life. It's a joy to bring into existence and too precious to destroy.* A plea, Mya thought, to any pig generals being chauffeured past.

Third day as Nan Pau, of avoidance and solitude, of the stupefying ache of losing family members she never valued enough until they were gone.

Mya wished she'd hugged her mother before she left for school, hugged her father before he protested the previous year. Told them both how much she loved them. That Thant had died more slowly so she could have told him that too. At least with her mother, and hopefully one day with her father, she'd have a second chance to do that.

Outside Moulmein the bus moved eastwards toward the rose-pink dawn that turned orange and paled yellow as the sun lifted over the rim of the world. Hpa-an was out there under all that new colour. Mya imagined it: a small town bordering a brown river, stilt houses and small fishing boats scattered along its banks; background of hills rising into grey limestone mountains; morning market starting to fill with school children and mothers, including hers. She had to be there – had to be. Further east was a war zone.

Though it was hardly a war zone where she was looking.

Her monk English teacher: *'Writing short poetry is about stilling the moment, probing it with words.'* The English word for where the edge of the earth and sky met? Started with 'h'. She got out her dictionary and found 'horizon', and checked on 'stubble'. She wrote:

> Rice field plain,
> Stubble now
> All the way to the horizon –
> Sharp –
> Like the edge of a plate.
> Walk too far,
> Drop off
> And never be seen again.

Hard to believe the world was round, she thought, as all that uninterrupted space held her gaze, the smell of harvested rice blowing in through the open windows, the road straight as the lines on her writing pad, the bus only veering to pick up passengers, avoid potholes and villagers on bicycles.

She relaxed a little and watched the driver reach for a cellophane bag filled with betel leaf. He took out a clump, inserted it between his gums and cheek and chewed; his periodic spitting of red phlegm out the window sounded like a pop-gun.

'Do you have extra?' the woman next to Mya asked the driver, pointing to the bag above the steering wheel.

He took out another clump and handed it to her.

The woman thanked him and dropped the betel in her mouth and chewed, her mouth soon turning as red as the driver's. She gave an impatient sigh. 'Very slow bus today,' she said to no one in particular, bouncing her toddler up and down. When the toddler started to cry, she turned towards the open window and asked, 'Could we switch seats?' Mya agreed and the woman leaned her head out and spat. She took the remnants of the betel from her mouth and rubbed it over the toddler's lips, hoping to stop its crying.

The bus slowed and creaked over a rusty bridge and the toddler shrieked.

Mya offered the woman a banana and sticky rice wrapped in fresh green leaves, telling her she'd already eaten. As a novice nun, her first act of charity for the day. The woman took the food and thanked her. With the first taste of banana on his tongue, the toddler went quiet, his eyes growing large with interest, his tongue pushing out for more.

'Try each day to smile. It is good medicine.'

And Mya did – her eyes on the toddler. The worst part was over, wasn't it? Someone would be in Hpa-an to meet her and she'd be taken to her mother's room. There they would grieve, yes, but over time find work and, as best they could, recover their lives together.

The mother and toddler finished off the banana and sticky rice and were soon asleep, the toddler sprawled across his mother's lap, the mother's arms over him. Betel was supposed to prevent sleep. That was why people like their driver chewed it. The woman must have been exhausted.

Mya looked out at the fields, the farmers and their water buffalo at mid-distance quivering in the heat waves, the far horizon now blurred in haze under a sun-bleached sky.

Time seemed to slow: the monotonous drone of the bus, the road's straightness and flatness, the constant travelling starting to feel endless.

'You can no more hurry life along than you can hurry the phases of the moon.'

Limestone formations started jutting up and merging into jagged, sheer-sided cliffs, stupas and their spires appearing on the most inaccessible outcrops. How builders got up to those places to build those structures was a mystery to Mya.

The woman stirred. She hooked an arm through Mya's and leaned her head against Mya's shoulder, all the time appearing to sleep.

The bus slowed. Up ahead a red and white boom gate. Heaped sand-bags encircling a propped machine-gun on one side, three soldiers – guns held loosely across their waists – on the other. Mya sank down.

'Wave to the soldiers,' the mother said, suddenly awake, before picking up her toddler's hand and doing it for him.

Seconds later the barrier rose and the bus drove through.

More boom gates and check-points appeared as they neared Hpa-an, but not once did soldiers board the bus. 'A different story going the other way,' the driver noted between check-points, as though Mya might need to know that.

Storm clouds were building, lightning flaring in the distance.

The bus entered Hpa-an, weaving through the narrow streets before shuddering to a stop in the central square. The door screeched open. Passengers piled out, though not the woman and her toddler. Boxes and bags were untied and came down from the roof, the passengers collecting them and moving off. When the doorway cleared, Mya got up and descended the steps, bus noise still lingering in her ears.

A tea shack was just metres away, two of its tables outside. A monk sat hunched over a glass of tea at one of them. The other table was vacant. Mya watched the monk spread his hands and stare at them like they'd suddenly become a mystery to him. She waited for him to look up, meet her eyes, but he didn't. Sitting at the next table seemed the logical thing to do, but if that monk wasn't there for her and started asking difficult questions, how long would it take for him to realise who she wasn't?

The woman disembarked and, strangely, stood beside Mya, toddler perched on her hip. Again she hooked an arm through Mya's, as though they were good friends or shared a family. 'Good to feel our feet on the ground,' she said.

Mya nodded, wary.

From the tea shack a man's voice called out, 'Mya!'

She answered, 'Yes,' then realised her mistake. Panic took her breath away.

'Good trip?' The man was sitting just inside, against the wall. Only his pressed trousers were visible until he stood up and moved outside, his stare like an animal's fixed on its prey. He put on mirror sunglasses.

Someone clomped down from the bus and stood behind Mya. She looked over her shoulder into the eyes of the whiskey drinker, a grin spreading across his big slab face. 'Surprised?'

The woman let go of Mya's arm and looked around, holding out her hand.

The whiskey drinker gave her some bills and she walked away.

Wide road. Little traffic. A market place a hundred metres or so to Mya's left.

'Save yourself the effort,' the whiskey drinker said, close enough for Mya to catch the smell of his breath. 'You won't get halfway.'

She was Mya Paw Wah again, fastest girl in her class. Nearly as fast as Thant, so midfield football player fast. And if she could reach that market place, she'd have a chance of escaping. Or should she just grab her rat poison instead? But the whiskey drinker was close. Getting the poison and swallowing it would take too long.

Mya looked at him like he was a rotten piece of meat, saying, 'Something's died in your mouth.'

She bolted, passing two motorbike taxis, leaping over a sleeping dog and a pot hole, weaving around bikes and motor scooters. She got to the market, chose the widest aisle and raced on, ducking and sidestepping, stalls flashing past, the eyes of *thanaka*-faced[*] women turning to stare at her. Sandals slapping her heels, people shouting – 'Sister', 'Daughter', 'What is wrong?' 'Why do you run?' Sudden silence when they see why.

'Watch out, watch out!' Mya screamed, darting left through a narrow opening. People jumped back, giving her room; her breath gasping, pounding boots closing in, until a hand grabbed her by the neck, pulled and threw her into a stall.

4

Mya stood in front of him, listening to the rain on the roof, eyeing framed portraits of generals on the wall, spots of peeling paint, warped floorboards – anything but his face.

'This girl could not invent the amount of trouble she is in,' Mister MI said from behind his desk.

Finally Mya looked at him as he studied her shoulder bag, writing pad, dictionary, rat poison, Nan Pau's ID card and a folder, its contents unknown to her. 'Would you agree, Aung Min?'

'I do,' the whiskey drinker answered from the open doorway, a cheroot pressed between thumb and forefinger.

[*] A yellowish paste made from the bark of sandalwood trees and used to prevent sunburn.

Mister MI stood. Hands on the desk, he leaned forward, eyes challenging Mya. 'I've been told by the old nun you shared a ride with in Moulmein and by the abbot of Thein Tan Gyi Monastery, before he was hospitalised, that you are a bright girl. So, that being—'

'Why was the abbot hospitalised?' she interrupted, her fear turning to surprise.

'Only speak when I am not,' Mister MI snapped. 'Otherwise learn silence. As a wearer of that robe, I should not have to tell you that.' His face softened a little. 'The abbot, I believe, had a heart attack. Most likely he's joined his ancestors. But maybe not. Either way, you'll never see him again.' He paused to let her absorb that. 'So, Mya Paw Wah, as a bright student, you must know what a proverb is.'

She gazed, dumbfounded. What sort of a comment was that?

'Well? Do you or not?'

'Like an aphorism, it's a short sentence that expresses something true in life.'

'A worthy answer from someone so young.' He sounded so superior, like he knew everything there was to know about the world. 'Now, as a student who has been top of her class and been reading the Tripitaka the past few days, I hear, perhaps you can give me an example.'

It took a while to think of one. 'When people show compassion for all living things, only then are they noble.'

A smile crept across his face. 'Bright as paint, aren't you? The abbot and old nun were right … about your knowledge anyway, as opposed to your actions. I have a proverb for you, Mya. Tell me if you've heard it before. Endings can be read in beginnings.'

She shook her head.

'I'll change the wording but keep the essence of the proverb intact. Actions result from thoughts. Or, decisions have consequences that a decision-maker must take full responsibility for. Appropriate to remember, don't you think, for someone who beat a policman unconscious, posed as a novice nun in an effort to escape and had to be chased down an hour ago only spitting distance from her destination?'

Mya vowed not to break eye contact until he did.

He picked up the folder and took out some enlarged photos. 'We'll start from the beginning.' He pointed to the first photo. 'Recognise it?'

'A protest march.'

'The protest march. Don't be coy with me. Next one.'

The photographer had to have been up a tree. She wanted to say something defiant, but nothing came. 'Me, my dead brother and a nun he was helping. She's dead now too.'

'Thant was his name, hers Nan Pau. Correct?' He tapped the ID card with his index finger.

Mya nodded and clasped her hands together to keep them from trembling.

'I take your nod to mean yes.' He pointed to the next photo.

'Me, a construction worker and the policeman who killed my brother.'

'How your brother and the nun died are anybody's guess. Wrong place at the wrong time in an illegal protest march they should never have taken part in. What is verifiable from this photo is the identity of the person holding a brick over the head of a collapsed policeman. Agreed? … I take your silence to mean yes. Next.' He tapped.

'Me … and a monk.'

'That monk being the abbot of Thein Tan Gyi Monastery. Next.' He pointed.

Mya felt sick. 'A nun getting off a bus at a market place.'

'The Hpa-an market place to be exact, the same spot you got off. Try again. Get the imposter nun's identity right and I'll tell you where she is.'

She drove her fingernails into her palms. 'You already know who she is.'

'Your mother, am I right?'

Mya glared.

'I take your silence to mean yes. Right now she is occupying a room at the back of the Soe Guesthouse, not far from here. Last photo, Mya.' He pointed. 'Who is this running towards the market place?'

'You know who.'

'With two policemen chasing after you, am I right?'

She nodded.

'Good. That was easy, wasn't it?' He sat, put his hand in a drawer, clicked a button and brought out a cassette tape and placed it on the desk. 'Endings can be read in beginnings. Decisions have their consequences. Your future is dependent on your past. In your case, a future as a long-term prisoner for crimes committed against the state: namely, involvement in an illegal march, vicious assault on a policeman, carrying a forged ID card and impersonating a novice nun while heading towards a war zone to join the Karen rebel movement.' He held up the cassette and photos. 'All here as passports to your and your mother's future inside Insein Prison, better known as the Iron Bar Hotel, as I'm sure you know.' He leaned back in his chair, looking satisfied, like he'd just finished a big meal. 'Happy with that?'

She felt numb, like a block of concrete.

'You're not smiling.' He continued to watch her, perhaps reading the fear in her face. 'Feeling overwhelmed and abandoned, are you? And I haven't even mentioned your father, currently serving a long sentence in a northern labour camp. You're from a family that refuses to learn the consequences of disobeying the law, of doing your utmost to destroy the country's peace and harmony.' He glared. 'As to your future …' He started picking his way through her things, letting her stew. 'Thirty years inside the Iron Bar Hotel sounds right to me. Two rice gruel meals a day, one bucket-wash a week, a rat stick to catch your meat with.'

Her eyes moistened. She clenched her teeth, held her breath. She would not cry – not one tear.

'Unless.' Mister MI gestured to the whiskey drinker, who tossed away his cheroot and came up to the desk. 'Are you a compassionate man, Aung Min?' he asked.

Aung Min seemed puzzled at first, then he grinned. 'I am.'

'Do you try to perform at least one merciful act a day?'

'I do.'

'When you look at me, Aung Min, what sort of a man do you see?'

'A man of great mercy and Buddha-like compassion.'

'Fine words. Thank you. Having established that, maybe we should perform today's merciful act together.'

The whiskey drinker nodded, understanding and grinning now. 'She is fit,' he said, 'her legs strong.'

Mister MI leaned forward and gazed almost tenderly at Mya. 'I have a proposal, one that will give you an opportunity to redeem yourself. And if you accept it, there will be no need to disturb your mother at the Soe Guesthouse.'

Seconds passed. 'What?'

'Perform a noble act, for the good of the country this time.'

'Doing what?'

He crossed his arms, heaved a sigh. 'You show no appreciation, no trust. You've taken up too much of my time the past few days. Forget the offer. We'll collect your mother and go back to Yangon together.' He picked up a mobile phone.

'No, wait. I'll … I'll do what you want me to.'

That smile again. 'Good,' he crooned, as though encouraging a child. He put the phone down, turned to the whiskey drinker and said, 'She's yours.'

5

Echoing cries of birds. The grunts of the old man in front of her, bent nearly flat under a basket of ammunition and supplies. His scratched legs spattered in mud, wearing a too-large singlet and blue longyi, he prodded the ground with a bamboo pole, a spike and two claws on its end.

Voices in her head: the whiskey drinker's as he escorted her to the truck where hollow-faced Karen captives – all of them male – waited in the back: 'Consider yourself lucky. MI peels skin from people who've done what you've done. But you've been spared, for the present anyway.' The officer's voice in the darkness hours later, at the end of a rutted road, as captives and soldiers – faces painted in black streaks – prepared to move out, the former acting as porters for the latter: 'Porters stay ahead of the soldiers. Do not stop and do not slow down unless you are told to. Break this rule and your ears will be shipped back in baskets to your families.' The old porter's voice after Mya had asked him why he tapped the ground: 'We do not talk. We do not look at each other. We do not give each other any thought at all. Then, when one of us is killed, that person remains a stranger.'

Half the previous night and all morning on this windy, undulating track, past the burnt-out ruins of a village, embers still glowing in the ashes, the supply pack and her sling bag cutting like wire into her shoulders. Her longyi and shirt saturated, feet mud-heavy and blistered, leech-bitten legs trickling blood. She tried to lose herself in memory: getting up in the morning, breakfast waiting for her on the table, parting her hair into braids and tying them off with ribbons, taking the bus with Thant and walking the rest of the way to school. Then came the lessons she was missing, the last time her family was together, what her bed felt like when last she slept on it.

Mya drew up a vision of herself and her mother leaving the Soe Guesthouse together, walking through the bustling Hpa-an market and out to the bank of that wide brown river. So much space and privacy out there that she could walk for hours and rarely see another person.

When she lost that vision she diverted to English, describing the things she saw in that language: leaves crunching under her sandals, patches of light and pools of deep shadow, the steepness and exposed roots of the next climb. Mya used the descriptions to write a letter, pretending her mother understood English, until the old porter veered onto a smaller track, avoiding a crater half-filled with water. The purpose of his pole hit Mya like a slap. She hurried to catch up, then drew an imaginary line from his mine detection pole, through him to herself, and did not waver from it.

Another hour, maybe, descending through bush and a tunnel of trees before a soldier confronted the old porter and pointed. 'That way,' he ordered. He grabbed the porter's pole and hurled it away.

Bush thinned, sunlight spread and soon they came to a large clearing – airless, hot and bordered by trees and jumbled rock. They were told to stop.

The officer came and ordered the loads to be dropped. Haggard looks soon turned desperate when soldiers pulled shackles and padlocks from three packs.

Minutes later, with all but one porter shackled together, including Mya, the officer spoke. 'Fifty, maybe sixty metres. Not far. If there are mines out there, you'll soon know. Respect them. Walk gently, avoid dips and stay close to bushes and saplings where the soil is root-filled. Do that and there's a good chance you'll get to the other side.' He raised an index finger in the air. 'But, though you'll need to walk gently, you must also leave footprints deep enough to follow so you won't have to return to get your packs. Our soldiers will carry them for you. And remember, if you stop or try to go beyond the clearing, you will be shot … Good luck,' he added, in a false tone of concern.

The taste of bile in Mya's throat, the air suddenly hard to breathe.

'Fear is to be expected,' the old porter muttered. 'It sharpens the focus of your mind. The challenge is not to be overcome by it.'

He sounded educated. Her eyes lingered on him, his mouth hanging open, wet singlet stuck to his bones. He was no longer the indifferent stranger he had tried to be. 'May the Buddha's blessings stay with you,' he added, looking at Mya now and smiling weakly.

Her voice quavered, 'And with you.'

'I am not here. The others are not here. Only you are. Keep your eyes on the ground and avoid any disturbed earth. Under it might be a landmine.'

Mya's throat locked against a surge of nausea. Blood thudded through her veins. She felt light-headed and took several deep breaths. Then she braced herself and stared out at the hard earth in front of her, struggling to concentrate on the best route across. Hers was the driest, sparsest section of all: barely a shrub or a sapling, just stones sticking out of the ground and small dips and rises from start to finish.

She asked herself what it would be like to step on a mine out there. Instant nothingness if she were lucky. Or thrown into the air, collapsing on the ground, feet gone, legs ripped apart, her screaming the last sound she'd ever hear. And away from this clearing, no one knowing why or when, only her mother and father at opposite ends of the country left to remember her name.

The order came: 'Walk.'

A bird shrieked, *'People coming.'* A vulture answered, its sharp eyes aimed, *'I know. I am watching.'* And everything poured out of Mya – hope, spirit, self-control. She felt weightless, wet between her legs, her body's betrayal no more than a passing thought. She stared at the ground – each crack, ripple, mound – and tried to lose herself in calculations. 'Fifty metres,' she mumbled, finding a strand of her voice, coaxing her muscles to do what her mind resisted, 'a hundred steps, each touching the ground like a feather, toe to heel, before pressing down.'

Shackles tightened and she walked, counting the steps, heart pumping, barely able to breathe for fear of disturbing the ground.

The still air carried every sound: distant birds, twigs crunching, shackles clacking, porters sucking air, until at thirty-four: *KAH-ROOOOM!* Then again: *KAH-ROOOOM!* Mya jerked her head around to where a few porters stood still as statues. Beyond them, under thinning smoke, two more porters – barely adolescents, bloodied, clothes in shreds, screaming and flailing on the ground. A third lay motionless.

Shouts from the officer: 'Get up, get up!'

How could they? Their legs were ragged flesh and exposed bones.

Shots rang out, puffs of dirt kicking up just short of the porters' heels.

'Go on!' the officer shouted.

'Concentrate,' Mya heard the old porter say as she struggled to control herself.

All the other porters looked from side to side. No one wanted to be the first to move. Two quick shots sent them diving for the ground and ended the screaming. The porter not chained to the others, who had been kept back with the soldiers, dashed out to the dead porters and unlocked their padlocks, freeing the corpses. He shortened the shackles and locked them again.

'Go on!'

The porters rose, Mya with them; heart and lungs doing their work, skin on fire, stomach ice. 'Thirty-eight, thirty-nine, forty …'

The old porter joined in, his breath coming in short bursts.

'Sixty-six, sixty-seven, sixty-eight …'

'Life is short,' the old porter gasped.

'Yes.'

'And death inescapable, and we have to accept that.'

'Yes.'

'I am Kho Noc.'

'I am Mya Paw Wah.'

'Eighty-two, eighty-three …'

A glimmer of hope that strengthened the closer Mya got to the trees. 'We're almost there, Kho Noc.'

'Not far, not far.'

Mya's shackles caught on something behind her. She moved her leg sideways to free it, glancing over at him, his head lolling, his feet dragging over the ground, leaving no prints at all.

'Eighty-seven, eighty—'

A flash of bright white light, a blast, a whoosh of air, and Mya seemed to be floating, the sky swinging sideways, dirt like rain showering down on her, the air itself quaking, before she slammed into the ground.

6

She woke to a blinding glare, itchy skin, ringing ears, a low throbbing noise coming closer and closer. Then WHUMP, WHUMP, WHUMP ... Dirt and bits of plant life flying around. A helicopter beating away all other sounds.

There came an image of grey limestone cliffs, stupas and their spires perched on the most inaccessible knolls and outcrops. Now she understood: helicopter, yes, that's how the stupa builders got up there, by helicopter.

Stupas and spires faded; so too the *whump, whump, whump ...*

* * *

Hot pain, like she'd been stabbed in the head, leg and arm. Grit inside her mouth that she tried to push out with her tongue. Mya opened her eyes, wondering why they had been closed, why she was on her back, the sun blazing down, the ground rippling in the heat. She raised her head until she couldn't.

Vague figures nearby.

Buzz of talk.

She lifted an arm and as she stared at the matted blood and red ants running up and down it, a shadow spread over her. A boot jabbed her in the ribs. A man shouted, 'This one's come to life.'

She tried to talk, but nothing came out.

Two figures, now like paper cut-outs against the sun, rifle barrels peering over their backs. Behind them a familiar voice, 'Unchain her. Get a stretcher made. She goes back with us.'

Her head lolled to the side. Below the two figures, a crumpled body, its backside and legs ripped open, bits of longyi and singlet scattered about. She stared, memory of Thant's body tunnelling her back. *'This is for Thant!' she screamed, belting the policeman below the ear.*

Her head grew heavy, like it was being buried under bricks.

Death: let it happen.

Her vision faded, the figures over her melting into the sun.

* * *

In a stretcher, bumping along, rocking side to side. Overhanging branches, patches of sky moving backwards. Smell of earth and sweat. Pain in her head, leg and arm. Ringing ears. Someone's laboured breathing. *'I am Kho Noc.'* She lay there, adjusting to being alive, then tried to lift herself up, but couldn't. She was strapped down, porters on each end, supply baskets fastened to their shoulders.

In her mind random images and sounds: screaming, explosions, shackles and locks. She tried to order them, fill in the gaps, before looking down the stretcher at her legs and feet still attached, left leg wrapped in cloth. Arms by her sides, the left one wrapped also. She clenched and unclenched her hands; thankfully they worked. Her bag was next to her, a section of robe sticking out. *'We're almost there, Kho Noc.'* Her head fell back. 'Are soldiers close by?' she asked the porter at her head.

'No. You can talk quietly. I'll tell you when to stop.'

'Where are we?'

'We left the combat zone hours ago. We're returning to the trucks. The great Burmese army has had another glorious victory, destroying another Karen village, killing more blood-sucking revolutionaries and leaving four porters behind for the vultures to watch over. Television interviews, photographs and front page newspaper headlines are sure to follow in Yangon and Mandalay reporting the number of medals pinned to our beloved officer's chest.'

More memory gaps filled. 'Medals for men who behave like monsters,' Mya added. There seemed nothing wrong with her ability to use words. She must have been born with a metal skull.

They crossed a creek, went up a rise.

'And me?' she asked.

'You, novice nun turned porter and mine sweeper? Sorry, only your compassionate self and our heroic officer would know the answer to that. What did you do, murder a general?'

'No … Not a general.'

He'd misunderstood her. As well, he'd spotted her robe. She thought about telling him why she had it, but decided not to. Her head wasn't up to it. 'What I mean is – why am I in this stretcher? I should be walking.'

'Landmine explosion. You suffered concussion, a gash or two, some lacerations. But nothing is missing, and you're thinking, talking and hearing alright. You'll recover because the officer wants you to. Maybe you're lucky, maybe you're not.'

The track flattened. The bushes thickened. 'In the clearing there was an old porter next to me.' Mya braced herself for the answer.

'He stepped on the mine that put you on the ground.'

'Dead?'

'Yes.'

They slowed to veer around low-lying branches then continued on. She asked, 'Did you know him well?'

'No. He kept to himself.'

'His name was Kho Noc and he was a good man.'

'He told you his name?'

'Yes.'

'Then feel complimented. He chose you to remember him … Soldier coming.'

* * *

Morning.

Mya's head slumped against a wall, her legs stretched out on another strange bed in another strange room. Yet, even with the sun streaming through the open doorway, it seemed marginally cooler here than in Yangon or Moulmein, so she still had to be in Karen State. That was something positive anyway.

A Chinese doctor was examining her; he moved quickly, his eyes darting about like time spent with Mya was costing him money. 'Cuts and bumps and bruising. But no broken bones. Your eyes are clear. There don't appear to be any after-effects from concussion. You're a very lucky girl.'

Lucky? Crossing a minefield? Witnessing people being shot and blown up? *Privileged and well-dressed – would you even know what a bush track looked like, doctor?*

'A few small scars as a reminder, nothing more.' He finished and quickly packed up his things. 'I'll leave the crutch on the floor next to you,' he said. 'Use it when you have to go to the toilet, which is out the door and to the right.' He placed a capsule of tablets and rolls of gauze and tape next to the crutch. 'Replace the bandages when they get dirty. I'll return in a week to take the stitches out.'

Mya could have worked all that out for herself. She asked, 'Where am I?'

He turned away as though deaf and walked towards the doorway.

'Anaesthetic, stitches, clean bandages and pain tablets. Who's paying for this?'

He stopped, scanned the corners where the roof met the walls. He returned, bent down and said quietly, 'The military. You're at a military police compound on the edge of Hpa-an. If you get the chance, get away.'

Mya had misjudged him. By the time she finished thanking him, he was out the door.

Her arm and leg were still anaesthetised, so she felt no discomfort in reaching for the crutch. She hoisted herself up, put the crutch under her arm and moved to the doorway. A soldier was sitting on a plastic chair, legs outstretched, head propped against the wall. In the distance a steel-mesh fence separated the compound from the town. A soccer pitch was just metres away; beyond that all things military.

The guard turned and Mya told him where she was going. He sprang up and followed her anyway. 'Do we go in together?' she asked when they arrived at the toilet.

'Be quick.'

She wasn't.

Back in the room, Mya tried to read her Tripitaka, then her English guide book, but kept reading the same passages over and over again.

Midday, and in came the whiskey drinker and a neatly-dressed, paunchy man with pitted skin and thinning hair. They stood over Mya, gawking.

'What do you want?' she asked finally, her nerves raw and stretched.

The whiskey drinker's mouth lifted into the thick-lipped smile she'd learned to hate. 'To settle your future, Mya.'

'You can do that by going away, taking the guard with you and leaving the door unlocked.'

'Sorry – not on the option list. Listen carefully and I'll tell you what is. Option one: as you've obviously impressed someone, consider this. Military Intelligence is looking for young people with your strengths and skills. The training is short and the pay is good, and you'll have a choice of where you'd like to work: Yangon, Moulmein or here in Hpa-an.'

Mya imagined a full-velocity roof fan dropping on him, his body parts flying. 'Doing what, working as an MI stooge, spying and informing on people I know?'

'Maybe observing and reporting deviant behaviour would be a better choice of words.'

'Go break a leg.'

'As I thought. Your future is settled then. Option two it is, as there is no option three.' The whiskey drinker turned to the man. 'Her wounds will heal with little scarring, if any. The bruises will be gone in a few days.'

'When do the—' the man pointed to Mya's stitches '—come out?' His Burmese was poor. Mya picked him for a Thai.

'In a week or two. Anyone with one eye working, tweezers and half a brain can take them out.'

'Is she a …'

'A virgin?'

'That's what I mean, yes.'

The whiskey drinker turned to Mya. 'Answer him.'

She pulled the sheet up to her chin, closed her eyes and wished them to go away.

'Mya's mother is staying at the Soe Guesthouse. Whether she is still there in a week, a month, a year, depends on her daughter. Could you repeat the question?'

The man did.

'He's waiting, Mya.'

'Not since I was four.' Mya looked at the man, the thin smile stretching his lips.

'A sense of humour as well as good looks, which will only improve once her hair and eyebrows grow back. I'll take her.'

'Fine,' Aung Min crooned, showing his pleasure. 'One opportunity leads to another, Mya. And this time you'll earn money and be able to send it to your mother. So you'll not only be helping her, but the Burmese economy as well. What a good girl you are.'

The man took a wad of money from his pocket and handed it to the whiskey drinker. Then he eyed Mya again, eyebrows raised. 'Can you swim?' he asked her.

She shook her head, thinking nothing could ever match the horror of the Yangon massacre or the minefield crossing. Or at least that's what she'd thought earlier. Now she wasn't so sure.

'Don't worry,' the man said. 'As pretty as you are, there'll be no shortage of men prepared to rescue you should you fall in the river crossing into Thailand.'

7

MAE SOT, THAILAND.

Mya sat on her bed at the Snake Skin, knees tucked up to her chin.

A banging on the door, and it burst open, ending her memories. Billy J swaggered in spouting his American DVD talk. 'Easy money tonight, girl, puttin' in bed time doin' nuttin'. You got ten minute ta get Gaga back on da payroll. Any questions?'

Payroll: an advanced word for him. 'No – no questions, Billy J.'

'Din get yar motor runnin'.'

Motor running too. Almost eloquent (today's new word for Mya). He'd been spending extra time with his DVDs and MP3 player.

Part Two

8

KAREN STATE, MYANMAR. CLOSE TO THE THAI BORDER
AND MAE SOT.

Its mottled brown head appeared first, forked tongue flicking below
its snout. It came out from under the tree's exposed roots and moved
over dead leaves until it found a pool of sunlight. There it lay, still and
flat.

The sunlight got stronger, the viper absorbing the heat until it
sensed an object approaching. It coiled and raised its head, tongue
flicking again.

The object formed, grew suddenly tall, moved into its light. The
viper lunged and struck, then reared back. Sound vibrations: high-
pitched in front, thrashing bush from behind. Its head wavering, the
viper swung around and targeted a shimmering blade of silver. But
the blade flashed down, striking first.

* * *

John woke no longer shivering. He looked around for Phoe Ni, but
there was only his sleeping mat. He looked down his body at his right
leg swathed thigh to toes in poultice bandage, thinking, *I'm not dead
yet. Local antidote must be working.* He stared up at the camouflage
sheet over him, thankful for his two metres of living space.

With nothing to occupy him, memories of home flooded back.
First-year uni holidays. Central highlands. No Maccas, kiosks, meet-
for-coffee culture up there. More concerning, no toilets either. Dad
dropping him, his bike and gear off in Hamilton, then climbing the
Lyell Highway to Tarraleah. After that his choice which hydro road
to follow, which lake to fish in, though he favoured that flat run into
Lake King William. Two nights there usually enough. Then back to

the highway, turn right. Just over an hour the first time, less each time after that, free-wheeling back down to Ouse; the cars, campervans and log trucks passing him only marginally faster. Start using the brakes a kilometre out or he'd blow past Dad and sometimes Ella, sometimes Nick, waiting for him. From Ouse half an hour until debriefing time on the deck, Dad reliving his own highland memories, barbie heating up, stubbies, tinkle of their guitars merging into Dad's sixties and seventies songs. By second-year uni he knew every back road in the highlands and revisited them in his Suzuki Sierra custom-made for a single driver, passenger seat dog, gear in the back, a kayak riding the roof.

He stared at a patch of sunlight forming on the camouflage sheet, watching it grow. In his mind a circle of candlelight, Lina lifting her head from the pillow and shaking out her hair. Like in that old Kristofferson song his Dad taught him. He whispered it: taking the ribbon from her hair, letting it fall, lying down by his side, helping him make it through the night.

A mossie buzzed his ear. He pictured its sensors and scaly wings working, on the same sweaty-skin approach as all the others before it, and just as blood-hungry. Ah, there it was, touching down on the back of his hand. 'Are you female, Anopheles and a malaria carrier?' he asked it. 'You're big and black, so I think you must be.'

'Go.' He waved his hand and the mossie rose in the air. Moments later the mossie landed on his other hand.

Just his thoughts now: *I'm watching you, Anopheles. Find a blood vessel. That's it. Inject your anticoagulant and malaria parasites. That's it. Your abdomen filling now, you must find my blood and viper venom to your liking. Hopefully you'll soon drop dead from your gluttony. But if you don't, I know this, big, black Anopheles, what you inject and take out will no longer harm me, though it will others you feed on later – poor bastards. You see my liver and blood are already full of parasites, my world reduced to staggering outside to relieve myself, to sips of water and spoonfuls of rice, to your buzzing friends and pain from my snake-bite, the headaches, fever and shaking.*

But the worst of it was that little girl shot in the stomach, and with nothing left to ease her pain, her moaning and crying just metres away.

John listened for the girl, but couldn't hear her now.

His eyes grew heavy. He dozed and woke, hand itching. *You're still with me, aren't you, Anopheles? Congratulating yourself for leaving your mark, and of course your parasites to settle in with all the others. Enjoy your remaining weeks on earth you miserable destroyer of lives. I hope someone rips your bloody wings and legs off, slowly, one at a time, before squashing you flat.*

A bony dog rushed in and nosed John's poultice bandage like it was a fresh bone. Seconds later, a woman entered and grabbed the dog by the scruff of the neck.

'Phoe Ni?' John asked.

In Karen, 'Tatmadaw* close. He go see.' She dragged the dog back outside.

John lay there, dozing, and woke to people shouting. Moments later came the *pop-pop-pop* of automatic weapons echoing off nearby hills. He watched the flap, wondering who would come in next. Phoe Ni? Karen fighters? Tatmadaw?

Sunlight spread over the tent. It got hotter. Sweat dripped off him.

The little girl started crying and his thoughts turned to death: hers, his. In song he was at heaven's door again.

Strange how those ancient, dad-taught songs occupied his head now. Bob Dylan; his old sheriff shot down, dying and knock, knock, knockin' to get in.

He doubted he'd be knockin'. Not after upstairs reviewed his church attendance. So what would happen to his body? Cremated? Or left to rot, the Tatmadaw encircling his remains with landmines to blow up the unwary? Or wrapped in a shroud and wedged between the boughs of a tree for vultures to feed on? It all depended on who came into the tent next.

He waited, his eyelids growing heavy again. Lunacy. At the cross-roads of life and death, love and an international singing career, and he couldn't even keep his eyes open.

He was outside, transformed into a Garuda, creature of the sky, preparing to ride the wind. He ran, spread his wings and rose into

---

* Burmese army.

the air flying over a battle zone, its flattened trees, a village burning, smoke rising up to meet him. He gained altitude, soaring over a winding river and tree-covered mountains, the Thai border and Mae Sot. He banked right and sped over the green plains of Thailand, its white sand beaches then the silvery blue of the Indian Ocean, its coral islands scattered beneath him, their bays and inlets gleaming like opals. On and on he went towards Australia, Tasmania and home.

9

GRETNA, TASMANIA.

The valley blazed, flames leaping up and coming his way fast.

Embers blew past. Fireballs landed, igniting the ground, searing his throat, sucking the breath from his lungs.

'Stay with me!' he screamed, coughing and slowing to let Ella catch up.

The air roared. The sky darkened. Smoke scratched at his eyes and clouded everything around him.

'We're almost there!' he screamed again, barely able to hear himself. He could only guess where 'there' was before spotting the dam just metres away, the debris-filled water moving in wavelets away from him.

'Just ahead!' He stopped and turned. 'Ella!' He leaned into the wind and smoke, shielding his face with his hands.

Branches hit him, embers scorched his skin and clothes.

'Ella!'

Spot fires were merging now; the heat like the air itself was on fire.

She knew where to go, didn't she? She had to be there, lying mud-caked in the shallow end, frantic for him to arrive. Not in the middle: no, please not there! She could barely swim. He turned and ran.

Over the embankment and into the water he went, screaming her name.

The bottom sloped downwards. At chest-level he went under, but not for long. Short of breath, his face broke the surface. He sucked air and sank down again, images of Ella behind him, not behind him, of his Mum and Dad leaving for New Norfolk hours earlier, Dad's 'Back soon', Mum's 'Want anything?' joining his thumping heartbeat and the firestorm about to come over the top of him. More horror thoughts, of having to choose between being scalded in the water or getting out and being consumed in fire. He rose, breathed deeply and realised the water – bathtub warm – was not getting any hotter, the firestorm no louder. He lifted his eyes to the falling ash, the orange-grey sky. The wind had eased and changed direction. He stood up, his legs shaky and loose. Still smoke and a distant roar, yes, but otherwise just the sound of his gasps and the muck and water dripping off him.

'Ella!' He waded, dragging his arms through the water, imagining her floating face-down on the surface. Finally he climbed out, sand-shoes squishing out water that hissed and steamed on the charred ground. The crackle of fire, sound of moving water, then from the dam a small, quavering voice – 'Nick.'

* * *

The kettle whistled inside the house, went quiet.

'Want anything, Nick?'

The words continually being asked of him, like he was too feeble to look after himself: two hours before the firestorm, driving to and from the Royal Hobart Hospital, and here on the front deck of his Aunt Jenny's, one of the few places around Gretna spared by the fire. Want anything? Change 'anything' to 'anyone' and the answer could be tattooed across his forehead – Ella and John.

'Nick, do ya want anything to eat or drink?' his Aunt Jenny called out again, her shrill voice penetrating his bones.

Be good if you could keep your voice down to a shout, he thought to say, sitting there on the edge of the veranda, legs dangling. He shouted back, 'No, thanks!' Followed quietly by, 'Commandant.'

Still the human megaphone jabbered away in there, as she had done since day one of 'Operation Stay-With-Us-For-As-Long-As-You-Like'.

Lately, she'd even started reminding him to wash his hands and brush his teeth, like he was still a pre-schooler too small to see over the wash basin. Next she'd be saying, 'Bedtime. Be sure to go to the toilet before saying good night, Nicholas.' Yeah, his mum was right. He should be bowled-over grateful to her and Uncle Pete (a shoo-in Order of Australia winner for unreal patience), and more importantly, show it. But beyond his barely-able-to-utter 'Thanks', he just couldn't muster up the emotion, sincere voice and wooden hugs to convince everyone he really was grateful. 'Still in shock,' he'd overheard his mother say to his aunt one night. *Yeah, too right I am, Mum, for more reasons than you think.*

He looked out at the rosebushes bordering the entryway, then at two honeyeaters fighting over bottlebrush territory to his right. The old tortoiseshell cat appeared from nowhere and sat next to him, gazing in the direction of that bottlebrush, its tail curled around its feet. Black cockatoos flapped past and landed in the top of the red gums, the only ones this side of Gretna Central not torched, he reckoned. They screeched and tore away at the leaves and blossoms. At least birds had survived what pets and livestock hadn't.

A few days earlier, he had stopped by their property and taken it all in. Like a huge incendiary bomb had been dropped. Not a sound. Concrete foundations, brick fireplace intact; otherwise the house and sheds just piles of charred rubble. Everything else blackened as well: the ground, outlying tree trunks, iron sheeting, animal carcasses (Sook's and Moonshine's?), mangled husks of John's Suzuki and Dad's tractor. No chooks, ducks, native hens. No fruit trees, boxing or play equipment, clotheslines, garden borders, fencing. He had wandered out to the far paddock and spotted his rabbit traps, one smothered in charcoaled rabbit, or something of similar size.

In his need for space, he'd taken to walking for hours over the blowtorched landscape, sifting through the remains, locating where things used to be. And sometimes during all that locating he'd turn in the direction of the river and his favourite fishing spot – his insides churning – and track the fire's path.

That landscape, this deck, night television, his designated mattress, the odd ride into Hobart and back – the extent of his world now. So, want anything, Nick? Yeah. To wake up in his own bed, pull the curtains back and see Ella planting something in her garden, or on the swing instead of being house-bound or in hospital getting her bandages changed. Otherwise nothing. Just being left alone would be good, thank you, Commandant. No one's arms around him, no one's confiding words that had about as much chance of clearing his head of the fire as the Sky God dropping off a cloud and fronting up for his birthday.

The deck creaked behind him, the footsteps recognisable. Two sisters: his aunt the stomper, his mum the creeper. He switched his brain to autopilot.

'You know what I'm looking forward to most?'

Yeah, he did. If his mum had a religion it was trees and plants and flowers. 'What, Mum?'

'Seeing the first new shoots and blossoms and watching the valley recover.' She sat next to him in her King Gees and city-bought t-shirt, beaming her hundred-watt smile; though he didn't look around to make sure, he just knew it was there. 'And the valley will recover. Its people will see to it. Such a tight-knit community. Few places in the world where you can go out and leave your doors unlocked and the neighbours will bring in your washing if it rains.' She was obviously having a good day.

'Well that won't be happening again anytime soon.'

'But it will happen.'

Mum the smiler. Brother John and sister Ella, the inheritors of her smiler gene, as well as her ease around people. Not him. 'You're so like your father,' newly-mets said to him on occasion; the newly-mets not bothering to add, 'Your father the quiet one, the paddock-wanderer.'

But his dad talked. He just chose the people he talked to and his talking places – mostly Rotary meetings, or up at the hotel – carefully. He had strong opinions too. Often expressed to himself when watching the news or a current affairs program. Opinions on politicians: 'Couldn't hold two thoughts in their heads on the same day.' Opinions on townie populations – their houses butted together, ghetto-blasters blaring, rat dogs barking, P-platers hurtling down the roads at Formula One speeds. And strongest of all, his opinions on 'new' technology. It challenged him, and he challenged the need for it. 'Where's all this technology taking us? Down the road to digital dementia …' or 'There was something I read recently about computer games and social networking amounting to conversation avoidance techniques that threaten to turn the next generation autistic.'

Dad wasn't into change. Reckoned after serving in Vietnam he'd left Texas for Tassie – 'the back of beyond and then some' – because he'd heard nothing changed here. Thing was, he still hadn't a clue Mum and the rest of the family were on Facebook and, when he was out, played computer games.

But what Dad lacked in ATM and computer appreciation he made up for in farming and handyman skills, playing his big, recently replaced Gibson guitar and perfecting his flat-tray driving skills by taking his kids – four to the seat, Ella the designated ducker – into town for weekend sport. He was a big reader too – 'A book with legs that man,' he'd overheard his Aunt Gas-bag say. 'Top of the valley's Dean's List in Paddock Reading.' – using the local library service (though not through internet) or buying secondhand books and stowing them under his tractor seat. Next morning he'd head out in his 'everydays' – shirt, overalls, boots, bush hat, all specially chosen for their frayed and faded look – a thermos of coffee in one hand, a hidden pack of smokes and matches somewhere else. He might tighten or repair fencing in the 'old bloke's' paddock for an hour or so, look towards the river, gaze at the sky and ground a while, before consulting his tractor library. He'd find a tree trunk to sit against, a secret fag to smoke, pour a coffee and read. Nick knew, but said nothing. His binoculars – strongest in the valley he reckoned – could spot a blowie lift its wings a hundred metres away.

'During my pregnancies,' his mum went on, ending her daydream interlude, 'your father would drive me into town to see Doctor Healy and we'd come home and always find something on the stove: a casserole or a pot of soup simmering away. Or, at the back door, a side of lamb from old Mick over the back paddock.'

'Low on maintenance, big on substance and tough as a two-dollar steak when she has to be,' was how Nick's dad described his mum, usually after a three-course meal and a couple of beers. That was about as wordy as he ever got about her, but it said a lot. They seemed good together: solid, never a sour word between them, at least when others were around. Didn't socialise much past Gretna. Dad's regular Rotary Club meeting in New Norfolk; a baking club one for Mum. Some Saturday nights an early parmigiana counter tea at the hotel where they might meet up with the rest of Gretna's Rotary and baking set: the Rodens, Patels, Foxes, Godfreys, Woodruffs. Then it was back home in time for the last half of AFL footy or a DVD.

'Later we'd get home from the maternity ward, my arms full of new life, and there'd be flowers and homemade scones and biscuits on the kitchen table. That night people would come around with more food and a bottle or two to wet the new head. Such warm, thoughtful people.'

Typical: Mum mouthing great long sentences in praise of the valley and its people.

Her of the power-of-friends and goodness-to-strangers school, as John put it, when he was home. 'Yeah, good people, Mum.' He recalled Ella asking her once how she'd met their dad.

'Just met him, that's all.'

'Tell me.'

She'd chewed her lip a moment. 'During uni holidays I worked at the hotel. He came in one afternoon and sat at the end of the bar.'

'A stranger?'

'A lonely-looking one, yes.'

'And so you decided to give him some company?'

'I suppose I did, older man that he was. I liked the look of him, the way he talked, though I had to do most of it at first. Anyway, he came back the next day, drank his beer, read a tattered book. Hardly country, I remember thinking then; wouldn't know which end of a spade to dig with.'

'And?'

'And I was wrong on both counts. He stayed. So did I. He built his world around a family, paddock, fruit trees and sheep. Later on joined Rotary, started building things for other people. Always a book going though, like reading soothed some lingering sore inside him.'

'And now?' his mum continued, 'Your aunt and uncle, us and no one else from the river to the main road.'

A familiar sick feeling rose up in his belly. *As an encore, you moron, why not try shooting a plane out of the sky.* 'Yeah. No good, Mum.' Memory-torture rode his brain again. One step too many while fishing and he'd been chest-deep in the river. Got out shivering and made a fire despite the total fire ban. No more than plate size, but big enough to mostly dry him out. Afterwards, he'd tossed handfuls of dirt on it. Just a few blackened branch ends left against the rocks, their middles burnt out, the tiniest wisp of smoke.

'It could be worse, Mum,' he said to fill the quiet. 'We could be homeless.'

Smell of eucalypts and distant hops. Outlines of blue gums, fences, livestock and distant houses (all gone now) as he rode his gear-heavy bike from the river towards the main road.

Thing was, the wind had picked up. Strong enough to re-ignite sparks from a tiny fire?

That was the question he couldn't stop asking himself. The answer: probably. With that wind at his back, getting over Paddy's Hill had never been easier.

'You're right, Nick. We could be … You hungry?' she asked.

'Not really.' When they still had a house, that question would come through his crack-open bedroom doorway, the opening she insisted on so the room stayed fresh, like his bedroom would turn into a sewage works if – shock, horror, 'Don't know how that happened,' – his door had actually spent a minute or two closed. No closed-door nag time since the fire though: no nag time at all. He could wear different-coloured socks, walk around in crotch-less underdaks with wax oozing out of his ears, snot out of his nose, and she'd just smile and look at him as though he'd stepped out of a Myer catalogue.

It was like she'd taken a knock to the head since the fire. Like now, she stared a lot, often at the most ordinary things: the kitchen sink, baking trays, fly-over birds that disappeared or the trees across the road.

He gave her another look: her elbows propped on her knees, chin in her hands, wavy salt-and-pepper hair running down her back. 'You're wrinkling well,' John would say, stirring her. So well, she was still a target for strange men's eyes. He'd noticed a few eyeing her off in New Norfolk recently and the few times they'd gone into Hobart together. Imagine, a bloke's own mother getting that sort of attention, especially while the bloke's walking along beside her. Unbelievable.

The screen door at the back slammed. 7HO radio went on: News on the hour. He listened, just nodding when his mum started on about whatever. Something on the radio about an opposition censure motion in State Parliament, a renewed proposal for a Mount Wellington chairlift, then – 'Fire Service authorities investigating the Derwent Valley fire are focusing their investigation on the Meadowbank Campground area …'

His fishing spot wasn't quite there, but still …

Someone messed with the volume.

'Jenny,' Uncle Pete called out.

'I'm in the laundry.'

Seconds later came Aunt Jenny's kookaburra laugh.

The radio volume went back up: something about government subsidies for drought-stricken farmers, followed by the traffic report, sport and 'twenty-two degrees in the city', then more of Hobart's Top 40. Hard for him to care now which new group had made the cut.

His mum leaned closer, picking something off the back of his t-shirt. She rubbed the back of her hand over his arm then across his cheek. 'Your burns have healed well.'

'My burns aren't the concern.'

She patted his hand. He took it back. 'I lost them, Mum: Ella, Sook, Moonshine. Me: the one supposedly there to look after them.' The repeat button again, like watching Harvey Norman ads on TV.

'I still remember your grandpop's mad terrier, Shooter, sniffing through our veggie patch once and latching onto the tail of a tiger snake and shaking it violently back and forth. Your grandpop running over with a spade and screaming, "Drop it, drop it, ya little mongrel!" Of course when Shooter did, the snake reared up and was about to sink its fangs when your grandpop took the spade to it. It all happened so fast. From dog sniff to decapitation in a matter of seconds. Later your grandpop said to me, "Fear can either paralyse you, Alice, or help you to move faster." It's obvious to everyone how you responded during the fire. Just like your grandpop did that day. Remember, Nick,

Ella's alive. Her burns will heal. She can feel, think, see, hear and talk because of you. A graft or two will take care of the rest.'

Ella – like Mum and John – so positive, full of ideas. Loving French at school. With plans to buy a beret and go to Paris, maybe study the language there, maybe teach English there, maybe this, maybe that, maybe everything.

Doors opened and closed inside then the house noises fell away again.

'Canberra rang while you were out walking,' she said.

Nick jerked his head around. 'What did they say?'

'He still hasn't returned.'

A crow glided over. He watched it until it disappeared. 'You know, Mum, I even miss him going gorilla on me in the mornings, scratching his ribs, grabbing my ears and handing me a banana.'

'No malice in it. Just big doses of brotherly love.'

Not quite how he'd read it. But he wouldn't be going on about it because an idea was forming – one that for the moment replaced his shame. 'Ban Thai Guesthouse, isn't it, Mum?'

'Last we heard.'

'Mae Sot, on the border with Burma?' He said this from habit. They both knew where John had gone. It had been drilled into them.

'Last we heard.'

'I read in my social psychology book once that it's normal for teenagers to get down on themselves, and when they do they often fantasise about being someone else, or living somewhere else, or both.'

'While performing great heroic deeds no doubt.'

'Yeah, that too.'

She watched him. 'Like who and where for instance?'

He knew the place was super-hot, the dry season now; that there was a medical clinic for Burmese refugees and lots of refugee camps nearby. He answered quickly, 'As a missing-brother finder in Mae Sot, Thailand.'

No surprise she lost her smile, her reply almost instant. 'You're in fantasyland, Nicholas James Stanish, if you think that's going to happen. You need to finish growing up first. A good thing school is starting again next week. It'll get your mind squarely back on reality.'

Nick thought of Basher Bates – self-proclaimed Derwent Valley Thug-of-the-Year – and his rat pack retards moving out from behind the demountable, chest-bumping and shoving each other, cracking up. They'd flicked away their smokes and headed his way, stooped, heads hooded, hands buried in bag-trouser pockets, their brains too small to go anywhere on their own. 'Some butt ends for ya ta suck on back there, dickhead,' one had shouted at him as he'd leant back against the fence trying hard to look relaxed.

'Enjoy your breakfasts, did ya?'

Basher's second in command: 'Fuck off.'

The pack had chimed in – same words, same volume – front to back in order of rank. All except the Thug-of-the-Year striding out in front of everyone else, like he was leading a parade, pleased with how the morning was progressing. If thuggery were a school subject he'd have earned a scholarship to university by now.

Hardly the reality Nick was looking forward to, another year of avoiding those drongo drop-kicks; along with the consequences of setting the Derwent Valley alight: coppers, fire investigation authorities, a magistrate, the Ashley Youth Detention Centre. 'What about the reality of not having a place of our own anymore, of not hearing from John for … for how long?'

'Four weeks, three days.'

'Yeah, that long. Someone has to go up there and find out what's happened to him, Mum.' He looked beseechingly at her. 'You and Dad can't. You've got too much going on here. So that leaves me. This is what I want, Mum – not to go back to school just yet, but to go up and find John, or at least try to.'

'Whoa.' She raised her hands as if to stop him from leaving that moment. 'Nicholas James, the last thing this family needs right now is another son gone missing.'

'Hardly missing, Mum. There're internet cafes up there and I'll have my laptop, so I'll keep in contact – promise. And it makes sense for me to go. And it's not like the school will go into mourning over my absence. Geez, Mum, the teachers will celebrate. It'll be like Christmas holidays all over again.'

'Don't exaggerate. You just weren't at your best last term.'

'But I will be this term after I get back. I'll really slog, Mum, and catch up on all my missed schoolwork.' In Ashley? 'I will – promise.'

'The answer's no.'

For reasons he obviously couldn't explain to her, he was desperate to get away, either to Mae Sot or somewhere, anywhere. 'What do you mean no?' Despite saying this, he understood her stunned look. But why shouldn't he go up there? He was old enough – just. 'I've got the money, and it's not like I'm asking you to let me climb Mount Everest or go sailing solo around the world. I've travelled. I've got a passport. I've been to Bali, Melbourne, the Gold Coast. I can do Thailand too, no worries – I know I can, I know it. Please let me go.'

She jumped up as if bull-ant bitten. 'No way,' she answered, escaping back into the house.

A minute or so later his dad came out and sat down, big hands gripping his knees. He scanned the trees, that drifty 'You care for the land and it'll care for you' look on his face.

'Your mother mentioned you're keen to go find your brother,' he said finally.

'Yeah, Dad, I am.'

'I read an article last weekend in *The Mercury* that pretty well summed up my view on travelling anywhere north of Hobart.'

Nick prepared himself for the 'Mum's totally right' lecture.

'It went on about how travel is mostly about eating and drinking and waiting in great long lines worrying about being late somewhere or losing things or getting sick. I reckon I could've written the article. Point is, there'll be nothing like a tropical paradise waiting for you up there in John-country. You know that, don't ya?'

Stunned, Nick stared at his father's face. 'Yeah, Dad, I do.'

'Then we'd better work out what we're going to say to your mother.'

10

THAILAND.

Sitting next to Jake 'from Cronulla by way of Broken Hill' made it near impossible for Nick to keep to himself. And he imagined what his family would say about the bloke if they were on the bus. His mum: 'He's like a car accident – you know you shouldn't watch, but it's hard to look away.' Ella: 'What a funny man.' His dad: 'Voice box the size of a silo.' John: 'Could talk underwater, like someone else we know.' Strange how much Nick missed his family now; had done since leaving Hobart.

'Grow a crop of Thailand's best out there, don'tcha reckon, dude?'

'Yeah, s'pose you could,' Nick said, having no idea what 'Thailand's best' was.

Jake scrutinised him up and down as if calculating his weight and height.

'What?' Nick asked of the look.

'Like, when I call ya "dude", I'm not like referrin' ta ya as a hundred per cent dude. Ya look a bit young and innocent to be that. I mean more a lesser dude. Maybe fifty per cent. Ya right with that?'

A hundred per cent weirdo, Nick thought, before answering, 'Yeah, fine.'

'Good man.' For bonding purposes, Nick presumed, Jake gave him a lesser-dude punch to the shoulder. 'But I'll say this, dude. I'm likin' your company.'

'*Awesome.*' Awesome if they could get to Mae Sot in the next half-minute.

Moments later the bus turned off the main road and Jake hopped up and shouted, 'The twelve-pack, flash-packer super-express about to disembark! Give the driver a clap, fellow farangs!' Only he did so; the Thais and 'fellow farang' backpackers on board either .yawned themselves awake or eyed him like he'd escaped a psycho ward.

Jake must have missed those looks though, or mistaken them for hero-worship, for with no loss of confidence he sat, turned all wide-eyed and beaming towards Nick, and jabbered on again, un-ignorable. 'I thought I'd grow wrinkles and like go arthritic before Mae Sot popped up on the windscreen. What a tragedy that would be.' He lifted his face, patted his cheek. 'More than just a haircut on board shorts, I can tell ya. Like I've spent twenty-three years honing these centrefold features.'

Laughing – for whatever reason – the freckled (like he'd been mud sprayed), auburn-haired (sticking up like he'd been dragged through the bush backwards) Jake tipped his head back, finished off his tinnie, sandal-crunched it and tossed it out the window. 'Might have a last beer to celebrate that fact, and our arrival. Like to join me, dude, for a wee small one?'

Warm beer, swaying bus, lumpy road: a recipe to vomit. 'No thanks.'

Jake freed a tinnie from his backpack and waved it in front of Nick anyway. 'Ah go on, say ya want one. Good for the pimples they are.'

Had Nick grown a few pimples since getting on the bus wouldn't have surprised him. Enough time to. Nick shook his head.

'Ya with the Mormons or somethin'?'

'Not yet. But I might be one day,' he lied.

'The god squad. Right. Like that, is it?' Jake ripped the tab off the tinnie and took a hard-thirst guzzle straight out of that VB ad back home. 'Mmm, keeps ya nicely jacked-up this time of day,' he said, blowing beery breath over Nick's face. 'Proof positive there's a god watchin' over us … Doubt he's a friggin' Mormon one though.'

Nick looked back out at the heat mirages and scrappy fields merging into corrugated iron shacks, a timber yard, motorbike repair shop, roadside fruit stalls. How Jake could drink beer warm like he'd been doing since leaving Bangkok boggled Nick's mind.

'Have a look at the rubbish out there!' Jake piped up again. 'The local tip, like, it's been carpet-bombed. And those buildin's over there saggin' with age, lookin' half-eaten. Ya wouldn't wanna like sell real estate around 'ere, would ya? Could be a short stay, unless …' His mouth went slack, his eyes big, like he was witnessing a holy act. 'I see visions, Nicko. And—' he cupped a hand to his ear '—somethin' else is comin' through … Would ya believe it? Patpong. Hear it? Neon-lit exotica thumpin' out do-it, do-it, do-it music as those goddesses of the silver poles buff their pleasure points radiant with G-string moves we'll never stop dreamin' about. Oooo-eee, how good were those Patpong nights? Our eyes about to pop their sockets, havin' ta gulp our Singhas down ta keep our love muscles from burstin'.'

'What do you mean "our"? I wasn't there.'

'No, dude, ya weren't, but ya should've been, so I'm like includin' ya in my golden moment memories.' He polished off his tinnie, crushed it under his sandal and tossed it out the window. 'Gotta be a Pussycat Club in Mae Sot. I've not struck a Thai town yet that didn't have one, or its equivalent. Have you?'

'Straight from Bangkok to here, so I wouldn't know.'

'Not even a short Patpong detour, like, just to get the juices flowin'?'

Patpong could have been in Africa for all Nick knew. 'No, not even that.'

'Tragedy.' Jake gave Nick a questioning look. 'So, whereabouts ya stayin' in Mae Sot?'

Alarm hit Nick hard. He'd hoped to just wave good-bye when they arrived, and that would be the end of it. 'Haven't decided,' he lied. Having Jake next to him 'on countdown time to his first Mae Sot beer and bonk' had eased his loneliness and anxiety, for a while anyway. Jake was entertaining (first time Nick had laughed in weeks). He slept, woke, rabbited on, downed tinnies, left to 'drain the dragon', came back 'rapturous' about the 'pure relief and feeling of ecstasy' the experience provided him with. Most importantly, he didn't ask probing questions – until now. So despite his distraction value, Jake wasn't the full-time travelling companion Nick was looking for. Nobody was. And if Nick did choose to enter a Pussycat Club, or some such place under-age, he wanted to do it on his own, in his own time. 'I might have a look around, see what's available.'

'I can save ya the trouble. Like, Lonely Planet reckons the Bai Fern Guesthouse is the Hilton by another name. Dead centre of town, clean, cockroach-resistant, big fridge. Can't be far from there to the nearest coldie and leggy lady serving it up, can it?' He paused for a breath, not an answer. 'Sample the merchandise, support the local tourist industry. How perfect is that? And not to worry, my man, like, as long as you've graduated from nappie-wearing ya're old enough to get in the clubs here.'

He took a mid-rant break to glance out the window before continuing on. 'A piece of advice though when ya do get inta a club. Either wear three pairs of yer strongest underdaks or yer baggiest trousers so ya got plenty of room ta grow, cuz ya will.' He winked. 'A vital statistic, mate: two-thirds of the local lads have their first below-the-belt experience wrapped up in the arms of Pussycat girls, or their clones.'

'Really?'

'Aaaab-solutely. Check it out on Google if you don't believe me: the girls' sole purpose is to share their charms and knowledge for the benefit of mankind, especially the under-educated ones.'

'At a price.'

'Yeah, well … poverty's sad, sadder than a three-legged dog, but what can ya do? Ya can go a lifetime with an empty brain, but not long on an empty stomach. Everyone's gotta eat. So not to fret, it's coin goin' to a good cause, and like no way will yer Pussycat experiences feature on Facey, Twaddle or Piffle, unless ya want 'em to. Ya can, like, take a mornin' to snap some photos: temples, boneheads, the market place, that sort of thing, then—'

'Boneheads?'

'Hairless ones. Monks, my man, monks.' He gave a nod towards the front. 'There're a few about ya know.'

And there were. Nick spotted four, the backs of their heads like great brown onions.

'So, what ya do is select yer best pics, break out the lappie and fire 'em off ta the rellies and friends back home. Or ya get back home and show 'em off personally while tellin' 'em all a Buddha story or two. "That's our Nick," they'll be sayin', elbowin' each other in the ribs, "gobblin' up the culture, gettin' the most out of his travels."'

Nick rested his head on the back of his seat and looked out the window again. Jake, on full throttle, was starting to grate.

'Anyway, Nicko, up the Pussycats. Up the Bai Fern Guesthouse. Up our Mae Sot budget plan! Like, what we save in sharin' a room, we spend hangin' out sharin' a culture.' He waited for a response that didn't come. 'Ya gotta toothache or somethin'? Ya're not lookin' that thrilled.'

'I want to have a look around the place first.'

Jake did a quick take of nearby passengers before eyeing Nick again. 'Right, that's cool … Mind if I tag along, just ta get a feel for the place too?'

The bus slowed and shuddered to a stop on the edge of a huge, crowded market place. Mae Sot was out there waiting for them.

* * *

Nick turned off the main road onto a crumbling laneway, Jake following at just above crawling pace, scanning left, right and behind. The sun's glare and oven-blast heat were starting to ease. People were appearing, sitting down in the shelter of shade. On a nearby goal-less pitch, shirts versus skins school-agers played hard soccer in a haze of dust and reddening sunlight. Beyond the pitch, a pagoda's golden spire, bell-shaped stupas and whitewashed walls stood out stark against the paint-starved town.

A skeletal dog, protecting a mound of rubbish, growled then attacked a smaller dog that dashed off yelping, nearly barrelling Jake over. 'Yo dog. Bugger off!' he shouted, his mouth back in gear after a lengthy pause. 'Eh, Nicko, you a dog-lover?'

A passing monk answered instead. 'Yes. Maybe you dog someday.' Like he was his own audience, the monk clapped and laughed, obviously delighted.

Jake regarded him like he was an extra-terrestrial. 'Your name Nicko, is it?'

'My name Phra Maha Sathienphongse. I thank you for me practise English.'

'Ah, right.' Jake leered at him, eyes squinting. 'Well Phra, can I ask you a question, one that at this time of day is very important for us to find the answer to?'

'Yes please.'

'Me mate and I are looking for a place that serves up cold beer. Is there such a place in Mae Sot ya could recommend? It doesn't have to be 5-star.'

'The Snake Skin.' Phra pointed in the general direction they'd come from. 'Not far – three street just.'

'Beauty! That's where me mate and I will be later on if ya're up for a drink and more practise – my shout.' He turned and shouted, 'Eh Nicko, drop your landin' gear a sec.' It was like Jake had signed up with him and wasn't about to let him out of his sight. He caught up and wiped his face. 'Sweatin' bullets I am. Big ones.' He looked back over his shoulder at the monk, made claws of his hands and spoke in a deep robotic voice, 'Totally weird boneheads with questionable fashion sense are wandering around out here unchaperoned. The vibes, my man, like not good.'

'Yeah, well, just another kilometre or two to go.' Nick turned and continued on, eyeing the old, two-storey wooden building on his left and spotting what he was looking for: a sign saying Ban Thai Guesthouse over the front entry. He looked away and kept going though, feeling a little smug leading a twenty-three-year-old around the back blocks of Mae Sot. After a hundred metres or so he stopped, dropped his backpack and made a point of adjusting the straps.

Jake drew level again, using a hand as a visor. 'Warm, wouldn't ya say?'

'You got any sunnies?'

'Nah. Hadn't planned on spending much time outdoors.' He straightened up and scanned the surroundings as a lookout would. 'Different postcode out here, don't ya reckon?'

'Yeah maybe. I just want to see what's up ahead.'

'Probably China.'

Nick thought he could hear voices coming from the back of the guesthouse. German male, he thought, followed by American female, without a doubt. Then an Aussie female, or maybe Kiwi, he couldn't be sure. 'Anyway, best to keep going before darkness sets in. You coming?'

'Ya need to know, Nicko, tropical sun has never been kind to my skin. Another five minutes out 'ere and I could grow inta one great blister.'

'Right.'

'And not only that, but in sun-fried places like this one, it's important to conserve energy, prioritise yer needs. Know what me priorities are?'

'I reckon I do, but go on and tell me.'

'Grog, air-con and chasin' women, at least those easily caught, and the prospect of satisfying any one of those is not lookin' all that bright at the moment.' He turned and fixed his eyes faraway. Seconds later he muttered mysteriously, 'Young nephew thought the sun shone outta my proverbial. The Amazing Spider-Man I was. Could do no wrong.'

What he was talking about, Nick hadn't the foggiest.

'Top little bloke.' Jake went on, 'And in our later years, if we're lucky enough not to have run off any mountain roads or crashed inta any trees, there're a couple of other needs we'll have ta consider as well, like a good telly and an armchair ta fall asleep in at night.' It was like a different person had put on his skin. He eyed the ground and continued on, weirding Nick out. 'Yeah ... not everyone lives long enough to like ... get to that armchair stage though, do they?' He stayed gripped in some other place for five seconds, ten, before his eyes found Nick again. He grinned and stated the obvious, 'Away in limbo-land there for a moment.'

'Yeah.' Nick watched him closely.

'Anyway, returning to the topic at hand ... Which was?'

'Prioritising needs.' *Like getting your head checked.*

'Course it was; just testin'.' His voice ramped up again. 'Know what happens when blokes ignore their basic needs?'

'Can't imagine.'

'Cretinisation syndrome sets in. Heard of it?'

'Not really.'

'A rapid thickenin' of the skull. Left untreated it'll constrict the brain like a grape in a winepress. For real, dude, for real. Like Google it up if ya don't believe me. And I'm gettin' cretinised big time out 'ere. Know what I'm thinkin'?'

'Shelter and drink.'

'Spot on, Sherlock. Place called the Snake Skin. Monk-recommended.' He pointed. 'Three blocks that way. On my radar now like a cane field for a cane toad. Croak, croak. Meet you there, alright?'

'Done.'

Jake headed off all springy and urgent now, his 'limbo-land' detour left behind as a curiosity. Moments later a motor scooter passed, trailing exhaust. As it closed in on Jake, he turned and signalled it to stop.

It did and he said something to the driver then hopped on the back and the scooter took off, Jake waving back blindly.

Seconds later, with Mae Sot gone quiet, Nick walked back to the Ban Thai. He passed through its lobby into a small courtyard dotted with tropical plants and small trees. Western men and women in cargo pants, t-shirts and sandals sat in the sweaty shade, drinks in hand.

A local hopped up and approached him, asking if he was looking for a room.

'A single room, yes. I'm also looking for my brother, John Stanish. I know that ...' The local lost his smile. The courtyard went quiet. 'I know that he was staying here up to about a month ago.'

'I can give you a room, but ...' The local glanced over at a girl sitting close by. She stood and came over, introducing herself in a slow Aussie accent as Lina Larkin. About John's age – mid-twenties – round face, big, wide-set blue eyes, lightly freckled skin and honey-coloured hair hanging in a thick braid down her back. He read her HEALTH IS A HUMAN RIGHT t-shirt then gave her his name.

'Tasmania, right?' she asked.

'Yeah ... Good guess.'

'I'm from Queensland, inland from Cairns.' She pointed to the lobby he'd just come from. 'It's cooler inside. Let's talk in there?'

He followed her into the lobby and they sat facing each other, Lina leaning forward like some school counsellor about to have a heart-to-heart with him, a pose he'd grown accustomed to lately. 'You have sisters, other brothers, Nick?'

That seemed a strange question from a total stranger. 'An older brother and a little sister. They're the reason I'm here.'

'How old is your sister?'

'Ten.'

'What's her name?'

Instead of answering he just looked at her, mystified and starting to get irritated.

Lina leaned back, clasping her hands together in her lap. 'Her name's Ella, right?'

'If you know, why did you ask?'

She studied him a moment. 'This might sound like a line out of a spy movie, but I just need to ensure you are who you say you are.'

The Snake Skin was starting to sound good. 'I've got ID if you want to see it.'

'Not necessary.'

'You working for INTERPOL or something?'

Her face took on an amused look Nick couldn't read. 'No, AusAid, like your brother, as well as the Mae Tao Medical Clinic and an organisation called The Burma Children Medical Fund … So what do you know about Mae Sot?'

'Not much. I've only been here an hour or so.'

'I'll enlighten you. It's largely a trading town: drugs, gemstones, weapons, teak, animal skins and of course people. Human trafficking and the sex trade are organised crime's third-largest money earner in this part of Thailand, after drugs and weapons selling. Stay a while and you'll meet all sorts of people. Some work for the benefit of mankind: missionaries, aid agency workers and volunteers. Others work for the benefit of themselves and their bank accounts, including Thai policemen – gotta love them – who request posting to Mae Sot to collect bribes, and also Burmese government agents, who aren't past paying the police or young westerners travelling on the cheap to collect information for them. Like where exactly has a foolhardy Tasmanian aid agency worker with a medical background – suspected of crossing into Burma illegally in the past – disappeared to this time? It's why you're here, right, because you've not heard from your brother for weeks?'

He took a moment to absorb all that, before nodding.

'No one here has.' She lowered her eyes, worked a silver ring up and down her index finger. 'He and I are … close. So I'm really worried about him too. In the past few weeks there's been fighting between Burmese soldiers and Karen fighters just over the border.' She leaned forward again, eyes boring into him. 'Two days ago word came out of the Mae La Refugee Camp north of here that a young westerner was seen by refugees in the Burmese mountains. Has to be John. He'd stick out like a three-headed ox. I've not been able to find out anything more, but I'm scheduled to accompany some refugee patients back to the camp tomorrow afternoon. So I plan to ask some questions and hopefully get some useful answers.'

'Can I go along?'

She shook her head. 'It takes three or four days to get a pass, even if you bribe the right Thai policemen. But I'll be back here this time tomorrow. We can meet and I'll tell you what I've been able to find out, if anything.'

'Thanks.'

'In the meantime, and excuse my bossiness, I think you should get to know Mae Sot a bit better, especially the people your brother and I and so many others are here to help – Karen refugees. You'll have to do it unescorted, at least most of it, as I'm working tonight and tomorrow. What do you think? Up for it?' She made it sound like a challenge.

'Yeah, sure.'

'Good. Start tonight. Lie about your age and go into the Snake Skin next to the Burmese market … You're smiling, why?'

'I've heard the name.'

'And?'

'And they serve cold beer.'

'Are you a Lady Gaga or Pink fan?'

He gave her a puzzled look. 'They're alright, I guess. Why?'

'Just curious.'

Just curious always meant more than that, he thought.

'To gain some understanding of Burmese working conditions in Thailand, especially for women, go to the Snake Skin and sit through a Lady Gaga or Pink performance.'

'Lady Gaga and Pink … here? You're joking.'

'Mae Sot, a world-renowned venue on the international celeb circuit.'

Was that a smirk on her face? Had to be.

'You didn't know that, did you?'

She was playing with him. 'No.'

'Anyway, that done, rent a bike or take a motorbike taxi tomorrow and go three kilometres along the Friendship Bridge road to the Mae Tao Medical Clinic. That's where your brother and I work. Look for a big sign on the left. Turn off and go down a dirt road. You can't miss it. Ask for me at the front office and I'll give you a quick tour of the place. Afterwards, continue on for another three kilometres to the Friendship Bridge. When you get there take the concrete walkway about two hundred metres south along the Moei River, sit down on a shaded concrete bench and watch the river activity, greet the day-trip smugglers from Burma plying their trade. Not a place you'll see featured on any Flight Centre travel brochures, but important to see, nonetheless, for getting a better understanding of the place. If you still have any curiosity and energy left, return to Mae Sot via the Burmese market place in the centre of town and have a wander. Accomplish all that, and you'll be ready to meet me here tomorrow for more debriefing, okay?'

'Okay.'

A slow smile formed on her face. 'If you don't accomplish all that, I'll meet you here anyway.'

II

Nick gawked, drop-jawed, finding everything and everyone mind-boggling: the loud voices, laughter and thumping sound system; the mass of shiny red faces reflected in the strobe lighting between a horse-shoe stage in one corner and a long, polished bar in the opposite one. To his right, what looked to be the bar-girl night shift descended a staircase to hoots and whistles and scattered applause. To his left, a cloud of smoke hovered over locals sitting in booths, seemingly incapable of breathing without cigarettes in their mouths.

'Nice,' Jake declared, his O-shaped eyes following a passing bar-girl in break-ankle heels, sprayed-on tank-top, breasts like side-on cereal bowls. 'We call 'em "skimpies" back on the Hill; girls flown in from the Gold Coast for blokes' birthdays, that sort of thing.'

The girl circled back, squealing when a hand reached out from the next table, latched on to her arm and pulled her onto a lap.

'Ooo-eee, playtime at the Gaga-dome!' Jake whooped, warming up to the night shift and its feature act. 'Queue starts at the door and ends at the Mekong River.' In show-pony mode again, his voice rocketed to presenter-level to include them in Lady Gaga's upcoming gig. 'And, ladies and gentlemen, boys and girls, slippin' into our awesome Lady's megastar slipstream tonight, all the way from Broken Hill and ...' He threw Nick a quizzical look. 'Where was it again?'

'Gretna.'

'Gretna Green, Australia, a round of applause please for the renowned Gaga-bloggers and Thigh-land nightlife brothers-in-arms, Jake Jones and Nick Stanisopoulos.' He shouted like he wanted to be heard outdoors, 'May our names long be remembered!'

While a few not taking phone snaps hoisted stubbies in the air in acknowledgement, Nick leaned over the table and said, 'Stanish, my surname's Stanish.'

'Yeah, well ... To quote a Pommie bloke long gone to worm meat, what's in a name? That which we call feet by any other name would still smell of sweat. But enough of legends.' He nodded towards the stage. 'That's the name we're here for.' He went for his stubby and stopped in mid-swig. 'Have a look at those magazine legs. Oooeee, I'm startin' to feel a fire down below.' He flogged an air guitar and sang a line from Lady Gaga's 'Bad Romance'.

And Lady Gaga was here – well, the Mae Sot version of her anyway – stepping onto the stage: honey-brown heart-shaped face, red bad-girl baby-doll dress, fishnet tights, mega-heels, long white wig, giant sunnies, thick red lipstick, cheeks painted in blue tears and lightning bolts. Moments later, spot-lit in red, she was Bad Romancing and silver pole-dancing to sound-system accompaniment loud enough to shake the speakers off the walls. A hand, a leg wrapped around the pole, slowly circling it, she ramped up her singing voice, wanting someone's ugly, wanting their disease, wanting their everything as long as it was free.

She stepped out of her dress and tossed it. In black lingerie under-wear above her fishnets now, she sang on karaoke-style, working her way up and down the pole. While others gaped, clapped and wolf-whistled, Nick just sat quietly. To him, she looked off: her heavily made-up and painted face more like a circus mask than the genuine Lady Gaga's. No emotion in it. No smile. No invitation eyes; no eye contact at all, just her targeted stare aimed somewhere between her audience and the strobe lighting as she belted out 'Bad Romance'.

She was obviously having a different effect on Jake though. 'Like two things, dude, that Thai women do better than the ladies back home,' he piped up, 'and one of 'em is singin'.' He cackled, head bobbing, fingers tapping.

Their stubbies arrived courtesy of a bar-girl in a red bikini bottom and tank top, BEAUTY IS IN THE WALLET OF THE BEHOLDER in white letters across the front. She set the stubbies on the table and stroked Jake's cheek with the back of her hand. 'Handsome man, what's your name?' she asked.

Jake gave her the slow once-over. 'Jake, Jacob, Jasper, your choice, darls.'

She ran fingers along the rim of his ear, took his hand and pressed it against her Bad Romance-grooving backside. 'You like what you feel, Jasper?'

'I do, I do,' Jake answered. 'Cheeks like … Let me re-assess.' He did. 'Like ripe melons ready for pickin'.' He stuck an index finger in the air and aimed it at her. 'Without a doubt, darls. Number one cheeks in all of Mae Sot - yours.' He took out some bills, stuffed them down her tank top and said, 'Give me mate over there a sample. A warnin' though: he's shy, like me, so needs encouragement.'

She moved around to Nick and repeated her introduction, 'Number one in Mae Sot - yes?' she asked.

Nick felt his skin warm, his brain too muddled to think in sentences. 'Umm … Yes. Very nice. Uh … thank you.'

She pulled away, smiling at Jake like she'd been waiting all her life for him to show up at that table. 'You number one too,' she said, massaging him with her eyes. 'Number one movie star.'

Jake gave her a wink and a puppet grin. 'In the absence of Johnny Depp, too right I am.'

'I come back soon and be with you, my movie star,' she cooed, cocking her hips and swivelling them back towards the bar - a crescent of shiny dark wood with a mirrored back wall and glass shelves. A line of pole dancers sat - brown thighs, thin ankles, stiletto heels draped over the bar stools - awaiting their performance turns, eyes fixed on a wall-mounted television showing cartoons.

Jake – his eyes still on Number One – yelped, 'Whoa, dude. You registerin' what I am? Enough movement in that girl's hip-roll to like generate electricity, light up the entire town. Ooo-eee. She's on the highway to my heart, and all points south. Love this place! Like a friggin' theme park for the thirsty and girl-hungry. Where do I buy their t-shirts?' His head swung right, then left, before he looked at Nick again. 'Mate, Patpong's history.' He raised his fresh beer in a toast. 'I give you the chilled Snake Skin stubby, a beer suckled by the gods. Could the sun rise without it? The earth rotate? The rivers run? The tides roll in?' He cast his eyes upwards. 'So bless it, oh Lord Buddha and whoever's up there with ya, for like makin' Thigh-land and Kanga-land the places they are today.' Clink went the stubbies and Jake took a big swig, then swooned and eyed the entertainment.

With Jake otherwise occupied, Nick scanned the place a second time.

No one with obvious corporate or Gretna-farming connections. Mostly locals and backpackers drinking and yapping on, occasionally whipping out smartphones to take a few snaps. Fourteen or fifteen tables wedged between the stage and darkened booths where older men clutched stubbies, their eyes on the attractions – everywhere. Bar-girls sat on laps, snuggled up, stroked arms, and ordered and poured drinks. No other females, just them, and Nick wondered how Lina came to know so much about the place. One thing for certain, he wouldn't be coming in here with her anytime soon.

In the nearest booth, three crim-types sucked on stubbies and cigarettes, surveying the passing girls like everyone else. One – bull-necked, buzz-cut hair on the biggest pumpkin head Nick had ever seen, his wrists and fingers glittering gold – was the clone of a crime boss he'd seen in *The Sopranos*. And it wasn't long before a girl was on his lap stretching her arms halfway around him, claiming him all for herself: a gorilla-size bloke for a pixie-size girl.

Local blokes in American t-shirts and back-to-front baseball caps occupied two nearby tables, though a couple of westerners – dreadlocked, studded and tattooed – sat at the closest one. Next to them, and eyeing them off, were two lady-boys (Jake's words) in red mega-heels, tight black jeans and singlets, their hair puffed up, their eye make-up rivalling Lady Gaga's. No one seemed to be enjoying themselves any more than they were as they sipped small, green drinks from long-stemmed glasses, chatted, giggled, compared non-existent biceps and took body-beautiful snaps while letting out peals of laughter.

As Lady Gaga pole-danced her way through 'Bad Romance', 'Just Dance' and 'Kaboom', two girls approached the westerners' table, hips moving as though on hinges. They landed on their chosen blokes' laps, put lips to ears and lap-danced their intentions while the lady-boys looked on and exchanged their own lip-to-ear commentary then clapped their hands and cackled some more.

Lady Gaga finished up and left the stage, and Jake took up his air guitar again, singing about watching them come, watching them go, there being a fire down below …

'Bob Seger.'

'Spot on, my man. A rock 'n' roll legend old enough to play Santa Claus.'

'My dad plays that song on his guitar.'

'Dude, only the elite do. Not for the amp-deafened, coke-snortin' gangsta rap …' He stopped. The girls at the next table were standing up, holding out invitation hands to a couple of blokes. Jake leaned closer to Nick and said in a stage whisper, 'Where to, do ya reckon?'

It was like being called on to give an answer in class when your brain was in another world. 'Dunno. The bar maybe?'

'I don't think so.' He reached for his beer and watched the girls lead their chosen ones towards the staircase at the back. 'Get out much in Green Patch, do ya?'

Nick stretched forward. 'Gretna. I live in Gretna.'

'Wherever … Well do ya?'

'Yeah, a lot. I go to school, fish, grow my own vegies most of the year, chop wood for our oldie neighbours, feed our animals, help my dad on the tractor sometimes, train my Labrador – Sook – and ride Moonshine my horse.' He felt his throat constrict. 'Or at least I … Anyway, I play a lot of cricket too in New Norfolk and Hobart during the summer.'

'Right … Good for you.' He couldn't hold back a smirk.

'Why are you smiling?'

'No reason, just smilin'.'

'You're so like my mum.'

'Really? Can't say anyone's said that to me before.' He kept his eyes on Nick for a few extra beats. 'So what would your olds say if they saw you eyin' off the leggy Lady Gaga about now?'

Nick thought for a moment. 'Dad nothing. Mum, probably something like, "Not exactly prime-time family viewing, is it love?"'

'Awesome. I like her already.' He drained his beer then looked left, right, found Number One and signalled for three more stubbies, like he feared the place might run out of them, before studying Nick again. 'So, up for all of this then?'

'All of what?'

'Like, look around, work it out. It's not that tough a question.'

Nick's confidence dipped. He'd felt cool, too cool for school and so in control as Mr Mae Sot Knowledgeable leading Jake through the streets and along the back laneway earlier – but no more. An invisible wall had gone up: Nick the clueless on one side, Jake and the rest of the bar-smarts on the other. 'Yeah, I'm up for it,' he said anyway, faking it. 'You?'

'Into it like a show bag. Can't do this back home, can ya?'

'Not in Gretna. Don't know about the rest of Australia.'

'Take my word for it, the rest of the country is, like, tea and scones and lace serviettes compared to Thigh-land – Kings Cross included.'

Nick nodded as if agreeing from his vast experience in such things. 'Yeah.'

Number One sashayed back over, her serving tray filled with stubbies and two small glasses of a tea-coloured drink, straws provided. She set them down. 'Break time now. You buy me and my friend drink, we sit with you.'

'Two drinks, no problem.' Jake stuffed more bills down her tank top and she sank onto his lap, wrapped an arm around him and rubbed his thigh. 'Ooohh, yeeess,' he swooned. 'I think ... Don't stop ... I think I've found my life partner. At least for the night.' He looked across the table. 'Bar babes, Nicko, one of humanity's three guiding lights.' He went for his beer, raised it in a toast. 'Along with the grog and retro rock and roll.' Clink again went the chilled brown stubbies and Jake swigged deeply before asking Number One, 'So where's your friend?'

She looked over at the bar, gave a 'come here' wave and pointed to Nick.

Lady Gaga glided over in a short, sleeveless lilac robe and what remained of her performance gear: lingerie, stilettos, white wig and hand-held sunnies. She sat on Nick's lap as she would a bar stool, placed her sunnies on the table and stared at them like they were about to hold a conversation with her.

Jake and Number One continued communicating mouth-to-ear, smiling and giggling, their hands getting to know one another.

Other than those two, Nick had no choice but to view Lady Gaga, her right shoulder and wig nudging his face. Under all that gunk, her face appeared widest across her cheekbones, her long eyes angling up at the outer ends. Thin arms and hands, long fingers, full lips, small nose and boobs, those scars ridging up from her left forearm. In truth, the bar-girls here scared him a little, but for whatever reason, this one didn't.

'How're yer trousers copin'?' Jake asked, glancing across the table.

Nick looked down. 'Yeah, fine. Haven't spilled anything on them.'

Jake's cackle drew looks from nearby tables. 'Like, just make sure nothing spills from the inside, that's what I'm thinkin'.'

Nick flushed neck to forehead, his skin hot with embarrassment.

'Drink to me only with thine eyes,' Jake spouted, ogling and squeezing Number One tighter. Again he cackled. 'Read that in a poem once.' He grinned like The Joker looking over at Nick. 'Some things just can't be helped. She likes me and her body has ideas my body's agreeing with.' He leaned forward. 'So ask me how my trousers are copin'.'

Nick did so with zero interest, and barely heard the answer. It had been a long day, probably too much of it spent in Jake's company. The beer in front of him would be his last. He sipped it, switching his thoughts to his brother.

Minutes later, with everyone's drinks but Lady Gaga's gone, Jake stuck more bills down Number One's expanding tank top. They stood and Number One leaned over and whispered something in

Lady Gaga's ear before blowing Nick a kiss. Then she turned and went to the bar.

'Takin' the stairway ta heaven,' Jake explained, grinning. 'Just ta check out the accommodation of course, see if it's up to Broken Hill standard.' He took a thumb-size, packaged item out of his pants pocket. His eyes met Nick's again. 'Means you'll be left here unchaperoned. You cool with that?'

Which, once Lady Gaga was off his lap, would make it easier for him to leave the place. 'Yeah, course I am.'

'Where are ya stayin'?' Jake asked.

After a moment's hestitation Nick told him the Ban Thai.

'What's yer room number there?'

No sense lying, he'd find out eventually. 'Four.'

Jake moved around closer to Nick as Number One returned. 'Tomorrow, by nine o'clock, if I'm not, like, number four knockin', ya'll know I'm still rockin' and in no mood for further exercise, of the daytime sort anyway. I'll meet ya here tomorrow night.' He shoved the item into Nick's front pocket and pointed to it. 'For when ya're throbbin' and bobbin' and ready to pop. But ya'd know all about that, wouldn't ya?'

Nick suspected now what it was. 'A condom?'

'Toppa the class, wonder boy.' Jake's grin lengthened. 'Ya don't suffer from a latex allergy, do ya?'

Nick shook his head, a look on his face like he'd just wet himself.

'And ya're not Catholic?'

'No.'

'Set then. If ya feel challenged, just ask your good lady here for advice. Sign language is all ya'll need.' He nodded at Lady Gaga. 'A girl ta turn yer peach-fuzz to whiskers, splinter yer bones, knock yer socks off if ya still got 'em on. And remember, dude, ya're not with her to talk and she's not with ya to listen.' He collected his backpack and eyed Number One. 'What is she here for, darls?'

Number One reached out and took his hand. 'I show you what.'

'Just think of it as huggin' with your hips,' Jake called out over his shoulder, before they burrowed between patrons and disappeared up the stairs.

Ten minutes passed without another word being spoken, while a second wigged pole dancer performed Pink's 'Sober' and 'Bad Bad Day', Nick sipping his beer, Lady Gaga – eyes cast downwards like she was about to jump off a building – not talking, not drinking, not doing anything at all.

So what was he supposed to say to her?

A tattooed local in a black skull cap, muscle t-shirt and jeans swaggered past scowling at Lady Gaga, who lowered her head again, seeming to shrink a little.

The 'chosen' from the next table returned, minus their girls. Big-eyed smiles and friendly abuse greeted them. A lot must have happened up there, because once the 'chosen' started yapping on, they couldn't stop.

When Pink finished up the noise increased, blokes herding together. Soon people had to shout to be heard.

Bar-girls passed by on the prowl for short-term partners. And as Nick watched them, he recalled a Rosanne Cash song his dad often sang on their pre-fire deck, a beer at his feet, his polished guitar gleaming in the late afternoon sun. About a girl offering up her body, just an open door, a fuel for other people's fancies: a body she didn't much need anymore. For something to do, he sang it quietly, no louder than a hum.

Lady Gaga turned, her eyes big like she was discovering his face for the first time. 'I like that song,' she said, her voice a little husky, like it had been sung out. 'Will you sing it for me again?'

Small miracle: she spoke – and in good English, with barely any accent at all. It took him a few moments to register she had. Then he did what she asked, though more self-consciously than before.

Once he finished, she tried to sing part of it.

Muscle t-shirt man strolled slowly past again, interrupting her. Lady Gaga watched him before returning her eyes to Nick, leaning into him, stroking his arm. 'You are handsome,' she said. 'I want to stay with you, for the memories.'

Nick seemed to nod and shake his head at the same time, his body screaming 'Yes!' from brain stem to tingling knees. But he was anxious about what 'stay' might mean; that he didn't know nearly enough to take the walk with her up those stairs, and beyond. He needed to think. He ordered another beer and another one of those tea-coloured drinks for Lady Gaga.

12

She knelt before her low table and faced the fist-size Buddha, his legs folded one over the other, right upturned palm resting on his left one, his eyes closed, face serene. She clasped her palms together and lowered her forehead to her fingertips, her lips moving without sound.

After a minute or so, she sat, pulled first one foot then the other onto her lap, and continued to watch her Buddha. If he were to open his eyes now, she thought, he'd understand how important his presence was. He was her focus, the burning candle and incense and lotus flower only there to highlight him. Nothing else on the table; nothing on the walls except for a lilac robe hanging from a nail above her bed; the white performance wig, folded clothes, bamboo pipe and other possessions were stowed under the bed.

Were it not for its location, thin walls and noise – thumping footsteps from above, heavy breathing next door – the room might well serve as a novice's cell. A fact reinforced now by her eyes closing, her joined hands rising above her forehead, dropping to her face, her lips mouthing more silent words.

She opened her eyes and scrutinised the Buddha again. As a young prince who had walked away from wealth twenty-five hundred years ago to wander India as a poor monk, he, better than anyone else, understood life's ironies. Like the irony of she, Nan Pau and Lady Gaga sharing the same body, kneeling now and praying in front of him. She imagined that his understanding was the reason for the small smile on his face as he listened to both her prayers and the racket going on around them.

Since she had bought him at the Burmese market six months earlier, he had seen her in this position most days, as well as in less pious positions, in less pious clothing or with nothing on at all. So he knew her, knew her heart, knew how hard she tried to keep it and her conscious mind separate from what her body was being paid to do: a body she no longer cared to know. Her prayers were constant reminders of that. Of course, her new-found pipe-smoking habit would be a concern to him, signalling that prayer was no longer enough to hold her together.

Would it be best then to turn him around to face the wall? Maybe.

Her mind wandered. If he could offer me advice right now, she thought, this is what I would like it to be: remember the lotus flower, where it comes from, how it overcomes obstacles, where it ends up.

She took her writing pad out from under the bed and wrote:

> From murky water
> A lotus flower blossoms,
> Reaches for the light.

Then she added:

> With patience,
> You can be
> That flower.

Shackled to the Snake Skin as she was, it helped to have a strong imagination.

$$* * *$$

Step gently, press down, step gently, press down … 'We're almost there, Kho Noc.'

KABOOOM!

A stench in the air: burnt clothes, burnt flesh? The voice of a soldier: 'This one's moving.' Two figures blurred by the sun. She looked away. Close up, propped over a small crater, Kho Noc's body: limp, ragged. Dark blood and body fluids …

Then, as always, she woke up to banging on the door, Billy J shouting to be let in. Since leaving Yangon, she thought, doors were rarely hers to open when she pleased. She got up, reached under the bed and took out the envelope containing her earnings then went to the door and opened it.

Billy J stomped in and planted himself, spread-legged. Never anything new in how he entered her room. Just the same intimidating scowl followed by three topics of monologue: threats, money and himself. 'I got no time bang all day,' he said, his voice gravelly like he had rocks in his mouth. A long night of drinking whiskey with his 'business friends', she thought.

'Next time break door, you pay fix it.'

He spoke no Burmese, she spoke very little Thai. Broken English was what they were left with, so broken she occasionally misunderstood him, which did nothing to improve his mood. He stuck out his palm. 'Baht – seven, zero, zero, zero.'

Should she inconvenience him by dying one day, she thought, he'd only mourn the loss of baht she handed over each morning.

'For rent, work permit, food and three last night customer.'

He certainly looked like the Thai boxer, street fighter and Snake Skin bouncer/enforcer the girls were constantly being reminded he was. Muscles stretching his Eminem t-shirt, arms and neck covered in tattoos, silver rings, chain bracelets, and as the only other Burmese bar-girl said before she disappeared weeks back, 'skull-capped American ghetto style'. Not that Mya fully understood what that meant.

She counted out the money and handed it over before sitting back down on the bed, drawing her knees up to her chin. She'd have to earn more the next few nights if she was going to meet her mother's expenses for the month. She expected him to grunt something, pocket the money and go. He didn't, but just glared at her.

'Boss not happy, so Billy J not happy.' He stuck three fingers in the air. 'Customer tree too long time. Boss say, again do, I take all night price for too long time.'

She nodded, mumbling more perhaps than she should have, 'Sorry. He was young, scared and wanted to talk and listen to me talk.'

He shook his head, his voice getting louder. 'You know rule. I already say. More time, more money. No different client. All same.' He scanned the room like he suspected someone or something illegal was hiding in it – a too-young Australian boy or a drug supply maybe? Rumour had it methamphetamines was another business he was involved in, as though all activities illegal and evil were his specialty. She doubted he was though. His clothes weren't rich enough, and why then would he be working in a place like this?

The pointlessness of everything struck her again: no stay-around people in her life, no joy, no foreseeable future beyond the Snake Skin. It was as if Billy J and this prison of a room were intent on squeezing every last bit of life out of her before … before what? 'Thais call it losing *khwan*, the spirit inside you,' the other Burmese bar-girl had said to her one night, before she disappeared. 'Losing *khwan* leaves you sad and empty, just like you are, Mya.' The girl's look had turned far away, as though she was lost. 'Bad things happen when you lose *khwan*.'

From her Tripitaka this: 'Joy follows pure thought like a shadow follows a person.' Not here. Not for her. Pure thoughts were deposited at the front door, only the shadows left to enter. As a distraction, yes, she still read her Tripitaka, or tried to, but lately it only served to frustrate her. She'd thought about writing a subtitle on the book's cover: 'Warning: Of no use to price-tag girls working in Thai bars.'

Sometimes – especially after he fined her for whatever he felt like fining her for – Billy J challenged her to complain, then he'd say something like, 'If you not like Snake Skin, can go back to Burma. Back to mountains, guns, snakes. Must go fast. Not let Network get you, Billy J get you again.' He made it sound like a game, one he'd enjoy taking part in, and winning. Of all the men who visited her room, she felt most diminished by Billy J: what he'd done to her that first day, so intent on crushing her, on controlling her every thought and action. And there wasn't a day he wasn't in her room.

Finished with his searching act, Billy J approached her, curling his fingers into a fist and jabbing her lightly on the chin. 'You not right do job, you do hate me.'

'I will never hate you, Billy J,' she said, 'Only what you do.' She asked herself, was that her Tripitaka speaking, or just her tired self wanting him gone?

Their eyes met and she imagined what his puzzled look was saying to her. That who he was and what he did were the same thing. That this dumb Burmese bitch was going to have to learn to speak Thai. That he'd bring a language book to her in the next day or two and charge her twice its market price: her choice how she wanted to pay him.

Or was her Burmese paranoia reading too much into his expression? For him there were Thais and westerners and Chinese bosses.

The rest of humanity – especially the Burmese – were equivalent to dogs.

'No work today, Gaga. Tonight start early – six o'clock. Not be late.' He reclaimed his swagger backing out and glaring pistol-eyed down at her.

All her time working here and he still didn't know her real name.

Alone behind the closed door again, she considered the day. So little to consider really; only ever two options: would she go to the Burmese market before or after biking to the Moei River?

* * *

Hard to walk straight and deal with his first-ever hangover at the same time. Halfway down the sun-blasted entryway, mouth dry like he'd eaten moths for breakfast instead of nothing, a hammer beating on his head, Nick stopped. He breathed deeply and waited for improvement. If it came, he didn't notice. He re-positioned his wraparounds against light sneaking in around the edges and watched poor-looking people standing around or sitting on tree-shaded benches and bordering walls.

'Right on time!' He heard Lina – as others had to – before he spotted her next to a big 4x4 Toyota fifty metres further along. She pointed to a series of flat-roofed, cinder-block buildings opposite the parking area and waited for him.

As he drew level with her, she lifted her sunglasses tiara-style onto her head and asked, 'Big night?'

'Yeah, s'pose.' Splats of red betel juice lay scattered along the ground and did nothing to soothe his stomach.

'Pleased you could make it then.' With a crisp heel and toe turn, and a 'Better get started,' the tour began, Nick following in her slipstream. 'The clinic's main goal, Nick, is to provide Burmese migrants and war-wounded with a complete range of health services from reproductive health to such specialities as eye, dental, HIV and mental health care. As well we have a prosthetic workshop for making limbs to replace those lost from accidents, land mines or gunshot wounds. Two other feature programs are health worker training and child protection.

Twenty different departments all up, around seven hundred full- and part-time staff and we see between four and five hundred Burmese migrant patients every day.' She stopped, regarded him as a teacher would. 'Any questions up to this point?'

Even in the shade he had to squint. It was like his eyes had shrunk, permanently. 'Do I have to sit an exam?'

'Nothing written, just oral. Sample question: why does this clinic see so many Burmese migrant patients each day? Answer: because no one else will.' She barely took a breath. 'Last year we delivered over two thousand, seven hundred babies. We do all of this on an operating budget of three and a half million dollars a year – thank you, aid agencies – and the incredible altruism and compassion of our volunteers.' She glanced over at him. 'There's a donation box in the front office if you'd like to help out. We take credit cards.'

Nick nodded absently. He reached into his pocket, fingering coins instead of the bills he'd started his Snake Skin night with.

'I'll ensure you get a receipt for tax purposes.'

'Right.'

They moved from one ward to another – eighteen in all – crammed with hard-looking wooden cots and patients and staff in white coats, Lina greeting those she knew with words he didn't understand. After a while his mind wandered back to the previous night, and just where a few beers had taken him. Which led to his next thought: how would he go drinking Coke or banana juice with Jake tonight? Even more to the point, how ready was he for a repeat performance with Lady Gaga – this time alcohol-free?

They entered a play centre, groups of adults and children engaged in board games and tossing and kicking soft, colourful balls to each other. 'Are these kids from refugee camps?' he asked, willing himself to appear interested, to put the Snake Skin behind him, at least for now.

'No. They have their own schools. Sometimes, with police permission, we're allowed to treat Karen refugees from across the border, some missing eyes and limbs, bullets and shrapnel still lodged in their bodies. But most of our patients are local Karen Burmese migrants who are doing it hard. They have no legal rights, so have no access to

Thai courts, hospitals, health care or schools and are often too poor to buy proper food. So we do what we can to provide for them.'

Inside the next building were two large work benches with hand tools scattered about and partial and full-size plastic legs, in various stages of completion, propped upright in vices. Craftsmen, wearing air-filtering masks, filed and sanded and brushed strong-smelling resins and glues on to the legs. At the back were a drill press, lathe and bandsaw. To one side were a set of parallel bars and a young girl amputee and her father sitting on a bench.

One of the craftsmen freed a lower leg from a vice and approached the girl and fitted and strapped the device to her stump.

'Her lower leg was crushed in a scooter accident,' Lina mentioned quietly. 'High-tech carbon-fibre legs cost upwards of fifty thousand dollars back home in Australia. Our locally-made ones come cheaper, about three hundred dollars each all up, thank you again, aid agencies.'

Holding her father's hand, the young girl stood and gripped the parallel bars with one hand then the other. She straightened her elbows and moved haltingly – right arm, left leg; left arm, right leg – to the end, turned and came back to discover her father had moved the bench a further five metres away. He sat down, extended his arms.

She hesitated, measuring the extra distance. Then she let go and shuffled in tiny, awkward steps to her father, propped her forearms on his thighs and rested, her eyes flicking around the workshop.

'I wonder sometimes what parents like hers are thinking at this stage,' Lina said. 'Their daughter a cripple, will she ever marry, ever find happiness in someone else's household? Anyway …' She pointed to the next building. 'Both adult and children's wards are in there. Between it and this place pass a lot of human traffic. Mae Sot Hospital, or even Chiang Mai Hospital up north, will do Burmese amputations, as long as they get paid. The amputees then come back here for post-operative care and prosthetic fittings.'

'John talked about mine victims on email and Facebook.'

'A topic he knows a lot about.'

His comfort level with Lina was starting to rise. In showing her softer side, she was less abrupt and challenging than before, their mutual interest in John drawing them closer. Nick went on, 'Studying tropical medicine up in Queensland, building things in Dad's work-shop, playing guitar, watching the footy, were the main things John did back home. I s'pose his guitar, the footy and cricket are … were all he missed out on here.' Nick was unsure which tense to talk about him in.

Lina's eyes wandered to the young amputee having another go with her new leg. 'Hyper-John. Energy of a bulldozer and about as subtle. ADHD – gotta be. Couldn't sleep eight hours to win a bet. Each new dawn the start of another adventure for him, though his enthusiasm can get ahead of his brain sometimes. As it did, I suspect, a month ago …'

The girl got to the far end of the workshop, turned as though on a rocking boat and started back.

'Like a searchlight, he can dazzle you with that energy, make your skin go warm, your girly bits buzz.' She looked at Nick now, a sugges-tion of a smile on her face. 'Sorry. I don't mean to embarrass you.'

'You're not.' Not totally true.

'Your brother can be a committed self-torturer too when he feels he's made a mistake. He often works through lunch and sometimes barely has time for a beer at night.'

'I remember him saying on Facebook once, "If you're too soft in this work you'll drown." '

'Really?' She thought about that for a moment. 'He's right. Not unusual for staff to request periodic resuscitation, meaning a few days off, or even longer. For me the worst of it is the kids who wander out from their villages in Burma and step on mines and by the time they get to us infection has set in. Not just limbs, but the amputation of gangrenous fingers and toes and hands is not uncommon, especially with the young ones built lower to the ground.' She walked. 'He said to me a while ago that he's thinking of giving away tropical medicine and specialising in orthopaedics when he returns to Australia. An informed decision: he's logged up a lot of hours helping blown-open Karen Burmese travel across mountains and the Moei River to get here. Doing that requires both toughness and softness, and it could be argued no small measure of stupidity. Anyway, he hasn't been shot, blown away by a mine or drowned yet. Or at least not up until …' She stopped and watched the girl sit down next to her father, lean her head against his shoulder.

'Is that where you think John is now, in Burma somewhere?'

'Yes.'

They entered the next building, the wooden cots either side pushed so close together there was barely enough room for the IV drips, much less staff.

Lina stopped at the end of a young bloke's bed. Maybe Ella's age, maybe a bit older. 'How are you today, Htan Dah?' Lina asked, careful to enunciate every syllable.

His eyes lit up, his smile frog-like. 'I am good, Miss Lina, thank you … Phoe Ni and Joan come?'

'Not yet.' She nodded towards Nick and introduced him to Htan Dah as John's brother from Australia. Htan Dah's eyes grew even larger. He raised his hand for a high five and Nick obliged him, taking note of Htan Dah's legs under the sheet, the right one stub-sized.

'There's a Burmese Migrant School not far from here that Htan Dah attends part-time. He's a good student and is in a friend of mine's class, aren't you, Htan Dah?'

'Yes.' He picked up a thin book from the bed and showed it to Nick. On the cover was a monkey high up a tree with a snake coiled around the trunk looking hungrily up at it. 'This is English book I read.'

Lina pointed to his crutches leaning against the wall. 'After returning from Chiang Mai Hospital, where his leg was amputated, he was fitted with a prosthetic leg. But it needs adjustments. As well, his stump has an infection, so that's why he's with us here for a week or so.' She looked down at Htan Dah, slowing her words and enunciating very clearly. 'Htan Dah can go anywhere with his new leg, except … except where, Htan Dah?'

'The river.'

She gave a thumbs-up sign of approval while muttering under her breath. 'Don't believe him. Like John, he'd swim a river rather than go around it – legs or no legs.'

On they went, Nick's hangover less of an issue now. He asked Htan Dah's age.

'Fifteen.'

So closer to his age than Ella's. 'Not much of him, is there?'

'Like most Karen people, spit on him and he could fall over. But what the Karen lack in size, they make up for in resilience and courage.'

'It surprises me they're taught English.'

'To improve their chances of resettlement in an English-speaking country.'

'Does it work?'

'I have students who were born in nearby refugee camps. They're adults now and speak English nearly as well as they do Karen and Burmese, but they're going nowhere.' She looked back at Htan Dah, who was watching them. 'Still, they live in hope and continue to attend classes each day, week, month, year.'

'Htan Dah seems happy enough to do that.'

'Coming from a life of avoiding landmines, forced labour, of seeing villages burn and people being killed, refugees like him do smile a lot from being here. But that could change. He's yet to spend his entire youth in a refugee camp asking, "Where do I go to start up my life again?" in between filling out endless application forms for asylum in western countries like Australia. There's a line in a Bruce Dawe poem – "A Voice from Limbo" – about grief and the fate of refugees. Such poems should be mandatory reading for aid workers here. Maybe for those stricken with COD in the west as well.'

'With what?'

'Chronic optimism deficit. Better known as "moaners' disease".'

They passed more beds, Lina greeting patients until she stopped next to a haggard-looking man – maybe fifty, maybe twice that age – sitting up, shaking a little, his legs curled into his chest. He said something Nick didn't understand.

Lina nodded and spread her fingers in front of him. When they moved on, she said, 'He's due for his methadone jab and is getting impatient.'

'Right … The boy back there mentioned Phoe Ni and Joan. I take it Joan is John?'

'Yes.'

'And Phoe Ni?'

She stopped. 'Have you heard of backpack medics?'

'John's mentioned them. They're Burmese who have been chosen by their villages to do months of medical training here. They're then sent back to their villages to provide medical care and train other Burmese.'

'That's basically it. About every six months backpack medics need to get re-supplied, so they travel for days to cross the border and get here. Phoe Ni is the backpack medic for Htan Dah's village. Or he was. About five weeks ago Burmese soldiers attacked their village. The villagers had been warned that soldiers were coming, but a few, wanting to salvage their chooks and what little else they owned, were slow to leave and were shot before the soldiers torched the village and crops. Three villagers were killed. Two of those were Htan Dah's father and uncle, and, as you could see, Htan Dah stepped on a mine trying to escape, most likely one freshly-planted by the Burmese army.'

She glanced around the clinic, her eyes lingering on patients she obviously knew well, including a toddler up ahead. ' "The comfort of horror happening to someone else" I read in my novel[*] last night. Better someone else than you. I can tell you that when the horror gets this close though – medical clinic close – your comfort level fades, no matter how tough an old croc you think you are.'

At the back door Lina turned and regarded Nick. 'Being a backpack medic is not for the faint-hearted or those planning for a long life. Since the program started ten years ago, seven have been killed and many more injured.'

They walked outside where two workmen were constructing a rock wall. One mixed mortar with a shovel, while the other scooped it up with his trowel, worked it into gaps then layered it smooth before positioning another rock on it. He jiggled the rock and tapped it into line with the end of his trowel, trimming off excess mortar. Something Nick knew a lot about.

'You look interested.'

'Back home I've helped my Dad build retaining walls.'

'Takes skill.'

'And patience. My Dad's got both, at least when he's building things.' They moved on. 'So did John help train Phoe Ni?'

[*] From *The Last Magician* by Janette Turner Hospital.

She nodded. 'And they became very good friends despite the language barrier. Five weeks ago word came in about the attack. In the mayhem that followed, the villagers scattered, and Phoe Ni hid in the bush with some of them, treating their injuries. After hiding out for a night, Phoe Ni hoisted a badly injured girl onto his back and carried her here. One of the other villagers Phoe Ni hid with was a young woman, seven months pregnant. Her husband was the third villager killed. Because the soldiers burnt everything, there was nothing for her or the other surviving villagers to go back to.'

Nick felt he knew where this story was going. 'So Phoe Ni went back into Burma for her.'

'After a brief rest and stocking up on food and medical supplies, yes, that's exactly what he did.'

'And John went with him?'

'Predictable, isn't he? Cramming more into his pack than Phoe Ni did, including a camcorder, notepad and biros.' She stopped and breathed a sigh. 'On top of everything else, your busy brother's involved with Human Rights Watch and a local media group called Karen News. He's intent on documenting Burmese war crimes for them and other appropriate databases – think UN Security Council or Amnesty International. Phoe Ni didn't exactly encourage your brother to go with him. But John said he'd find out where the village was and go there on his own if he had to.'

'That so sounds like him.'

'Yeah – introverted, non-assertive.'

'Not even in his sleep.'

'Anyway, whether Phoe Ni believed him or not, I don't know, but the fact that John could carry in as much as Phoe Ni, and that the wounded included children and perhaps a new-born baby, tipped the scales. John got what he wanted, though not without a debate.'

They found their way back to the car park.

'A half tour for today I'm afraid. I need to get back to work.'

'No exam?' Pure bluff. He craved water, sleep; nothing that could stress his brain.

She smiled. 'We can arrange a time once you've completed the course.'

'I'll study my notes tonight then.' He thanked her and looked towards the road where two Thai policemen, in their peaked hats and tight tan-and-gold braided uniforms, stood at the top of the entry-way. Bar workers, girly-blokes, the military and police here all in their skin-tights. What was it with Thais and their shrunken gear look? 'So I guess all we can do is sit around, wait and hope, huh?'

'As frustrating as that is, though the sitting isn't mandatory. Where are you off to now?'

'Third page of your get to know Mae Sot itinerary: the bridge and river border.'

She nodded and watched him a moment. 'How did you get on at the Snake Skin last night?'

'Yeah, fine.' Could he have said that faster?

'Stay long enough to see a floor show?'

'A bloke I met coming up here on the bus was there. We had a few beers and talked … and yeah, saw a floor show.' He added, smiling a little, 'Typical nightclub magnet that I am.'

'Uh huh.' She kept her eyes on him, like she expected him to say more. He didn't and to his relief, she jumped topics, 'Remember last night I told you about Burmese government agents and their inform-ers who wander around Mae Sot?'

Trade the word 'told' for 'grilled', Nick thought. 'Yeah, I do.'

'We think they've even been in the clinic, posing as someone else. The point is, please don't utter a word about John to anyone anywhere near Mae Sot or along the border, okay?'

He mimed zipping his lips, thoughts of Lady Gaga next to him on the edge of her bed still pin-balling around in his head. *Why are you in Mae Sot?* *To look for my brother.* *Mae Sot is not so big. Why can't you find him?* *He's an NGO worker at the Mae Tao Medical Clinic … or he was. But about a month ago he went missing …*

Lina's voice brought him back. 'An aid worker captured in a Bur-mese war zone while helping the enemy would either be imprisoned for about a hundred years or earn a Gina Rinehart-size bribe for the military government.'

He'd need to have a word to Lady Gaga. 'Right.' Who Gina Rine-hart was he hadn't a clue. Probably one of those Bill Gates types who own half the world's money, don't know what to do with it, so start ploughing it into aid projects. Rich people, guilty consciences. Safe bet though he'd not be meeting up with any of them here, or on a Thai bus, or in Jetstar economy class. He asked, 'What do you think a captured senior high school student would fetch?'

She gave him a look that said he had to be joking.

13

The drop-off was her main reason for being on the walkway today. But she came regularly for other reasons as well: privacy and anonymity, the sounds of the river, the colours of the low mountains – Hpa-an on the other side. And, much closer, to watch the smuggling going on right in front of her, like at this very moment.

Young women mostly, carting baskets brimming with cartons of cigarettes and bottles of whiskey, were doing exactly what she'd had to do a year earlier: take off footwear, step over the silt into the water then onto a giant truck-tire tube, the river being too low in the dry season for long boats. When the tube was full and the fares paid, two men paddled them across. Two minutes later they disembarked in Thailand and, using footholds, tree branches and a vertical rope, scrabbled up the steep embankment, stepped over a metal railing on to the concrete walkway and made their way towards the main road and Mae Sot. As easy as that, as if the heavy police and military presence at the Friendship Bridge border crossing were a hundred kilometres away instead of just around the next bend.

The absurdity of sitting on this concrete bench and watching smugglers going past so openly and untroubled irked her. Only twice had she seen policemen here, and when they got the bribe they wanted, they vanished. Not once had she seen a smuggler arrested. The law meant nothing in the face of money, did it? Money-hungry men play-acting as MI agents, policemen and border guards, while employing tough-looking bribe collectors or simply holding out their hands while looking away to collect their payoffs. In her own play-acting as Lady Gaga, she too looked away – at the window, the candle, her small Buddha – though the rest of what she did for money hardly invited comparison. And because she was Burmese, she had to pay twice what the Thai girls paid to the police for her so-called work permit, which she'd never seen and doubted existed. That's the way things worked with powerful people, swinging their power around like a club, indifferent to who they hit. And the more vulnerable you were, the harder you were hit.

She stretched forward and could just make out the Friendship Bridge – its thick concrete pylons and thin guard rail – going into the town of Myawadi, where supposedly an uncle she'd never met lived. Not for the first time, she asked herself what would happen if she descended the embankment, rode a tube over to the other side and walked into Myawadi? She'd have five or six hours, if she were lucky, to either locate that uncle or take a bus to Hpa-an before a phone call went out to Mister MI. Enough time? Probably not. And the penalty for getting caught? Prison time in the Iron Bar Hotel, its hot cells, rats and sweaty walls.

Across the river a woman in a blue longyi and white blouse caught her eye. She watched her walk quickly along the dirt road before cutting between stilted huts and going down to the river's edge. She obviously had enough money to be brought over on her own, so waded in and was helped up onto a tube just for her. She sat and glanced in Mya's direction and Mya thought about waving, but didn't. Why draw attention? Instead, she scanned the walkway on her side for any policemen or MI types. Not surprisingly, there were none. Just a couple of older women on her right and, further on, what appeared to be a western male: all three, like her, sitting on concrete benches river-gazing. Satisfied, she took some bills from her shoulder bag, rolled them up in her fist and waited.

* * *

Incredible. Five minutes after Nick realised he had to talk to her again, she biked past him at the junction to the main road heading towards the Friendship Bridge. Or at least he thought it was her in sandals, jeans, t-shirt, dangling shoulder bag, buzz-cut hair, those same giant sunnies and weird-looking yellow splotches – like sea shells – on her face. It was her hair, or lack of it, that puzzled him most. His hangover was almost finished punishing him, so he gave her a fifty-metre start then followed, closing the gap when the huge bridge loomed up ahead, rumbling trucks and vans and scooters filling the road, market stalls on both sides doing a brisk trade.

Lady Gaga – or her lookalike – weaved in and out of traffic until she came to a large sign warning in different languages of long prison sentences for people caught smuggling. She went left along a concrete walkway running parallel to the river and pedalled on, passing women carrying baskets full of merchandise, like they'd just looted a warehouse. Lina's 'day-trip smugglers' obviously.

Minutes later the girl stopped, dismounted and sat on a concrete bench under a tree. While she stared across the river, Nick studied her – his mind on replay – convinced now she was Lady Gaga.

As they sat on the edge of her bed, she asked, 'What did your friend give you?'

He felt his face heat up, his heart beat hard. He fumbled for words, barely knowing what was happening to him. 'Um … oh … just.' He lifted the packaged condom from his shirt pocket then put it back quickly.

'Have you used one before?'

'Yeah, sure … Lots of times. Um … Are you … ?' He took in her face, her cat-like eyes. 'Have you worked at the Snake Skin for long?'

'A year maybe.'

'Oh … You're a good singer.'

She moved closer, placing a hand on his knee and coaxing him along. 'You paid to be with me for half an hour. We have talked for some of that time. What else do you want to do?'

He looked at the bed then at her again, too nervous to do or say anything but – 'Your English is good. Did you learn it at school?'

'Yes, in Yangon.' She took her hand away and eyed him curiously, like a cow might when being approached. 'Do you know where that is?'

Gaga-clone, pole-dancer, bar-girl – yeah, all those things. But what else? That's what kept his mind buzzing. At the Snake Skin it had taken all of a micro-second to see how different she was from the other bar-girls, who appeared programmed to work in such a place.

Besides her near-perfect English, she moved – what was the word? Gracefully. Like a model. And she almost totally kept to herself. Even around other people she looked alone.

He continued to watch her, the light catching the side of her face. Then she turned towards him, forcing him to look away.

'Always good to joke with them first up,' he'd overheard girl experts at school say. Like 'them' was a different species, which they sort of had been for him. If he could sit closer, or what about this? Walk past her, glance around and acting surprised say, 'Oh, hello,' then, to loosen things up, maybe joke about her hair before sitting down and getting on to the topic of John. He got up nervously and started walking his bike towards her just as more river-crossers climbed up the embankment and stepped onto the walkway. A woman in blue and white gear veered towards Gaga and handed her something, and got something in return, before continuing on in his direction. When the woman passed he noticed wadded-up money in her hand.

He quickened his pace and got to Gaga just as she stood up. 'Hi,' he said, putting on a smile.

She caught his eye then looked away, scowling a little.

He placed his bike on the ground and rubbed his head. 'What sheep shearer gave you that haircut?' Nice one, he thought too late. Sheep totally don't exist up here. He grabbed his ears and tried again. 'Sometimes my older brother calls me "Monkey" because my ears are like jug handles too.' Better. Plenty of tree-climbers about.

Her eyes turned stony. She dropped a small package into her shoulder bag and made for her bike.

'I got hold of an atlas last night,' he said, chasing after her, 'and found out where Yangon is ... Mandalay, Bagan – all sorts of places in Burma, or whatever you call ... Umm, what's Burma's other name?'

She stopped, drawing a deep breath. 'Myanmar.'

'Yeah, that. Please. If you've got a minute, I need to talk to you about something really important.'

She turned and faced him, an impatient look on her face. 'What?'

'My brother. It won't take long.'

He pointed to the bench and she followed him back. They sat in awkward silence, before she asked, 'What do you want to say to me?'

So Nick talked, quickly at first, like she was a bird ready to fly away the moment he stopped. He just assumed she knew what he was talking about and after explaining why she couldn't say anything to anyone about his brother, he jumped to Ella and the fire. Easy to do. He didn't want her to go and Ella was one reason he was here in Mae Sot. Towards the end of his account, the sun and river and warm breeze started to slow him down, make him feel drowsy. He decided against mentioning who was responsible for the fire, saying instead, 'So no more Gretna Sunday Market for home-grown and home-made everything,' as though she'd been born in the Derwent Valley.

'You found your sister,' she said in a low voice, proving at least that she had been listening. 'So you should feel good about that.'

'If I'd kept her with me in the first place, she'd be free of skin grafts now.'

'When you are in the middle of something very dangerous and feeling pan ... What is the word?'

'Panicky?'

'Yes, that. And your heart is beating like a ...'

'A drum?'

'Yes. Knowing what to do is not easy. And later, when things are quiet and peaceful again, like now, it's easy to think about what you should have done and feel bad about yourself.'

The breeze had picked up. Quick clouds cast moving shadows.

It occurred to Nick that in two sittings he'd said more to this Gaga bar-girl than to any girl he'd ever met, and he still didn't know her real name. 'Your English is fantastic. You must have had the best English teacher in all of Burma.'

'I had three teachers.'

'Three of the best then. And when they called out your name, did they say, "Read from page one of the English language newspaper please?"'

A faint smile formed on her lips, or at least he thought so. Encouraged, he went on. 'Or, "Would you please read your excellent English story to the class?"' Her eyes and mouth stayed the same, which encouraged him even more. 'Or, "Lady Gaga – world's number one superstar – would you please lead the class in a rousing rendition of 'Bad Romance'?"'

Like the flick of a switch she launched herself towards her bike.

He jumped up. 'I just ... I was just trying to find out your real name.'

She was on her bike and pedalling hard.

'My name's Nick!' he shouted at her back. Then he recalled having told her that in her room.

* * *

Town, Friendship Bridge and back to town again by way of the Burmese market, a vast area of crowded chaos under huge tarpaulins slung between poles.

Nick got off his bike and wandered past stalls selling fruit and vegetables, caged birds, fried insects, pickled snake, pigs' heads, hunks of hanging meat, bowls of wriggling eels and fish. In narrow spaces beggars begged, dogs scavenged and stacks of merchandise forced people to detour. Car horns from the gridlock of surrounding traffic joined the shouting vendors, the clatter of motor scooters, the sound-duelling loudspeakers atop utes screeching out music and what seemed to be lottery results and advertising slogans. Front row Baskerville Raceway back home was a library stall in comparison.

He vowed to give the market a wide berth in future while making his way to the bike rental shop, the one place that was easy to get to.

After that he returned to the Ban Thai and waited in the courtyard for Lina. Someone offered him a beer, which he declined. Someone else asked about his day. 'Good,' he answered, before he found a corner to himself. As the sun dropped and darkness set in, Lina appeared, looking nervy, seemingly in need of a quiet recovery corner too. When a bloke held up a tinnie for her, she grabbed it and took a swig before spotting Nick. She approached, sat down next to him and asked, 'A productive afternoon?'

He nodded.

'Get to the river?'

Another nod.

'And?'

'Someone in Thailand must be smoking a lot of cigarettes and drinking a lot of whiskey.'

'Amongst other consumable products you probably didn't see. Did you get to the Burmese market too?'

'Barely. So not like shopping in New Norfolk.'

She laughed, before her beer-provider called out from across the courtyard, 'Bring back any picture postcards?'

To her playful smile, she added a quick two-finger salute. 'Typical of you, Brett, so last century.'

Brett clasped his heart and play-acted being mortally wounded.

'So you got to the refugee camp?' Nick asked.

'Uh huh.'

'And?'

'You got money in the bank?'

He'd never talked to anyone more incapable of having a straight, stick-to-the-topic conversation. 'Why? Does INTERPOL want to investigate my finances?'

She studied him, a smirk on her face. 'You want a beer?'

'No, I want my brother.'

'So do I; so do the rest of the aid agency establishment here … Are you thinking of going to the Snake Skin tonight?'

He felt like screaming, *Like where are we going with this?* 'Maybe,' he said.

'Sounds like you can afford a spare twenty-five dollars then to get into the Mae La Refugee Camp. Am I right?'

'Maybe.'

'If you can afford a bit more than that – say another ten or fifteen dollars more – I could probably get you into the camp tomorrow.'

'This is about my brother, right?'

She nodded. 'There's someone there I think you should meet, someone who could be a big help in finding him.'

He got out his wallet. 'Baht or dollars?'

'Your choice.'

He handed her two twenties.

She thought a moment, then handed back one of them, saying, 'We'll do this together.'

* * *

From schoolgirl to bar-girl, the three constants in her life: an English dictionary, a pen and a writing pad.

She'd looked up the word 'gaga' one day. First meaning: over-excited. Second: senile, mentally deficient or confused. Extend the second meaning to 'going mental' (patrons said this) or mentally dead, she thought, and there couldn't be a more suitable name for her. Sometimes she could go for hours barely thinking, though not now.

As she looked out her window she recalled two other words she'd looked up recently: 'futile' – an adjective meaning useless or having no purpose or importance, as in 'my futile life' – and 'despair' – noun or intransitive verb meaning loss of hope or to be without hope. As in, 'My despair growing, I feel the nothingness in my life.' Or simply, 'My dreams gone, I despair.'

No doubting which way her mood was going.

She glanced around at her table. Days earlier she'd decided that when a patron came in, or before she got out her pipe and smoking imple-ments, she'd stow her Tripitaka under the bed and turn her Buddha around to prevent him from watching her. Now all that seemed stupid. Where her Tripitaka was located meant nothing and her Buddha would know exactly what she was doing whichever way he was facing.

She went over to the table and turned her Buddha back around then sat on the edge of her bed and put on her wig, changed into her Gaga lingerie and shredded red dress. Another Lady Gaga night and the same issues clawing away at her: waiting for nothing but more of the same, reading her future in the late-night eyes of the other bar-girls, having to act like half her brain was missing while sitting on patrons' laps; this cage of a room that she could only escape to 'per-form', use the bathroom, or go to the market or river for a few hours most days. Back in her room after five pm and Billy J either threatened or fined her for being late.

'Your life is the sum of the choices you make for yourself,' her father had said on occasions. 'Not here,' she answered him now, gazing at the floor. The next day, week, month, year, as arranged by her, was unimaginable, and she asked herself: what more could the Snake Skin take away from her other than her blood and the rest of her worthless life?

She lay back on her bed wishing she could sleep forever. She couldn't remember the last time she'd smiled or laughed through sheer joy, or when she had said more than a few words to anyone, or given or received genuine affection. Not in Mae Sot, anyway; her life here was either solitary or shared with men who passed through her room as quickly as possible, never asking anything about her, never knowing she'd been one of the best English students in Yangon, or that her brother had been killed and her family destroyed trying to make Myanmar a better place, or that she'd been forced to work as a porter and mine-sweeper – like she'd been forced to work at the Snake Skin – and nearly blown apart.

Outside the Snake Skin no one cared to know her either. At the Burmese market – Gaga-sunglasses hiding much of her face – she listened to others talk, watched them with sideways glances while wandering aimlessly around thinking about the lives she wasn't living and the one life she was.

Mothers, especially, held her gaze. How they squeezed the hands of their youngest whose other hands sisters or brothers squeezed. How they fed and hugged their babies, biting the ends of their fingers and toes to make them squeal and laugh. She watched and listened to young couples too – the Karen Burmese longest – who walked past, eyes beaming in on each other, their hands and shoulders touching as they chatted away about what music they liked, who said what on Facebook, what they wanted to buy or become. The first stages of intimacy, she thought, though how would she know? She'd never had a boyfriend – someone she could wrap her arms around from the back of a bicycle or scooter, someone who gave her his full attention, who really listened to her, who she could spend contented hours with, or hours daydreaming about. 'Look at me, touch me, talk to me that way,' she'd whisper, imagining herself belonging to someone too.

At times, in frustration, her whole body seemed to scream out – 'Here I am standing on the edge of other people's lives, occupying space but attached to no one or anything but Billy J and the Snake Skin. Or my next lit pipe.'

She often felt invisible at the market, like a sewer rat people turned away from, until she caught sight of a man, or men, glaring at her. In her mind the message: 'Lady Gaga, bar-girl, singer and five-minute body. What's she doing here?' Her emptiness complete, she'd quickly buy what she needed and leave.

Outside her window, the red neon light flashed on-off, a patch of it hitting the wall behind her. No music. No squealing, shouting or laughter. Except for the occasional passing truck, the quiet period now before things got busy again.

She looked over at her Buddha and recalled a story about him struggling to reach the light of dharma, how he cut off his eyelids to stop himself from sleeping. Where his eyelids fell there grew the world's first opium poppy, symbol of the falsehoods – false rest, false visions – a person had to cast off in their quest for truth and Buddhahood.

Her memory surged. The word 'dematerialise' came into her head. She'd heard it used downstairs the previous night. Just typical of her scatty brain, wasn't it? In the blink of an eye her thoughts jumping from the Buddha back to the Snake Skin.

'That word, what does it mean?' she asked the white-haired Australian who had used it and whose lap she was sitting on.

'Ya don't wanna know, love,' the man across the table shouted. 'It's like what battery acid does ta ya after it's been thrown in your face. Not much left above the shoulders, if ya know what I mean.'

'Don't listen to him. He's just havin' ya on,' the white-haired man said, smiling. 'Dematerialise means to disappear, become non-material, to enter a higher world – a spiritual world if you like – if you believe in such a thing.' His arm tightened around her. 'Not something you're meant to know about though.'

'Never met a whore who did,' said the man across the table.

First time she'd heard that word too, though she was certain she knew what it meant. At times she was struck by shame so overwhelming that she felt like it would break her.

She looked at the block of opium next to her leg: her recipe for dematerialising, for escaping the Snake Skin unpunished, for riding the golden cloud, at least for a few hours. Either that or what? Scream? Scratch her eyes out? Buy a syringe? The good Buddha, she'd convinced herself weeks earlier, would understand her despair, the need to light up her pipe to keep her mood from plummeting further.

She locked the door, took a straight-blade razor from under the bed and cut a small fingernail-size pellet from the opium bock and put it in a small metal dish. She wrapped her right hand in cloth and used a lighter to heat the dish until the pellet sizzled, dissolving into paste. She scooped the paste up with a knife and stuck it on a little barb over a hole in the metal bowl of her pipe. Lying back on her hip, she placed the lighter under the bowl and sucked in the rich, oily smoke, holding it in her lungs. When she could hold it no longer, she exhaled slowly through her nostrils, thinking her soul was in that pellet dispersing into smoke, lingering in different shapes then disappearing like a ghost. She let out a sigh, felt her stomach loosen, her heart slow, relaxation seeping into her all the way down to her toes.

Her skin cooled, moistened.

Background noise faded.

The walls drew closer.

Time went blank.

Billy J and the rest of them were out that door somewhere and from the way she was feeling the somewhere could have been Africa, and that made her smile.

She inhaled and exhaled, and too soon the paste was gone.

She dropped the pipe to the floor and lay flat on her back, emptied of thought, of tension, her body light as air, ready to lift and float. She stared obliquely at the roof fan, followed its rotations, sensing it slow, feeling its draft penetrate every part of her body. It felt good – just so good.

There came an image of that bony old man, chin perched on the end of his walking stick, sitting on that riverside bench only metres away. A week ago? A month, a year? Both she and her supplier had ignored him as they completed their transaction. After her supplier left, the old man – staring out at the river – had spoken.

'Up north there is a legend about the opium poppy. Have you heard it before?'

'No.'

'It goes like this. There was once a Lahu* who fell in love with a

* The name of one of the many hill tribes living in northeast Myanmar and northwest Thailand.

farang girl. The girl died and out of her body there bloomed an opium poppy. The Lahu said, "The sap of the poppy is sweet, as sweet as she was; the sap of the poppy relieves my sorrow, as she did." But the legend ends there. It does not go on to describe the Lahu's addiction. So be careful young girl,' he went on, *'too much of what was meant to relieve sorrow can soon create more – create a living death. Believe me, I know.'*

'Don't worry, old man,' Mya said now. 'A little bit from time to time will always be enough. Never any more. Promise.' She cast off that dreary old doom merchant.

'Try each day to smile. It is good medicine.' She did so now, slowly singing, picturing Lady Gaga – as if Lady Gaga were someone else – silver pole dancing, the stage lights casting her in red, a wall of red faces staring up at her, mouths agape, hungry for her. But – they – could – not – have – her, – could – they? – And – they – never – ever – would – when – she – felt – as – far – away – from – them – as – this.

She gazed at the opium, the string, the poppy-leaf wrapping, as if unsure where they came from. Then dimly she remembered. Then she forgot what it was she was thinking about. One of the pleasures of opium: it didn't let your brain linger on anything for too long.

The image of that old man on the bench came back, and she said to him, 'In a good world, old man, opium is bad, but in a bad one it is good – just so good.' She wanted more. Smoke another pellet and her mind could leave this place for days. No flashback nightmares. Just sleep and dream and float, dreaming of home, school, her family, as though she'd never left them. The present merging with the past and staying there. No other dreams but those. If only ...

From somewhere there came a bang on a door, followed by a too-familiar voice. Sadly, Billy J was back from Africa.

'You got ten minute. Got that? Ten minute.'

Another bang, harder, feeling closer this time. The click of a key in her door, the hinges squeaking. She just had time to shove everything under the bed before Billy J stepped in doing his usual hands-on-hips scan of the place, his nose lifted in the air like the giant rats of her nightmares. 'You do somethin' here, not tell me?'

His script rarely changed. That rat nose of his sniffing the opium-sweetened air. He knew. He just play-acted he didn't – with her, with all the girls. Even in her stupor, Mya had an answer ready for him. 'Be accepting. Be patient, Billy J. You can no more hurry life than you can hurry the phases of the moon.' Then she sang the chorus from 'Bad Romance', a strange strand in her voice making her ask herself – *was that me?*

'Oh, Billy J, do not look at me like that,' she added in a playful tone, as though they'd grown up together.

'Like what, girl?'

In her mind a spot-billed pelican swooped low over Yangon's Inya Lake and the many swans there swimming in pairs: their looped necks, stilled heads, fixed red eyes. She flapped her arms. 'Like I have grown wings and am about to fly away, never to return, not even to visit my favourite door-knocker and money collector – Billy J.' Floating in her opium-slowed mind, it was easy to feel affection for people, even for him – just like her Tripitaka said she should do.

The protest march drifted back, the monks and students chanting. What? Then it came to her. 'May all living beings be free, be free,' she chanted, 'May all living beings be free from harm. May all living beings be free from …' She couldn't remember the rest, so whispered to herself, as a naughty girl might, 'from the Snake Skin.' She slowly sang the chorus from 'Bad Romance' again and smiled. 'Ignore me, Billy J. I am just practising, just getting my head-space right. Like you sometimes tell me to do.'

'Yeah? Get it done din, girl. Cuz you got five minute get yor funky arse down stair, and da clock's a-tickin'.'

'Ah yes, my funky arse – whatever that means, because I cannot find "funky" in my English dictionary.' She squinted at him for a moment. 'Every day you collect and count money, Billy J, so you must be good at math. I want to ask you a math question.'

'Quick. Gotta move.'

'How many kilometres do you think my funky arse has travelled going up and down the stairs since I first got here?'

'Dat for you to work out and for me to see you doin' it.'

'All that work-time walking and climbing and I have got no further than the stage downstairs and this bed. I could go blind and my life would not change here, not a bit.'

'Yeah, it change, girl.' He grinned. 'You a blind Gaga, I gotta get you a walkin' stick.' He snorted with laughter before his face turned 'tough guy' again. 'But you not. Not yet.' He held up a hand, fingers parted. 'You can see dis, can't you? Dat much minute. Dat what you got.' He did his hard-glare act backing out.

'Thank you for your visit, Billy J,' she said, though he'd disappeared out the door, down his grate and back into his hole. 'And for your inspiring conversation.' She smiled. That word 'inspiring' pleased her. At least something about her was improving.

14

Nick sat where he had before and let his eyes wander, asking himself – was there anywhere on Planet Earth more unlike the Mae Tao Clinic than this place?

'How's life at the Ban Thai minus a fridge, plasma set and Xbox?' Jake asked.

Which reminded Nick that he'd forgotten to check on his laptop for fire investigation updates. He'd have to do that before going to bed. 'I'm adjusting. What about you at … wherever it is you're at?'

Jake nodded, a self-satisfied look on his face. 'Excellent.'

Their drinks came and moments later Lady Gaga stepped on stage, wrapping a slow hand around the silver pole, leaning outwards and eyeing her audience before breaking into 'Bad Romance'.

'Ever notice, Nicko, how men sweat and women glow on stage?'

'Yeah.' Not really.

'Ooo-eee. Still winnin' at life, are we not?' Jake took up his air guitar pose again and burst into a rendition of The Doors' 'Light My Fire' with 'Gaga' substituted for 'baby'.

Heads turned. Someone shouted, 'Shut it!' Jake stood, took a quick bow, sat and went quiet.

Watching Gaga, Nick imagined how she'd ended up here, organising pieces of her life he'd witnessed or felt fairly certain about. Young, smart and a super-English speaker, her family still over in Burma. So something had made her flee the country. The most likely reason was poverty and the need to provide a family with money. He pictured the river smuggler, the money rolled up in her hand as she passed him. Drugs for baht – had to be. One thing that didn't fit though – unless she'd had nits or had gone through chemotherapy – was her cropped hair.

'Get that down ya,' Jake called out, 'then we'll get friggin' serious.'

Nick raised his Coke in the air, took a sip. 'This will do me.'

'Ya're jokin'?'

'Nah.'

'Actually, ya're not lookin' all that bright. Get wrecked and hurl chunks around town last night, did ya?'

Nick was mystified, and must have looked it since Jake explained with a glint in his eyes, the twitch of a grin. 'Five shades of purple?'

'What are you on about?'

'Ya spew?'

Could he ask that any louder? 'I wasn't that bad.' He peered into his Coke sensing patrons' eyes on him. He'd known high school students like Jake: in-your-face, frantic-to-be-noticed types who tossed words out like matchsticks to fire up controversy, passed out rude songs on the school bus and sang them just below driver detection level, dropped blue-tongued lizards in girls' school bags, farted when the teacher's back was turned and pointed to the meekest girl in class, saying, 'That's the third time, Elizabeth. Like how am I supposed to concentrate?'

Surprisingly, Lady Gaga finished up quickly, left the stage and went over to the bar, a drink there waiting for her.

Jake raised a hand and indicated two more beers to Number One, hovering like a blowfly next to him. 'So how'd things go upstairs last night? Up to your imagination?' he asked, studying Nick closely.

Had to come, didn't it? 'Sensational.'

Jake waited for more, but Nick didn't provide it. 'Sensational as in what?'

Nick shrugged, starting to feel cornered.

Jake flashed a grin. 'Goin' all non-disclosure on me, are ya? That's cool. Part of bein' true blue, keepin' yer feelin's stored up inside, not yappin' on. Well, like, for some anyway. Ask me how I went.'

Nick did, without interest, and Jake took the next couple of minutes to provide the details.

'I'm happy for you,' Nick said, when Jake finally drew a breath. No mistaking the tone in his voice.

Number One set two beers down, smiling her smile at Jake, who smiled his back while adding to her tank top. 'Stay close,' he said to her. She rubbed his cheek with the back of her hand and he whispered something into her ear. Her eyes lingered on Nick for a moment before she turned and went back to the bar.

Jake passed a stubby over.

Nick passed it back. 'No thanks.'

Jake swigged then watched Nick like he was trying to work out some mystery about him. 'There's a better way to fix yerself up,' he said. 'Called a depth charge. Two shots of Sorehead Whiskey, a shot of invalid gin tossed into a long glass of ice and Coke. Yer jump-start to drinking yerself cheerful. Non-tasteable. Like ya won't even know it's gone down till yer head and stomach message back for more.'

'Not for me.'

'Right … Leaves ya with more coin for other things then, doesn't it?'

Nick shrugged and looked over at the bar where Lady Gaga and Number One stood shoulder-to-shoulder, Number One doing the talking. Typically Gaga looked the outsider, her eyes fixed on the floor. If he offered to buy her a drink she'd be obliged to sit with him, wouldn't she? He could then apologise for whatever it was he'd said that sent her rocketing off earlier in the day. If that worked, he might even try to solve the mystery of her hair. As Nick was about to get up, the girls came over, Number One carrying two tea-coloured drinks on her tray. No sooner had she placed the drinks on the table than Lady Gaga plonked herself down on Jake's lap, wrapping an arm around him.

As Nick watched, stunned, Number One sat on his lap, arm around his shoulders and pressed her glossy lips to his ear. 'You buy drinks, I give you good price for boom-boom.'

Blindsided, Nick barely heard.

'Everything sweet over there?' Jake asked, grinning like he was having the experience of a lifetime.

Nick could only stare in disbelief, feeling … what? Disappointment for sure. Jealousy too? How dumb was that?

'What's wrong, my man? Ya look like ya swallowed a redback spider. Eh, it's me, Jake Jones, remember? Here ta work out life's best options for ya. Like I'm the closest person ta Santa Claus you'll find in this town.' He flashed Number One an approving look before eyeing Nick again, nodding. 'Up to your imagination, I guarantee it. A girl ta walk your eyes around a room, and as that old song goes …' He eyed Number One, singing 'Light My Fire' again, this time substituting Nick's name for 'my'. 'So chill, my man. Mormon eyes are elsewhere … Now, about that whiskey and Coke? Guaranteed ta set ya right.'

Nick shook his head, unable to take his eyes off Gaga as Jake tightened his arms around her and broke into song again.

Bodies shifted. Heads whipped around. The same person as before shouted, 'Shut it!'

'Annoyin' ya, am I?'

'Too right you are.'

'How sad.' Jake sang on.

'Shut it!' The shouter repeated, adding a mad-dog look to his threatening voice.

Jake sent back a grin and a wink. 'Just stirrin' the possum, possum, nothin' more.'

'I'll be stirrin' the street with ya if ya don't shut up!'

'Now why would ya do that?' He lifted his stubby in the air. 'Good beer, good bar, good company.' Jake pointed to Nick. 'Besides, me mate here has a heart condition. A bit of aggro directed our way might do 'im in.'

'Ya know what to do ta keep yerselves outta the morgue then, don'tcha?' The shouter placed an index finger over his mouth. 'Ssshh.'

Jake stretched across the table and said quietly, 'Escaped his cage, don'tcha reckon? Either that or someone's planted a knife in his scrotum?'

Pink stepped on stage. But before she got started, a mystery hand reached over Nick's shoulder, depositing an Australian twenty-dollar note on the table. He jerked his head around to view Lina Larkin, her face set like stone. She lowered her mouth close to his ear. 'I don't mean to disturb your party. I tried your room before coming here. No need to go to the refugee camp. Your brother is back and occupying a bed in the Mae Sot Hospital until morning.' With that she turned and couldn't get out of the place fast enough.

Jake: 'What was that about?'

Nick was too gobsmacked to reply. Half a minute later he lifted Number One off his lap and got to his feet. 'I'm off.'

'What's the rush?'

'Gotta see a man about a plane ticket,' he answered, not looking back.

Nick out the door, Jake said to the girls, 'It appears I'm double-booked.'

Number One grinned, while Gaga got up despite Jake's efforts to prevent her. 'Bathroom,' she said, twisting out of his hands. She gave him her standard 'back-in-a-minute' smile then strolled towards the staircase keeping her eyes on Billy J talking to customers at the bar. Up the stairs she went, continuing to check on him. Once in her room, she placed her incense, candles and Buddha on the floor and jammed the table against the door. She went to her bed, reached under it and got out her opium and smoking implements.

15

Nick's nerves kicked in the moment he entered the hospital's men's ward. This won't be easy, he thought, as questions bombarded him. *How will he take seeing me? What'll he ask about first? What will I say back?* His brother seemed like a total stranger to him now.

Had Lina not been sitting next to John, Nick would have walked right past him. Only his face and arms were visible, a white sheet over the rest of him, drip tube attached to his wrist. With matted hair, scrappy beard and a scratched, thinned-down face, he looked like a death-camp survivor out of a World War Two documentary.

'Recognise him?' Lina asked, glancing up from her chair.

'Barely.'

'You need to know he's sedated, not dead.'

'How … ? What … ?' His voice caught in his throat. He fought to keep from tearing-up.

Lina started talking in her usual mine-of-information style. 'Phoe Ni brought him back, marvel of a man that he is. Malaria, snakebite, and as you can see, involuntary dieting as well. Snakebite's the worst of it. Russell vipers are as deadly as cobras, but more aggressive and responsible for more human deaths than any other snake in the world. Its haemotoxic venom is a powerful coagulant that damages tissues and blood cells before attacking the kidneys and lungs. Fortunately the hospital stocks anti-venom and Phoe Ni just happened to have a vial of it in his pack.'

'And that's what saved him?'

'Along with assisted resuscitation, a compression pad and traditional Karen poultices to draw out the poison. Still, there's more to do. He's due to have dialysis treatment to flush out his kidneys, and necrosis has set in where he was bitten on the calf, that'll require surgery at the hospital in Chiang Mai. He's booked to go up there with two other patients in the morning.'

'Necrosis?'

'Rotting flesh.'

Nick's stomach moved.

'He's lucky. Most viper victims die before they can reach help.'

Events back home paled in comparison. 'How long will he be in Chiang Mai?'

'A week or so. Then he'll need to spend another three or four weeks, probably at the clinic, for post-op treatment and physio. That's the theory anyway. Any ideas for ensuring he stays in bed and does what he's told?'

Nick shook his head. One thing for certain, if John caught sight of him he'd know something was wrong, and if not chained to the bed, he'd be up, crutches under his arms and on his way to the airport. 'Have you talked to him since he got back?'

'No. Word came through to the Ban Thai just after I'd finished work. I went straight to your room then—'

'Yeah, well,' Nick interrupted. 'About me being at the Snake Skin, I—'

'Next topic.'

'Right ... So John has no idea I'm here in Mae Sot?'

'Not yet.'

Nick moved closer to Lina. He'd have to do this quickly then get to the internet cafe in town – a quicker option than his laptop – before it closed. 'I need to tell you about something that happened back home a few weeks ago, and why it would be better if John didn't know about it, for now at least, or the fact I've been up here looking for him.'

* * *

The cafe proprietor came over as he was logging on. 'Close five minutes,' he said.

'Okay.'

He checked *The Mercury* website first. Nothing about the investigation.

No Skyping or Facebook, just email. Though he hated it, email gave him time to work out what to say and he wouldn't have to answer continual questions. He clicked on the icon and stared at the screen. How much could he tell his parents about John without lying or alarming them? He wished he had John's or Lina's, or even Jake's, ease with words.

> Mum and Dad –
> No problems geting to Mae Sot from Bangkok. Good news – Johns okay. He's been working in a realy remote place with bad roads and no Internet conection. He's suposed to be back in Mae Sot in about a week. Will rite more later.
> Miss you all, Nick

He sent it and got up. Where to next? Two choices: his room, where he should go, or back to the Snake Skin. Thing was, he didn't feel like being on his own just yet. Plus the image of Lady Gaga sitting on Jake's lap still troubled him, and he had no idea why.

* * *

Nick nodded to the doorman like he lived at the place and entered the roar and babble inside. He stopped and looked over to where Jake was sitting, Lady Gaga still on his lap, the chair opposite still vacant. Everywhere else the usual: patrons drinking, arms reaching out for bar-girls, raised voices and loud laughter. He glanced at the bar and spotted Number One talking to the same bloke in tight jeans and muscle t-shirt who'd hovered around his table the previous night. Had to be the Snake Skin's head-banger, he reckoned. He looked back at the table. No way would he be telling motor-mouth about John, so he stood there a moment planning what he would say. That done, he went over to the table and sat down, ready for debriefing.

'Ahhh, welcome back to Ratbag Central!' Jake shouted, his eyes glazed, a goon-like grin on his face. 'Ya're obviously in need of a drink.' He pushed a spare stubby Nick's way. 'Get yer lips around that.'

'Nah. I'm good.'

'In this world, dude, what doesn't kill ya makes ya stronger; but your call.' He swigged, watching Nick. 'Brilliant.' His stubby banged the table. 'Not a bad looker, that over-your-shoulder sheila. Had that look of authority about her, like she could stop a Grand Final in mid-kick. Is she, like, the one ya got the horn for?'

'You ever thought about writing poetry?'

'Yeah, when I'm in the grip of dementia and can't remember where the friggin' fridge is … or what's in it.'

Hard not to smile. Another thing he'd learned about Jake, he never took offence. 'She's just someone I met at the Ban Thai. I told her I was coming here. The Ban Thai's mucked up their bookings and want to give me a smaller room for the next couple of nights. Anyway, no worries, it's sorted.'

Lady Gaga sucked her tea-coloured drink through a straw, blotched lipstick running outside the lines of her lips. From kissing Jake? She looked up – eyes glazed – and cocked her head to one side before raising her hands in the air, as if surrendering. 'Are these my hands?' she asked, out of the blue. Not waiting for an answer, she replaced Jake's hands on her breasts with her own. 'Are these my breasts?' She ran her hands down her body, slowly. 'Are these legs mine? The answer: sometimes yes and sometimes no.'

Jake looked around at her like she'd grown a second head. 'Wadda ya on about?'

With tranced eyes, tranced voice, she went on, ignoring him. 'Right now fingers and hands …' – she held them up – 'breasts …' –

she cupped them – 'the rest of my body …' – she pointed – 'are not mine. They belong to the Snake Skin.' She nodded to confirm that. 'Do you know what that feels like?'

'No,' Nick answered automatically, while Jake just gaped.

'Sorry. Bad question. No man or boy would know … So, what can I call mine? My name, Mya Paw Wah, is mine …'

Jake: 'Stay with Lady Gaga. Like at least I can pronounce it.'

She went on, not caring her voice was rising. 'My smile is mine. You should try each day to smile.' She put on a dopey one and held it for seconds. 'And my memories, they are mine. Thant shot dead and Nan Pau too; the abbot taken away, my mother and father, now far apart.' She went totally still, her eyes appearing to enter another time zone. 'One of the worst things in life is to have a family, a place to live, then … suddenly, not have anyone, or anywhere to go to … but … but here.'

Nick nodded. And surprisingly, Jake did too.

Lady Gaga gazed at Nick then cupped her palms like she was holding out a bowl. She stood, leaned across the table and placed the 'bowl' on Nick's head. 'My memories,' she said, 'I give them to you.' She sat back down and frowned, perhaps fearing the bowl might fall. 'No, sorry. Why would you want them? Why would anybody want them?' She took them back and placed them on the table in front of her. 'These memories are mine, all mine. Like my name is mine, my smile is mine, my thoughts are mine.' She turned and looked at Jake again, her forefinger aimed over her shoulder at Nick. 'He cannot have them.' She continued to shake her head, child-like. 'You cannot have them. The Snake Skin cannot have them. But if you want to pay for—'

'Not tonight, darls. Whatever ya're on, wherever ya're at, I want no part of it.' Jake stood, sending Lady Gaga sprawling to the floor.

Heads turned. Patrons stared.

'Change of plan,' Jake said, looking down at Gaga like she was deranged. 'I'm outta here.' His eyes met Nick's. 'You with me?'

Nick pictured himself as a trained chihuahua, lead around his neck, tail wagging, Jake leading him out the door. 'I think I'll stay a bit longer.'

'Suit yerself.' He stayed where he was though, long enough to offer Gaga – getting up awkwardly – a helping hand. But she refused his help, grabbing the table instead, hoisting herself up and hobbling a few steps, favouring her right ankle.

Billy J approached, nodding his head to the beat of Mr Thai Mafia's shouts. 'Bar!' Billy J shouted, pointing and moving into Gaga's face. As she turned, a push in the back got her going.

'Shoulda been drowned at birth,' Jake mumbled. 'IQ of plankton.'

Nick's eyes flicked from the head-banger to Jake and back to the head-banger, appealing to him. 'She's hurt her leg.'

Billy J: 'She can walk, she can work.'

Jake: 'The grunt, shoulders and hangin' jaw of a gorilla. Neck thick as his ugly head. Like someone ya'd threaten small children with.'

Billy J looked over at the boss-man, on his feet now, his face a balloon about to burst. He pointed and Billy J put the gesture into words. 'No, Gaga! Room! Now!'

'A lesson in sensitivity trainin' wouldn't go astray,' Jake muttered, a notch louder. He ignored Nick's alarmed look and took a giant stride into Billy J's personal space, calling out, 'Like grow a brain, ya miserable toe-suck.' He tapped Billy J on the shoulder and asked, 'You always this stupid or are ya just havin' an off-night?'

Billy J glared sideways at Jake, his eyes travelling up and down him like he was a side of meat.

To Nick's amazement, Jake stood his ground, matching the head-banger's dagger stare with one of his own. 'Ya can try yer luck with me if ya wanna,' Jake growled in the voice of a Terminator. 'A warnin' though ...' He jabbed his chest with his thumb. 'Ex-Australian Army SAS, otherwise known as The Snake Eaters: mad, bad and dangerous to know. Two years recently served in Tarin Kowt, Afghanistan. For the geographically-challenged, like you, that's a long walk west of here. Ya gettin' this, Ratbreath?'

While Nick quietly freaked, Jake boxed the air: bobbing, weaving – jab, jab, cross, hook, uppercut – all the time shouting, 'Who dares wins, bum-face. And I dare! Mess with me and I'll eat ya for breakfast and spit out yer bones.' Then he stepped back into Billy J's space and went eyeball-to-eyeball with him again.

Not a voice, not a sound; everyone rubber-necking, until Jake – x-ray eyes not budging from Billy J's – said to Nick, 'How're ya readin' this, dude?'

'As a hospital admission – yours.'

'No guts, no glory. See any weapons about – drawn knives, pistols, that sort of thing?'

Nick glanced right, left. 'No.'

'Good. I'm into gladiator movies. So trust me.'

'Try something safer then, like bomb disposal.'

'Next time.'

Gaga crooned, 'Come along, Billy J, and put me away.' She veered left, right leg slower than the other, and started up the stairs holding onto the railing.

'Yes, go along, Billy J, and read her a story and tuck her in nice and tight.'

A smile stayed on Billy J's lips. 'You be here. I come back,' he said.

'I'm goin' nowhere.'

Billy J drew a finger across his throat, made a fist and moved it under Jake's chin, nodding. 'You go. Soon. Pow! Bye-bye.'

'Ya got more chance of makin' the Olympics than knockin' me over.'

Billy J caught up with Lady Gaga on the steps and seized her by the elbow.

'Gently!' Jake screamed.

As Gaga pulled away, she overbalanced and toppled over the railing, crashing onto a table and falling to the floor.

* * *

Nick pounded a third time and the door cracked open, Lina's sleepy face looking out. 'Why am I looking at you and thinking Snake Skin?'

'Lady Gaga has had a nasty fall. Nobody there would help her, or even get a doctor or … do anything but try to get her out of sight.'

Lina's face sharpened. 'Where is she now?'

'Out front, in the back of a ute.'

'Is she conscious?'

'Sort of.'

'I'll be right out.'

16

They sat together on the low stone wall, stubbies wedged between their knees, Jake gazing upwards. 'As a member of the local high-wire act,' he said, raising his voice to get over the morning market noise, 'I'd have a few options about which wire ta strut my stuff on up there, don'tcha reckon?'

Nick's eyes rose to the maze of bare, low-hanging wires attached to electricity lines higher up. For poaching other people's power, the walking Wikipedia had informed him. 'Not all that far to fall either. About Gaga distance.'

'Yeah, true.' Jake polished off his stubby and looked at his watch. 'I'm fallin' right now – fallin' behind.' He dropped the stubby in his backpack. 'World looks a different place without a half dozen stubbies in the belly by mid-mornin'. Ready for another?'

'Nah, I'm good. Not my usual brekky drink.'

'Should be. Puts hairs on yer chest.'

'I've got enough already.'

'Really? Give us a look. I might borrow some for transplants.'

Nick – at first believing Jake was serious – refused, and Jake chuckled as he pulled another stubby from his backpack and opened it. 'Mate of mine big on the science of digestion mixes his brekky beer with tomato juice. Calls it a "red eye" and swears it cures all possible ailments while primin' his stomach for what's comin' down later in the day. Anyway, here's cheers.' He took a swig and sounded his approval before looking at Nick again. 'It's good of ya ta come and see me off like this.'

'Yeah, well, I'm not exactly booked out this time of the day.' Nick glanced around at the market then let his eyes follow a passing truck until it disappeared around a corner. 'Can I ask you a question?'

'Affirmative.'

'Are you really ex-SAS?'

Jake grinned. 'Me in the military? About as likely as spottin' a nun lap-dancin'. A good mate of mine in Broken Hill is though. After a few beers, he tends ta debrief. I reckon I'm as clued up about the SAS and Tarin Kowt as I am about Cronulla or the outback of New South Wales.'

Nick was starting to twig there was more to Jake than he'd realised, much more. 'So you were bluffing last night?'

'Yeah, though not without a purpose in mind. It's called diversion. Me sister used ta use it when her young bloke went off the rails, the purpose being to deflect high emotion elsewhere.'

'From Gaga to yourself, for example?'

'Pet hate of mine – being stood over by bottom-of-the-food-chain blokes like Billy J. About as useless as human beings can be. Should be hung up on meat hooks by their colons, the lot of 'em.'

'Brave move. What if she hadn't gone over the railing and Billy J had fronted you – what then?'

'Point to the exit, tell the bastard I'll meet him outside once I've drained the all-powerful dragon. Don't know if ya noticed the big, open window in the loo. Leads out onta a laneway that loops around to connect with the main road. Prime spot for peekin' around a corner at that big Snake Skin neon outshinin' everything in sight, and that boofhead and his entourage under it waitin' ta punch my lights out. Have ta pinch myself ta keep from crackin' up.' He paused for a grin, obviously picturing the moment. 'The lesson being, my man, if ya decide to go rogue on the side of the angels, always scout out the turf first, get the lay of the land. Good for ya ta remember that.'

Lady Gaga on the side of the angels? Nick liked that. 'You ever considered an acting career?'

'Not much I haven't considered.' He kept his eyes on Nick longer than usual. 'I'll say this. Ya showed steel gettin' the Lady out and things sorted last night. Right up there it was.'

'Not quite up to your standard.'

'Don't sell yerself short. When trouble started, ya coulda bolted, but ya didn't. Ya manned up and together we scored a small win for the forces of justice and fair play … or at least until the Lady went over the railing.' He took a short swig. 'And that's when ya really dominated play. You were the dude. Hundred per cent. Toss ya on my shoulders, do a victory lap 'round town if I had the time.' He smiled. 'Or had the shoulders … When things get ugly, Nicko, ya're a good bloke to have around.'

'Thanks … You too.'

Moments passed in silent thought.

'So, back ta the clinic after ya leave here?'

'Yeah, I reckon.'

'You seemed to know the place well last night.'

Nick nodded, wondering how much he should say. 'Lina gave me a bit of a tour earlier.'

'Did she?' He waited for more, but it didn't come. 'Well, can't be a better place in Mae Sot, I s'pose, for the good Lady to recover in.'

'Actually, it's the only place.'

'Really?'

'She's Burmese.' Again, saying any more would take Nick where he didn't want to go. Bicyclists passed, a family on a motor scooter, a smoke-belching truck. 'So do you want me to relay any messages to her?'

Jake stared at the ground. 'She's a strange one, for sure.' His voice went unusually soft. 'Tell her I'm, like, sorry. I didn't mean ta get her in strife. I'd have told her that myself, but yeah, well, she wasn't exactly up ta hearin' much last night.' Jake sipped his beer, showing little interest now in reaching his mid-morning quota. 'Still, we've had some fun, haven't we?'

'Yeah.'

They watched passers-by before Jake looked down at his stubby between his feet and muttered, 'Sittin' in the bar at the Hill's Palace Hotel a few days ago, this mate o' mine, Tony Zucco, says in his most profound Sicilian-Aussie accent, "Why do we drink, amico mio, why do we do it?" I wasn't in a good space at the time, so said to him, "Because we hurt." Probably not the answer he was searchin' for.'

Nick didn't know how to respond to the sudden sombreness in his voice. 'Right.'

Jake finished his beer, eyed off the empty stubby. 'Swallow your joy from a chilled brown stubby, eh?'

'I s'pose … So what's the plan from here?' Nick asked.

Jake lifted his head, blew air through his lips. 'Not really in the country to explore my ultimate purpose in life, or think too hard. Might run with the pack a while, my karma rating continuin' ta slide. Chiang Mai, Chiang Rai, Chiang somewhere else.' He grinned, seemingly more from habit than joy. 'World's Best Practice Pussycats on most every street corner up north, or so I've been told.'

'And once you've done them all, then where?'

'Wanderin' bloggers report that Luang Prabang and Vientiane in Laos show promise. Then maybe Phnom Penh. Heard of it?'

'Capital of Cambodia.'

'Well done you ... I might chill there a while, compose a mission statement. Call it "The Traveller's Gospel According to Jake Jones". Include in it the rental of a house, a visit to the local brewery to stock up, employment of a cook and a cleaning lady with the right qualifications.' He stared at the ground and started to nod as if agreeing with something the ground had said. 'Yeah, on a bit of a spree up 'ere, ya could say. My family would, if they ...' He stopped, took a deep breath, his eyes lingering on Nick. 'Ya compared me to yer mum our first night at the Snake Skin. Made me laugh. Yer dad still about?'

'Yeah, sure.'

'Whadda they do?'

'Mum's an infant teacher. Dad's an orchardist; runs a few sheep as well as doing renovation and building work for friends in the area.'

'Busy people.' He looked in his backpack, rummaged past stubbies to find a biro and scrap of paper. He wrote something on the paper and handed it to Nick. 'When ya're ready ta finish yer education, Facey, text, email or whatever me care of Jake Jones. Thailand, Laos, Cambodia, Sydney, wherever – your choice.'

'Education?'

'Girls, grog and retro rock and roll. The unholy grail on which to base a ... a certain sort of life anyway.' He'd lost his spark, the energy gone from his voice. 'Well, that's if ya don't morph inta a certified three M-er first.'

Nick gave him a baffled look.

'Marriage, mortgage and midgets. The three Ms. Can happen before ya know it, people tell me.'

Nick held up the paper Jake had given him. 'I'll keep this close to my heart.' He put it in his shirt pocket.

'As you should, my man, as you should.' He stared a while before giving Nick a grin. 'Anyway, remember another one of my mission statements. For the Green Patch Flash, accommodation and recreational advisory services – whether in Asia or Aussie – will always be available and affordable. Your dividend for puttin' up with me prattlin' on these past few days.'

Green Patch. Gretna. Close enough. Why Nick felt complimented by Jake's offer, he didn't know. 'Actually, I mostly enjoyed it.' He couldn't help smiling. 'Those advisory services, like, will they recommend barrels of beer and front row seats at more pole dancing performances?'

'Always make for a decent night out, don't they? And in between performance drinks you can, like, tell me a story or two. Maybe start with your brother and the reason you're here, like now, in Mae Sot … Or maybe not. Again, totally up to you.'

Not a topic Nick would be pursuing. He diverted. 'So, long-term Asia. I'm envious.'

Jake let the comment pass and looked around at the traffic chaos, at locals further along the wall chatting away. 'Have ta pull the head in when the money runs out, or my liver explodes.' No grin; just his head drooping now, his face vacant. He blew out a long breath before eyeing Nick with a brand new look: serious, very serious. 'Then I'll head back to Cronulla, buy some flowers and put 'em on my parents', sister's and young nephew's graves before headin' back ta the mine, rejoinin' the under-life.' A bus turned onto the market road and came their way. 'They were killed in a car accident a few weeks back.' The bus pulled up and Jake stood and hoisted his backpack over his shoulder. 'So no, not all champagne and sunshine for the Jake-man back on the Big Island. Anyway, on that cheery note …' He presented his palm for a high-five.

Nick – stunned – was slow to respond. 'I'm sorry.'

'Yeah, well … It can addle yer brain, cut through ya like a piece of ragged tin at times. But what can ya do other than try to stay distracted … brain-dead?' Jake's eyes misted up and in the next second he had sunnies on; sunnies he wasn't supposed to have. He slapped Nick's half-raised palm then offered up his fist. Seconds later he shook his head and asked, 'Yer arthritis playin' up or somethin'?' He took Nick's hand, made a fist of it and bumped the knuckles with his own. 'Ya'll need to practise up on that before we next hang out together.'

17

Mya's eyes opened to red and blue spots twirling in her vision. She closed and opened them. Still the spots. She looked around at the ward, the wood slab beds pressed together along the walls, maybe a dozen women occupying them.

The Australian boy moved into her line of sight giving her an appraising look. Same look, same across-the-table stare he'd given her at the Snake Skin before ... what?

'Hello.'

'Hello.' Not for the first time she tried to sequence disordered images, voices. *'Come along Billy J and put me away ...' 'She can walk, she can work ...' 'No, upstairs, Gaga!'* The left side of her face pulsed. She touched her cheekbone, brow and eye socket – all sore, puffy.

The Australian raised a hand, tucked his thumb in and spread his fingers. 'How many?'

'Four.'

'No worries about your eyesight.'

The boy had been with another Australian who'd challenged Billy J. 'Where is your friend?' she asked.

'No worries with your memory either. Jake left for Chiang Mai earlier this morning. He asked me to apologise to you for how he ... treated you last night.'

She was on the floor next to feet. A man's voice: 'Change of plan. I'm outta here. You with me?'

'You're in the Mae Tao Medical Clinic. You fell off the Snake Skin staircase last night.'

The words 'Snake Skin' stilled her until she realised no one else in the ward could understand what they were saying, even if they were listening. 'How did I get here?'

The boy raised a hand.

'Thank you.' She recalled him in her room and later at the river telling her about a fire, someone being burned. What was his name? It wasn't a question she was used to asking herself in Mae Sot. She watched him eye the floor then glance around the ward like this was his first time here as well. 'First time' struck a chord. First time in

Mae Sot she'd woken up outside the Snake Skin. First time she'd had a visitor who didn't work there or hadn't paid for her time. And though sore and dazed and having no idea what was in store for her, she felt a sense of freedom, like a claw had dropped away from her throat and she could breathe easier.

A western woman entered the ward with a crying baby in her arms. She rocked it, talked to it, before she said to the boy, 'You're spending about as much time here as I am, Nick.'

Yes. He'd said that name in her room, shouted it at the river.

The baby went suddenly quiet and the woman introduced herself as Lina Larkin, an AusAID nurse. What AusAID was, Mya didn't know.

'Nick tells me you speak English,' the nurse said. 'So how are you feeling this morning?'

'Free' was the first word that came to her mind, though she doubted the nurse would understand why. 'Sore,' she replied. 'My head feels …' She couldn't think of the word, so moved a hand back and forth.

Nick: 'Wonky, wobbly?'

She nodded, adding, 'And heavy.' Though not heavy enough to stop her brain from processing the opportunities available to her, an ember of hope starting to smoulder away inside her.

Lina handed the baby to Nick and it started crying again.

'What am I supposed to do with this? Nick asked, holding the baby at arm's length, as he might a baby monkey.

'Entertain it.' Lina took out a biro and held it vertically in front of Mya. 'Follow this with your eyes.' She moved it slowly at first, back and forth and around, before speeding up. 'Alert. Good.' She pocketed the biro. 'So, nothing broken, and your eyes are clear and responsive. You should be able to leave in another day or two. But you'll need to rest after you do leave. Do you think that'll be possible?'

'Do you know where I work?'

Lina took a moment before nodding.

'They sometimes say to me "no work, no pay".' Then, like a barred door suddenly opened for her, she was gripped by a secret excitement. An idea took hold, followed by the beginning of a plan. She raised the sheet and looked down the length of her body like she was rediscovering herself. 'No clothes.'

Lina: 'Yes, your second need, your first being a good clean-up.' She met Nick's eyes. 'I'll take care of the clean-up, if you ...' She paused. 'As you no doubt have a better idea of where she keeps her clothes than I do, would you be good enough to go and get them for her?' She rescued the baby from him and it went quiet again.

The boy looked stung, and answered shortly, 'And if I'm not allowed into her room, what then?'

'Maybe you don't ask. Maybe you just find another way to get to where you need to go. I'm sure you've picked up a few clues from your time there.'

Nick gave her a stony stare and she caught its meaning. 'Okay. Bad idea maybe.' She thought a moment. 'The Snake Skin's top act knocked unconscious and ignored by staff. Can't be a good look for business there, can it? I know a local artist who'd have no trouble depicting the cold indifference of that on a poster, meant for duplication, and posted on every street corner in town.' She thought some more. 'But maybe we should start with something a bit less confronting. I reckon a note from Doctor Cynthia on Mae Tao Medical Clinic letterhead might prove persuasive.' She turned and started off. 'I'll be back soon.'

Mya called out, 'Excuse me.'

Lina stopped, looked around.

'If it is okay, could the doctor write that I will be here for many days – maybe seven? Then I can rest like the doctor will want me to.'

Lina kept her eyes on Mya a moment before answering, 'Okay.'

They watched Lina leave before Mya muttered Nick's name softly, like they'd just become friends. 'My clothes and things are under my bed. But some things are not for other people to see or know about.'

Nick shrugged his shoulders. 'Okay. No worries. Just tell me what you want and I'll leave the rest.'

'My small Buddha from the table, and from under the bed my two books, writing pad, shoulder bag, pink robe and everyday clothes and shoes and sandals, and also my money that is in a plastic bag. Please ig- ... ignore everything else.'

'Right.'

'And you must be careful. A man named Billy J, with many tattoos, will be there and—'

'I know who he is,' Nick interrupted.

'If he sees you with the money, he will take it from you.'

Nick looked as though he wanted to say something, but his confident expression was quickly followed by anxiety, reluctance.

'So you will have to be careful … have to be …'

'Sneaky?'

'Yes, that.' As encouragement, she added, 'My English improves when you are with me.'

Lina returned baby-less and handed him a note. 'Doctor Cynthia is away until tomorrow, but the Snake Skin won't know that.'

Nick glanced at the note. Mya saw it was written in Thai. 'So who wrote this?' she asked.

'A friend,' Lina replied. 'The Snake Skin won't know that either. So how are you feeling – up for it?'

Mya didn't understand that expression but Nick gave a long sigh.

* * *

Door and windows open, light beaming in. TV on the wall showing video clips of gangsta rappers. Bar-girls in skinny jeans and t-shirts, brooms and rags in hand, doing the cleaning up. Number One brushed past him with a mop – eyes averted, hip-roll gone – like he was just another blow-in off the street. Which he supposed he was.

Billy J looked up from the forged note, shaking his head. 'Crazy that girl,' he said, jabbing his skull with a forefinger. 'Spiders in head.' He locked his gaze on Nick and asked, 'Where your friend?'

'Gone.'

'Where?'

Nick shrugged. 'Back to Australia I reckon.'

Billy J nodded like he understood why. 'You see him again, say come back to Snake Skin. See Billy J. Free drink if he do.'

Free knife between the ribs as well. 'Sure.'

Lina, growing impatient, placed exhibit B – her own drawing – on the bar next to Billy J's dark-coloured drink. 'Falling off stairs, knocked unconscious and ignored by the staff until a young Australian took matters into his own hands to get your feature attraction into a vehicle and on to the Mae Tao Medical Clinic. Can't be a good look for business, can it? Especially after my artist friend makes up more of these posters, showing your Lady Gaga sprawled out on the floor, and attaches them to every building and tree trunk from here to the Moei River. So, up to you or whoever you work for about what happens next.'

Another thing about Lina. Tattoos and muscle-shirts didn't intimidate her, or soften her voice. Hard to know how much Billy J understood. From the sullen, bleary-eyed expression on his face probably not much. But at least he didn't shake his head like he did when presented with the forged note. He reached for his drink now, glancing down at the drawing for a second time. He took a sip, stirred the drink with his finger then read the forged note again.

'Just her toiletries and seven days' worth of clothes,' Lina reminded him. 'They won't take more than a minute or two to collect.'

Billy J propped his elbow on the bar, head in his hand. 'You say to her five day, no more. Then not come back, no job.' He pointed upwards. 'Room one. You got three minute and da clock's a-tickin'.'

'You coming?' Lina asked him.

Billy J's focus was on the TV. He shook his head.

* * *

'Not The Lodge in here, is it?'

Nick didn't know what The Lodge was. 'No,' he answered anyway, while on his belly, his arm extended under the bed. He fingered two silky items, a tubular object – like a baton but rough-edged – and next to it a small square of something hard and half-wrapped in foil. He brought them out into the light. A pink garment, a brown sash, a long pipe and what looked to be a small packet of black cheese, but might have been some sort of incense. Then he thought about her cropped hair, her dazed voice and appearance just before she fell off the staircase. Without knowing why, he shoved the pipe and 'cheese' back just far enough so Lina wouldn't see them. He looked over and saw her gazing out the window. 'That's it,' he lied. 'All cleared out.'

Lina checked her watch. 'Two and a quarter minutes and "da" clock's a-still-a-tickin'". Towards what, do you reckon?' Her voice went cowboy American. 'Shootout at the Snake Skin Cor-ral?'

'I doubt he has the energy.' He sat up and leaned back against the bed, waiting and thinking.

Deadline time came and went, and another minute passed before Lina said. 'You seem to know our host pretty well.'

'He and Jake – the bloke I was with – had an encounter last night just before Lady Gaga went over the railing.'

'Want to tell me about it?'

'Not really.'

'Then I s'pose we'd better get moving or someone might get the wrong impression about why we've been up here … so long … together.'

'As if.'

Like Jake, she couldn't hold back her smirk. She collected the small Buddha from the table and stuffed it and Gaga's things into a bag. While she did, Nick tossed the hidden items into his daypack.

18

The Australian came back and placed the bag of clothes next to her bed, and she thanked him. He reached into his daypack and brought out the pink garment and held it up. 'I didn't know if you wanted this. There's a brown sash as well. What sort of dress is it?'

'It is not a dress. It is a robe.'

'A robe? Like for wearing around the house … in your room, I mean?'

She shook her head, thinking: at the Snake Skin, at the river, treating her like she was someone special; asking her questions, telling her about himself. He'd got her out of the Snake Skin as well when no one else would, then gone back and got her things. And here he was at her bedside again. Yet he had no idea who she was – really was. 'The robe belongs to a novice nun.' She watched his puzzled look as he placed the robe on the bed.

'Buddhist?' Nick asked.

'Yes.'

'A friend of yours?'

How could he understand, or anyone understand, unless they'd been with her from the massacre until her Billy J delivery day? 'No.' In the light streaming in through the window he looked about fifteen. She asked him his age.

'Twenty … two.' She stared and he broke eye contact. 'Well, at least in the Snake Skin I'm supposed to be. Actually I'm seventeen.'

'Me too. But if people ask, I have to say I am twenty … or had to say. I have an identification card that says I am.'

'The legal age for working in a bar here?'

'Yes.'

'The robe's yours, isn't it?'

She nodded.

'How can you be both … that and Lady Gaga?'

And there was Mya Paw Wah to account for too. Part of her frustration in Mae Sot came from being a stranger to everyone. Yet now that someone really did want to know more about her, she felt uncomfortable, scared even. To confide in someone meant getting closer to them, trusting them. Apart from the abbot, she'd not done that with anyone since leaving Yangon.

Yet this Australian boy had twice confided in her, and she'd not be here now if it weren't for him. And as she had said to Billy J, this boy was different from the other westerners she'd been with at the Snake Skin. Okay, so without flooding his ears with words, where to start? As Lady Gaga there was little about her he didn't already know. But as Mya Paw Wah and Nan Pau … 'The answer to your question is very long and confusing,' she warned.

'Try me.'

'Okay. I will. But you must tell me when you have heard enough.' She glanced down at her hands folded on her lap. 'Life can turn against you in seconds,' she started, mimicking what her father had said to her in the past, 'and put you in … sit-u-a-tions and places not even your nightmares do. Over a year ago …' And in a low, slow voice, she went on to describe the four monks who'd passed by on Sule Pagoda Road that day and Thant knowing the one with the limp and scarred face. Initially she skipped the rain, how the protesting monks looked coming down the road, what they were chanting, how crowded the footpaths and buildings were behind her. But the further she went, the more her emotions took hold, the more she paused to think, the more detailed her story became, her words turning bitter at times like it was all happening again right in front of her.

At times she blinked, suddenly and repeatedly, as if to clear her eyes. She stopped now and then to gauge whether the Australian boy had heard enough and was too polite to say so. But he just looked straight back at her waiting for more.

A half hour maybe – certainly the longest period of time she'd ever spoken English in one sitting – before she got to the part of being taken from the river to the Snake Skin, Billy J there to 'welcome' her. She paused and stared across the ward. 'Like living in the bottom circle of hell since then,' she muttered, before facing him again. 'Anyway, you know the rest.'

He didn't feel he did, but was too tongue-tied to say anything more than, 'Incredible.' Then he said, 'How suddenly things can happen that will haunt you forever. My mum said that to me after the fire.'

'Haunt?' she asked.

'Bad thoughts or memories that you never forget.'

At his words, her head sagged.

* * *

Lina, the super-charged, bounced back in, her voice box erupting, 'How's the patient?' It took them a moment to re-adjust to her.

Mya – he'd finally gotten her name – replied, 'Good, thank you.'

'Lunch is coming. We've got a big carton of mangoes in. Would you like one?'

'Yes, thank you.'

Lina looked over at Nick, her eyes bright, a slow-growing smile on her face. 'Want the good news?'

'Only the good news.'

'Just got word that John is doing well and will be back in six or seven days.'

His smile came first, then: 'Awesome.' Though he didn't think another week of waiting around for John was awesome at all. Maybe he should take a bus up to Chiang Mai to visit him and wait there.

'How's your sister?'

'As of yesterday, still improving. Actually, I'd better go and check in with the family.' And also check on bus times to Chiang Mai, he thought. He stood and looked down at Mya. 'I'll be back this afternoon.'

'Okay.' She smiled. 'I will be here.'

He grabbed his daypack, having forgotten about the pipe and 'black cheese' in it, and made for the exit.

* * *

The next two days Mya left her bed early and walked along the clinic's perimeter developing her plan. She refused to think about it failing, knowing only she would not see the inside of the Snake Skin again, no matter what.

Nick put off going to Chiang Mai and went to the clinic instead, mid-morning, then again mid-afternoon. They walked, sat in a court-yard – sometimes silent, sometimes chatting about small things.

On the third morning, Mya woke before dawn, her skin flushed and tingly. She knew the symptoms, the slight addiction of her opium pipe calling. First line for a haiku: *Beating the dragon.* And that's just what she was in the process of doing. She took her shoulder bag, left the clinic and went out to the main road where she caught a motor-bike taxi to the Friendship Bridge. She shopped at the stalls there, not bothering to bargain, each item bought contributing to her excite-ment. Then she paid a stall owner to store her things for her.

Early on the fourth morning she walked around the ward and exchanged brief words with the Karen women there. In one of her fanciful moods, she thought briefly about asking Lina if she could work at the clinic, doing anything to earn enough money for food and the rental of a room. Then reality smacked her hard: Billy J would come, wouldn't he? He'd harass and remind her of the big sum of money she had to earn to support her mother, remind others what she'd spent her time doing the past year at the Snake Skin.

No, living anywhere near Mae Sot would be no escape.

Nick came – daypack dangling from his shoulder – and, surpris-ingly, asked her to go to the Burmese market in town with him. That was another 'first' here in Mae Sot. She shook her head.

'Yes, do.'

She shook her head again, more insistent.

'Please,' he said, not unlike a little boy when he wanted something badly enough.

She'd been duped, almost killed, and bought and sold like a piece of meat since coming to Mae Sot; the same experiences that could happen to any Burmese woman considered an enemy of Myanmar. In a sense, though, she'd been lucky. She'd not been killed, or lost any limbs. She'd not ended up in a labour camp or the Iron Bar Hotel, though that could still happen. But what was so unexpected was this boy's insistence on staying in her life. He should be at home in Australia doing his homework, meeting girls, kicking a soccer ball or whatever they kicked in that country. Again she shook her head, this time adding, 'Someone might recognise me.'

He picked up her robe. 'Wear this. Wear sunglasses. I'll make you a bargain. If after ten minutes you don't like being there, we'll come back and I'll never ask you to go to town, or anywhere else with me again. Promise.'

Why it was so important to him, she couldn't begin to understand. She breathed a sigh, reached for her Gaga-sunnies and took the robe from him. They left and rode their bikes up to the road, where she turned left towards the bridge.

Moments later, Nick came alongside her shouting, 'Wrong way.'

'Either the bridge market or no market,' she answered, eyes on the road.

He stayed with her and said no more, at least until they arrived. Then he opened up, continually asking questions about things on sale, the merchants selling them, forcing her to use words she could barely remember. And when she got stuck, he gave her the words.

He bought chicken satay and fruit for them and they sat in a private corner and ate and watched. It felt strange being Nan Pau again, walking and sitting shoulder to shoulder with a male in public and talking about everyday things in English, which, even more than her Tripitaka and stone Buddha, connected her with school and home. Strange too feeling seventeen, almost a schoolgirl, almost innocent again.

When they returned to the clinic, Mya changed and they sat in the courtyard and watched people go by, mothers breast-feeding their babies, amputees trialling new legs. She grew fanciful again and thought about postponing what she was about to do. But she couldn't, her time was running out.

After Nick left, she wrote him a note, putting nurse Lina's name on it and asking her to give it to him. She placed the note on her bed and, almost sadly, went out to the road and caught a motorbike taxi back to the Friendship Bridge.

Had Nick not met up with Lina and the clinic's founder, Dr Cynthia, and had a curious woman in the ward not seen Lina's name on the note and immediately delivered the note to her, Mya might have drowned in the Moei River.

19

Nick left the clinic in a hurry and spotted Mya turn in the direction of the river and walk along the main road. As he debated whether to call out to her, she disappeared. He ran and reached the road just as she got onto a motorbike taxi.

He waited on the roadside for another one to come by.

* * *

Mya collected her supplies, packed them into her backpack and made her way quickly along the walkway. Focused as she was, it took her a while to notice how deserted the walkway was. No watchers, smugglers, other walkers, and as she neared the river crossing zone, no passenger-carrying tubes either. Something had happened. The start of the dry season had lowered the river a little, but it was still high enough for tubes to cross. There were a couple of marooned tree trunks in the river, but such obstacles had never stopped crossings in the past. Then it struck her: a border police crackdown. She knew they occurred when high-ranking officials from Chiang Mai or Bangkok were visiting the area. She glanced back towards the market stalls and felt her skin bristle. Nick was jogging towards her, daypack bouncing over his back.

He pulled up next to her, catching his breath. 'Hi … How are you?' he asked, as though surprised to see her.

'What do you want?' she asked, scowling at him.

'Backpack, huh?' He forced a smile. 'Going somewhere?'

She glared, and he made a performance of glancing up and down the walkway. 'A bomb go off or something? About as populated as the moon here. Where is everyone?'

'Gone. You need to go too.'

'Maybe we could go together, head back to the clinic or … wherever?'

Why was he installing himself in her life? He knew what she did, what she was. She shook her head, both puzzled and annoyed by his persistence. She looked down at the river: low, full of eddies and cross-currents, foam riding the surface. So close now, she craved getting to the other side. She glanced up the walkway and saw two men, darkly dressed, heading straight for them. 'Good-bye', she said, turning and bolting for the smugglers' rope. She grabbed it and descended the embankment, dislodging dirt and small rocks in her rush to get down.

On the river's edge, she searched for a way across then stepped into the water and sank quickly to her waist. She leaned forward, used her arms as paddles and began to wade unsteadily to the other side.

* * *

Nick spotted the two border policemen, their eyes scanning the river. They quickened their pace, shouting something at Mya that only prompted her arms to move faster. She stumbled, sank to her chest then found a shallower section, stepped onto it, before dropping into deeper water again. As she struggled to stand up, her pack shifted and she fell over, getting swept metres down the river before grabbing onto a bough and scrambling onto rocks. There she stood, battling the current to stay upright.

The policemen slowed. One put a mobile to his ear.

Nick searched through his daypack for his passport, certain they'd want to check it. He pulled out Mya's pipe and foil-wrapped 'black cheese' instead. The pipe was weird, he realised now. Bamboo stem, a metal bowl at the end with a hole at the bottom encircled by a tar-like residue. It had to be for smoking drugs – had to be. His mind in turmoil, he had about seven seconds to make a decision. Toss them? But the border police would see him do that and the 'cheese' was light and wouldn't carry far. Follow Mya? Thing was, once in Burma everything would be out of his control. Stay and probably be searched? Schapelle Corby and how many other Aussie druggies were rotting away in Asian jails? *'Fear can either paralyse you, Alice, or help you to move faster.'* He glanced down at Mya, still stranded, her pack big enough to drown her if she got swept up in the current again.

Ropes and trees and embankments and Derwent River-wading were sport for him back in Tassie.

He went for the rope.

* * *

MYANMAR.

They huddled amongst the scrub and low-lying trees, the hum of flies, the sun hammering down.

The Thai policemen were studying where they'd exited the river, about fifty metres away, like they expected them to re-appear there.

'You okay?' Nick mumbled, glancing over at Mya.

She nodded, her head on a swivel checking out five directions at once.

Like a continuing episode of *Australian Survivor*, he thought. The boy from Gretna surviving a firestorm, Jake and a 'Snake Skin education', now hiding with the nightclub's star attraction on the wrong side of the Moei River, police searching for them.

'Why did you follow me?' Mya muttered, renewing her glare.

'You were in trouble. Pushed a few more metres and you'd have been on your way to the Indian Ocean.'

'You need a geography lesson. I was okay.'

'Yeah, well … I might not have been okay if the policemen had searched my bag.' He reached into his daypack and took out the pipe and 'black cheese'. 'What are these for?'.

Her eyes bulged. 'You are not supposed to have those.' She grabbed them and shoved them into her backpack. 'Now you can go back to Thailand.' She eyed the policemen again, 'As soon as they go.'

'What about you?'

'You do not need to know.' She added in a sad tone, 'And you need to stay away from me – please.'

There came the sound of a high-revving engine, tires spitting gravel. They listened as it closed in on them. Brakes screeched. Doors slammed. A voice called out.

'Border police, I think.' She moved crab-like into thicker scrub then hopped up, grabbed her pack and ran.

Without options, what else could Nick do but follow? Along a path they went, that turned away from the river and up into the mountains.

On a low ridge they stopped, their breath ragged, clothes still sodden. They looked back down from where they came. No one was following – close up anyway. Mya dropped her pack, lay down and propped her head against a fallen tree, her body unwinding, her eyes going teary for a few seconds.

Nick sat next to her.

Quiet up there, like a classroom during exam week.

A lizard emerged from under the tree trunk and basked in a bar of sunlight. Two butterflies danced in front of them.

Nick looked at Mya, her thin fingers, half-moon nails. 'You climb better than you swim.'

Out of immediate danger she grew grateful. 'I should have thanked you earlier for helping me out of the river.'

'Done.'

She pulled up a cuff of her jeans, sat up and eyed a bloated leech attached to her ankle. She reached into her pack for a box of matches, lit one, blew it out and pressed the match head into the leech and watched it curl and fall to the ground. Nick squashed it with a rock, then took off a shoe and sock and pressed the sock against her leech wound. When the bleeding finally stopped, Mya took the sock and told him not to move. She leaned into him and rubbed at spots on his forehead, cheek and chin, telling him, 'There is dirt on your face. Here … here … and here.'

Like his mum used to do, Nick thought, when he was about four years old. He almost expected to hear, 'Now that's a good boy.' Yet he warmed to her closeness, her concern.

Finished with his face, she took out a water bottle and drank and passed it along. Water, like whatever food she had, was going to have to last. So he took only a mouthful.

They listened to the quiet, watching sunlight beam in through the trees, before Nick spotted a line of ants that, unlike him, knew exactly where they were going – straight for his sock.

'Talk,' Mya said, looking less grateful now.

'About what?' he asked, putting his sock and shoe back on.

'How you are going to get back into Thailand. You do not have permission to be in Myanmar, or a … a …'

'A visa?'

'Yes, that. You do not have one, do you?

'No.'

'Do you have your passport?'

Her officiousness brought to mind the walking Wikipedia who, hopefully, was starting to wonder where he was now. 'I do.' He patted his bag. 'Just here in a plastic cover – so still dry.'

'You must show your passport on the Myanmar side of the Friend-ship Bridge if you want to return to Thailand. But without a visa stamped in it you will be in big trouble.'

No greater authorities than Snake Skin patrons had obviously told her that. Thing was, being reminded only ramped up the fear he was trying to suppress. 'So where are we going?'

'Me, not we.' She recalled: *'Better you don't know that until you're nearly there. That way, if you're arrested, you can't divulge your mother's whereabouts.'*

'You then.'

She pointed to a crosscut of tracks just up ahead. 'West.'

'West? Those tracks are going in all directions. How would you know west from east, north or south?'

'From experience,' she said. She reached into her backpack and brought out two rice-balls, each wrapped in newspaper. She thought for a moment, then handed him one. 'You need to eat.'

'Right. I didn't exactly come prepared, did I?'

She scrutinised him like a problem, before glancing away.

They ate and minutes later Nick jumped up, grabbed the backpack and his daypack and headed west, or wherever, Mya in pursuit.

'There could be landmines,' she called out, catching up.

He stopped. 'Ah ... right. No worries.' Yes there were.

She reached for the backpack, but he pulled away and gave her his daypack instead. She must have thought it was not the time to argue. 'I will go first,' she said. 'But tomorrow you must go back.'

They climbed on, immersed in their own thoughts.

* * *

Late in the day, with birds shrilling like the intrusion of humans was big news, they made it to the summit and level ground and a boulder to use as a backrest, rice-balls to eat, water to drink.

Weary and foot-sore, Mya could have slept right there, on the ground, in a tree, the next day and all its anticipated problems too distant to worry about. Yet, at the same time, she was flushed with a sense of accomplishment – her soreness good soreness; her weariness to be expected; the police, Billy J and the Snake Skin far down below consigned to memory; her mother a day closer. She looked over at Nick, a far-away look on his face. 'What are you thinking about?' she asked, ready for talk now.

'Gretna, where I live in Australia, and what my parents would say if they saw me now, like on a Skype link-up.'

Light was fading, darkness rising from the ground. 'I do not think they would be happy about where you are or who you are with.'

'Don't think I'd tell them. I'd just ask, "Want the good news or the bad first?" They'd go the good, I know. So I'd put you in front of the computer and say, "This is my good friend and travelling companion. Mya is her name. She's brave and smart and good-looking, even though she's missing some hair." Then I'd swing the camera around at the trees and everything, and say, "Actually, there is no bad news. Top viewing spot here, isn't it?" Then I'd describe where we are, that sort of thing.'

'You have a good imagination. I hope you would not name the country, or why we are here.'

'Probably not.' Birds chorused and they listened before Nick asked, 'What would you say to your mother?'

'I will be with you soon.'

'In Hpa-an?'

She stared in thought. 'Yes.'

'How far away is that?'

'About seventy kilometres.' Her thoughts turned to him here with her, that the longer he stayed, the less she wanted him to leave. And that frustrated her. The sun – to be avoided earlier – was setting now, the last light gone from the tree tops, the sky streaking red. Soon it would be just them and the darkness and night animals.

'I've never slept the night in a strange place, not having a clue where I was.'

'I have,' Mya replied. 'And I have heard that villagers sleep outside in these mountains,' she added, lying in order to comfort him. 'I have a large plastic sheet. It is big enough for two people to sleep on.'

'Oh.' He grinned. 'Do you snore?'

'What is snore?'

'Making low growling noises while you sleep.' He gave her a demo.

'I do not. Do you?'

'Not if I have a pillow or something to put under my head.'

At that moment he reminded her of Thant, teasing, manipulating, but in a fun sort of way. She shoved her pack his way. 'Use this. I do not need anything for my head.' She lay back against the log, her tired mind reviewing the day before considering the night animals – both the four- and two-legged varieties – here and in Mae Sot. She'd read about bears in this area. But better them, she thought, than the Snake Skin patrons down below. No matter what, she was never going back to that pit, that hell hole. Living there as a stranger to herself. Her body just 'an open door' for men to thump and squeeze her sore; their sweat and alcohol breath; her ridiculous wig, make-up and cheap perfume. Like now, she often wondered if she'd ever be capable of making love to someone she was attracted to, of getting married, of mothering a child as she'd been mothered, of just living normally.

She looked over at Nick and saw he was watching her. 'Plastic sheet, eh?' he said.

She reached into her backpack and pulled it out. 'We need to collect leaves and put this over them so the ground will be soft to sleep on. But we must collect them from under trees, not the middle of the track.'

She wanted him to ask why, and he did. 'Land mines,' she answered, in the belief they would discourage him from going any further in the morning.

* * *

Ten minutes later they lay next to each other, cicadas chorusing through the trees, the two of them staring up at the first stars.

'I think I'd prefer hearing your voice to what's around us now,' Nick said.

She was slow to answer. 'What do you want me to talk about?'

'Whatever … What about yourself?'

'There is no more about me to say. I have told you how I got to the Snake Skin. You have seen me there. You have been in my room. You have sat with me on my bed. So I think it will be better if we do not talk about me.'

'Your room, yeah. I know nothing about sex.' Away in his thoughts, that just escaped his mouth. His face flushed. He felt like crawling in a hole and burying himself.

'I do not think it is hard to learn; the movements, anyway.' She eyed Nick a moment. 'Besides that, I know nothing about it either. But it must be good when you feel strong a fiction …'

'I think you mean affection.'

'Yes, a-ffection for the person you are with. Maybe we will meet again sometime, feel strong a-ffection and teach each other.' She must have realised how suggestive that sounded, and quickly added, 'In another lifetime I mean … Another lifetime.'

'Yeah ... That would be good.' Though he was partial to this life-time. But no way would he say it. Instead, he lifted his nose, sniffed the air as a dog would. 'Not a bad patch of ground here, is it? Cool now. The smell of trees.'

Surprisingly, she laughed.

'What's funny?'

'Billy J would fine us if we gained weight, or broke something, or tore our clothes, or if we didn't sit straight at tables, or men didn't buy us drinks, or if a patron complained. Every month the girls had to pay two hundred baht to help bribe the police. But because I am Burmese, I had to pay four hundred.'

'And that's funny?'

'To laugh is to make that not so important, to push it into the past and make it go away.' Moments later she sniffed and turned away, her breath quickening.

He lay there feeling awkward. Finally he asked, 'Are you okay?' What else could he say? Shut your face?

'Yes ... okay.'

He waited until she started to breathe normally again. 'Talk to me about your childhood.'

'It would take half the night.'

'I do have a few hours to spare.' Talking would distract her, maybe ease what was troubling her.

'I will make a bar ... a bar ...'

'Bargain?'

'Yes, that. I do not think we will be together for much longer. But if we are tomorrow night and we have not stepped on any mines or been eaten by bears or tigers and are not too hungry or thirsty to talk, I will tell you about my child ... hood if you tell me about yours. Okay?'

'Okay. And that done, what'll we talk about the following night?' In fact, he was starting to feel conflicted about going any further, and not just because of the talk about mines and animals. John was due back any day. 'I mean, if we're still together?'

'That is a long time away. We might be dead.'

A mosquito buzzed Nick's ear. He slapped the spot.

'Sshhh. We must be quiet now.'

'No worries.' He put the sheet over his head, aware of how close he was to Mya – almost touching.

'Good night.' She was clearly still troubled by something. 'You are in Myanmar illegally,' she said to him eventually. 'If you are caught, you will be asked many questions. Like who you have been with and where you were going and why. I do not want anyone to know that. Can you understand why?'

He lifted the sheet from his head. 'Yes. But there's no way I would tell anyone anything about you.'

'Not even with a gun in your face?'

'Not even then.' Playing Mr Up-for-it again, wanting to impress her, win her praise. How could he know what he'd do? 'Anyway, not to worry, I've already forgotten the place. Except, I reckon there'll be buses there that go to the Thai border.'

'Yes. But you will not be allowed to cross the Friendship Bridge.' She sounded exasperated, like she was losing patience with him. 'It won't be like what happens in western countries. In Myanmar police beat people and put them in prison for a long time.'

'I crossed the river once, I can do it again.'

She gave a frustrated sigh. 'You are … diffi-cult.'

'I know.'

'I don't want to talk anymore.'

'Okay.'

'Good night.'

'Good night.'

'Try not to listen to anything or maybe you will not sleep.'

Night sounds were coming from everywhere: strange birdcalls, the trilling of cicadas, the squealing of something else, like the something else was being eaten. So how could he not listen? 'Okay.'

'Good night.'

'Good night.'

'I sometimes have nightmares. If I scream do not be scared.'

'Right. I thought you didn't want to talk anymore.'

'I do not. Good night.'

'Good night.'

* * *

Chased in Hpa-an, caught, imprisoned in the Iron Bar Hotel. Wedged in a corner trying to avoid the faces ogling her through the bars …

Mya woke with a start, birdcalls intense. She laid there calming herself before rolling onto her elbow and looking over at Nick, still sleeping on his back, mouth open, and yes, snoring a little. Above them the pre-dawn light, bright enough to make out individual trees. She got up and moved into them.

Out on open ground again she located the right track then returned and placed her Buddha on the ground and sat intending to pray. She didn't. Then came the sunrise and continued chorusing of birds and right there and then – above all the difficulties, all her fears – she felt a surprising sense of lightness, happiness even. She'd survived the past year and life suddenly, overwhelmingly, felt good to her. If she could, she'd have stopped time to keep feeling the way she did now, valued even more maybe because she knew the feeling couldn't last. There was still so much to do to get to Hpa-an, so much to overcome, so little she could count on.

In those few minutes, in the soft, slanting light, she felt she understood something about the Buddha's enlightenment under a Boddhi tree in India twenty-five hundred years earlier. Though that understanding wasn't something she planned to share with Nick, starting to fill her thoughts as he stirred, woke with a grunt, stretched and sat up, giving her a finger wave.

'You snore,' she said.

'And you twitch and … scream. Like twice.'

'I told you I might do that.'

He tucked his arms behind his head. 'Yeah, and you weren't lying.' He wrinkled his nose like he smelled something bad and sniffed his armpits.

She pointed to the closest clump of trees. 'Toilet.'

'Yeah, I've worked that out.'

When Nick returned, he started packing up while Mya boiled water for rice and tea.

They ate and drank, each waiting for the other to speak. Finally Nick said, 'Besides my mum when I was a baby, you're the first person I've ever slept with.'

She smiled, watching him. 'And you are the first one I have ever slept with too; really slept with. It was good. I will remember it.' Hurting a little, Mya added, 'But … there is nothing you can do to help me now. So you must go back to Mae Sot.' She got up and started folding up her plastic sheet.

'Who'll carry your pack?'

'Who do you think?'

'Who'll give you English improvement lessons?'

Now she looked over at him, smiling. 'Yes. You are good at that too. And because you are I will give you two rice-balls and water for today. Remember, you need to cross the river tonight so no one sees you. I think you will be the first westerner to ever swim across.'

'Twice?' he asked.

She nodded then went quiet, having said everything she could without making their parting more difficult.

He reached into his day pack, got out a biro and a scrap of paper and wrote on it. He handed her the paper, pointing. 'This is my travelling Gmail address and this is my email address at home. Are there internet cafes in Hpa-an, do you think?'

'I think so. I have seen them in Yangon and Bago.'

'Then I'll check my email. And I'll write back. One thing you need to know though is my spelling is no good. It'll take some work to make sense of it.'

'Try me.' The words he'd said to her at the clinic.

He must have remembered too, because he smiled and said, 'I will.'

Outside of her family she'd never done what she was about to do. 'Please, I want to do this.' She stood on her tip-toes, placed a steadying hand on his shoulder and kissed his cheek. She stepped back. 'Thank you, Nick. I will miss you.'

'Yeah, me too.'

She retrieved her things and started down the track, not looking back.

* * *

A sudden loneliness swept over him as he watched her disappear. He thought about leaving too, but getting to the Moei River before nightfall made little sense, so he sat down and thought about all the things he'd like to have with him up there: computer, MP3 player, Tassie fishing book – anything at all that could distract him. Gradually he settled, taking in the occasional sound of a bird, the tentacle-like roots lining the track. A scorpion moved out from under a leaf in front of him, its tail arched upwards like a miniature dragon.

He found another place to sit.

Time passed, his thoughts gradually returning to Mae Sot, the prospect of going back there starting to feel good: the food he was going to eat, the comfort of his Ban Thai room, seeing John again. He dozed, woke and heard small track sounds; soon voices. He scrambled further into the trees.

Villagers appeared as if out of the earth: three young women in longyis and ragged t-shirts, babies strapped to their chests. Further back came two young blokes – black ink tattoos trailing up their calves and arms – carrying a makeshift bamboo stretcher. In it was another bloke, blood-stained bandages twisted around his leg. A half dozen old men and women – bundles strapped to their backs, walking wearily, sticks prodding the ground – brought up the rear.

He let his pulse settle before moving out onto open ground and greeting them with 'Hi.'

They stopped, their faces turning in his direction, but without alarm, like he was just part of the landscape.

'Neek?' one of the women asked.

He wouldn't have been any more surprised if she'd followed up with his Gretna address.

The woman approached. She handed him a note and Mya's tinfoil-wrapped 'black cheese'.

He read:

> Nick
> Do not worry. These people will not eat you. Burmese soldiers have attacked their village. They are escaping. The women and old people are going to the Mae La Refugee Camp. They know how to get there. But the boy in the stretcher has been shot and has lost lots of blood and is feeling lots of pain.

You are good at helping people. Please help him get to the Mae Tao Clinic. I hope you have money. As much as five hundred baht for bribes. You have the pipe and opium. When the track gets rough give the opium and pipe to the boys carrying the stretcher. They will help the boy smoke it. It will take away the pain and maybe even put him to sleep.

Mya, the opium authority.

When you get to the river, throw away the opium and give three hundred baht to one of the boys. He will bribe someone to paddle them across to Thailand. You must cross before they do and go to the clinic and get help to take the wounded man from the walkway to the clinic.

Like the walking Wikipedia had written the note.

The boys know how to swim, how to get to the Mae La Camp. And the border police should not stop a refugee who is badly hurt from getting to the clinic. But if they do, two hundred baht should make them go away.

Thank you and good luck.

Mya

And she was going on about him teaching her English?

He glanced in the direction of Mae Sot then regarded the villagers, drawing up an image of being caught and arrested by border police. Other images followed: falls, landmine explosion, river-crossers refusing to paddle them across, being caught in a cross-current and swept away.

'Fear can either paralyse you, Alice, or help you to move faster.'

Yeah, yeah, yeah.

To the mother's beseeching look, Nick nodded and said, 'Okay,' and the mother smiled her reply and returned to the others.

The oldies, reluctant to leave, reached out to the young ones and held on to them. Not something meant for him to watch. So he turned and headed slowly back down the track.

* * *

Mae Sot, Thailand.

She'd be at the Ban Thai, Nick reckoned, but even if she were still working, he needed to get out of his saturated clothes and get something quick to eat and drink, for himself and the three villagers waiting for him at the bush end of the walkway.

He paid the motorbike taxi driver in wet baht and entered the foyer and ran up the stairs. He banged on her door and Lina answered in seconds. 'I need help,' he told her.

'Of course you do, why else would you be here at this hour?' She looked him over. 'Off to the river, are we?'

20

Karen State, Myanmar.

As Mya descended, the terrain grew more rugged with screes and sun-baked slabs and buttresses of rock rearing up either side of her. Above, buzzards glided in the invisible currents, watching. She stopped often, drank from her water bottle and scanned the landscape listening for sounds, especially men's voices. After a while she took the container of rat poison from her pack and put it into her front pocket. There were worse things than dying and she had experienced some of them. She'd not experience them again. So, three possibilities: she would get to Hpa-an unhindered, step on a mine or meet up with the military. Her poison – quickly accessible – ensured the third possibility, like the second, would be brief.

On she went, Mae Sot growing more distant, her mother nearer.

The track flattened, rose again then plunged steeply, her tiny sideways steps struggling to grip the track. The landscape turned green, vegetation thickening. Out of the sun she entered a cooler world of dampness and dappled light, where as many plants seemed to grow from trees as the ground. She came to a stream and sat and drank and ate; dragonflies hovering, the sound of the water from deeper in soothing her.

Rested, she walked on, climbing the next hill's twists and turns and crossing a bald knob before descending again into more trees and finding another stream where frogs chorused and monkeys shrieked in the distance. Tired and sore and facing another climb, she spotted a small animal track to her left. She followed it – the ferns giving way, the ground damp and sunken, insect hum in her ears – before meeting up with the stream again. She waded up it until the stream deepened and widened into a pool so still and clear she could see her face in it. She hoisted herself onto a rock and stretched out in shade, blissfully aware that no one in the world could know where she was. She was unreachable, wonderfully alone, the spiders of her mind long gone. And into her thoughts returned Nick: his shy looks, determined manner; hopefully waiting now to cross the river with the villagers.

She got out her dictionary, pen and pad and wrote:

Australian boy
With courage
And kindness
Kills spiders
And straightens
Their tangled webs.

'When writing creatively you have to be patient,' her ex-monk teacher reminded the class. 'Digging a well with a pen requires no greater amount of patience and concentration.'

The thirteen-word poem took her an hour to write – an hour of pleasure. Though, if anyone asked her about those last three lines, she'd find them hard to explain. Something to do with symbolism and her nightmares and how Billy J and Nick-types could affect people. Of course, no one would be asking, because no one else would be seeing the poem.

A tear rolled down her cheek, one of pure relief. She knuckled it away and lay back down, smiling a little, gazing at the thick-trunked trees above her.

The light dimmed.

Birds warbled and whooped. Mosquitoes buzzed her.

The first bats flew overhead, swerving in the twilight, wings pulsing.

Bang! A gunshot pierced the air. For seconds it echoed, and moments later came another one – *bang!*

She packed up quickly and scampered further upstream until she spotted a small cave above her, water trickling from a rock overhang above its entrance. She climbed, entered the cave and sat down amongst charred wood and the stains and acrid smell of bat excrement, picturing solitary monks meditating there.

She dropped her pack, gathered leaves from outside, and – as bats flew in, circled and flew out again – she made up her bed, all the time conscious of scratching noises from further inside. Cave rats, she thought.

She ate a rice-ball, drank some water.

The cave darkened.

She took off her wet boots and socks and wrapped herself up in her plastic sheet. Soon she was dreaming of earlier times.

At some point she woke to rustling noises, like leaves stirring at her feet, before the rustling moved away. She tightened the sheet around her and slept until well past dawn.

* * *

'Welcome to King Cobra country.'

She stopped, rigid. Had she stepped on one coming out of the cave, she would not have been more startled. Her head shot around to where a thin, long-haired man in sandals, worn trousers and t-shirt sat on a rock, eyes fixed on the stream. A rifle, a machete and a darkly-stained cloth bag lay beside him.

'Did you sleep with any last night?' he asked, still watching the stream as if something was about to rise out of it. 'Because cobras are attracted to body heat and one or two are normally in there.'

She recalled sounds in the night and shuddered.

'There is enough venom in their bite to kill an elephant in minutes ... That they shared their cave with you means they must like you and your town clothes and your town pack. They don't like the Tatmadaw though.' He turned and squinted up at her. 'If I were Tatmadaw, you'd be getting a lot of close attention about now. But I'm not.' He stood. 'Only the Tatmadaw, returning home, walk through these mountains from one end to the other. Are you lost?'

She stepped away from the cave mouth into warm morning light. 'No.'

'Because, town girl with the town pack, this is a war zone.'

'I know.'

'Then you are very stupid, or stupidly brave, or a Tatmadaw informer.'

'I am none of those.' She adjusted her pack. 'Good-bye.' She walked down to the stream, rock-hopped to the other side and returned to the track, the freshness of the new day and a desire to get away energising her.

As she started to climb, the hunter came up alongside, cloth bag, machete and rifle strapped to his back, the smell of animals and dirt on him. 'Another possibility,' he said. 'You cannot travel by bus and are walking from Mae Sot because you are afraid of meeting up with police or the Tatmadaw.'

Now she began to fear him. 'Please, I just want to keep going.'

'Me too, and we are going in the same direction, for a while at least. I can walk ahead of you or behind you. But if I were going to Hpa-an along this dangerous track, I would welcome someone carrying my pack and staying a few metres ahead of me, showing me where to step, so ...'

'So as not to step on mines,' she interrupted. 'I know about that.' Irrespective of who he was, she was not about to let him take control of her.

He smiled. 'And maybe to look out for stray Tatmadaw too.'

She thought of telling him she could do that for herself as well. But if she had no choice but to share this track with him, it would be better to have him in front of her. She stopped and waved him past, saying, 'Okay, you can lead. But this town girl will carry her own town pack.'

* * *

Upwards out of the trees they went, shades of green reverting to grey rock, the track seeming to rise forever. At times the hunter tried to initiate conversation, but Mya offered little in return, often breathless or pretending to be. Finally – lungs burning, streaked in dust and sweat – they made the summit. They sat and drank, their eyes wandering over mountains lifting in peaks, plunging into valleys, and ahead of them huts perched high above the dark thread of a river.

'My village,' the hunter said, pointing. He passed her a water bottle and she drank from it and passed it back. He talked about his family and asked about hers. When she didn't respond, he asked, 'Why are you so afraid of the authorities?'

She'd prepared herself for just such a question. 'I've been working in Mae Sot and don't have permission from the government here to come back into the country.'

He asked what sort of work she did.

'There is a medical clinic for refugees there. I cleaned and cooked and sometimes helped the nurses.'

He rubbed a hand over his head. 'Your hair, there is not much of it.'

'I got an infection and it fell out. But I'm healthy now and it is growing back faster than ever.' As Nan Pau she recalled the Moulmein whiskey drinker sitting close, asking similar questions. She got up and walked on, the hunter's choice whether he wanted to stay or follow. Half a minute later he passed her.

The track descended gradually, wound around the edge of the river valley then dropped sharply. They crossed a small suspension bridge – the rushing river below – then climbed until the track levelled out again and divided. The hunter stopped and nodded to his right. 'That is the way to my village. It is the last village before the flatlands. Maybe you would like to stay for the night.'

Her first thought was that she didn't. But she was bone-sore. The sun was dipping towards the horizon, and the village's sleeping arrangements had to be better than what she'd experienced the previous two nights. That is, if this hunter spoke the truth and was genuinely trying to help her. 'Is your village safe?'

'Usually.'

'From cobras?'

He watched her a moment, a smile showing on his face. 'No. But I'll have a talk to them, assure them you mean no harm … My name is Bo-An.'

She decided to chance it. 'I am … Nan Pau.'

* * *

Twilight. Stretch-necked chickens raced off the track and into the bush as they approached a barbed-wire perimeter interspersed with deep, rock-walled trenches. 'To welcome the Tatmadaw when they come to visit,' Bo-An said, pointing. They stepped onto a wooden plank and crossed over a trench into the village of ladder-propped, woven bamboo and timber huts.

Barefoot children played. Women sat by cooking fires, a couple plucking feathers from headless chickens. Men skinned animals or stacked wood or dozed in hammocks slung between trees, their rifles hanging from branches or leaning against posts.

They veered left and continued on, children following, a couple of the braver ones running up and tapping Mya's hand and greeting her in Burmese before scampering back to the safety of the group.

A goat bleated. A rooster crowed.

A woman stood in the doorway of the end hut, baby on her hip, eyes darting between the two of them. Bo-An said something and she stepped back. They went up the ladder, discarded their footwear and entered the hut, its bamboo-strip floor creaking under their weight. Bo-An introduced his wife, May May, who simply nodded. 'Many Karen people either don't know or don't like to speak Burmese,' Bo-an said. 'My wife has never learned the language.' He took the baby from his wife so she could clear a spot in the corner, roll out a sleeping mat, and arrange a makeshift mosquito net over it.

Back outside they sat on wood stumps while Bo-An emptied two dead monkeys from his cloth pack and skinned and gutted them and tossed one into a water-filled pot steaming away on red coals. May May leaned over and poured rice, bok choi and tea into three smaller pots.

Night came on: lamp-lit huts, subdued voices, cooking fires and the red embers of cheroots piercing the darkness. They ate, May May chewing steamed rice and bok choi and meat from the monkey's head into pap before feeding it to the baby.

Two men approached, one with an arm that stopped just above his wrist. They squatted and Bo-An brought out cups and a small bottle of strong-smelling drink. As they drank they talked.

'They are curious about you,' Bo An said to Mya after a while, the men gazing glassy-eyed into the fire. 'Most people here rarely see town people. But these two do. They travel regularly to Hpa-an with produce to sell to the shops.'

'And what did you tell them about me?'

'What I know, which isn't much. What interests them is that you're trying to avoid the authorities. Because they want to avoid paying bribes, they are experts at doing that.' He sipped his drink and kissed his baby before May May took the baby into the hut. 'They are going to Hpa-an tomorrow and are happy for you to go with them, at least as far as the river on the town's outskirts. From there you'll have to get into Hpa-an on your own. Are you interested?'

Like a starving person is interested in food, she thought. 'Yes.' She thanked the men, though they seemed more interested in their drinks than her response.

Next morning roosters announced the dawn and a pig grunted replies from behind the hut. Bo-An and his wife got up and within minutes Mya was fed and ready to go, her water bottles filled, a small packet of rice and two boiled eggs in her pack, the two traders – huge packs on their backs – waiting for her by the plank bridge. 'How many hours to Hpa-an?' she asked, as they crossed over the trench.

'With luck you should be there by nightfall,' the man missing a hand said.

'My mother is there,' she confided, her excitement escaping her. It felt good saying this, indicating how much she valued their help, how thankful she was. 'She's been living at a place called the Soe Guest-house for over a year.'

The two traders exchanged glances, and said nothing.

And they walked; the track descended into teak forest; the forest into rutted roads and fields and tin-roofed villages with barking dogs and sagging power lines.

Eventually they came to a wide brown river.

21

HPA-AN, MYANMAR.

She'd gone up and down staircases all her life. Her earliest memories were of holding her parents' hands and being lifted up and down the staircase between their third floor unit and the housing block's entry. And while her progress was always encouraged and praised, Thant's was not, their father or mother having to appeal to him to slow down, to stop being so reckless. A front-runner at school, at football, it seemed he needed to be one everywhere else as well. Thant, always on the move, like he had so much to do and there was never enough time to do it.

Once-a-week steps to climb also at the Sule Pagoda and most sacred Shwedagon Pagoda, like a golden mountain watching over Yangon.

A staircase too at the Snake Skin.

She hadn't expected to see one here though, especially one so narrow, long and closed-in. She stood there under the guesthouse sign giving herself time to settle, to savour the warm sense of achievement coursing through her.

She looked back along the street; a few lights beginning to come on. A year earlier she'd run past this very spot trying to escape, and just down the street, lying abandoned and quiet now, was the open market where she'd been caught. If she were to walk through it in the morning – head covered, Gaga-sunnies on – buying food and whatever else they needed, would she be recognised? Because she wasn't prepared to live in Hpa-an like a prisoner. And if she were recognised, would those who recognised her turn informers? Hpa-an was mostly populated by ethnic Karen, people who'd been forced to accept army occupation, and who, at best, only grudgingly accepted government control now.

So she thought she and her mother would walk through the market in the morning, keeping a practised eye out for any soldiers lurking in the shadows, for any prolonged stares and quick exits made by possible money-seeking informants.

Mud-spattered, covered in track dust, she felt like the dirtiest person in Hpa-an; conspicuous too, carrying a pack when no one else was, her face in full view.

She turned and climbed the creaking steps, anticipation rising. She felt she needed her mother more than ever now, and in her mind an image formed of a slow opening door. Her mother peering out. Her eyes growing big. Her hands pressed against her cheeks. Shrieking and reaching out and embracing Mya and pulling her inside. Their next embrace a tearful one. All this, yes, the shock, joy and relief, before her mother composed herself enough to sit her down, sit herself down and start asking the questions that had to come: the where, when, what, who, and finally how she got to Hpa-an. Everything Mya had prepared elaborate lies for, knowing the effect the truth would have on her.

Mya slowed on seeing a small counter, a young female attendant and poster-filled walls. She and the girl exchanged looks and, strangely, the girl turned and went into a back room, where a light went on. Seconds later the door closed.

Joy turned to wariness. With her last three steps, the view widened: a dark hallway to the right, a magazine-topped table on the left, two cushioned chairs at either end – one empty, the other occupied by a man in a blue and white checked longyi, expensive sandals, white shirt with a pair of mirror sunglasses poking out of the pocket. He had a magazine on his lap, but wasn't reading it.

'You made good time getting here,' Mister MI said.

* * *

MAE SOT, THAILAND.

John, clean-shaven now and sitting up, spotted him coming. 'I've been waiting for you,' he called out, though Nick was still a good distance away.

'Yeah, well I …' Then he twigged. How could John know? He sat down on the side of John's bed and looked him over. From comatose and cadaverous only days earlier, to clear-eyed and alert now. 'How'd you know I was here?'

John pointed to his laptop, half covered in sheet beside him. 'Also Lina's not that good at withholding information. You may have noticed, as you two have met, I've been told.'

'We have … So do you know what's happened back home?'

'In summary, no house and a burnt-out valley. But we can take heart, can't we, little brother? The house was insured. And you know what Dad's like facing up to a new building project. His nose is no doubt into every home-building journal and magazine article published in the last decade. Building a replacement will keep him finely-tuned and agreeable. He'll write a song about it. No replacing you or Ella though. If you hadn't done what you did, no replacing you two. Better start preparing your speech, little brother, because I reckon you'll be wearing a big medal around your neck after the next Australia Day Bravery Awards are presented.'

Nick felt slightly sick. 'That won't happen,' was all he could bring himself to say.

'I'll wager you two airfares and admission tickets to a top-line rock concert or AFL match in Melbourne that it will happen. But whether it does or not, what's crucial is our family's still intact because of you and there is no way I'm going to let you shy away from that fact from now until your bravery award is presented, so start getting used to it.'

For a moment Nick thought about telling him the truth, but didn't. 'Snakebite. Malaria. Pretty gutsy effort getting back to Mae Sot, from what Lina's told me.'

'Maybe that's why I'm so happy to see you. From saving Ella, to finding your frazzled brother, to helping out the local version of Lady Gaga, from what I hear. We have a lot to talk about.'

Unsure how much John knew about Mya, Nick resisted setting him straight about her. He glanced around the ward looking for Htan Dah, but didn't see him. Probably back in a refugee camp, he thought.

'What about this?' John continued. 'A Nok Air flight leaves here day after tomorrow with seats available to Bangkok. Lots of them. Odds-on we'll survive the flight. The company's not had a crash in months.' He laughed seeing the alarm on Nick's face. 'Naw. Not really. Just seeing how hard you are to shock these days. Anyway, another bonus, little brother. There are still seats available on Jetstar flights Bangkok to Melbourne the following night and to Hobart the next day. Tickets as close as the lappie. Mine as part of medical leave entitlement already paid for, yours to go on my Visa card as a reward for services rendered to the family.'

So like his girlfriend. Up-front, 'exuberant' (the word his mum used for him), the more he talked, the more excited he got. Nick wondered, between John and Lina, which one carried the highest energy reserves. Dead heat, he reckoned. 'You're okay to travel then?'

John pointed his thumb at a pair of crutches leaning against the wall behind him. 'Those and a bag or two of tablets and your continuing rendered services should get me back to Tassie without further difficulty.'

'Be warned, a mattress on the floor and burnt-out paddocks is all there'll be to welcome you back.'

'Can't be any worse than where I've been and where I am now. Anyway, family hero, it's good to know they've got the bastards, isn't it?'

'What ... are you talking about?'

'You haven't heard?'

'What?'

'The two blokes responsible for the fire. Apparently they walked into the New Norfolk cop shop a couple of days ago and turned themselves in. You can read about it in yesterday's *Mercury* if you want to fire up a computer. They claim their small campfire, near the Lake Meadowbank car park, got away from them. Their slug-size brains obviously got away from them too. Can you believe it, lighting a campfire during a total fire ban? As part of their sentences they should be providing free labour for all the rebuilding and replanting that needs to be done, the idiots.'

First the shock, then, 'Yeah ... idiots,' Nick muttered, feeling the weight of guilt lift from his shoulders, the skin-tingling relief.

* * *

Hpa-an, Myanmar.

The shock, like seeing the dead body of someone she knew – Thant's. Her nerves humming, she looked down the staircase measuring her chances.

'Like the last time, policemen are across the street—' he could be lying; she hadn't seen them '—but they're anxious to go home to their families, so let's make things easy for them and ourselves, okay?' He put on an agreeable smile – obviously forced – and pointed to the chair opposite him. 'Come and sit down, Mya. You look as though you could use the rest.'

The pig hypocrite sounded almost father-like in his concern for her. 'Where's my mother?'

'Come and sit down.'

'What have you done with her?'

He eyed her a moment, his face hardening. 'A better question would be, what have I done *for* her? I'll consider it asked. I've provided her with a proper cremation.'

She glared, horrified, doing all she could to keep her emotions from bursting. 'You're lying. I've been sending money to her here every month. Tell me where she is – please.'

'Six months ago your mother died of cancer, which she chose not to get treatment for. You can confirm that fact with the desk attendant if you don't believe me. As to your money, a part of it, I suspect, was skimmed off to supplement the income of someone called Billy J in Mae Sot. You obviously know him. Of the money that got here, some of it went for painkillers, some went for your mother's cremation, and some, you might say, as compensation to a policeman bashed with a brick during last year's illegal march. But the policeman is back in uniform and anxious to meet you … or at least he was. Your kind donations in support of his recovery, which I've informed him about, seem to have cooled his anger.'

Mya leaned back against the wall, staring but seeing nothing. She sank slowly to the floor, drained of will, of hope. Visions formed: her mother alone in bed, destitute, dying in pain. She buried her head in her arms, but would not cry, not in front of him.

When she raised her head finally, she summoned her dignity and asked, 'Her ashes, do you know where they are?'

'Buried next to a small pagoda out along the riverbank. Stay here tonight and I'll get them dug up and bring them to you in the morning.'

As an assassin's would, his offer caught her by surprise: the apparent concern, the kindness. As Mister MI, he was trained to deal with people's grief, tears, high emotion, not soften in their presence. So, as always, his motive had to be self-interest. What did he want? She studied his face. No surprise that it remained unreadable. 'After I get my mother's ashes, then what?' she asked. 'Do I go back to Mae Sot? Yangon? The Iron Bar Hotel?'

'That's up to you, though you've already served a sentence of sorts, and to your credit you've survived. Resilience, it would seem, is what you have a lot of. It's your decision where you go from here, but it won't be Yangon. From there you're banned, banished, exiled.'

So was that his motive: a mother's ashes in exchange for quietly-accepted banishment? A small part of her felt relief, a part she was reluctant to admit to.

'I take it you know what those words mean?'

'"Proverb" was the last word you quizzed me on. Remember? And what followed after that day hardly gives me encouragement to provide you with another answer.'

He stared, his eyes unmoving. 'Your mother knew the meaning.'

Tears threatened to blur her vision. If this was a contest of inner strength, he was winning. 'Kicked out, or expelled from a country … or a city it seems.'

'Your brain doesn't seem to have suffered from your recent experiences. Not only were you the youngest bar-girl in all of Mae Sot, I suspect, but the brightest one too.'

'But not bright enough to avoid discovery in coming here.'

'Our border police are well trained and highly-skilled, as are others we have in that area. But you got here, and you can be thankful for one other thing as well. Your Australian schoolboy friend is back in Mae Sot, feeling pleased with himself. Next time you make contact with him, tell him if he tries to cross the border illegally again, he'd better do it with the Thai army in support, or plenty of prison time and money to spare.'

She didn't acknowledged that, or look unknowing. 'My father,' she said.

'In a labour camp up north.'

'Yes, for over two years. He won't know what's happened. And when he gets out he'll go straight to Yangon and where … we lived, once.'

'If … If he gets out, you will not be there to welcome him back. It took the policeman you bashed three months to recover enough to return to work. If I ever see you, or hear of you being in Yangon again, I'll hunt you down and arrest you and do everything I can to ensure you spend the rest of your child-bearing years miserable and barren in the Iron Bar Hotel. Can I be any clearer than that?'

A question not meant for answering. Back to the tone she expected out of him, yet it seemed he was still planning to let her go. How noble. This man she loathed, next he'd be congratulating himself on his Buddha-like compassion. So how did he expect her to respond to his 'generosity'? By grovelling? Presenting him with a bouquet of flowers? Kneeling down and touching her forehead to the floor as though he were a second Buddha? No chance. She stood up, closed the distance between them and held his gaze. 'The Iron Bar Hotel,' she said, almost sneeringly, 'no longer holds any fear for me.' She considered the rat poison her most valuable possession now. 'And it never will.'

'Then you'll have no trouble adjusting to it when your cell time comes. But for now I've arranged for you to stay here. I'll be back around nine in the morning with your mother's ashes. If you cannot give me a simple assurance by then that you'll never return to Yangon, then your mother's ashes will be the second last thing I give you, your Iron Bar Hotel cell being the last.' He got up, brushed past her and descended the staircase.

The counter attendant came out. Without looking at Mya, she placed a key, a travel bag and a sealed envelope on the counter. 'The key is for your room, number three, the same room your mother was in,' she said. 'The bag contains your mother's belongings and in the envelope is a letter she wrote shortly before she died. She asked me to save her things and the note for you for as long as it was convenient. That was the word she used – convenient. She was like that: polite, considerate.' The girl looked up at Mya, her palms pressed together. 'I'm sorry.'

* * *

Like a cocoon, this little room, she thought. Absolutely no evidence of an outside world, just four walls, a low roof and pure quiet. Like her Snake Skin room, but without a window, so no flashing neon light reflecting off the walls. No passing trucks, loud laughter, shouting or gasping either; and of course no Billy J – who she did hate more than ever now.

She dropped her pack, sat on the edge of the bed and opened the letter.

> *Dearest Mya,*
>
> *You've finally made it to Hpa-an. I prayed you would. My beautiful daughter – like my husband and son – so determined, resourceful, and for Myanmar nowadays dangerously idealistic too. My family, it seems, wasn't born to grovel to tyrants.*

She re-read that last sentence, surprised it had come from a mother who had always counselled caution and acceptance over protest. Actually, she didn't entirely agree with her mother. Her father and Thant were the idealistic ones, not her. Head down, staying out of trouble, concentrating on her studies, working towards becoming someone important – she was of the no politics, no protest school. At least until Thant's death. She read on.

> *I want you to picture me over your shoulder, my arms around you, reading this note too. Because that is what I'm picturing as I write this.*
>
> *My body is telling me I'll need to write a little bit at a time. Yes, there is pain, but the people here are watching over me, and seem to have an unending supply of painkillers and soup and spoons to feed me with and rubber mats and clean sheets to replace the ones I soil. At first a Chinese doctor came to see me. After I was diagnosed, I made a decision. Something cheap for the pain, thank you, but nothing else. But I didn't consider what a mess I'd be making, how I would affect other people. I know that in western countries there are places where the dying are cared for. As it's turned out, I'm certain I'd get no better care in one of those places than I am getting here, and yet I can barely remember my carers' names. They are two young women who work here, I know that.*

And sometimes there's a male voice having words with them. Someone has to be paying, at least for the rent and bottles of painkillers, because I'm not.

I must stop now and sleep and wake up and write some more.

Don't ramble, stay on task; isn't that what I and your teachers used to say to you? You're here reading this, aren't you? And I could not be happier that you are and that you've survived whatever life has thrown at you compliments of MI.

One of my biggest regrets is that we couldn't have lived together here in Hpa-an, at least for a little while. That was the plan, wasn't it?

It's happening again. Concentrate, silly woman, stay on task. There's something else I want to tell you. But it might have to wait.

Awake again and the magical tablets are working for me. Each day I take a few more than I did the previous day. Something I said earlier I've been thinking more about. Had we 'lived together', Mya, you would have had to look after me. So maybe separation was best after all.

'No.'

Now to what I'm determined to tell you before I drift off again. On that horrible day, as the train made a last stop before arriving in Moulmein, an elderly nun sat down beside me. She glanced around like some disguised MI agent then mumbled a coded sentence close to my ear – 'Myanmar is beautiful this time of year, don't you think so?' I suspect you may have had a similar experience. And yes, she was an agent, an unlikely, abbot-chosen one entrusted with getting me to a guesthouse.

We spent time sitting together at the Moulmein train station. I took her into my confidence and talked and talked and cried and talked some more because I needed to. When she got the chance, she talked as well.

At one point she told me about her life in a small nunnery surrounded by green hillsides and caves, pagodas, shrines and stupas. Looking at me, disguised as I was, she said, 'Your head shines and you wear your robe comfortably. If ever you feel the need for quiet reflection in a place far away from the problems of this country, you might consider entering such a nunnery.' If I had been free to do so at the time, I think I would have. I've always thought that in the dreadful event I lost my family, there would be no better place to retreat to than a nunnery. Convenient also, I suppose. After my mother died, her ashes were spread in the garden of a nunnery in Bago. Such a place, or the ocean, is where I'd like mine to be spread, though near a pagoda anywhere will be alright too. Better than being kept in a table-top jar serving as a curiosity item for family and friends.

I wrote the name of the nunnery down on a slip of paper, but of course I can't find it now. I do know it's about ten or fifteen kilometres south of Moulmein and close to a big monastery. Did you meet such a nun on the train approaching Moulmein? Was the code sentence the same?

'Yes.'

Did you stay at a double storey guesthouse next to a motorbike repair shop?

'No.'

I remember also sitting next to a young mother with her baby on the bus to Hpa-an. We talked. She seemed anxious to befriend me. Were people like that with you too?

'I might walk the streets here looking for that young mother, whose thin face and shrill voice I remember well.'

Oh here I go again, wandering thoughts, wandering pen, and all my stored-up questions wanting to spill out. Questions I don't have the energy or the time to go on with. Yet, imagining my arms around you, I want to keep on writing. If I stop, you're gone.

She clenched her eyes, sank her teeth into her lower lip.

The reason I've told you about the conversation I had in Moulmein is, well, being the bright girl you are, you've probably worked it out. But let me feel useful by mentioning the main ideas: quiet reflection, far away from everyday turmoil. Since saying good-bye to that compassionate old nun, I've been carrying a premonition that such a place might benefit you.

There, I've done it. I'll sleep now then write more later.

There was no more. She read the letter again then put it in the envelope and the envelope inside her Tripitaka. There it would stay.

* * *

Mister MI handed her the box made from teak. It was finely-carved with a Boddhi tree, mountains, a pagoda, small Buddha, stupas and spires. It must have been heavily wrapped while in the ground, for there wasn't a speck of dirt or a scratch on it.

'Who paid for it?' Mya asked.

'You did.'

'It's beautiful.' He probably deserved to hear that.

'Won't be many in the Iron Bar Hotel who'll think so.'

She ignored that.

'So what's your decision?'

'My mother left a letter for me.'

'Did she?'

'In it she said she couldn't have had better carers while she was ... dying here.'

'Did she?'

'I don't know what planet you're on, and to tell you the truth I have no regrets at all about taking a brick to that policeman who was beating the brains out of a construction worker. But I can't help suspecting that the man responsible for my mother being ... exiled here, for forcing me to become a porter and a bar-girl prostitute, for helping himself to my money, is the same man who was responsible for my dying mother's daily care. If that's true – only if it is – then I want to thank that man.'

'So what's your decision, Mya?'

'Moulmein.' That her mother was dead allowed her, in fact required her, to make a new start somewhere else as someone else. She'd write to her former neighbours, give them an address and ask them to pass it on to her father, should he ever arrive back there.

'And you'll never again enter Yangon?'

Why would she? It was death-haunted, a city of ghosts for her now. 'Never again.'

'Prison time deferred.' He glanced at his watch. 'There's a bus leaving for Moulmein in half an hour.'

'How convenient you should know that.'

He looked at her like he'd reached the limit of his interest. 'You're low on my priority list, Mya. Next to nothing. Know that, and keep in mind that MI priorities and plans can change very quickly.'

'I need you to do something for me.'

'I'm a man in the service of justice, not charity.'

Exploiting and imprisoning the powerless at the behest of the generals, that was justice? But it was hardly the time to voice such thoughts. 'On the bus from Moulmein last year there were lots of military check-points to go through. We got past alright, but the driver said that going the other way passengers were constantly being checked. Authorisation for me to be on the Moulmein bus will ensure I get there.'

Impatience showed on his face, irritation in his voice. 'I'm looking forward to you disappearing.' He took out a card, went to the counter and grabbed a pen. Seconds later he handed her the authorisation along with an envelope addressed to the Soe Guesthouse. She looked in it and saw a roll of Thai baht: last month's payment, less Billy J's cut, she suspected. She started to say something, but was interrupted.

'You know where to go. So get your pack and get to the bus.'

At least now, she believed, the Network would leave her alone.

* * *

MOULMEIN, MYANMAR.

It took her a while, but she finally found an internet cafe next to the Moulmein Star Hotel. She walked in, showed the man at the counter Nick's email address and asked for help in getting one of her own. Five minutes later she sat down in front of the newest-looking computer, stared into the screen's blue glow and began to write.

Dear Nick –

I know you got back to Mae Sot. Do not ask me how I know, I just do. I hope your brother is well and that the two of you are back in Australia (I cannot remember where in that country you live) or are about to go there.

I got to Hpa-an and to the Soe Guesthouse where I thought my mother was living. But she was not there. She died of cancer about six months ago. I am now in Moulmein, southwest of Hpa-an (a short geography assignment for you, if you are still interested in this country). I have my mother's ashes. I am going to take them to a nunnery south of here. While I am there I am going to ask for permission to stay. I hope I can because my thoughts do not go any further than there.

I have an email address now. It is: nanpau@mptmail.net.mm I do not know if there is an internet cafe close to where I am going, so I do not know when I will be able to check if you have written to me or not. But I will check sometime, even if I have to come back to Moulmein to do it.

There will be many things I will miss where I am going. One thing will be English lessons if you do not write back. But I have my English book and dictionary, and I think I can get more English books somewhere. So do not feel obliged (I have just looked that word up in my dictionary) to write back if you do not feel comfortable doing it. I will understand why.

I need to tell you that the 'nanpau' in my e-mail address is my novice nun name. I thought it would be more suitable than 'ladygaga'.

I will not say good-bye, not yet.

Yours sincerely,

Nan Pau (but still Mya to you)

22

After going so long disclosing nothing about herself because no one wanted to know, she was now in the middle of her second massacre-to-the-present story in a little over a week. This time though, her listener's disinterest irritated her.

Despite having to speak English to Nick in Mae Sot, she thought how much easier it was to talk about herself to him. True, she barely knew him, but they had talked earlier and he had got her to the medical clinic. Plus she'd been so relieved to be away from the Snake Skin that she'd felt like talking, and Nick – voicing little 'ohs' and 'ahs' – had obviously wanted to listen.

Here, in her brown-boarded kuti, the abbess – her face the size and shape of a small shovel and about as expressive – sat at her table still as a painting, her half-lidded eyes gazing through Mya like she was a pane of glass. If a fly had landed on the abbess's nose, would she have known about it? And yet the abbess – somehow knowing about the protest march and massacre and her fleeing Yangon in disguise – had asked her why she wished to enter the nunnery.

'I want to live away from the outside world,' she'd answered. How obvious was that?

'So tell me about yourself,' the abbess had said.

So why couldn't the woman at least pretend interest? If anything, her stony silence deepened as Mya talked, like she'd fallen asleep with her eyes open.

Maybe the abbess asked for the account only out of duty, and was only partially listening, or maybe partially listening and partially meditating (was that possible?), and once Mya finished she'd be offered a glass of tea or water then be told that, for some made-up reason, this nunnery wasn't suitable for her and she should try somewhere else.

Growing restless and frustrated, Mya decided to end her story quickly and forget about showing the abbess her mother's note – her best chance for gaining admittance. She was not about to grovel for acceptance, especially by sharing something so personal with someone so indifferent.

She provided a single sentence to being a porter and omitted the minefield entirely. When she got to Billy J and the Snake Skin, she let her imagination take over. Billy J became 'a manager', the Snake Skin 'a cafe/nightclub', she 'a cleaner/dishwasher' there. She did send money to her mother. She did return to Hpa-an, though she didn't mention how. Yes, she'd met up with MI, but she said nothing about what happened with her money. And yes, her mother had died. Finally, she had always thought she'd like to enter a nunnery one day, though she didn't mention why.

That ended it. A flicker of eye movement from the abbess, but nothing more to indicate she was fully conscious, her mouth staying shut, an iron bar needed to prise it open. The utter quiet again, like the sounds of the world were being absorbed by the trees and fallen leaves outside.

Switching her thoughts to insecure living again, Mya said, 'Anyway, thank you for your time.' She wasn't thankful, she was irked. She set her pack upright and stood up, the floorboards creaking from her effort.

'I lost my father when I was six ...' A button was pushed, the abbess activated. 'It was like losing part of my heart.' The abbess leaned forward, looking up at her. 'What's it been like for you?'

'Like ... falling into a black hole.'

'Will you sit with me a while longer?'

Mya sat, taking note of little lumps and dents on the abbess's newly-shaven head.

'The nun who met and escorted both you and your mother had been with us for almost sixty years before she died last month. At the time, after she was questioned by police, she of course told me about the two of you. It saddens me to hear about your mother.'

The word 'detachment' came into Mya's head. Exhibiting it was an important part of being a monk or nun. She suspected now she'd confused the abbess's detachment for disinterest. 'That nun was very good to me.'

'She was to everyone. People like her perennially shine. They make you feel better about living. So interested in everything and talkative and sociable. I often wondered why she stayed a nun. But she did, so it must have suited her, and now everyone misses her. Later, if you like,' the abbess went on, 'I can show you where we scattered her ashes.' She leaned back, face etched in thought. 'But if you're not too tired, I wonder if you'd be kind enough to tell me a little more about what happened after you got to Mae Sot? From that point on, certain things you said confused me. For example, I had no idea Mae Sot had become so westernised that they have such things as restaurant nightclubs now. And while I can't remember when, I'm sure I've heard the name Snake Skin mentioned before in relation to Mae Sot, but I don't think it was used as the name of a cafe.'

That afternoon, while sitting on the tiny balcony of her assigned stilt hut, called a *kuti*, the new novice Nan Pau would, dictionary-assisted, write this quick poem and pin it to her wall:

No better place
To use words carefully,
To speak with honesty
And sincerity,
Than inside this nunnery.

* * *

As it turned out, she didn't need to be reminded how to speak. Here, as at the Snake Skin, she barely spoke at all. But unlike at the Snake Skin, the other women barely spoke either, absorbed completely in whatever they were doing. It was like talking shrank their brains, restricting thought and reflection. Sick of feeling lonely and depressed, she initiated conversation with the three other novices her first few days there, but only got brief, hushed replies. Pray and meditate together. Accept charity. Provide solace. Maintain cleanliness and neatness. Yes – all that. But discuss the world outside the nunnery's gate, rarely, and with difficulty.

There were times in the first couple of weeks she imagined her weeping filled the nunnery. No other sounds, just hers. Then silence again. Yet, as the weeks merged into months, Nan Pau took comfort from the quiet, order and routine, the aromas of incense, lamp oil and jasmine, of finding acceptance in the close, harmonious company of so many pious women. She recalled the abbot's mystifying comment that day – 'Feel yourself grow invisible in your stillness'. And she thought she understood that now, the need to withdraw, to live a life based on simplicity, compassion and forgiveness. Occasionally, though, negative feelings swamped her and she'd fret and rage to herself about what the country had done to her family. In addition, certain questions continued to pre-occupy her. And the most nagging one was this: what were the limits of forgiveness? How could someone – the Buddha even – feel compassion for people who had killed their brother, forced them to become a mine-sweeper porter, a bar-girl prostitute? From compassion, supposedly, came forgiveness, the true test of a Buddhist's changed heart – a test she continued to fail and thought she always would.

While she was working in the vegetable garden one day, the abbess walked up and asked, 'Have you been able to work out in words, Nan Pau, why you wish to become a nun?'

The question surprised her. What she wanted was the polar opposite of what she'd had in Mae Sot. No more than that. The nunnery was, possibly, just an escape. So it took a while to form a suitable answer. 'I want to scrape away what's happened to me, learn how to control my mind, and …'

The abbess continued to watch her. 'And?'

'And … and once, when I was working at the Snake Skin, someone said to me, "You're beyond redemption." I want to prove that person wrong. I want to get close enough to the Buddha to find redemption.'

'Nun for a lifetime close?'

She lowered her eyes and shrugged her shoulders.

'If you are still here in three months, I will ask you that same question again.'

One afternoon Nan Pau got permission from the abbess to take a motorbike taxi into Moulmein. Just metres outside the gate a middle-aged woman on a motor scooter stopped next to her, asked where she was going and offered her a ride. She hadn't been on the back of a motor scooter since leaving Yangon and it felt good to be on one again, absorbing the openness, the wind in her face, the world around her speeding past.

With all its computer game sounds and noisy participants, the internet cafe made her realise just how accustomed she'd become to slowness and quiet. She checked her email, hoping. And yes, Nick had replied.

> *Hi Mya,*
>
> *After I red your email I relised first up I needed to apoligise for my speling. I'm totaly remediel when it comes to riting and with speling my brain is like a blender, allways mixing the leters up. I get two kinds of reaksions at school. One from teachers who no I'm dyslexic (mening my speling will allways be hop-less) and who are prety good to me, and anuther from a few blokes who call me (or did) dys-stupid and try to unmake my days. Maybe they stil spel beter than me. But I fite a bit beter now. Dad was in American Spesal Forses during the Vietnam War. The day he piked me up from the school bus stop with blud runing down my face was the day he started me on wayts and self defence befor mum got home from infant teaching most days.*
>
> *Konfrontasion day came again at lunchtime and the teachers and prinsipal at my school weren't to pleased about it. I was warned after the first tiff, then two days later suspended from school after the sekond one. But so was the bloke I had the tiff with, wich was fare enuf. Anyway, that's my speling and school problems storey. I rekon you no more about me than anyone else outside my family. You who are so good at English. Hopfully you wont get to frustraited reading this.*

I was realy sad to here about your mum. I think of you as sumone who has serviced evryones worst nightmairs, and if there is a balence in life between the good and bad times (so says my dad), then I rekon you've got a lot of good times a head. Anyway, I hope things are working out beter for you.

I got on Internet and did some reserch on Budist nuns in Burma, so I no a bit about your nunnery life there, like wake-up early in the morning, like all the meditasion that goes on and that you don't eat after mid-day. But I woud realy like to no more.

I got the three vilagers across the Moee River and to the medical klinic allright. The two carrying the strecher were incredable, like so payshant and strong.

A cuple of days later my bruther and I took off for home wear we are now. He is still useing cruches, but less and less each day.

Things are realy good here now. Like – 1/ Ella got three skin graffs on her legs and arms, but nowear else. She's back at school and cant get there fast enuf in the mornings.

2/ Rebilding has started in the vally wear I live. Evrybody is helping evrybody else. For my mum, who loves the vally and evryone in it, it's like the gods have arived with there work belts on. And my dad has allready started to bild our new, fire-resistent house. Cant wait till its finished.

3/ School hollidays have ended and mum's back teaching agin and I'm going to matric college (years 11 and 12). It's called Claremont College and its just out-side of Hobart. I'm doing Information Tecknology (computer study) and what's called a Tecknology and Trades corse. Dad rekons it will skil me up for helping him bild the new house. I'm also taking gitar lesons after school and I've got my lerner's lisense and I'm driving dad's flat tray around the vally. Its my driving he's supervising now, not my fite trayning.

I hop after you have to batle to read this, youll still want to rite to me. By doing that you mite help me improov my speling. I'll be in charge of spoken English improvment, you can handel the riting. Seems fair to me. Okay?

Good luck Mya. I think about you lots.

Your good frend,

Nick

So much to say to her; she couldn't help feeling complimented. Her eyes lingered on the words 'Your good frend'. Yes, she supposed he was. Certainly he was the only 'friend' who knew both what she was in Yangon and Mae Sot and what she had become. He was also the only 'friend' she was still in contact with, and it seemed unlikely she'd be acquiring any new ones outside the nunnery anytime soon.

She wouldn't answer Nick's email immediately. It required further study to work out the words she didn't recognise. She printed the email, planning to write a long reply at the nunnery. It might take weeks to do and email back, but time was of no consequence now.

The lady who gave her the ride into Moulmein came past as she was walking towards a motorbike taxi stand. The lady stopped and motioned for her to hop on the back. She did, sitting side-on and thanking the lady, and they headed back to the nunnery, Nan Pau feeling happier than she had in weeks, maybe since that first night in the mountains with Nick. The parameters of her life now: a father in a labour camp somewhere in the far north, Nick in Australia, and of course the nunnery and everyone in it. And as the day's bonus, a generous lady with a motor scooter looking out for her.

If she were still in the nunnery in thirty years' time, she thought, then that would be fine by her.

23

It was the long first draft for an email she might have written to her parents rather than to a boy in some faraway country, especially a boy she had only known for a few days. As she sat outside under a banyan tree or beside her single candle at night writing, revising and constantly double-checking her English accuracy, she gave more and more thought to the abbess's questions: 'Have you worked out in words, Nan Pau, why you wish to become a nun?' And – 'How close?' So the email took on a second purpose: that of reinforcing in her own mind why she was there.

It took her weeks to finish and check over, and as a description of her everyday life written in her very best English, she was pleased with it. But that was the easy part. As an explanation for why she wanted to get close to the Buddha, she was less satisfied. Was there any greater reason than just wanting to escape her recent past, to feel safe again? If there was she couldn't seem to find the right words to clearly explain it.

She arranged with the abbess to go into Moulmein one afternoon. The same lady as before – her benefactor now, half-filling her begging bowl with rice each morning and offering her transport 'any time of the day' – was at the gate at the arranged time to take her to the internet cafe. There she wrote her finished email:

Hello Nick,

I was happy to read that your life is good now in Australia, that your brother and sister are healing, that your parents are well and you are all building a new house and that you will soon be driving a car. I am getting used to my new life in the nunnery little by little, and every day I get a little happier. To answer your questions, yes I do have to wake up early. This is my schedule for each day:

4 am – Wake up. Tidy my kuti. (That is my small room. If I stretch my arms out I can touch the walls either side. If I reach up I can touch the roof). It is built from the wood of fallen trees, not those growing from the ground. It stands on stilts to keep out snakes and flooding. Shave heads. Once a week a novice shaves mine, I shave hers. Here is my brilliant haiku about it.

> Pour water, rub soap.
> Razor placed in my bristles.
> Skull shaved back to front.

Exercise. Sitting meditation (We are told we must go deeply into ourselves and to imagine a lit candle floating in front of our third eye, which is supposed to be in the middle of our foreheads. Mine either wants to stay closed or is somewhere unfindable. We have been told meditation is the main reason for people entering a nunnery or monastery and that the purpose of living in such places is not to escape the outside world but to prepare a person to re-enter it as a committed Buddhist). Thirty-minute rest or study period. Leave the nunnery to beg for food (Usually uncooked rice. We are not like monks who are given cooked food. Nuns have to cook what they are given).

7 am – Sitting meditation watching the sun rise while – Do not laugh – practising breathing and smiling ('Breathing in, I calm my body. Breathing out I smile.' We are told we must smile at our sorrow and when we can do that we will become peaceful and happy and everyone around us will benefit) and appreciating the wonders of the world around us. Then sweep the walkways.

8:30 to 10 am – Mealtime. Sitting and walking meditation while concentrating on the senses (The touch of the earth, smell of leaves, sound of running water, wind and birds in the trees).

10:30 am – Thirty-minute bathing, study and drink time (Tea for me). Use rainwater in our shared barrel to wash myself, or in the dry season a bucket of water from the nearby stream (Across the stream is a monastery and monks who are forbidden to look at us, but their dogs do and bark and bark). Sitting meditation. Mealtime (You are right, we cannot eat after mid-day, but we can drink as much water or tea as we want. We are told food is what you want, water or tea is what you need).

1 pm – Walking and sitting meditation. (If I want to leave the nunnery to go to Moulmein and I can get the abbess' permission, this is when I go. The same lady – my 'benefactor or 'donor' – who fills most of my begging bowl each morning also takes me into Moulmein on her motor scooter. Benefactors give monks and nuns food to earn credits for their next lives. Monks and nuns cannot refuse offerings from anyone, even if they are criminals. In exchange for food, monks and nuns are sometimes asked to settle disputes or offer moral advice. Can you imagine Lady Gaga doing that? Thankfully I am just a novice and not a nun yet.).

3 pm – Chores – like weeding the garden, sweeping the walkways, picking stones out of the next day's rice, cleaning my kuti again and scrubbing my toilet, all the time being careful not to step on ants or beetles or worms, or drown any gnats, or slap a mosquito like you did the night we slept together. I never knew how complicated the vow of not killing any living creature could be. Last week a senior nun stepped on a snake and said to it, 'Excuse me.' Yesterday there was a rat in my toilet. I said the same thing and asked myself how was I supposed to get rid of it without killing it? And if I did not kill it, which I could not do, how was I supposed to use the toilet again? (If you are interested in how the problem was solved, then ask me in your next email). Wash clothes. Study (like English). Read Buddhist texts.

4 pm – Outdoor meditation time, both sitting and walking (This time concentrating on the rhythm of lifting right/left heel, lifting right/left foot, swinging right/left, stepping left/right. This is not my favourite activity. I keep thinking how dumb I would look doing this in the middle of Moulmein).

6:30 pm – Watch the sun go down. Instruction from our abbess.

7 pm – Thirty minute period for rest or study or visiting other novices in their kutis. Bathe (It is too dark for the monks across the stream to see us even if they wanted to). Clean toilet. Exercise. Sitting meditation.

11 pm – Sleep (Usually I cannot wait this long. I fall asleep during sitting meditation, roll over, wake up and crawl to my sleeping mat. We cannot sleep on any soft or high surfaces).

There are many things I miss, but never enough to want to leave the nunnery – at least not yet. Do you know what I sometimes think about during medita-

tion? Answer: my Lady Gaga songs. Sometimes I hear her (Is it her? Is it me?) singing away inside my head.

In my third week here the abbess asked me why I wanted to become a nun and how close to the Buddha I wanted to get. I mentioned the word 'redemption', but mostly I could not think of the right words to give her a good answer. She said she would ask me again in three months' time, which is almost now. So can I practise some words on you? You are the only person in the outside world I still communicate with. But maybe reading about nunnery life will bore you. So, as you Australians say, 'No worries'. I will understand if you do not read the rest of this email.

Right now I cannot imagine living without Buddhism. A Buddhism that will bring peace and order to my life. That will allow me to find what is good inside me; that will allow me to get rid of the bad. This is called 'redemption'. Often people need a special place to find redemption, like a monastery or a nunnery, which are open to anyone – even Lady Gaga – temporarily or permanently. So if my reason for being here is just to escape the past through isolation and meditation, then that is okay. But there might be other reasons too. I feel better now than I have for a very long time. It is like cracks in me are filling in. I am learning things, like smiling at my sadness and finding the strength, understanding and knowledge to follow a worthwhile path in life. I know that before I can do that I need to accept what has happened to me; that the massacre, the minefield, the Snake Skin are over and only memory makes them real again. I say to myself the passing of time will lessen everything: the good, the bad. And as time passes you will find other things to do and think about.

But I get frustrated because I still cannot forget. Sometimes, instead of the Buddha filling my mind, bad memories do. I still have trouble accepting what has happened. Maybe I just need more time to get closer to the Buddha.

Did you know that 'buddh' means to wake up, to know, to understand? The ability to do all that, as well as to love and show compassion, lead to a Buddha nature. Maybe this is what I will tell the abbess when she asks me that question again. I want to acquire a Buddha nature. It is as simple as that.

Anyway, I do feel peaceful here. So smiling practise must be working. But I know that if I leave, the challenge will be to keep my peace and acceptance and understanding (if I ever get them) inside me. If a person can sit and meditate and learn wisdom in a place like a nunnery, then return to the outside world and look for a weapon when they see people who have done bad things to them, then what use is wisdom?

This email is becoming a book, I know. Just two more things I want to tell you, okay? I have received permission from the abbess to buy some Karen language books in Moulmein and to study that language. Also, the abbess has asked me to teach English to other interested novices and nuns for an hour three nights a week. Lady Gaga, now a novice nun, a Karen language student and an English teacher. That makes me smile without even trying. So that is what is happening in my life. What about your life? How is your school? Is your new house built yet? Is your brother completely recovered? And your sister too? I hope life is good for you and your family and that you are smiling without having to practise it.

Your good friend,
Mya

* * *

In the next six months Nan Pau requested permission to go to the internet café in Moulmein on four occasions. On her last visit an email was there waiting for her.

Hiya Mya

Good to hear things are going well there.

You should know my girlfriend is helping me with my spelling for this email. So you won't go blind and bonkers (Australian for crazy) trying to read it.

She stopped reading and realised a place in her heart had started to open up for him, and that both surprised and saddened her. 'Stupid girl,' she mumbled. 'He lives on the bottom of the planet. What did you think would happen? He's happy. And he deserves to be. So be happy for him.' She couldn't tell whether she was or not, but read on anyway.

Sorry it's taken me so long to write back. So many things are happening. Like our house has a roof now and we're sort of living in it. And I'm driving a 2005 Holden ute around. Great wheels. A carry anything, go anywhere super-machine – including to parties, lots of them. John's gone back to uni. He broke up with that nurse girlfriend of his, Lina. Remember her? Something about her going somewhere in the Middle East where there is a war going on and maybe not coming back. Something like that anyway. John's pretty cut up about it. He's been talking instead about returning to Mae Sot, or somewhere else along the border when he gets the chance.

School is good, although we have exams soon. I haven't missed a day yet this year and I'm also doing a bit of work on the house with dad on the week-ends.

And surprise, surprise, yes, I've got a girlfriend. Her name is Annie and we've been going out for weeks, lots of them. She's a student too and studying sub-jects like English Studies, Sociology and Psychology, Indonesian and Australia in Asia and the Pacific. She's really brainy (as she's doing the proof-reading, I thought I'd better mention that) and really interested in Asia. She's doing a section on Buddhism now in her Australia in Asia course and it was when I was telling her about you that I remembered your last email. I hope you don't mind that I let her read it. She can't believe your life.

Anyway, must go. Have to get Annie home to get ready. We're heading into the northern suburbs of Hobart tonight for a session with some mates (Remember your Australian? Mates means good friends).

Keep the faith, Nick

She took out her dictionary, searched and found the English word she wanted: 'equanimity' – an evenness of mind or temper; compo-sure, resignation, acceptance of fate. Along with detachment and compassion, the essence of what she was trying to acquire at the nunnery.

She wouldn't wait. She decided to write back there and then.

Dear Nick,

Thank you for your email. I am happy that you are happy and that you have a girlfriend and you are doing so many good things together.

Everything is the same at the nunnery, except that soon I will not be able to leave it to visit this internet cafe for maybe a long time. Like people who make offerings of rice or coins in a begging bowl, I want to make an offering of my life to the Buddha, at least for a while (six months, a year – I do not know yet) by going on a retreat. I hope the isolation and constant meditation will get rid of the anger inside me. I hope I will be able to better understand the types of people who have caused my anger. I hope I will be able to see life differently and acquire more of a Buddha nature so I can stay close to the Buddha for the rest of my life.

Still, she'd enjoyed Nick's company, the adventure of sharing those first twenty-four hours in the mountains with him. No one could have helped her more, treated her any better than he had. Maybe they could remain distant friends. She should offer him the opportunity.

If you want to know more about retreats, or would just like to write about any-thing, please email me in the next two weeks. Okay? I hope you do.

Your friend,
Mya

She had only really thought about seeking permission to go on retreat. But now, once again, she felt a strong urge to escape. As soon as she got back to the nunnery she would ask for permission.

Two weeks later, retreat permission approved and arranged, she returned to the internet cafe. There was no email there for her, so she read the email she had spent many hours preparing to the screen: *'To retreat, Nick, is to go into the forest or into a cave and live and meditate alone for a long period of time. I will go into a cave. Done correctly, meditation develops concentration and understanding and lets us see deeply into things and into ourselves. It allows us to change our hearts and our minds and how we view life. It teaches us to look at everyone – strangers, friends, soldier killers, people like Mr MI, Aung Min and Billy J – through compassionate eyes. The more we see, the more we understand. The more we understand, the easier it is for us to demonstrate compassion.'*

She stopped when she sensed someone over her shoulder. She looked around to see her benefactor smiling down at her.

'I can come back later,' her benefactor said.

'Thank you, but there is no need to. I'm ready to go now.'

24

Along the worn stone path she went, carrying a small backpack and shoulder bag full of essentials, her mind a mix of curiosity, fear and excitement. A breeze stirred the trees and sent the prayer flags over her flapping, wind chimes either side tinkling away. Novices and nuns – some of them rostered to re-supply her – glanced up from their gardening and smiled their good-byes. Typical. She couldn't recall a face in the nunnery that didn't smile back at her nowadays, even the abbess's. Especially hers.

The path merged into stone steps that climbed in a sweeping curve past sandstone Buddhas, tree shadows, potted orchids, hibiscus bushes and lemongrass. Above the tree-line the steps gave way to a dirt track that angled sharply upwards. She stopped once to rest and look out over the distant fields lying everywhere below her, still hearing distant motor scooters, the yelping of monks' dogs – the last sounds of other living beings she would hear until she returned.

She recalled coming here, distressed, confused; the abbess's watch-fulness, her slow-to-show understanding. The abbess's counselling of the previous day played again in her mind. 'You'll be going to a place that's as much inside your head as inside the earth. So no great discoveries up there other than what you find is inside you, inside the blackness of a cave, what you learn to see, to feel that others don't. Hopefully the experience will help heal wounds, prepare you for a fresh start in whatever you decide to do with your life. But don't think you'll find a mountain paradise up there. It can be hard and lonely and oh so boring isolated from the world in all that silence. The first week or so will be the worst. Remember that many others have been up there before you, and that they all felt the same fears you'll be feeling. Some found the Buddha inside them up there, including one novice who stayed for five years. Not surprising when you recall the Buddha meditated in the caves of northern India. Jesus Christ was resurrected in a cave. Mohammed received the Koran in a cave outside Mecca in Saudi Arabia.'

The abbess had stared a moment, smiling at some thought before she went on. 'If you persevere, my young, talented novice, you'll learn as much from the environment up there as from the books and scrip-tures you have with you. Arguably the most important lesson you will learn is just how simply a person can live. You will have food, water, clothes, shelter and oxygen. Whatever else you feel you need must come from your mind.' She'd paused and watched Nan Pau for a moment, before taking some battered-looking books from her book-shelf and placing them on the table. 'Have you heard of Tin Moe?'

'He's my father's favourite poet, his "The Years We Didn't See The Dawn" one of his favourite poems.'

'For which Tin Moe was sent to prison. That poem is in this col-lection of poetry, his last one. Take it with you.' She'd passed over the book then looked down at the others on her table. 'And William Shakespeare? Have you heard of him?'

'The greatest English writer ever. In English class, before the mas-sacre, we were going to study—' Surprised, she'd pointed at the title of one of the two books. 'That one – *Romeo and Juliet*.' She'd glanced at the title of the other one: *Romeo and Juliet Made Easy.*

'From my grade twelve year,' the abbess had said, smiling. 'It's good to know he is still being studied in schools. Take them with you also. They may offer a needed diversion, a chance to recover what you missed out on in school.'

Nan Pau had taken them, thanking the abbess.

'And finally this. You must remember the cave is not meant to be a prison. You're not required to stay for a prescribed period of time. When you feel you've experienced enough, your abbess and nunnery will be here to welcome you back.'

The Place Above is what she'd named where she was going. Feeling the tug of the nunnery, so not daring to linger long, she continued upwards towards it.

An hour maybe before the track began to flatten out.

She crossed a shallow creek – her source for water and bathing, she'd been told – so knew she was close. She veered around two more bends with crumbling edges, vertical rock and deep drops, and came to the cave's markers: two large boulders separated by a low rock shelf. This was where, after the first week, food supplies and cooking wood would be left. To her left, beyond the shelf, a rock outcrop ending in a deep chasm. To her right, under a bluff overhang, the mouth of the cave, facing west into the afternoon sun. She approached it nervously, and ducked her head to enter; the smell of dampness was immediate, the air cooler, the light going ever-greyer before cutting out in the crawl space further on.

The cave's compactness surprised her: slightly smaller than her Snake Skin room, but high enough at its centre to stand upright. The bed further in was a triple layer of reed mats, a candle stub on a piece of tin beside it. More reed mats covered the uneven ground, their edges looking chewed in places, probably by mice. She stroked the walls that were covered in paintings of golden Buddhas and scenes from Buddhist texts, interspersed with a monitor lizard – all teeth and muscle – and a cobra arching its hood, giant rats, hand-sized spiders and scorpions.

'Welcome to King Cobra country.'

A wave of panic hit her, her body stiffening, her eyes blurring with tears. She'd had dreams about this place. But in none of them was the cave as small and ugly as this one. 'So stupid girl,' she reprimanded herself, 'you of all people should know the difference between dream and reality by now.' She struggled to take control of her breathing, to concentrate on what the abbess had told her – '... *they all felt the same fears you'll be feeling.*' She took out her Buddha and placed it on the mat bed, then jumped back as a tarantula emerged high on hairy legs spread like fingers. She threw a sandal to one side of it and it scurried away, disappearing at the back.

She knelt, touched her forehead to the ground and prayed for spiritual growth to flower in her head, quickly – very quickly. After a minute she got up, struck a match and extended it into the dark angles, the crevices and ledges where animal droppings collected and spiders' webs hung with husks of insects.

One comfort at least: there was no sign of bats.

A rat suddenly launched itself in an arc from a ledge to the ground, darted forward, stopped and stood on its hind legs, sniffing the air. She clapped her hands and the rat scurried off in the same direction as the tarantula. Learning to love the earth and all its creatures didn't have to start immediately, did it? Affection could develop gradually – ever so gradually – surely.

Satisfied there were no more animals sharing her living space – for the present, anyway – she dropped her pack and shoulder bag and went out and sat on the rock shelf between the boulders, noticing again how high up she was, almost level with distant summits. Silence was absolute, like she had arrived in deep space.

Dark descended, lights from Moulmein coming on. To downplay her fear, she tried to joke with herself, muttering things like, 'So quiet I can hear my hair grow, hear the rat urinating.' Staring down at the lights, she recalled something else the abbess had said the previous day: *'Life can be no more than just breathing up there.'* And it was the abbess's reassuring voice she continued to hear.

'I know of no one as young as you going on retreat. But then age is not always an indicator of experience or readiness, is it?'

'A westerner at the Snake Skin said to me once, "Lady Gaga, too young, but old enough".'

'Yes ... well ... I can only imagine how bad it must have been for you working at such a place. But you're here now. You're Nan Pau, taking your first step towards Buddhahood. When you arrive at the cave feeling scared, think of the monks who go on retreats with only their umbrella and a mosquito net. Think how they meditate and depend on the forest for food and water, and sleep on the forest floor with only their two possessions for shelter.'

The abbess had paused, raised her eyebrows and gazed again into some neutral zone.

Though she was smiling, her voice had turned unusually strident when she spoke again. 'Sometimes these can be the same monks who believe only they and madmen deserve to live in isolation, who decree that women are incapable of going on retreats to advance themselves to higher spiritual levels, that our bodies are impure and forbid us from ever obtaining enlightenment. They say women only serve to lure men away from Buddhahood. They say women need children. They need love. They need comfort and security. They need this, they need that. Need, need, need. There is nothing to stop women from learning to love the natural world as much as they love children. But of course some monks, in their male wisdom, consider them-selves more advanced than nuns, and that our main aim should be to earn enough merit in this life to be re-born male in our next one.' She'd huffed, 'What is it about having a penis that is so essential for enlightenment?'

Nan Pau could only stare.

The abbess had seemed to deflate then. She'd taken a deep breath and let it out, 'Ahhh', as though disappointed with herself. 'By letting their emotions get away from them, people can make life complicated, can't they? Sorry. This old woman's tongue escapes her sometimes.' She'd glanced over at the open door. 'Let's hope no one outside heard or I might have to join you on retreat.' Her smile broadened. 'I can feel confident, can't I, that where you're going you'll be telling no one?'

Nan Pau had nodded more vigorously than she'd needed to.

Sometimes the abbess seemed too ordinary to be an abbess, Nan Pau thought now. She spent half that night sitting on the rock shelf facing the mountains, the stars, the spread of tiny lights below – her fear coming and going in waves.

* * *

She'd never known such intense silence. The rock seemed to manufacture it. Silence was for sleeping, for doing homework, for free reading or exam sessions at school. Couldn't there be reflection and meditation with just a little less silence? Especially that edge-of-death-like silence that had her talking to herself, debating herself (Why am I punishing myself by coming here? Should I have to withdraw from the world to find ways to deal with it? How stupid is it trying to regain faith in people by hiding away from them?), howling Lady Gaga songs just to hear her voice before the silence swallowed it up, drawing up images of people she'd known and talking to them about anything that came into her head – just like crazy people did.

Seeking distraction, she wrote haikus about the silence, like:

> Water drips on rock,
> 'Drip', stillness, 'drip', stillness, 'drip'.
> How far a bird call?

And:

> Only monks, nuns know
> Of such isolation, silence.
> Who else would want to?

A world for just one up there. The starkness of the place too, like there was nothing man-made left in the world except what she'd brought with her, what her providers provided, and the poor excuse for a toilet around the next bend.

Then there was the issue of the two-metre marble-skinned python coiled next to her legs when she woke up one morning. The same one she'd seen stretched out above the creek where she bathed. It had obviously taken a liking to her. In a sense, with a snake, a snake-proof rat and spiders sharing her cave, she wasn't completely alone, was she? A fact that became more and more important to her as her perceptions of cave life changed up there.

There was so much she wanted to talk about, the first time her provider visited, that she almost wept in frustration at having to remain silent.

One afternoon, sitting on the rock shelf, her emotions broke. She should have known better. Cut off by all the rock and space and silence, living up there was just too hard. She didn't need solitude, she needed people. People she warmed to, she could learn from. Still weeping, she packed up her things and left the cave, getting as far as the creek before stopping. Stretched out on its rock, the python was sunning itself, head pointed in her direction. She watched it and the sunlight shift over the rock greys and browns, the pale grey creek, while memories of the abbess – who she suspected had survived five years up there – filled her mind with words of encouragement.

As the snake straightened and moved into warmer light, she thought of herself, alone, passing the seasons, how she would cope. One thing: the snake was friendly. It probably wanted her there, would miss her if she left. That made her smile. She steadied and decided to stay, to assess her retreat a day at a time.

Gradually, her confidence grew. Cave life turned ordinary, non-threatening. She discounted the weirdness of sharing a cave with a snake, of how her lips moved with her barely knowing what they were saying. Time was entirely hers to fill, and she developed routines to do it. She adjusted to the absence of things, to living life inside her head, to non-clock, non-calendar time. After all, being isolated and lonely were hardly new to her, and far better her own company up there, she often told herself, than that of some forced on her down below.

'Another way to write short poems in a foreign language,' her monk English teacher said to the class one day, 'is to focus your poem around an advanced word.'

She checked 'chasm', found the word 'immense', practised them then wrote:

Cave mouth to chasm,
Stage for immense surroundings,
Meditative thought.

The 'immense surroundings' a constant reminder of how small and insignificant she was, like her cave companions, invisible to the outside world. What she had – books, writing material, novice clothes, a longyi, sandals, a jumper and socks for the cool nights, a small torch, gas cooker and cooking implements, soap and a razor to shave with, something to eat and drink out of – was enough. So too what she did: smiling at her providers and just watching and reading and day-dreaming and meditating and drawing and writing as silently as nearby spiders spun their webs. Was it possible to live more simply, more predictably, her inner self filling all her time?

Life, she'd learned, could change in an instant, shattering into a million pieces down below for innocents caught up in a massacre, walking across a minefield, having to prostitute themselves, languishing in prisons or dying in small, windowless rooms. But not on her outcrop, not in her Buddha cave. The life she'd started with up there, she would surely end up with, plus there were bonuses: improved resilience, confidence, and ability to meditate; a sense of creation from her rock wall art and poetry; improved knowledge of English and Karen and her Tripitaka. And this: what had once unnerved her most up there, the stillness, was now a source of contentment.

Initially she tried to blank out the massacre and her fugitive past, as though the silence could cure bad memories. Recalling the abbess's words, she told herself to live in the moment. Yet a part of her couldn't do that, the part that kept answering back, 'But some memories cut too deep to forget.' And she recalled her vow that horrible day: *'If by chance you survive, remember all this. Remember every detail.'* Recalled too her eighty-eight steps across the minefield and Kho Noc giving her his name.

Besides, often there was little for her to do but remember. So yes, all that happened, she ended up saying to herself. But it's over. Looking out over the barren hills and mountains, there could be little doubt of that.

Sometimes she'd divert unwelcome recollections by memorising and reciting something from her books. Like from Tin Moe, her father's favourite poet (and probably Thant's too if he'd ever stopped long enough to read a poem). Or she'd recite stanzas she mostly understood from *Romeo and Juliet*.

One afternoon, as a storm turned the cave mouth into a temporary waterfall, she stripped naked and went out, her face lifted, palms up as if weighing the rain, the close thunder filling her ears, the flash of lightning filling her sight. The storm passed; the wide silence and sunlight returned. She gazed at the steaming rock, the dripping crevices and far down at the wet green of the trees re-emerging bit by bit from out of the mist. Her heart swelled. She cupped her hands and drank the water that streamed from the cave mouth. She inhaled the crisp air as she would a market stall of herbs and spices and wondered if, since the massacre, she'd ever felt more at ease with herself. Feeling as close to euphoric as she ever had, she put on her Gaga glasses and stretched out on the rock shelf and let the sun warm her legs, belly and shoulders.

'Sometimes it's better to use the tanka form to express feelings,' her teacher said. 'Five lines with a 5-7-5-7-7 syllable structure.'

Warmed through and through, she found the word 'deluge' and wrote:

After the deluge
Trees emerge as sun-touched glass,
Puffs of mist rising.
All the world wet and warm.
God light gleaming over me.

That night, as moonlight paled her outcrop, she wrote:

Thank you sun and moon
For chasing away the rain,
The whiskey drinker,
Billy J, Mister MI,
And for warming my soul.

She loved English more than ever now, loved the challenge of finding just the right words, told herself how 'eloquent' her writing was, then laughed.

From the abbess: 'Thought thrives best in solitude.' And it did, sharpening her senses, focusing her energy, her ability to observe and imagine. She noticed how small things, little changes, could focus her attention for long periods of time: the texture of stone, the interplay of light and cloud shadow on the rocks and trees below, the timelessness of the night sky. And from that awareness came more poetry.

Rather than just tolerating her solitude, she was learning to prize it.

Though she did most things randomly over the ensuing months, one thing never changed: her single meal of rice, vegetables, nuts and occasional fruit eaten while watching the sunrise. Often during the day, she couldn't tell if she was dreaming or meditating. Maybe that's what led her to prefer walking to sitting meditation, though she did give some thought to walking over the edge and dropping off the mountain as she had the Snake Skin staircase that night. To her activities she added practising English to her companions: the hidden tarantula, the returned cave rat, the marble-skinned python next to her by night, above her by day. In her silliest of moods she imagined seats, lights, curtains, scenery, costumes and an audience emerging from out of the chasm, all surrounding her, as she recited more from *Romeo and Juliet*. Like:

> O observant rat, see
> How she leans her cheek upon her hand!
> O, that I were a glove upon that hand,
> That I might touch that cheek!*

She filled her writing pads and diary, pretending she had a friend who would one day read them. When her provider next arrived, she gestured for more to be brought up.

A week later, in large letters, she wrote on her new diary covers: *Settling my past through solitude, silence and writing. The reason I am here.* Just in case she needed a reminder. She increased her writing, mostly in the form of haikus. After she got out of her cave one morning, looking out at her own private horizon, she wrote:

> *Watching the new dawn*
> *Spread, probe the misty shadows –*
> *Deep, dark, resistant.*

The next afternoon, after another storm:

> *Through exploding clouds*
> *A sudden shaft of sunlight*
> *Flashes off treetops.*

A day later, with distant thunder rumbling:

> *A rainbow omen –*
> *Sharp-edged, bright as coloured glass –*
> *Bridges my world.*

---

* *Romeo and Juliet*, Act 2, Scene 2, lines 23–25 (Pelican Shakespeare edition, 1960).

Sometimes she grew uneasy if she couldn't fall asleep quickly at night. She'd never entirely got used to the cave's relentless darkness. With nothing visible, she often felt entombed. Night demons penetrating her thoughts, she'd leave the cave for the rock shelf. One night, straining her eyes for want of light, she wrote:

> Night cluttered in stars
> Trembling white across a sky
> Polished in blackness.

The next morning, emerging later than usual into the soft sunlight:

> My night-dark cave that
> Starlight cannot penetrate,
> Though my python can.

Three days later:

> Sleeping inside rock,
> Sheer blackness, utter quiet.
> Python prods my feet.

She remembered: *'Digging a well with a pen requires no greater amount of patience and concentration.'* In her stretched state of mind she set herself the task of completing one short English poem or haiku every second or third day about her surroundings, her feelings, her stubborn memories too.

When her provider appeared one day, Nan Pau waved her inside the cave, showed her haikus, pointed to her wall drawings and again used gestures to request a brush and paints along with more writing pads. A week later her requests arrived. Hers were the first haikus, the first English writing, ever written on the cave's walls.

'Nowhere else,' she often said now to the space and rock. The solitude, remoteness and her sleeping companion were what she had in mind.

Time slipped by, season gave way to season, when one day her provider handed her a note and surprisingly stayed put.

> Dear Nan Pau,
>
> It is with regret that I disturb you. Weeks ago a man claiming to be an acquaintance of your father visited our office. When I told him where you were, he said he did not want to interrupt you.

Yesterday he returned. When he learned you were still on retreat, he asked when I thought you would finish. I told him I did not know. He thanked me and left. I think you should know about the visits. He told me he is living in Moulmein and can be found most mornings at a certain tea shop for which I have the address.

If you wish to stay on retreat, do so. But tell me what you would like me to say to him if he returns again.

Abbess

Strange how her sense of calm had just lately been disturbed by bouts of restlessness, a growing interest in what might be waiting for her down below. And now this note.

Feeling giddy at the prospect of returning, Nan Pau pointed to the sky then to herself and broke her retreat silence by reciting a haiku written the previous day:

'Eternal silence
Above man's guile and greed.
Nan Pau in between.'

She knew her provider didn't understand English and probably thought she'd gone cave-crazy (and maybe she had), that once down below she might go scurrying around on all fours shrieking and howling, going manic. So she recited the haiku again in Burmese and explained it; her social voice, for so long dormant, sounded weird to her.

'Life can be no more than breathing up there,' she recalled the abbess saying. And for so much of her retreat that's all life had been – her breathing and the passing of time as marked on the cave wall: the two hundred and forty-two risings and settings of the sun, eight waxings and wanings of the moon, fifty-two afternoon or evening storms; everything else the by-products of her solitary mind. The experience had changed her, given clarity to her thoughts. There were things she had learned and re-learned about herself, things she vowed would not be taken away from her again, no matter what. Though, holding onto her new self in the difficult world below would test her, she knew that.

'Sister, can you wait? I want to pack my things, say good-bye to my friends and go back with you.' She laughed, not knowing why, while her provider just stared.

Soon Nan Pau descended the mountain listening for the first, welcoming sound of a distant motor scooter, or a monk's dog. She felt good about herself, better about the world, though a little scared at the prospect of finding a place in it. Not unlike how she'd felt climbing up to The Place Above eight months earlier.

25

Nan Pau had no way of knowing who he was, so described him as a big, round-faced man in his late thirties or early forties. The boy server knew instantly, saying the owner was expected to be in soon. She thanked the boy and her suspicions took over: *'Inside or outside the gut, it's the best disinfectant in all of Myanmar.'* But she largely discounted them as a product of her paranoia. She sat at a table out of the sun and inhaled the cooking smells from inside. Still morning, barely, so she ordered a tea-leaf salad with her water and waited, memories of similar teahouse settings stealing into her mind.

She didn't dwell on those memories for long though, jolted back to the twenty-first century by a smoking, backfiring truck rattling past, the close proximity of strangers and smells of rot, spices and exhaust fumes that stung her eyes. Two days down from her cave and her senses still hadn't adjusted; each passing face, sudden smell, movement or loud noise turned her head.

Her water and salad came. She ate and, despite the clamour, small things held her attention.

In the tree shade, just metres away, stood a thin woman in a faded green longyi – her hair frizzy and snarled as though electrified, her big eyes darting around at every potential customer appealing to them to buy from her. On a plastic mat next to her was a baby and the sunglasses she was selling.

Nan Pau took out her pen, writing pad and dictionary. As if still on retreat she wrote:

> Tiny and wrinkled,
> Encircled in sunglasses,
> Cloth-wrapped baby sleeps.

She went over and bought a pair of wraparounds from the woman.

Back at the table she put them on and looked across the tree-lined road at an old man on a bench. He seemed to be talking to a dog stretched out beneath him. He scratched himself, looked in her direction. She wrote:

Bench-seated, gazing,
Old man with tree branch crutches,
Street dog at his feet.

Another old man with a walking stick shuffled along to the bench, stopped and felt his way into a sitting position, sparking memories. *'Yeah, it change, girl. You a blind Gaga, I gotta get you a walkin' stick.'* His eyes – appearing glassy and grey – stared straight ahead. His lips moved, and soon the two old men were exchanging words, nods and smiles.

Talk too from nearby tables. A man with a bandaged calf described getting his leg ulcer treated. Another talked of a boat he was leasing out to a local fisherman.

A monk was reading a newspaper at the next table, something that the old man with the walking stick would never do. She stared at the paper trying to recall the last time she'd seen one. When the monk finished, she thought of asking to borrow it. Just five words: 'May I borrow your newspaper?' One less than the daily maximum allowed from a nun to a monk. But he would most likely just ignore her. She recalled the abbot at Sule Pagoda, his life-saving goodness, his indifference to a spoken word count.

She glanced at her side-on reflection in the folded glass door opposite her, and took in her appearance. How long had it been since she'd done that? Thinner without a doubt, her knees gone bony, her nails cracked and broken. Yet she felt strangely comfortable with who she saw. She might find a stall later that sold nail clippers and hand mirrors. That she could think of doing that made her smile.

'Down from the mountain, I see.' The voice over her shoulder startled her, before she realised who it belonged to. She stiffened. Her paranoia had been justified.

'Welcome to my teahouse, Mya Paw Wah – or should I say Nan Pau now? Or possibly Lady Gaga?' He sat down on her right, grinning like a lizard.

The enemies of her well-being had circled back into her life: Mister MI a year and a half earlier, now the whiskey drinker. Might Billy J be next? Like living in hell again having to meet up with these people. She concentrated, meeting the whiskey drinker's eyes and returning a smile as dishonest as his. 'Aung Min, isn't it?'

'Well done.'

'Interesting who you remember in life and who you forget.'

'So no re-introduction is needed then, is it? Except … you'll need to instruct me. Which one of your names are you answering to these days?'

'You can use whichever one you want.' She could no longer will her lips to smile. 'I answer to all three with equal pride.'

'Do you? Well then, Lady Gaga appeals to me the most as you sit there in your novice robe, your bare skull reflecting the sun, as though enlightening itself.'

Good: a put-down. He was reverting back to his true self. She'd have to be careful, yes, but she would not pander to him, nor allow herself to fear him or be dominated by him like before.

'And tell me, Lady Gaga, where did you find those beautiful almond eyes of yours? While on the mountain meeting the Buddha face-to-face?'

'You've seen them before.'

'Not with the light on them.'

'They came out of my mother's womb with the rest of me.' She watched the traffic as his laughter turned into a cough. When he stilled, she turned and asked, 'You do remember mentioning my mother to the Thai Snake Skin agent that day in Hpa-an, don't you?'

His smile shrunk only a little. 'I do. But the past is past; now is now.'

'For some maybe.' Ironic, wasn't it, how practising Buddhists and a man like Aung Min could share the same view of time? Though for very different reasons. 'I have ten minutes before I must go. What is it you came to the nunnery to say to me?'

He leaned closer, as though they had secrets to share. 'I'm disappointed. I was hoping we could eat and relax together. You've lost weight. You need to eat more than just a salad. Like the prawn curry, a specialty of ours. Of course it would be served with the compliments of my teahouse.'

'Another time.' About as likely as snow falling on Moulmein. 'I really can't stay long.' Yet she was curious. 'How did you know I was living at the nunnery?'

'You of all people should know the answer to that. The Network, the same one that's allowed you your freedom since you got back from Mae Sot.' He turned and snapped his fingers at a boy server.

A woman had stopped to look at the sunglasses. She sampled a pair and bought them. A second sale in a matter of minutes. The baby would eat well tonight, either through its mother or from her hand.

The old men and dog across the road hadn't moved. First line for a haiku: *Old men of Moulmein.*

The boy waiter placed a small glass of whiskey in front of Aung Min. He took a sip, then sat back, folding his arms on his belly. 'You are aware, aren't you, that Aung San Suu Kyi has been released from house arrest and is running for a seat in the new parliament in upcoming elections?'

She nodded. 'News powerful enough to keep even our nuns talking.'

'Understandably. Great change is coming to Myanmar as we open up to international investment, development and tourism. Such a change as you would not believe. Think Kentucky Fried Chicken, Coca Cola, Heineken, Samsung. And Moulmein, with its magnificent pagodas, scenic hills and coastline, will have every opportunity to share in the development, to become a second Pattaya or Phuket even.' He sipped his whiskey, glancing over at her.

She recited the lines from "In the Quiet Land of Burma" about the country's generals profiting from foreign exploitation of the land. The look on Aung Min's face, like she'd suddenly grown a beard.

'From a poem by Mother Suu,' she explained.

'Ah.'

'You visited my nunnery. You told my abbess you had information about my father.'

'I did, and I'll come to him … While Moulmein has many attractions, Lady Gaga, what it doesn't have is a large airport, western-style hotels and nightclubs – nightclubs like the Snake Skin in Mae Sot. The government is going to build the airport and hotels. I want to build and operate the nightclubs, starting with a nightclub conversion of this place.' He sipped and continued to talk like the minefield and the Snake Skin had never happened. 'I have the financial partners I need and the plans have been approved. Construction will start in a couple of weeks. I have one problem though. I need people working for me who have had experience working in western-style entertainment businesses, smart people who are capable of occupying leadership positions and who I can trust to run a nightclub efficiently. Like you.'

So that was it. Even coming from him, the suggestion stunned her. Her lips tightened. She fought to retain some semblance of calm detachment. 'You want me to manage bar staff in your nightclub?'

'You're a survivor, Lady Gaga: smart, tough, fluent in English and at a very young age already skilled in dealing with the sort of people my business will be depending on. As a retired ...' he paused, letting his smile linger, 'bar-girl, you are just the person I need to advise and supervise my female staff, while teaching all of them the English they'll require.'

Trade her, sell her or employ her: he would use her any way he could to his advantage. And again – despite the hundreds of hours of Buddhist instruction and study – Nan Pau bristled with anger, her equanimity unravelling. His whiskey breath, smug face and controlling manner; his greed and the ruthless way he set about benefiting from the misfortunes of others. She thought how morality and money started with the same letter in the English alphabet and amounted to the same thing in people like Aung Min, who obviously saw himself as a man of rising influence and status. Though in her eyes he'd never rise above crab bait. 'And this time I'll be allowed to remain untouched, will I?' she asked. 'As untouched as a ...' She wondered if he could make the connection.

He couldn't. 'A what?'

'A nun.'

He laughed like that was the funniest thing he'd heard all year. 'Your choice entirely, Lady Gaga.' A smirk stayed on his lips.

'A choice I didn't have at the last place you arranged for me to work in.' As to his plans, Billy J came to mind, and she thought of saying, 'Give me a monkey and a bag of bananas and I'll give you back a bar manager,' or perhaps she'd suggest a name for his nightclub:

'The Aung Min Pig Pen'. But she did neither. Self-recrimination set in. A voice in her head: *Think better. Be kinder.* From her Tripitaka: *Holding on to anger is like grasping a hot coal. You are the one who gets burnt.* And she was.

All that time away from everyday people it was easy to feel compassion for them, to be a friend of the world. First stop out of the nunnery, meeting up with Aung Min again, and she was feeling no closer to Buddhahood than when she'd attacked that policeman with a brick during the massacre. She might as well have never entered the nunnery, or gone on retreat.

'Have to start on the bottom and work your way up in this sort of business,' Aung Min said, laughing again for whatever reason. 'And you have, Lady Gaga, you have: from fugitive to bar-girl to novice nun to prospective English teacher and bar and entertainment manager. An impressive range of activities and occupations already experienced at such a young age … And as a bonus you'll earn enough money and gratitude in the job to be able to bribe your father out of jail. You do know he's nearby, don't you?'

It was like seeing the ghosts of Thant and her mother sitting at the next table. She gaped at him, her silence – born of astonishment – stretching out.

'He was transferred to the Moulmein Prison a few months ago.' He raised his glass and held Nan Pau's stupefied gaze, his smile that of someone in total control. 'Here's to opportunity and a title – yours.' He drank the last of his whiskey. 'I don't need your answer right away. Visit your father. Take some time to think about him and my offer. You can come back and see me in the next week or two.'

26

As the prison's razor wire-topped walls came into view above cramped, double-storey housing, certain possibilities entered Nan Pau's mind. That Mister MI and the whiskey drinker were still 'in business together'. That Mister MI was responsible for getting her father transferred to Moulmein. That her father's eventual release depended on her working in Aung Min's night club. Besides a cave or a nunnery, was there anywhere in Myanmar she could escape the legacy of that massacre?

Nan Pau's thoughts turned to the abbess, two days earlier, when she'd told the abbess about Aung Min and her father: the abbess's stillness, her calm detachment. Because, along with a bucketful of courage, that's what she would need in explaining to her father what had happened to their family. And though she'd chosen – with her abbess's permission – to wear jeans and a t-shirt to the prison, she'd have to account for her recently shaved head. So yes, bend and edit the truth. And the abbess had agreed with her. Tell him about the massacre, about Thant, about how she and her mother fled to Hpa-an, where they lived together until her mother died and she came to Moulmein to enter the nunnery. Spare him the rest.

She got off the motorbike taxi by the iron entry gate and guard post and, for the first time since entering the nunnery, paid for her transport. Not a place she'd wanted her benefactor to take her. She approached the guard post and showed her abbess-arranged pass. Her shoulder bag was checked and she was escorted across an open compound, past the high, barred windows of her nightmares, to the door of an annex attached to the main prison. Inside, under fluorescent lighting, was a padded bench against the wall and four tables about two metres apart bolted to the floor, stools either side of them. Otherwise the room was empty, the walls bare.

The guard pointed to the last table. 'Sit there. You have ten minutes. Do not stand or touch the prisoner. If you do, your visit will end and the prisoner will lose visitor rights for the next month. Any questions?'

She shook her head, a swirl of emotion running through her: tension, fear, anticipation. She went to her stool and sat down, drawing up images of her father – how he would look, how he would react to her – and rehearsing what she would tell him, along with the answers to questions he might ask.

Minutes passed with near-unbearable slowness before the door opened and in he came, a guard following.

Sudden pain in her throat. Itch of tears.

Long chin-whiskers and neck-length hair going grey; he was smaller, thinner, more stooped and older than she remembered him. And for an instant she thought he was someone else. The guard said something in his ear before he approached in short, stiff steps. He stopped next to his designated stool and glared at her, eyes aglow.

It was all she could do not to jump up and run to him. She had to say something, had to, but after all her rehearsing, the words wouldn't come. 'I …'

'Ssshhh.' He held up a callused hand, sat down and leaned forward. There were new lines between his eyes and from his nose to the corners of his mouth. 'First, I know about the protest and massacre,' he said. 'I know about Thant. I know about your mother, and about you.'

She shook her head, stunned, not understanding.

'Your abbess visited yesterday. She thought it would be easier if I heard about what's happened from a neutral source.' He paused, eyes fixed on her. 'I can't imagine the horror you've been through, see-ing Thant shot, your mother die slowly and now having to visit your father in prison.' His eyes explored her face, seemingly trying to catch up with who she was. 'Anyway … your mother would have approved of you going into a nunnery. Did she encourage you to?'

'She mentioned it, no more.'

'And will you seek ordination?'

'I don't think so.' Her father, not the Buddha, was her priority now. 'I'm thinking about leaving the nunnery and finding work in Moulmein. I can't go back to Yangon.'

'No. I can't either.' He didn't elaborate. 'What about Myawadi? My brother and his family are there, and I've heard fighting in the area has stopped, hopefully for good.'

The suggestion surprised her. Myawadi, on the Thai border, all of eight kilometres from Mae Sot, the Snake Skin and Billy J. At the river she'd spent hours daydreaming about her stranger uncle, of using Myawadi as a first stop on her way to finding her mother. But that was not something she could tell him. 'I'll go wherever you go, whenever you get out of here.'

He managed a smile. 'Which might not be too long. Since Aung San Suu Kyi was released from house arrest, labour camps like the one I was in up north have closed. Political prisoners have been released; a few hundred already, and according to prison gossip, more will be released in the next few months.' He paused, watching her. 'Right now I want to leap over this table and wrap my arms around you.'

Her first smile for the day, a wet-eyed one. 'You can't.'

'No. And I'm not much good at leaping nowadays … Tell me, are you still able to study English where you're at?'

'Yes.'

'Good. We live under a government suspicious of knowledge, so be careful with it.'

She nodded. And they talked about Hpa-an (for which she was prepared), the labour camp and prison only briefly, the nunnery and Nan Pau's retreat, each preferring to ask the questions rather than answering them. Finally, he asked, 'Do you have access to a computer?'

'There's an internet cafe in town.'

He took out a slip of paper and held it up so the guard could see it. 'My brother's postal and email addresses,' he called out to him. 'You can check it if you want to.'

The guard came over, gave the paper a cursory glance and returned to the padded bench by the door.

'A few weeks ago I would have been … let's say reprimanded for carrying such an item on me. More reason to think I'll be out of here soon.' He showed the addresses to Nan Pau. 'Take this and write to your uncle, telling him you're thinking about going to Myawadi. Ask if you can stay with him and his family for a while. I know they'll be very happy to have you, and when I am out that is where I'll go … Another thing. If you should get an offer of work from anyone here in Moulmein who you think may not have your best interests at heart, assure me please you won't accept it. Okay?'

What else had the abbess told him?

'Okay?' he asked again. 'Agree and I won't ask anything else of you.'

She nodded.

The guard approached, indicating time was up.

Life was suddenly speeding up and getting complicated again. She now faced a dilemma. 'I want to come back tomorrow.'

He smiled. 'There should be time available on my visitors' schedule.'

At least he could still joke.

* * *

Back at the nunnery, by way of the internet cafe, Nan Pau went looking for the abbess and found her with others inside the temple, kneeling, heads bowed in benediction. So she retreated and sat on a bench under the tamarind tree, breathing in the incense, listening to the birds and insects.

When the abbess came out she spotted Nan Pau and went to her, and sat and stared back into the temple. 'Detachment, Nan Pau,' she said finally. 'There's a need I think to constantly re-evaluate it in our dealings with the outside world.' It was as though she knew why Nan Pau was there waiting for her. 'That when a clash occurs between detachment and compassion, compassion should always take priority.' She turned Nan Pau's way. 'Any thoughts about that?'

'The abbot who carried me away from the Yangon massacre said the same thing.'

'It's heartening to know others in charge of Buddhist facilities struggle to stay detached.'

'And the thousands of ordinary monks who protested that day chose compassion over detachment, and many were killed.'

The abbess recited some lines of verse about the spoiling of life's beauty, and asked, 'Know who wrote that?'

'Tin Moe.'

'From your father's favourite poem I believe.'

A bird high up chirped away. One of the sounds she'd missed most on retreat; the other a fast-flowing river. 'I want to thank you.'

'Ah … And how was he?'

'Better for you having visited him yesterday.'

'It occurred to me after I told him about your nightclub employment offer that I should have stayed more detached.'

'I'm pleased you didn't.'

Silence now, the sort when a moving leaf can attract attention. And Nan Pau knew then how much she would miss the nunnery.

'We had another novice here while you were on retreat,' the abbess said eventually. 'One day she told me she was ready to leave the nunnery, and she finished up by saying, "I could stay a lifetime here and still feel more a guest than a resident." Such a perceptive thing to say … So, Nan Pau, from retreat to renewed involvement with the outside world. First stop Myawadi, yes?'

'There's a problem.'

'You mean besides the obvious one of how to make your way through the world again?'

Nan Pau nodded. 'If I don't accept Aung Min's employment offer, he could use his influence to keep my father in prison.'

'Ah yes. What did Tin Moe say?'

'We do not worship learning. We worship power.'

'He did.' She glanced at her watch. 'Time for things less mind-testing, like chores. Let's talk more. Come to my kuti during study period, okay? Say about nine o'clock.'

Nan Pau arrived at her door at exactly that time and was called in. She sat on a mat, legs folded, and waited for the abbess to continue their earlier discussion. 'A feature of Buddhism, Nan Pau: choosing a pathway to a meaningful life. You have the experience, compassion and ability to make an impact on some small part of Myanmar ... or better yet the Thai border region. I can see you working as a counsellor for exploited Karen women, or a teacher of English, Karen and Burmese at a school for migrant children, and—'

'But—'

The abbess held a hand up for quiet. 'When you were in Mae Sot, did you ever hear of a Doctor Cynthia Maung?'

'There would be few there who haven't. She founded and is in charge of the Mae Tao Medical Clinic there.'

'Yes. She and I have a mutual friend who lives close to that clinic and knows her well. That friend is also the principal of the Hsa Thoo Lei Burmese Migrant School in Mae Sot and has a son who is currently overseeing the building of an additional room there. Apparently the school is in need of an English teacher who—'

'But—'

Up went the abbess's hand again. 'I believe I can arrange a Thai work permit for you through a ... a certain network of people I have access to. Best for you not to know anything about them. But first you need a passport. Do you have one?'

'No.'

'I would have been surprised if you did. So that will be our first task.' Her lips curled into a grin. 'Do you recall me saying earlier this afternoon that detachment was over-rated?'

'I do.'

'You can understand why now, can't you? And why that part of my job description troubles me most … Mmm. Now, to the problem of your employment offer. Do you have any ideas about how to deal with it?'

'I can't go to Myawadi thinking I'll never see my father again.'

'So you're considering accepting the offer?'

'I have no choice, at least until my father is released.'

'The youngest girl ever approved for retreat by this nunnery, followed by another precedent. I don't recall any of our novices working in nightclubs either side of living and studying here.' Her coy smile showed the comment was light-hearted. 'But then people can't choose their positions in life, can they? Circumstances do that for them.' She sat still as wood for half a minute or so, before asking, 'What do you know about tuberculosis?'

Nan Pau gave her a puzzled look. The abbess might just as well have asked what she knew about dark energy and black holes in the universe for the lack of connection tuberculosis had with what they were talking about. She replied, 'It's a disease of the lungs caused by a bacterial infection, and lots of people in Myanmar get it, and some die from it.'

'Yes, and it's largely spread through coughing and sneezing. In its advanced stage, a person's mucus contains blood. It might be fanciful, but tell me what you think of this idea. Wait three or four days, then go back into Aung Min's teahouse. Sit, making sure he sits with you. Order tea. Ask him if you can have a few more days to make your decision, all the time coughing and spluttering, and maybe with the help of some chilli or pepper between your fingers, sneezing and constantly clearing your throat. Eventually you have a coughing seizure and you take out your handkerchief that's spotted in blood – chicken or pig's blood, but he won't know that – and use it to cover your mouth. You put your handkerchief away. You finish your tea and leave. A few days later I go in, sit down and order tea. I wave Aung Min over and tell him I have a message for him. You've gone into hospital suffering from suspected … what?'

A look of understanding passed between them. Then a big smile broke over Mya's face.

'Worth a try, don't you think?'

'You're the best person I know and someone I will never ever forget.'

'Perhaps we should see if the plan works first before you become so appreciative.'

27

The essence of Buddhism, Nan Pau thought on the road to Myawadi, is the impermanence of everything: what is new growing old; the turning of the wheel, the wheel of life; the way forward being the way back.

And once back there, what? A place to live deeply in – boyfriend, husband, children, walking through the Burmese market hand-in-hand with them? Doubtful, and much too fanciful to waste time thinking about, especially considering how close Myawadi was to Mae Sot and the Snake Skin.

So two goals only when she got there: a room of her own and a job. A small life, but enough, at least until her father joined her. And as an incentive to keep her thoughts from straying, this fact: how badly had she miscalculated her future the last time she rode a bus from Moulmein to Hpa-an?

Admittedly, she was no longer a disguised fugitive on the run. Far from it. Now she wore jeans and a t-shirt and in her shoulder bag she carried an ID card, a Thai work permit, a letter of introduction and directions to her uncle's place should he not be there to meet her. So she had every reason to feel optimistic. Yet experience had changed her. The unexpected could ambush you at any time. That little girl with her story-book dreams and imagination, who thought everything she wanted for herself would be hers in time, was long gone. Be wary, take life one careful step at a time, had become her mantra. And for now the one step included getting to Hpa-an while watching the rice field plains outside, reading Aung San Suu Kyi's 'Letters from Burma' (a cause for immediate arrest during her last trip on this bus) and waiting for the right opportunity to test her new ID card's acceptance. There was little sense showing it at the Thai border if it didn't first pass inspection in Myanmar.

But inspection didn't happen on the bus. There were only two military check-points to pass through – both missing their sandbagged machine-gun emplacements. Soldiers still wore automatic rifles, but didn't bother to board the bus or order anyone out – only waved them on.

No demand for her identification in Hpa-an either, where she had a two-hour wait for a *songthaew** to Myawadi, so she drank tea at the table where Mister MI had called out to her that day. Despite nearly three years having passed since her capture, she couldn't help looking out for that girl with the crying toddler when she went for a walk past the Soe Guesthouse to the market and on to the river. From the river she went another kilometre to the chain-linked perimeter fence of the military base – looking abandoned – where Mister MI had sold her to Aung Min and later Aung Min had sold her to the Thai agent.

As she stared through the fence at the faded brown door of the room she'd occupied, her spirits slumped. And for the first time since her early days in the Buddha cave, she felt fear. Up there, at least, there had been certainty and safety and nobody but providers to deal with. But now she had to deal with entering another strange town; meeting an uncle and his family she'd never met; being recognised as Lady Gaga; possibly meeting up with Billy J again as she had with Mister MI and Aung Min. Small town Myawadi only eight kilometres from small town Mae Sot; gossip-mongers moving between them; the river and border crossing no barriers to the opening up of her past.

Maybe it was useless to have hopes, she thought gloomily, even when they were as small as hers.

Back at the cafe-side terminal, the *songthaew* to Myawadi and the bus back to Moulmein chugged away, side by side, passengers and their bags and boxes and caged animals boarding both of them.

She climbed into the back of the *songthaew*, though if there'd been transport going anywhere else – other than Yangon – she might have chosen differently.

Half an hour out of Hpa-an, the *songthaew* drew up to a military check-point, sandbagged machine-gun emplacements either side of

* A utility truck used for public transport, with an arched, metal canopy and two length-wise wooden benches at the back.

the road. A soldier ordered the passengers to get out and line up at a documentation table. Papers and possessions – sacks of vegetables, boxes of scooter parts – were inspected. Only Nan Pau was detained after the soldier at the table scrutinised her. 'Have you come from a nunnery?' he asked.

She nodded, clasping her hands together to keep them steady.

'Which one?'

She told him.

'Yet you do not wear a robe.'

'I have completed my novice training and I'm spending time away from the nunnery to consider possible ordination.'

He studied her ID card again then pointed to her left arm. 'It appears you've fully recovered from your wounds.'

Her head jerked up. First the shock, then a cold fear gripped her. 'Yes … I have.'

'Maybe two, three years ago, you were the only female porter carrying military supplies into the mountains behind me. Yes?'

The past circling back. She nodded, the present suddenly everything to her.

He tapped the palm of his hand with her card appearing to mull over what to do next. Finally he handed the card back to her, saying, 'I hope your trip is more comfortable this time.'

'Thank you.' She returned quickly to her spot on the bench, wedging in shoulder to shoulder again and not daring to look back.

The *songthaew* climbed on, the temperature dropping, passengers swaying against the roll of the vehicle, a few speaking quietly beneath the noise of the engine.

Two ways to try to calm herself. She consulted her dictionary for a word meaning 'tied up' and found 'tethered'. The jolts and bumps made writing no easier than meditation. So it was in her head first that she wrote:

> Up the mountain road
> Songthaew rumbling thunder.
> Smell of trees, turned earth.
> Along the roadside
> Rhesus monkeys, blue peacocks,
> Tethered buffalo.
> Further in raised huts,

Spirit house and pagoda,
Villagers at work.

Feeling pleased with what she'd composed, she drew up an image of herself walking along a corridor at the University of Mandalay. First day of the academic year. In a student bag dangling from her shoulder, writing material, English dictionary, second-hand laptop, Shakespeare's *Macbeth*, Charles Dickens's *Great Expectations* and George Orwell's *Burmese Days*. Other students meeting her eyes, smiling greetings and entering the English Literature lecture hall with her. Rows of seats descend from the back to the front. Sitting at the front, peering around to see if anyone, including the lecturer behind a lectern, looks happier than her. No one does.

Two tarpaulin-covered trucks roared past, snapping her mind back to reality. The night closed in, cold; the canopy of the *songthaew* shut out the stars.

Over the summit they went, picking up speed and winding their way downhill, passengers donning shawls and hunching over for warmth, their flat stares perhaps counting down the many bends they passed.

As they closed in on Myawadi, Nan Pau felt a surge of excitement. Her uncle and his family would be waiting for her. She would find work. Her father would be released soon and join them. Family, work and everyday life again and before long she and her father would have enough money to look for a place of their own. If not in Myawadi, then maybe somewhere along the remote south coast, far away from military check-points and sandbagged machine-gun emplacements.

They entered Myawadi, passing little open-fronted shops, a scattering of food stalls still doing business and groups of young men squatting or sitting on upturned buckets and talking and smoking.

They stopped at the terminal building, its front door padlocked, a low outside light left on. The tailgate swung down. Nan Pau waited while the others got out, before disembarking into the semi-darkness.

From a few metres away came a male voice. 'Mya Paw Wah?'

She turned, relieved to hear her family name spoken. 'Yes.'

'You're under arrest.'

* * *

MYAWADI, MYANMAR.

Still chortling away, her Uncle Zarni blasted the air with a couple of throttle bursts and they were off back down the main road, the scooter coughing exhaust fumes, its headlight cutting a weak funnel into the night. While Mya – she was no longer Nan Pau now – clung to her uncle, Thiri, his wife, clung to her, mouth close enough to her ear to chew on it. 'Joke, joke, your uncle is always joking,' she said loud enough to get over the engine noise. 'Sometimes when he does I want to kick him because he and I are the only ones who know he's joking. Then I have to apologise to people while he continues to enjoy his joke.' She shouted out, 'Isn't that right, you silly man?'

'Can't hear you.'

'I barely took any notice,' Mya lied, the shock of his 'joke' still lingering. 'I think I'm too tired to pay attention to anything but the chance to sleep.'

'And eat, hopefully. Your uncle's favourite fish curry will be ready for serving up in about three minutes' time.'

'I haven't eaten since early morning.'

'Perfect. So first we eat, then to bed, and tomorrow will begin the first day of your new life in Myawadi. Our sons are working in Hpa-an, and our house has felt so empty since they left, so we're thankful that you'll be taking their room.'

They turned onto a narrow, twisting dirt road, veering around potholes before stopping next to a double-storey place with a staircase at the side and a narrow balcony above. A sign – Zarni's Scooter and Cycle Repair Shop, hanging over large doors abutting the edge of the road – was visible in the headlights.

Zarni led them to the side of the house and through a door into darkness; the peppery smell of teak filled the air. 'Mya in Myawadi,' he said, 'I present your room; may you always think of it as home.' He reached up, tugged on a string and the bare light bulb came on.

Mya looked around the low-roofed space, her skin warming with gratitude. It was no bigger than her room in Yangon, but after the Snake Skin and life in a kuti and a cave, it was luxury. Freshly-painted in lime green, it had a teak bed with a mattress, a teak chair and table and lamp. Opposite the bed was a shelf for her belongings and a mirror big enough to take in her face, chest and shoulders. Her bicycle 'with special new tires', the outside toilet and shower were only metres past the door towards the back.

'It's wonderful. Thank you.'

Uncle Zarni said, 'Good, good. We've received a letter from your father. He can write one now every month. So, before you unpack – which with what you brought could take a full minute if you go very slowly – and we eat, let me just say how much we admire anyone who can spend more than an hour living in a cave. As for someone spending eight months in one, well, that's bordering on the super-human, or Buddhahood.'

'Not really. It wasn't that hard.'

'Oh yes, really. You're being modest. And while living in a cave up there among the clouds, my brave young niece, you no doubt had encounters with some of nature's less popular creatures, as our Lord Buddha did after he turned his back on wealth, prestige and influence. Yes?'

'Yes. But not dangerous ones.'

'Still, a word of warning. No cockroaches on this earth grow bigger than Myawadi's. So this is my advice for when you meet up with one: first, don't feel you have to pet them when they stand up on their back legs, and second, don't put your head in their mouths. Heed my advice and you shouldn't find them difficult to share a room with. Okay?'

Mya glanced over at Thiri, who was shaking her head and scowling.

'Okay.' As Uncle Zarni laughed, Mya added, 'But would it be permissible to whack a couple over the head and use your kitchen to cook them up? With lime leaves and fish paste, they were the most delicious food I ate in the cave.'

'Ahh.' Uncle Zarni suddenly looked perplexed, and said in a soft voice, 'The problem is lime leaves are expensive to buy here.' He went quiet and stayed that way as they climbed the creaky staircase to the living area and only spoke a few words while they ate – Thiri doing most of the talking.

After helping to clean up, Mya returned to her room, turned on the light, sat down at her table and viewed herself in the mirror. Picturing

Thant's 'girlfriend for a day', with her near waist-length, braided hair, Mya speculated on how long it would take for hers to reach that length: a year, two? Whatever time it took didn't matter. But before it got that long, she would learn how to braid it tightly and keep it braided.

She recalled the time after school that she'd slipped into the Trader Hotel's lobby through a back entrance and spied on Thant in his door-man's clothes. Spied as he opened the thickly-glassed, gold-handled door and greeted guests. Spied how rarely the guests gave him a glance. Thought about his ten-hour work shifts standing between giant bowls of lilies and the hotel entry: how monotonous, how sore his feet must have got. If he had to die young, better out on the street protesting for a better Myanmar than as a robot door-opener.

She got out her pad and wrote as if Thant were beside her:

No soundproof glass,
Bowls of lilies,
Gold-handles here, Thant.
Just family and kindness
And the world's biggest
Fictional cockroaches.
Home is belonging.

Home was also a place to settle into, absorbing the new smells and sounds and routines – her Uncle Zarni opening up his work-shop early, Thiri away most of the day working in a nearby tea shop. That first week Mya wandered around Myawadi re-adjusting to town living, trusting to luck that her past wouldn't connect her to a passing Snake Skin patron – if that happened, she'd prove to herself how detached and resilient she could be.

Each afternoon she sat on the same log by the riverside and stared across at the walkway and, yes, watched smugglers – including her former opium supplier one day – ply their trade. The memories would flood back. It seemed incredible that she, as someone else, had once used that walkway to escape Thailand forever. And now look at her, re-acquainting herself with the place from a different angle, readying herself to return.

Biking home, she stopped in at Thiri's tea shop to check on what to cook for the evening meal. That decided, Thiri handed over left-over ingredients, commenting again on how pleased they were Mya was living with them.

In the evenings, while sitting on mats and eating on the balcony, they chatted to neighbours opposite them, talked about Mya's future plans, her father, the border wars and sudden changes taking place in Myanmar. Television followed, before Mya excused herself and went down to her room and curled up on her so-very-soft bed, feeling almost guilty about how comfortable she was.

Home was a place to contribute to also. She'd already started doing that by cooking the evening meal and sweeping out the house, her room and the workshop. Next came rent, though her hosts disagreed. She had little money left from what Mister MI had handed her so long ago. So her thoughts turned to presenting her ID and passport at the Friendship Bridge and, if allowed to cross, determining if there was a livelihood for her in – of all places – Mae Sot.

Part Three

***

28

Mae Sot.

Wearing a floppy hat, t-shirt, jeans and sandals, the Australian visitor Mya was expecting stuck his head in the open doorway, his attention caught first by the English alphabet, colours and animal posters filling the walls, the many mobiles hanging from the ceiling, before looking at the schoolchildren, barefoot in their uniforms of white shirts and bright blue dresses or trousers, as they sang:

> 'Here we go
> Round, round, round,
> Round, round, round,
> Round, round, round.
> Here we go
> Round, round, round,
> So late in the morning.'

'Keep going,' Mya shouted in Karen and English, before signalling to her visitor that she'd be with him soon. She'd been told an Australian aid worker was coming from the Mae Tao Clinic, bringing along a young amputee. But the amputee was either outside or hadn't come, as the visitor appeared to be alone.

The children repeated the chorus then stopped circling, dropped their hands and sang on, patting their appropriate body parts –

> 'With an ear, ear, ear,
> With an eye, eye, eye,
> With a nose, nose, nose,
> With a mouth, mouth, mouth,
> With a bottom, bottom, bottom.'

Three times 'bottom' sent them cackling and giggling, some of the boys almost falling over themselves, before they all linked hands and started circling again.

> 'Here we go
> Round, round, round,
> Round, round, round …'

Each time they repeated the song, they sang it faster and faster until the circle finally broke up again in high-pitched squeals and laughter.

'Break time,' Mya called out. She moved to the door. 'Welcome to the junior primary class. Only about three minutes to go,' she said to the Australian.

'No worries. They're all looking healthy and happy. I thought I might see a few about with stick legs and swollen stomachs.'

'There are some who came to us that way. But they soon fill out.'

'Well, I've got one with a composite plastic leg just outside sitting on a bench.' He looked out and frowned. 'Or at least he was on a bench.' He shouted, 'Raju!' then glanced back at Mya. 'Sorry. I'd better go chase him down.'

The class ended, the students left and Mya went outside and sat on a bench, welcoming the lunch break more for the opportunity to rest than eat. She shared the junior primaries with another teacher and today was her only full day at the school. Two other mornings and an afternoon filled out her timetable there.

This new way of feeling, she thought, watching two of her girls, was good – just so good. As a teacher and a translator, she'd sensed people's respect, their need for her, her own self-esteem building. In the year since leaving the nunnery, she'd written only one haiku and read just three pages of her Tripitaka. Her life – no longer dominated by ideas and imagination – had turned practical and very busy, her obligations increasing, time and timetables regaining importance for her. She'd completed a ten-month primary teacher training course, rented a room in Mae Sot, and started teaching part-time, and she was also getting regular translation work from *Karen News*, an online magazine that regularly sent digital copies into Myanmar. At their suggestion, and with their help, she'd even organised her own website showing the words 'Mya Paw Wah, Mae Sot, Thailand, translator of English,

Burmese and Karen languages', her photo (with hair, now grown), two photos of the Burmese market, and her uncle's email address for contacting her. It wasn't long before she'd started getting job offers from western media groups wanting to report on the Mae Tao Clinic, nearby refugee camps and the many Burma-linked agencies like the Association of Political Prisoners, the Karen Women's Organisation, the Backpack Medic's Office and the Thai-Burma Border Consortium.

She'd been surprised by how influential the abbess's recommendations had been. It was like the migrant school, clinic and agencies had been forewarned a girl with amazing language talents was about to land on their doorsteps desperate to work just for them.

But her greatest satisfaction was finding a place away from her uncle's house where she was wanted and valued. While going from one workplace to another on roads furthest from the Snake Skin, she often muttered a thank-you to her abbess, feeling that now she was the person she would always be.

There was little such busyness at night though.

Occasionally some of the female teachers invited her to a cafe or the night market in the centre of town, or for a meal at their house. But she always declined, fearing being recognised by a Snake Skin patron in town or that the teacher's husband or boyfriend may have a Snake Skin connection, despite her changed appearance – long braided hair, Moulmein-bought sunglasses and teachers' clothes. If that happened, she thought, please let it happen after her father had been released so she could tell him a lie and they could go off and live somewhere else.

Her weekend reward for hard work and night-time solitude? Escaping – legally – back across the river and being treated like royalty by family.

Ironic, wasn't it? The upturn in her life, how good she felt here and now. Each day so purposeful; her life filling up with the stories of her students, their parents, Burmese activists, her weekend family.

'Found him.'

She looked around at the Australian, smiling broadly, and the young amputee, his head slumped, leaning against the Australian's side. She made room on the bench and they sat, the amputee using the Australian as a shield against her.

'I'd better introduce myself before Raju here attempts another escape,' the Australian said. 'I'm John Stanish and over the four-month Australian university holidays I'm here working for AusAid, largely at the Mae Tao Medical Clinic and hospital in town, but also in nearby refugee camps.'

He held out his hand and she shook it thinking, could it be happening again, her past circling back? Though that Australian boy, Nick, had never mentioned his last name and she knew 'John' was as common a first name in English-speaking countries as Mya was in Myanmar. Still, she baulked at giving him her name. 'Is this your first time in Mae Sot, John?'

'Second.'

She took hold of her braid, draped it over the front of her shoulder and worked at it with her fingers. 'Where do you live in Australia?'

'You know Queensland?'

'From maps.'

'Brisbane?'

She nodded, picking a hair off her red blouse, another off her blue silken trousers. She scanned the playground but took little notice of the students.

'I'm studying orthopaedics there. I actually grew up in a place called Tasmania.'

The knot in her stomach tightened. 'Land of Tasmanian Devils.'

'You know it.' He looked surprised.

The wheel was working its way back. So, Nick's brother – had to be. Incredible. 'From television,' she said quickly. Would Nick have told him anything about her? Her real name, for example? Still, there was no way she could give him a false name. He'd be at the school daily dropping off the boy, who was leaning forward now, peeking around at her. 'Tell me about Raju.'

'He's an orphan. Eight years old. His parents and sister were killed in a Burmese military attack on their village about five years ago. Raju suffered lower leg and hand wounds that, by the time he was rescued and brought to Mae Sot, had become gangrenous. His left leg below the knee and three fingers on his left hand had to be amputated.' He reached back and put an arm around Raju and drew him closer. 'If you have to have an amputation, though, three years of age is not a bad time. Not much memory of how you got around before your leg was amputated, how you tossed a ball or dressed yourself minus three fingers. Anyway, up to a couple weeks ago Raju was living with an uncle in the Mae La Refugee Camp. Have you been there?'

'No.'

John took his arm back. 'A hard place: massive, full of despair and boredom; so drugs are the pacifiers of choice and addiction a big problem. Apparently Raju's uncle was one such addict. He eventually died. So Raju is now living in an orphanage boarding house close to the medical clinic, which offers him one advantage. As he grows and his prosthetic leg needs replacing, he's only around the corner from the local producer.'

'And what have been the effects on him living with a drug addict?'

'He seems untroubled, at least on the outside. At his age though, especially where he's been living, what differentiates normal from abnormal behaviour is often not clearly understood. He is shy and a bit solitary and certainly needs time to adapt to the changes occurring in his life; but according to his refugee camp teacher he's very curious and smart and eager to learn.'

'So are you looking after him full-time?'

'As his designated daytime minder, just about, at least until he starts school here.' He paused, keeping his eyes on her. 'It's Mya, isn't it?'

'Uh … yes.' She sensed her past about to spring open. 'I apologise for not introducing myself earlier. With everything going on in the classroom …'

'Not a problem.'

'How did you find out my name?'

'Raju and I went to the principal's office first. While I filled out admission forms, she gave me your name and room number. I caught the Mya part, but missed the rest. When I was last here, my young brother visited Mae Sot. While I … was away for a few days he met a girl whose name was Mya: Burmese as well. Had a bit of an adventure together, apparently, the two of them. Anyway, the girl is back in Myanmar now. In a nunnery, last he heard. Can't remember where.'

Not even with a gun in her face would she be telling him. 'You need to know I only teach the junior primaries part-time. Raju can meet his other part-time teacher tomorrow afternoon.'

'That's something else I wanted to talk to you about. Would you mind if we delay that meeting and you being his only teacher for two or three weeks, or at least until he's adjusted to all the changes going on in his life? A part-time teacher for a part-time student. I mentioned this to the principal, and she said if it was fine by you, it would be fine by the school.'

'Okay.'

'I'll get him here and I'll make sure either I or a motorbike taxi picks him up.'

Raju was watching students playing soccer, maybe gauging if he was good enough. A ball rolled up to the bench, followed by a couple of boys there to retrieve it. 'Kick it,' John said in Karen.

Smiling, Raju stood and right-footed the ball, getting it past the boys.

'Score one for Raju Beckham,' John called out, as Raju sat back down looking pleased with himself.

'Your Karen is good,' Mya said.

'I had a good teacher last time I was here, but only for the basics.' He, then Raju, stood up. 'Anyway, I'll drop him here tomorrow morning. And do you mind if I ask you one more favour?'

'Please do.'

'If you could give him a bit of extra work each day as homework, I'd appreciate it, and I'll make sure he gets it done and back to you. He's bright, so hopefully with an education he'll have some sort of a future to look forward to.'

'No worries.'

He smiled. 'I like the way you said that. You'd do well in Australia.'

'Really?'

He nodded. 'Sounds as though you've had a good teacher too.'

'I did.'

29

Myawadi.

Her weekend routine was so predictable that the bridge's border police quickly grew to recognise her and just waved her through during her crossings, no longer checking her documents, never once demanding a bribe. Going home, she'd enter the workshop, greet her uncle, then go into her room to drop off her things. From there she went upstairs to see what Thiri had left for her to cook up for the evening meal.

One Friday afternoon though, she crossed the bridge so pre-occupied she barely knew where she was. Every day she'd worked at the school the past two weeks, aid worker John Stanish had brought Raju in before the other students arrived and prompted conversation while she was trying to arrange her room. Initially he asked about Raju's progress. But over the past few days he'd started asking her questions about herself. Where was she from in Myanmar? How did she come to be teaching in Mae Sot? Did she go out much during the weeknights? One day she caught him looking at her scarred arm and, thinking she'd get a question about that as well, prepared an elaborate lie to tell him. But he didn't ask.

She thought about asking him questions too. Politeness called for it. Yet, though he was an intelligent, good-looking man with sky-blue eyes, a ready smile and a compassionate heart, she thought it vital to keep her distance from him. Her job and welfare in Mae Sot depended on her remaining as unknowable as possible.

Then, just that morning, he said to her, 'I've got some free time this afternoon so I'm planning to take Raju down to the Moei River, have a walk and get something to eat at a food stall. Why don't you come with us, okay? Raju thinks it's a great idea.'

Rattled, she shuffled through papers, making a show of being busy. 'Thank you for the offer,' she said finally. 'But I cannot. Every Friday I return to my uncle's house in Myawadi.'

'How do you get there?'

'By bicycle.'

'So it would take you what … forty-five, fifty minutes to get to the bridge?'

'Yes.'

'Do you live nearby here during the week?'

'Yes.'

'What about after school we go to your place, get your things and your bicycle, toss them in the back of my ute and head straight for the bridge? Only take ten minutes, meaning you'll have half an hour at the bridge for something to eat and drink with us.'

At first, feeling trapped, she could think of no other excuse but to say that she didn't want to go. And that wasn't entirely true. Then she relaxed a little. The river wasn't the middle of town. Her anonymity would be as safe there as anywhere else around Mae Sot. 'Okay,' she said finally. 'But I won't be able to stay longer than thirty minutes.'

'I'll guarantee it.'

So came the first change to her strict Mae Sot to Myawadi and back routine.

As they drank tea and ate fish soup at a bridge food stall, Mya grew conscious of the eyes either side of her: Raju's darting around everywhere, John's holding steady as if trying to work out something about her. Her Lady Gaga connection maybe? She concentrated on keeping him talking; his tone, as always, was friendly and familiar, as if they'd known each other for years rather than weeks. Half an hour went by in a flash; a passing thought saying 'too quickly'.

And it was this thought that pre-occupied her an hour later when she arrived back in Myawadi, went upstairs and entered the living area to see Nyan, her father – *her father* – standing by a simmering pot on the kerosene stove, spatula in his hand. A thrill such as she'd not felt for a long time ran through her, gripping her chest. He turned her way, smiling, and said – as though his presence there was completely normal – 'Hope you don't mind taking a break from the cooking.'

Mya was too overwhelmed to respond.

'Recognise what's in the pot?'

She could smell the ginger, see the skins of a catfish and garlic on the cooking table.

'Mohinga.'

'Your mother's favourite.'

Tears came. 'I know.' She dashed to embrace him, quickly made aware of how thin he was.

'Only one more ingredient still to put in,' Nyan said into her ear.

'Shallots.' She almost laughed.

'Uh huh. And lastly?'

'Boil up the rice noodles.'

Nyan stepped back, placed his palms on her cheeks and kissed her forehead. 'You look so good to me. Even better than a bowl full of Mohinga.'

She gave a self-conscious shrug. 'Life here must suit me.'

'It must, and I want to hear about everything you're doing, which I've been told is a lot.' The staircase creaked with Uncle Zarni's heavy footsteps. 'But first we better finish the cooking.'

It wasn't long before the four of them were sitting in a circle on the balcony's boards, legs folded and slurping Mohinga. The specialness of the night limited talk, long silences prevailing before someone complimented the food. Meal over, Mya rose automatically and went inside and poured her father a second glass of tea. She returned and placed the glass in front of him as her mother used to do after he'd finished eating. He looked up, held her gaze.

Mya sat and Uncle Zarni turned to her and said, 'Why don't you tell your father what you're doing over in Mae Sot? Though, he's been in prison for so long you might need to get a map to show him where the place is.' Only Uncle Zarni laughed.

So Mya talked about her work and Nyan smiled when she told stories about her more rambunctious students.

Then, predictably, Uncle Zarni took over, talking as fast as the others could listen about expanding his business – if he had the right sort of help. He cast a quick glance at his brother, perhaps as a cue for him to respond. But Nyan stayed quiet, eyes lowered now, the ring of silence around him almost palpable. Even Uncle Zarni knew not to press him, at least just yet, that his brother needed more time to adjust.

* * *

Sitting by the river with her father the next few weekends, Mya was struck again by her good fortune. A working life in Mae Sot, a family one in Myawadi. In the evenings her father made up a bed on the balcony, calling it his 'after-prison lounge', and listened to the night sounds – televisions, chatter, neighbours closing shutters, passing scooters and trucks. By day he tapped into his long dormant mechanical skills to help out in the repair shop. He gained weight. Business was brisk. Mealtimes were filled with talk – future plans, ideas and feelings all tumbling out in conversation. Though not much from Nyan. He smiled, but said little, and never anything about prison. He just listened agreeably or stared out at some spot along the tightly-packed road.

One dry-season Saturday, sitting with her father on the same log by the river, Mya sketched his face in her pad and wrote:

> Slow river watcher.
> Sense the sadness in his bones.
> Mind still imprisoned.
> Rats, sweaty walls, screaming guards.
> Before his hand squeezes mine.

She read the tanka to him in both Burmese and English. He squeezed her hand and said, 'As fine a poem as any of Tin Moe's.'

'Stop it.' Yet it pleased her he should say that. And on Friday nights thereafter, when they started their ritual cooking of Mohinga, one of them recited a stanza from a Tin Moe poem and the other would get a point for naming the poem, and two points for reciting the next stanza. It was agreed that the loser would wash up after the meal, though in practice neither ever did that on their own.

Uncle Zarni finally decided it was time to expand his business with or without his brother's vocal support. He travelled to Yangon and negotiated with western-dressed managers in big-window offices to become Myawadi's sales agents for Honda and Yamaha motor scooters and Lanying Chinese bicycles. After that, mealtimes lasted well into the night as Uncle CEO Zarni discussed profit margins and business options. Thiri chipped in with the latest shop gossip and how well her prawn and tomato curry was selling. While Mya, at her father's request, told stories about her teaching and translating week. And though she mentioned Raju from time to time, she said nothing about his transport arrangements or the person responsible for them – the same person who continued to take her to the Friendship Bridge food stalls on Friday afternoons.

But those afternoons couldn't last. Soon she'd have to say 'no' and lie to John about why. That wouldn't be easy. It felt good getting such attention from him. His blue eyes that studied her. His lingering smile, like she'd been specially chosen to receive it. His playfulness and the stories he told about his work and encounters with people at the clinic and in the Mae La camp. Though she did at times wonder what sort of fanciful image his brain was conjuring up from what his eyes were taking in. That she was a stay-at-home virgin maybe – innocent, vulnerable – placed on this earth especially to share a Friday food stall table with him and his amputee orphan until … when? Until he asked her to spend more time sharing more places with him? Delete the Snake Skin from her past and she had little doubt she would. As it was, she had no choice but to end it. Whatever 'it' might be.

30

MAE SOT.

Mya realised quickly how much Raju doted on one-to-one instruction, how eager he was to please, be praised, succeed. And despite her efforts at impartiality, he took on a special presence in her eyes.

After school one Friday, but still in the classroom, she praised him for getting a number puzzle right then passed him a two-part language exercise to complete. She backed away and watched him label the items, using the English words on the board, then colouring in a Mae Sot-style house, tree, bus, car, motorbike taxi, Burmese clothes. She glanced at her watch. Twenty-five minutes late already and if John didn't come soon, she'd have to put Raju on a motorbike taxi, or maybe on the back of her bicycle to get him back to his dormitory.

When Raju finished the exercise, he stuck the coloured pencil between his prosthetic leg and stump and scratched around. He withdrew it, put the end of the pencil in his mouth and looked up at the questions on the whiteboard written in Karen and English.

Mya said in Karen, 'If you can read and answer the questions for me in English, I will allow you time on the computer.' Such time for him was like uncovering a bag of gold. She went to the whiteboard and pointed to a question and he spoke slowly and quietly. 'What colour is de house?'

She praised him then asked for the answer.

When they finished Raju got his reward. She watched him, his nose nearly touching the screen as he played a computer game with the skill of someone older, though effort took precedence over accuracy.

Another fifteen minutes passed.

She decided against waving down a motorbike taxi, with its anonymous driver. The dormitory wasn't far out of her way so she decided to bike Raju there after making a stop at her room down the road.

'Shut down the computer, Raju. I'll take you home.' She preferred the word 'home' to 'dormitory', which seemed so impersonal.

She invited him into her room while she packed for Myawadi and filled a bottle of water. But Raju stood only just inside the door, eyes scanning the place for hidden dangers. Soon they were off back down the road, Raju riding side-on across the rear rack, an arm around Mya's stomach. They turned left on the main road and hadn't travelled far before a ute beeped its horn as it passed them on the opposite side. It stopped and John's head appeared at the window. 'Stop, you two. I'm coming for you.'

As the ute drew up in front of them, John jumped out and shouted, 'Sorry, sorry. Let me explain why I'm late.'

His concern drew a smile from Mya. 'There is no need. It does not matter.'

'It does to me.' A laneway intersecting with the road caught his attention. He pointed. 'The Casa Mia is just in there, only fifty metres away. We can get a drink and some food there.'

'I am already late.'

'Yeah, I know. But just give me half an hour then I'll drive like the wind to get you to the bridge. Promise.'

It was happening: the offer of a different place. She needed to be firm and say 'No', followed by 'Thank you', followed by 'Good-bye', then get on her bike and go.

'Twenty-five minutes then,' John said.

Raju was looking at her as intently as John was. The absolute last time, she thought. 'Okay.' Next week, away from Raju, she would end this. 'But not a minute more,' she added.

'I'll guarantee it.'

In the car park, bike propped against a tree, Mya suddenly realised Raju was no longer beside her. She looked back and saw him staring at a baby elephant at the edge of the trees. He moved cautiously towards it, extending his hand and touching its ears. Then he laughed, turned and caught up to her. 'Pretend elephant,' he said, reaching for Mya's hand and looking up at her.

'Yes. Made of cement. So no need to feed it.'

The Casa Mia was a large, open-walled restaurant set back amongst the trees. A long, curving bar on one side, an assortment of bamboo tables and chairs everywhere else. John arrived and led them in, a voice from a table of westerners to their right shouting, 'Yo bro, John-man, the bone-man, the Ban Thai geee-tar man. How ya doin', ol' buddy?' The man hoisted his stubby in the air.

'Yeah, good, Matt. Stress levels being dealt with satisfactorily there?'

Mya slipped her wraparounds back on and looked out at the car park.

'You bet. Best stress-reduction table in Mae Sot, so come and sit yerselves down.'

John glanced back at Mya, taking notice of where she was facing. 'Like to a bit later, Matt. Got some urgent business to tend to first.'

'Looks like the sort of business we could all take an interest in.' Laughter. 'Be sure to let us know if you need any help with the figures.'

'Yeah, thanks.'

They headed for a table in the farthest corner. Mya sat down with her back to John's friends, took off her wraparounds and asked, 'Aid workers?'

He nodded. 'This is their hang-out. Did you pick up on Matt's accent?'

She shook her head.

'A Texan-American one, like my dad's. He's from a place called Waco and he can get a bit cowboy frisky towards the end of the week. He's a top bloke in his job though. You've heard the word "bloke" before?'

'Yes.'

'Good. Important for you to keep your Aussie English up to scratch.'

Teasing was permissible now, she thought, even expected. Their friendship seemed to have moved to a different level.

The server came. They ordered tea and a rice dish for Raju.

'I think I better warn you,' John said, meeting her eyes again, 'I'm enjoying these Friday afternoons.'

She looked at her watch. 'Twelve minutes to go.'

'Ah. I'd better get started then. Two reasons I was late.' He raised a forefinger. 'One, I met up with an old, very close, friend of mine at the clinic. Do you know about backpack medics?'

'Yes.'

'Well Phoe Ni is one of the best. He and I spent …' He paused and thought a moment. 'We spent a lot of time together when I was here last time. Also, it turns out his village is close to our friend's here.' He nodded at Raju, but Raju was too busy digging into his stump with a spoon to take notice. 'There's the possibility he could take Raju back. So you can understand that we had a lot to talk about.'

It struck her what John didn't tell her. 'Would Raju want to go back?'

'I'll have to pick a time to ask him, but it wouldn't surprise me if he didn't.'

The rice dish and tea came.

'Next time you're late, if you call the school and leave a message, I will make sure Raju gets back to his room.'

'Great. Thanks.'

They sipped their tea while Raju, who normally ate like he hadn't seen food in a week, just picked at his meal.

'Raju, okay?' John asked him.

He nodded slowly.

'You mentioned a second reason.'

'I know where I can buy a second-hand computer for a very cheap price. Do you think Raju is ready for one?'

'Does the village he comes from have a reliable electricity supply?'

John smiled. 'Ah. Good point. No, it doesn't. But the dormitory does. So do you recommend a computer now, or do we wait a while?'

'You are more qualified than I am to answer that.'

'There is also the issue of his school teacher. My qualified opinion is that even without a computer, Raju would refuse to return to what's left of his village. Do you know that I'm actually speaking a bit of English with him? He loves it.'

'I am pleased. It is good practice for him.' She sipped her tea, making a point of looking at her watch.

He bent his head to hers. 'Can I ask you a personal question?' He didn't wait for an answer. 'Would you consider going out with me … um, some night – one that's convenient for you? Maybe here or to another cafe or the night market or just take a walk along the river?'

She'd relaxed and was enjoying the past few minutes, until now. She drew back, that familiar anxiety moving through her, knowing – despite Raju's presence – that she couldn't postpone revealing her full Mae Sot self any longer. The situation would only get worse. 'There are things you do not know about me. Things no one at the school or even in my family know. So I need to trust what I am going to say to you now will be kept secret.'

'Yeah, sure.' To her surprise he appeared little interested. 'How much time do we have left?' he asked.

'Six minutes. What I need to say will not take long.'

'Raju looks to have lost his appetite.' He hopped up, dropped money on the table. 'C'mon, you two. We should just have enough time to do this.'

'Do what?' she asked, collecting her wraparounds.

He took her hand and led her outside, Raju hanging back to wave good-bye to the elephant.

* * *

John turned off the ignition, and as Raju – seated between them – watched people passing by, he and Mya stared across the road to where the Snake Skin once stood.

'So you know,' she said finally, surprised and embarrassed: her secret known, her teacher's job threatened.

'Not at first. But when I described you recently to brother Nick, he suspected and suggested I check out your left arm for scars.' He glanced down at that arm. 'Evidence of a landmine explosion, I believe.'

Two automatic glass doors over there, one leading into a 7-11 store, the other into a western-style clothes shop, like something normally seen in Yangon, not Mae Sot – or at least the Mae Sot she thought she knew. 'I was told once that Thailand has over a quarter of a million monks and twice as many prostitutes. I do not know why remembering that makes me feel better about myself.' Why she said that she didn't know; maybe no reason, just thoughts escaping as words, or maybe as a simple acknowledgement – to herself as well as him – of what she had been. For clearly now she would need to make him understand the effect public disclosure would have on her life.

'Nick's talked a lot about you,' John said.

That wasn't the response she expected. She fixed her gaze on him.

'The girl he slept with in the mountains.' He almost smiled. 'And more to the point, the girl whose brother was killed in a protest march, who used a brick to dissuade a policeman from beating a construction worker to death, and who, disguised as a novice nun, was apprehended and sold first to the Burmese military then later to the Snake Skin, which, as you can see, no longer exists.'

Something in her warmed to him; his desire to please maybe, the thoughtful, gentle way he disclosed what he knew about her. The obvious compassion. 'Your brother was good to me, helpful, protective, but also foolish in following me into Myanmar.' She felt she knew John well enough now to say, 'Like big brother, like little brother, I believe.'

'Yeah, well … I did find myself over there on one or two occasions. Got some skin taken off me whenever I got a bit silly.'

She'd learned that too about Australians at the Snake Skin, their knack for understatement ('No dramas'), not taking themselves or their friends or even life itself too seriously ('Stop big-noting yourself, ya great galah', whatever a great galah was). Humility of a sort, she thought. 'To be a doctor, you must come from a very caring, protective family.'

'Mum's both those. Scratch your hand and she wants to ring up an ambulance. She's a teacher too; teaches the same age group you do. Dad's more a loner, protective from a distance, I s'pose you could say.'

Business was picking up across the road, people almost bumping into each other going in and out of the shops.

'How long has the Snake Skin been gone?'

'About a year apparently. Rumour has it there's now a Snake Skin in Chiang Mai.'

'If I had not escaped,' she muttered, as much to herself as him, 'I would be up there now or … somewhere worse.'

'Instead of studying in a nunnery then moving on to become a teacher. I reckon you'd know more about the best and worst in people than anybody I know.'

'My father used to say, "The best people deserve reverence, the worst defiance."'

'A wise man.'

'That was just before he and my brother joined a big protest march. The problem in Myanmar is some of the worst people are the ruling generals. If you show defiance and are caught, you are sent to prison.'

'As your father was.'

'Yes. Although he is not a prisoner anymore … Not a lot of things anymore, except in his memory.'

'To have lived through what you have and not gone stark-staring mad is a tribute to your mental strength and courage; to your Buddhist character as well, I reckon.'

'Tribute' had to mean something like 'compliment'. 'Mad' had two meanings. One was 'crazy'. She thought of that other Burmese bar-girl at the Snake Skin who had told her about losing *khwan*. 'What is so different now is to wake up every morning and feel joy at starting a new day. It is like stepping out of a nightmare into a dream.'

'A dream shared by your students from what I've seen.'

She smiled, welcoming the compliment, even though it sounded a little overstated. There was still her vanity to account for, she thought.

'I think you have only seen the good times in my class and not the bad ones.'

'Maybe. But I reckon there wouldn't be many bad ones. If I were a writer, Mya, I'd want to write your biography, sell it to the world.'

Her face lost expression. 'I could lose my teaching job if people find out what I did at the Snake Skin.'

'Yeah, well, I'm not a writer, so there'll be nothing to learn from me. Not here anyway.'

'Promise?'

'Promise.' He gave her a smile, and it struck Mya how often he did that. *Try each day to smile. It is good medicine.* John had enough medicine stored up to start his own pharmacy.

John went on. 'Got to admit, a degree of self-interest comes into play here. With no Mya Paw Wah at the school, I reckon Raju would refuse to go. Besides, what does Buddhism say about incarnations and the passing of time? Live in the moment is one thing.' He chuckled at what came into his head next. 'Back home there's a plaque above my grandfather's fireplace that reads, "Let's think about tomorrow tomorrow." Love it. Though it wouldn't surprise anyone to learn he's not a Buddhist … So what's another saying about time?'

To the windscreen she said, 'The past is quietly gone, the present flies like an arrow, the future slowly draws near then suddenly slips past.'

'From your Tripitaka?'

She eyed this man of surprises like he'd just sprouted wings. 'Yes.'

'Nick mentioned you carried one … Anyway, I like the idea of the past being quietly gone, though certain memories can be hard to part with sometimes.'

The way the windscreen held his gaze made her think he'd learned that first-hand too.

Raju shifted his prosthetic leg and gave a little yelp.

Startled, John bent over, pointed to the leg and asked. 'Hurt?'

'Hurt,' Raju admitted.

'The first English word he learned, I reckon.' He checked Raju's eyes then placed the palm of his hand on his forehead. 'On the warm side. I better take a look.' A foul odour filled the cab as John unstrapped the prosthetic leg, took it off and shifted Raju's stump towards him for a better view.

'Ouch! Inflamed and infected. I should have noticed earlier. Tissue necrosis can develop from infections like this one.'

She remembered Nick using that word by the river one day. 'Like from a snakebite?'

'Yeah.' He gave her a curious look. 'You and Nick obviously talked a bit.'

'We did.'

Had Raju not been in pain, he might have pushed the conversation along. As it was he nodded at Raju. 'Can you ask him how long his stump has been like this?'

She put an arm around Raju and asked. 'Five or six days,' she told John.

'Yes, I heard.' John started the ute, beeped the horn and swung out into the traffic. 'Will you be right to bike from the medical clinic to Myawadi?' he asked.

'I reckon.'

He smiled, but only briefly, taking notice of a motor scooter that had pulled out with him and was following close behind.

* * *

In Myawadi that night Mya found the words 'inevitable' and 'dwell'. She wrote:

> Inevitable
> My bar girl past revealed,
> I dwell on my cave.

The next morning she dwelled on John and Raju; for the first time since living weekends in Myawadi, she was anxious to get back to Mae Sot.

31

MYAWADI.

Sunday morning on the balcony. Shutters flung open. The sounds of the neighbourhood around them. Motor scooters. Someone hammering. Boys kicking a soccer ball on the road below.

Mya stepped away from the railing and explained why she wanted to leave early. Her uncle and aunt nodded, while Nyan said, 'I wish I could go with you to see your amputee student, watch you work, help you cook Mohinga over there. But I think you already know that.'

According to Thiri, her father was best when she was there, but was okay when she wasn't, that he didn't need her to be there to look after him. Still, she always felt a little guilty leaving him. 'I do,' she answered.

There were times when she wondered if it would be better to confess her Snake Skin past, that she should hide nothing from him, that he would understand. But often he seemed slow, dazed, drained of *khwan*; the legacy of prison-life and the deaths of her mother and Thant affecting all he did. Who she was – or at least who he thought she was and had been since the massacre – seemed to go some way, at least, towards balancing the hurt inside him. Confessing might tip that balance the wrong way.

* * *

MAE SOT.

After crossing the Friendship Bridge Mya went straight to the Mae Tao Medical Clinic. John was sitting on the end of Raju's bed, Raju's freshly-bandaged stump exposed above the sheet, his face lighting up at the sight of her. She sat across from John, pointed and asked Raju in Karen and English, 'Still hurt?'

He nodded slowly, as if unsure whether to admit it or not.

She turned to John, the one person in the region she could be totally honest with now, and asked, 'Good weekend?'

'Quiet.'

She looked around the crowded ward, her eyes lingering on two other amputees, before returning her gaze to John. 'You spent most of it here, I ... reckon.'

Not surprisingly, a smile. 'Keep using words like that and Australian English will be the next language you'll be teaching, I reckon.'

'Said the Buddha: learn first, teach later.'

'Like your father, a knowledgeable bloke.'

That touched her, prompting a warm glow. 'If I ever do teach it, I will owe my Australian language education to you and your brother.' She gave him a little bow. 'So thank you.' In a past life there were of course other far-less compassionate Australians she had learned from too.

'What are you doing for lunch?'

'Today?'

'Today.'

She shrugged her shoulders and deferred answering, looking at Raju instead. 'What is happening with him?'

'Three treatment options. We're trying the first one now: a five-day course of antibiotics. If that fails there is traditional larval therapy to consider.' He stopped, expecting a question, but didn't get one. 'Not something widely practised in western countries. Should be, I reckon. The use of maggots to clean an infection can be very effective, though I'll not be advocating the practice on any exam paper back home.'

'Or the third option?'

'More amputation. Hopefully minimal.'

'So a week before we know?'

'About that.'

Raju answered, 'Lots,' to her question, in Karen, about how much schoolwork he'd like her to bring in.

'Good.' She told Raju what a fine student he was, then exchanged a look with John. The three of them, drawing closer. Or so it seemed. She had what remained of her family. She had work friends. But no non-family male in her life, particularly one she felt drawn to. So she wondered if she was reading John right. That in his eyes she was more than just Raju's teacher, just a friend with a secret in his care. Or was her inexperience playing tricks on her? She recalled his brother Nick saying something about Lina, the nurse at the clinic who John was close to, or had been. But she was obviously somewhere else, and there didn't seem to be any evidence of that relationship now. So the answer, she supposed, was to push past her awkwardness and go along with whatever was drawing them together. See what happened. Determine her feelings as they went along. Though of course their closeness would only be temporary, wouldn't it? He was returning to Australia soon.

'About today,' John reminded her.

'Today I am going to organise schoolwork for Raju.'

'Ahh … right.'

Feeling emboldened, she added, 'But what are you doing tonight?'

His face brightened. 'Tonight?'

'Yes, tonight.'

'Thought I might go out for a five-course banquet, maybe in town somewhere, or to the Casa Mia.'

Despite the Snake Skin being gone, Mya still felt uncomfortable about going into the centre of town. 'What if I meet you at a quiet Casa Mia table at six o'clock?' She paused before adding, 'My shout' – her smile a private one.

* * *

In his room singing the Van-man's 'Queen of the Slipstream', John showered, shaved and got dressed. With half an hour still to kill came decision-time: another Van-man download, a drink with the first end-of-day beer hunters and gatherers in the courtyard, or an over-due look at his emails. Get the quickest over first, he thought: go the emails. After that a download then a beer and finally extended time with Mya Paw Wah, lady of substance, intelligence, soft smile, soft voice, soft looks.

He fired up his laptop, scanned his inbox and abruptly stop singing. Three emails, one sender very familiar to him:

Gobsmacked, he brought up the email.

John,

'Time is a healer and routine makes good bandages' I read in my novel when I got a moment to myself last night. Maybe that idea has encouraged me to contact you.

A mountain of bandages here at the Zaatari Refugee Camp, Northern Jordan. But with over half a million Syrian refugees in the country, about 130,000 of them here with us and our inflatable tent hospital, future bandage shortages are a distinct possibility.

But off bandages and to the 'why' of this email. I'll keep it short. Yes, I've thought a lot about our last night and how we parted, and the horrors of the Syrian conflict haven't deadened my missing-you-ache. And yes, I'll under-stand if you decide not to answer this email. But what I DON'T want is a reply filled with obligation and mock politeness.

Never thought I'd get to the point of saying 'aid work sucks'. But that's where I'm at now. No place for a moaner here, so it's a good thing I'm coming to the end of my contracted time with Save the Children. Obviously need a break. I leave for home in a week's time and am having a three-night stopover in Bangkok where I plan to walk the streets (though not to earn money), brave the traffic, eat market stall curries and take cruises up and down the Chao Praya River to try to get the worst of the past year out of me. If you would like to meet for an obligation-free Bangkok break, or for any other genuine reason, then I'd be very interested in getting a reply from you in the next few days.

Just Lina

He read the email again, recalling that last night in Maroochy-dore on Queensland's Sunshine Coast. *Final night of their three-night stay. Candle-lit beachside table. Sound of small waves. Paradise really. Yet Lina was strangely subdued, like a part of her was somewhere else. Meals finished, last sips of their wine. She scanned the beach, crumpled her serviette. Then, starting in mid-sentence (had he missed its start?), came the shock: 'That's the thing about aid work, isn't it? It's so all-consuming it can push everything else out of your life.' She looked over the table at him. 'What I feel for you, John, I've never ever felt for anyone else. But tomorrow we head off in very different directions. So I think ...' She glanced down at her lap then at him again, eyes glistening. 'I think we should end it.' Her voice quickened like she had just seconds before losing it. 'The demands that will be on us, the huge distance between us, just won't be suited for maintaining a relationship like ours, and what I absolutely don't want is to go through the slow torture of a dying six-thousand-kilometre relationship poisoning the memories of what we've had.' There, she'd said it, her look seemed to say, before she lowered her eyes, toyed with her crumpled serviette. It was like his heart and tongue had been cut out.*

He sat in front of his laptop now, staring. It was only in the past few weeks that he'd begun to let go.

* * *

First time ever Mya had been on what she'd overheard Snake Skin patrons call a 'date'. Her mind racing, both excited and a little scared, she was barely conscious of the traffic as she rode her bicycle to the Casa Mia. Her long braid swinging, her new white blouse and patterned blue-and-white longyi fluttering in the head breeze, she played out scenes of their corner table, of John and what they would eat and talk about. Halfway there she looked at her watch and started pedalling faster, not wanting to be even a minute late.

Only a couple of motor scooters and a four-wheel drive in the parking area. No AusAID logo ute. She perched her bike against a tree and waited, unsure whether to go in or not. More motor scooters arrived, two with local couples, another with a pair of westerners – aid workers most likely. She walked up the couple of steps and peered inside. The 'stress-reduction' table was occupied, along with four others. Thankfully the far corner table was empty, like it had been reserved for them. She turned and walked over to a low rock wall and sat down on it.

Ten minutes passed, the parking area growing shadowy in the twilight. She got up and wandered further down the laneway approaching a giant fig tree, its above-ground roots like a mass of twisted snakes. Under the tree, beside a scooter, a man squatted, shoulders hunched, a wrench in his hand. He glanced up, stopped what he was doing and stared at her.

She looked away, and as she passed he started singing 'Bad Romance'.

She walked faster, rounding a bend before realising there was nothing for her up ahead. She had no choice but to retrace her steps.

She turned back and as she passed by him again, he called out, 'Lady Gaga.' He spoke in Thai, words she didn't understand, before saying, 'Where you be? Mae Sot want you. I want you. Be with me.'

She decided against just quietly walking on. She slowed and gave him her sternest 'drop dead' look, saying in English then Burmese, 'Good luck with what you're doing because you either need a blind man's stick or a new set of eyes.' Seconds later she added, 'No problem with your singing voice though.'

He laughed and shifted his attention back to his repair work.

Back in the parking area Mya grabbed her bike and was about to ride off when John drove in, screeched the brakes, parked quickly and ran over to her saying, 'I've done it again,' and apologising for his lateness.

'It's okay. No worries,' she replied, though there had been. She returned her bike to the tree.

'Second time I know. But I got … Anyway, I'll tell you about it inside.'

At 'their' table he ordered a stubby, she a mango juice. For a time they were silent, Mya monitoring the serious look on John's face that didn't disappear. As he sipped his beer she was struck by the thought that she hadn't shared a table with a man, a stubby in his hand, since the Snake Skin. Though that's where the comparison ended.

A stool scraped the floor.

She glanced around to see the man from the laneway sitting at the bar. She heard him order a beer.

'She worked for AusAid too …' John was saying.

Realising she'd missed something he said, she gave him her full attention.

'A couple of years ago back in Australia we broke up. Her idea. She was heading off to work for an aid group called Save the Children on the Syrian border, and didn't think our relationship would survive the experience. Why there I don't know. Just desert. About as alluring as a cow pat.' He sipped his beer. 'Anyway, I've just read an email from her. First contact since the breakup. She's heading home next week and is having a three-night stopover in Bangkok. She suggested we meet.'

That she liked and trusted him was a given. So too that if he asked she would go with him again to places around Mae Sot before he returned to Australia. But what he said wasn't a surprise. Nick had mentioned this girl, Lina. And this solved the dilemma of him for her. Theirs was a friendship, she was a part of his social life. And that was fine, she told herself. Wasn't it?

'So I'm thinking of flying to Bangkok to meet up with her.'

She smiled, pretending to be happier than she felt. 'Good.'

'Yeah, well … I'm not sure how it will go. Anyway, I need to ask you a favour.'

'The answer is yes.'

He watched her a moment. 'Whether or not Raju will need re-amputation will most likely be decided while I'm gone. You and I, we're who he responds to. So …'

'Easy. I will visit him every day except Saturday. I will need to collect and give him more schoolwork to do anyway, so no worries.'

'No worries, eh? … Thanks … I'm hungry. Let's order up big.'

The bar stool scraped again. She waited a few seconds before turning. The laneway man was leaving, his empty glass still on the bar. She wondered if he'd mentioned the name 'Lady Gaga' to the girl who had served him.

When the same serving girl came to their table to take their order, Mya watched her for some sign. But there was none, the girl business-like and friendly. After 'Lady Gaga', the word 'paranoia' entered her mind and stayed. Four syllables. Put 'My' in front of it and she'd have her first line for a haiku.

'Besides visiting Raju,' John interrupted her thoughts, 'have you got anything else planned for after school tomorrow?'

* * *

Back in his room, John fired up his laptop and went onto the Nok Air website. A daily two pm flight to Bangkok, seats available all the next week. He got into his email to send Lina a reply, but the name Nick Stanish, subject 'Thai-bound brother', stopped him.

He opened Nick's email.

Hi John –

Got room for me for a few days? Suprise I now. The bilding trade is on holidays until the end of the month – even the aprentises. Got in touch with that bloke I told you about – Broken Hill Jake. He's on holidays to for longer then me and is in Phnom Penh now. Were going to meet up in Chiang Mai in five days time. Ive bout a Jetstar round trip Bangkok tiket. I was thinking Id fly to Mae Sot to see if your copping alright without me there – then bus it to Chiang Mai. Plus it would be good to say hello to Mya again to. Cant beleve shes there doing what shes doing.

All that OK?

Nick

Besieged by the world outside, or at least that's what it felt like. Of course besieged was an exaggeration and the answer to both Lina and Nick was 'Yes.' But from there it got a bit complicated.

The next afternoon, as they sat on a concrete bench overlooking the river, John told Mya he was going to meet up with Nick, also in Bangkok, and they were coming back to Mae Sot together.

'Your brother and I have sat on this bench together too,' she confided. 'And we hid from border guards together.' She pointed. 'Just across the river – there. It will be good to see him again.'

If Lina didn't exist for him, he might have discouraged Nick from coming to Mae Sot and suggested that they could meet up in Chiang Mai instead. The thought of brotherly rivalry made him smile. As it was, he said to Mya, 'I can tell you right now it will be good for him too.'

32

Mya's routine loosened further. First time ever she had crossed the Friendship Bridge on a Saturday, or any day other than a Friday or Sunday. She didn't have to: Raju had enough schoolwork to keep him going into the next week. But John had left for Bangkok the day before and the thought of Raju being on his own for an extended period troubled her. Besides, the workshop had been extra busy the past week and there were lots of overdue bike repairs still to complete. No disguising the fact her father felt badly about leaving Uncle Zarni on his own to do the work. And it was obvious Uncle Zarni knew that too. 'No, no, you go to the river with Mya,' she heard him say to Nyan twice. 'Sit and relax and enjoy the view. Don't worry about me and all the work to be done here.'

At the Snake Skin she'd heard westerners use the term 'guilt trip'. A term that Uncle Zarni obviously knew about too. Still, there were positives in her uncle's growing reliance on Nyan to handle the bulk of the mechanical work while he concentrated on 'sales and administration'. It kept her father focused on fixing things, and it seemed that things inside him were slowly being fixed too. His skills were needed and appreciated, like hers were in Mae Sot. Clients warmed to him, Thiri had told her, and sought him out for advice. Since Nyan had started working there, business had never been better.

Ever so gradually he was pulling himself back into the present, probably accepting that confinement could linger in a person's mind and eyes long after they were released from prison. He started walking in his free time, along village tracks to temples, back to tea shops and the market. He started sleeping indoors. He talked more, though never about the political changes taking place. They were saving money. They'd started discussing a shared future. Though on which side of the Moei River that would eventually occur remained undecided.

Entering the children's ward, Mya saw that Raju was sleeping. She sat on the edge of his bed and tested his cheek and forehead with the back of her hand. He was hot. She looked around at parents sitting on beds and at the play area at the back filled with balls, balloons, a mini-slide and climbing bars. She noticed a black laptop peeking out from under the small pillow next to Raju. John had obviously bought it for him, and perhaps Raju – wise to the practices of refugee camp thieves – was trying to hide it. She lifted the pillow. To her surprise, there were two more laptops – three in all – each with extension cords and a mouse. A note with her name on it was taped to the top one.

Mya –

Best not to ask too much about these. Let's just say three for the price of a very cheap one. And one of them is yours. Back home there's a saying about such things falling off the back of a truck. If these did, they had a very soft landing. Two use English, the other Burmese. I'll let you determine which is which. Also, they are server and email-connected. If you fire up an English one, I'll guarantee there will be at least one email from Bangkok, written in my very best grade two English. Don't want to impose on your lesson plans for Raju, but thought if he was up to it, you could translate the email into Burmese and he could write a reply that you could translate and send in English.

Could be a Casa Mia meal in it for the both of you when I get back.

On a different note, last word I got on Raju's infection was that it started with a split in his stump, caused by an overly-tight prosthetic leg. Not days, more like weeks ago, and that it became infected and the infection has spread. It would have been painful for him. Treatment options you know about.

You two are in the front row of my thoughts.

See you soon,

Mister John (John to you)

She folded the note and put it in her shoulder bag and sat there, Raju's flat cheeks and long lashes twitching occasionally. Not unlike sitting by the river or on her rock shelf high above Moulmein, she thought, before she became aware of someone standing behind her. She turned and looked into the face of a man, everything about him an extra degree of darkness: eyes like small dark stones; ink tattoos, sun-exposed skin; lank, shoulder-length black hair. He carried a black shoulder bag and wore loose-fitting khaki trousers and a black t-shirt inscribed with an animal resembling a giant red rat, above it a name in red: TASSIE DEVIL. She'd forgotten his name, but remembered what he did – the backpack medic. John had told her about him.

'Sleeping,' he said in Karen.

'Yes, and still hot,' she answered in Burmese, testing his language range. 'It seems the infection is acute and hasn't improved.'

He broke into Burmese. 'The antibiotics probably need a few more days to be effective. You are Mya Paw Wah?'

'I am. I believe we share a friend.'

'Mister John.'

She gave a nod. 'And you are a backpack medic whose name I've forgotten, but whose reputation I haven't.'

His smile formed creases around his eyes. 'Phoe Ni.' He extended a rough hand and she shook it. From his bag he took out a pocket-size game board and a small box that rattled of small pieces inside. 'Do you play chess?'

'My father tried to teach me when I was little, but not very successfully.'

He asked if she was planning to stay a while and she said she was.

He placed the board and the box on the floor by the side of the bed. 'I'm at the clinic for a couple of days before returning to Karen State. Mister John asked if I'd check on the boy. I have and it seems he's in good company. I'll come back later and if he's awake and willing, I'll give him his first lesson.'

'May I watch?'

He smiled again, showing his teeth – neither decayed black nor betel reddened as with many villagers, but intact and looking service-able well into his old age. 'You'd be most welcome to.' He looked at the pillow, recognising some of what lay under it. 'Or maybe we can make an arrangement. I'll teach you chess and you teach me about computers.'

'With Raju between us?'

'Good for everyone then.'

Supposedly, backpack medics came across the border every six months or so to stock up and rest, before returning to their villages in Karen State.

He smiled, stepped back and said, 'It's been good to meet you. You'll be here when I get back, yes?'

'Maybe.' And with that he left as quietly as he came.

Minutes passed. She began to look for a power outlet along the wall and found one with an unused extension plugged into it. Perfect for a computer.

Raju opened his eyes, watched her a few moments, then went to sleep again.

She took out her pen and pad and wrote:

As he lies here –
Young orphan amputee –
Sleeping, waking briefly,
Infection hot,
Tender with pain.
Does he ever ask,
'What future for me
After the care,
The comfort
Of this clinic ward bed?'

Phoe Ni returned and sat down next to her. In between talk of everyday things, he gave her a chess lesson and got a computer game lesson in return.

33

Sunday morning and no other visitors in the ward but Mya, until Phoe Ni came in, a female western medical student trailing behind him.

He set a small sandalwood box down on Raju's bed, took off the lid and showed Mya the squirming contents. 'I believe they're called maggots in English,' he said.

Mya didn't look for long, though the medical student standing beside her did.

'Like hairless, white caterpillars,' the student commented, her anticipation showing.

Phoe Ni: 'Hungry ones.'

'Maggot therapy isn't a feature of the medicine course at Flinders University.'

Phoe Ni looked questioningly at Mya and she translated for him, though she knew he spoke some English and probably understood.

Phoe Ni looked at Raju and spoke softly to him. 'You've seen maggots used before, haven't you?'

'Yes.'

'Is it okay if I use a few to try to get rid of the infection in your stump?'

Raju drew a deep breath, eyeing the roof. 'Yes.'

Phoe Ni uncovered Raju's legs and took the pressure bandage off Raju's stump, undeterred by the strengthening odour. 'The treatment is used in Karen villages when there are no antibiotics available,' he said, 'or when the antibiotics are not working well. Maggots are collected, fed and raised especially to treat infection. So they are always available and familiar to villagers. They will not eat live tissue, only dead tissue.'

Bandage off, Phoe Ni used a damp towel to moisten the wound. 'Can you recognise the dead tissue?' Phoe Ni asked the student through Mya.

'Yes.'

He handed her a pair of forceps. 'Would you like to place the maggots where they should go?'

'I would, yes.' She could be placing rich jewels in the wound, Mya thought, and her look could not have been more eager.

'A lecturer's position for you soon at the University of Yangon's Medical School?' Mya asked Phoe Ni, teasingly.

'As a Karen infiltrator. I'll hire you as my guide, personal secretary and bodyguard.'

'Sorry. By order of MI, Mya Paw Wah is never to set foot in Yangon again.'

'Ah, yes. I have heard about that.'

'John?'

He nodded. 'But there are always lecturing opportunities in this clinic and on the street corners in Myawadi.'

She smiled, enjoying the banter. 'It must be satisfying to have such maggot skills. Won't you tell us more about the therapy?' She almost called him 'doctor'. Which, in a sense, he was, at least for those living in and around his village in Karen State.

He sniffed the air at a higher level and cleared his throat. 'Pay attention now and I will,' he said.

As the medical student lifted each maggot out of the box and placed it on a portion of inflamed, pus-yellow flesh, Phoe Ni continued to inform, while also nodding his approval of the student's work. 'The maggots are in the wound to clean, not heal it. Their saliva has antibiotic qualities and often maggots can clean wounds more effectively than anything else, except surgery. But surgery is expensive.' From a cloth bag he brought out a white, finely-meshed device the size, shape and rigidity of a small, plastic rubbish bin. 'The wound's dressing. Once all the maggots are in place, this is placed loosely over the stump. Not only must the wound be kept moist, it must also have a consistent supply of oxygen.'

After a final look at where the maggots were squirming and burrowing further in, Phoe Ni fitted the dressing over Raju's stump and fastened it with surgical tape. 'In two days, when they've grown to about five times their original size and cannot eat any more, the maggots will be useless. So they and the dressing must be changed. Depending on the extent of the infection, maggot therapy can go on for a couple of weeks.'

'And if the therapy isn't successful after that time?' the medical student asked.

A question Mya knew the answer to. Phoe Ni spoke quietly so Raju didn't hear, 'After finding the money from somewhere – re-amputation.' He turned to Raju and asked in a bright voice, 'Okay?'

'Okay.'

'Your choice. Do we play chess or set up the computers?'

An hour later, Phoe Ni mentioned he had a borrowed motor scooter out front. He asked Mya if she'd like to go to the Friendship Bridge food stalls with him and buy some lunch.

* * *

Sitting on the concrete bench, she thought if the river had ears and a memory, she could talk to it about the times she'd been beside it, on it, even in it: as Mya the hostage, as Lady Gaga, as Nan Pau in her final days, and now as Mya again, the teacher and translator. And as her life had improved, so too had the men she shared the river with: Nick, her father, John, and soon Phoe Ni, once he returned from packing his backpack. Lunch had been good and had lasted much longer than she'd expected. He'd told her he was returning to Myanmar that night, and that maybe they could just sit and talk a while before nightfall. Sunday, so that suited her.

She watched, knowing the river well enough to account for its obstacles, its moods – from sluggish to dangerous – and its subtle changes in colour. Now the colour of light tea, it moved steadily, twisting into whorls around the uprooted trees, but high enough to cover anything else. Still navigable, but only by outboard-powered long boat, like the one making the crossing now.

'Welcome back.'

The shock, like a conscious nightmare. She knew the voice, as she'd known Aung Min's in Moulmein. But how Billy J could suddenly materialise next to her made her question her faculties. She recoiled, scooting out of grabbing range, watching him. He seemed reduced, face slackened and yellow-tinged, eyes glassy and red.

'You good?'

'Yes.' She worked to settle herself down. 'You?'

His smile hadn't changed, though his teeth had, confirming her suspicion: he wasn't just dealing in drugs but using as well.

'Billy J always good, teacher. Always good.'

Teacher. He knew what she did, so had to know where she worked. Knowledge he would obviously use to his advantage. 'What do you want?' she asked, part of her there, part of her entering the principal's office, a resignation form in her hand.

Behind Billy J, Phoe Ni was approaching.

'For you.' He handed her a business card. 'New Snake Skin in Chiang Mai now. Boss want you come back. All you do forgot. Free meals and accommodation. Monday night off. Work seven to twelve. Ten thousand baht a week to start – no upstairs duties. Unless you want.' He grinned, then said, 'Much more money as Lady Gaga than teacher. You call Boss in five day, or I come see you and go your school. Any questions?'

She thought of saying, 'My name is Mya Paw Wah, not teacher, not Lady Gaga. Better you know that for when you return and go to my school.' She didn't, saying instead, 'No – no questions, Billy J,' as in times past, but then said, 'You can tell The Boss I won't be contacting him. Not today. Not ever.' At least once the school found out, she'd still have her translation job, though it was only ever for a few hours a week. The Karen-Burmese welfare groups were interested in her language skills, not her history.

Billy J glared his hard-eyed look, but before he could say anything, Phoe Ni stopped next to them, gave an actor's smile and said, 'Hello.'

Billy J's eyes slid sideways, a grimace of irritation on his face.

In that time, Mya thought of an idea. Sensing her advantage, she spoke in Burmese, telling Phoe Ni to pretend he was the person she was going to introduce him as, that she would explain later. 'Phoe Ni, this is Billy J,' she said in English. 'He was my boss when I worked as a bar-girl at the Snake Skin here in Mae Sot. Billy J, Phoe Ni is the Director of the Burmese Migrant School I work for. One of his duties is to hire and dismiss teachers. So you can save yourself another trip back here by saying what you wish to him now.' She wasn't sure how much Billy J understood, but judging from his scowl, it appeared to be enough.

Phoe Ni's toothy smile wasn't entirely forced, Mya thought, as he extended both his hands, clasped on to Billy J's right one and gave it a near-violent shake. 'I am very pleased to meet you, Billy J,' he said, as though reading from a play script. 'Mya friend my friend. Ha, ha, ha. What is it you want to say to me?'

Billy J stood, looking disgusted, and Mya asked him, 'Any questions, Billy J?'

He turned and left, fuming.

As they watched him head towards the main road, Mya mentioned to Phoe Ni what Billy J wanted, and what he was prepared to do to get her to Chiang Mai. She asked, 'Before now, did you know I once worked at the Snake Skin in Mae Sot?'

He shook his head. 'I assume it's what westerners call a nightclub.'

'Yes. And I was called Lady Gaga.'

'I've heard the name.'

'And I performed her songs and did all the things bar-girls do.'

'Burmese girl working in a Thai nightclub. Not something usually done voluntarily. Tell me about it.'

She told him over a meal at a Friendship Bridge food stall, after which Phoe Ni insisted on dropping Mya off. Outside her room, he asked, 'Another meal when I return to Mae Sot?'

She said she would like that.

34

There were times when the school principal reminded Mya of her abbess. About the same age, both were the heart and brains of the institutions they ran, their compassion unending for those in their keeping; their small offices both had books and lists tossed around everywhere, but unlike the abbess, the principal had a computer as a feature on her desk. She also taught the grade sixes for an hour each day and was a solitary watcher and walker around the school during breaks and lunchtime. When she did sit down, it was for the purpose of talking to a student. And not once could Mya recall seeing a student walk away from such a talk looking grim or upset. No doubt that stemmed from how the principal ended the talk. Whether the student was in kindergarten or grade six, the principal insisted on shaking the student's hand as a final gesture of appreciation or congratulations, or that an agreement had been struck between them.

Australians used the term 'up-front', and the principal was. For that reason Mya always felt uncomfortable, something of a fraud, hiding her past. When she'd got the job, yes, an agreement handshake had taken place. But out of self-interest, talk went back no further than her time at the nunnery. Her choice: a job as opposed to the possibility – strong now – of her Snake Skin past lowering the school's image.

The thing was, Burmese migrant organisations didn't need any more negative publicity. They were already the focus of strong Thai resentment, with many Thais advocating the sending of all Burmese 'illegals' back to Burma. Though for Thai plantation owners it was all in the timing. They objected to the 'illegals' being sent back until a few days before they were due to pay their Burmese workers for their six months of daily harvesting work. Then the owners contacted the police saying they were unaware until now that their workers were 'illegals'. Such a scam. Money changed hands, yes, but only between the owners and the police before the police drove their loaded vans away and the owners went back into their big houses to arrange for the delivery of more Burmese 'illegals' for a period of slightly less than six months.

Anyway, whether Billy J believed Phoe Ni was the director of the migrant school or not, his threat only pushed Mya into doing something she'd been thinking about doing for a long time. First thing before school on Monday morning she went to see the principal. She was asked to sit down, and as she wanted to get the explanation over with quickly, she got straight to the point. 'I need to tell you that in the next week or two you might be contacted by a person telling you that I worked as a bar-girl at a night club here called the Snake Skin before it moved to Chiang Mai.'

The principal displayed no visible emotion, which surprised Mya. 'Do you know who the contacting person might be?'

'Billy J works for the Snake Skin. He might be the one to contact you. Or the owner of the Snake Skin might do it. Though I worked for him, I don't know his name.'

'And let me guess why they might be doing this. They obviously want to punish you for something. Would it be that they want you back as a bar-girl and you've refused?'

It was like Mya had been emptied of breath. She nodded.

'And they think the stigma of one of our teachers having been a bar-girl in the past will tarnish our reputation to such an extent that it will create an uproar amongst our students' parents. Am I right?'

'Yes.'

The principal frowned. 'Just shows how ignorant they are of our parents. As I've heard westerners say when challenged, "Bring it on." And if they do, this is what will happen. Firstly, I will inform the person I am fully aware of your bar-girl history, and exactly how it came about. You probably need to know, Mya, that your abbess in Moulmein and I have known each other for a very long time. That we are probably much closer than you realise.

'Secondly, if the person threatens to contact parents, which I'm certain would be the emptiest of threats, I'll tell him to please do so. I'll also mention that our Burmese migrant parents are well-acquainted with people trafficking and Thai exploitation of Burmese migrant workers, as many of them have been, and continue to be, exploited. I'll remind him of the time you spent in a nunnery and on retreat, which second only to dedicating one's entire life to the Buddha, brings great esteem to the participant.

'Thirdly, if the person is still listening, I'll tell him that playing Lady Gaga must do wonders for a girl's teaching potential because you're an outstanding teacher, the staff and parents know it, and in a few weeks' time the school will be offering you additional teaching hours for next year. There are a few other things I could say to the person as well, but in my position it would be best not to show my aggressive streak. So … are there any other issues you wish to discuss?'

Mya didn't know whether to laugh or cry. 'No.'

'Good. Because there's something I want to talk to you about.' She glanced at her watch. 'We have a few minutes. Tell me, how is Raju getting along at the medical clinic?'

Five minutes later Mya walked out of the principal's office feeling like a person cured of cancer.

* * *

Mya had got a message at school that John and Nick were back and would meet her at the clinic. What a good day it was turning out to be, her happiness at what had unexpectedly occurred in the principal's office augmented by that message and the prospect of seeing them both.

Raju was asleep when she arrived. Sitting on his bed, she watched as John and Nick approached, Nick trailing behind. John looked around and slowed, allowing Nick to catch up, and she saw them exchange a few words. Nick held up a white crinkly bag he was carrying.

When they spotted Mya, she clapped her hands and smiled brightly. 'Hello, hello,' she greeted them, standing. Her eyes stayed fastened on Nick, searching for the changes in him. His hair was longer. He had filled out and had three or four days of whisker growth: looking more the man now than a boy pretending to be one.

John spoke. 'Raju's starting to stir … How's he been?'

Mya sat again and told them about Phoe Ni's use of the maggots. Then she placed a hand on Raju's forehead, on one cheek then the other, while he watched her, staying perfectly still. 'You're not so hot today, are you?'

'No. I – am – good.'

'Raju, this is my young brother, Nick,' John said in Karen. 'He's visiting Mae Sot for a couple of days and he's brought you something from Tasmania, Australia.'

Nick leaned forward and put the crinkly bag beside Raju. 'For you,' he said in English.

'Thank – you.'

'Yeah, you're welcome.'

'You know where Australia is, don't you, Raju?' Mya asked, reverting to Karen.

'Bottom of the world.'

Mya took out a blue shirt from the bag and held it up in front of her. It was far too small for her, so obviously was meant for Raju. She passed it to him.

John pointed to a word on the shirt and said it slowly: 'Tas-ma-ni-a.'

Raju tried saying it and after he did, the three of them chorused, 'Good, good.'

Then John pointed to the animal, like a huge, black rat, below the word. He looked at Mya and asked her to explain it to Raju. She said, 'This is called a Tasmanian Devil, Raju. It's ferocious and eats other small animals. Tasmania is an island that belongs to the country of Australia, and the Tasmanian Devil only lives on that island.'

'Oh,' said Raju, looking perplexed. At the migrant school Mya had used a big map on the front wall to show everyone where Thailand and Myanmar were in the world, and also where Australia was, because some people there gave money so more school rooms could be built. Mya made a mental note to point out Tasmania on the map when Raju got back to school.

John turned to Raju and said in Karen, 'I want to look at your leg, okay?'

Raju smiled, replying, 'Okay.'

John pulled the sheet down, ripped the tape off the stump – which didn't hurt Raju because that part of his stump was numb – then took off the bandage. Nick looked like he was about to throw up.

Mya took this opportunity to take two strange furry animals out of the crinkly bag. 'These must be for you, Raju,' she said.

One was grey and was a sort of bird. The other looked like nothing Mya had ever seen before. It was brown and had little arms and giant back legs and a long, long tail. 'Animals from Australia,' she said to Raju in Karen, and then in English she asked Nick, 'What are they?'

As she pointed to the grey animal, Nick said 'Kook-a-burra' for one, and 'Kang-a-roo' for the other. Then Nick said the names very slowly again, and Raju tried saying them, and the three of them sang out again, 'Good, good,' like nothing he could ever say would be bad, bad.

Then John started singing a song called 'Skippy the bush kangaroo'.

'Skippy is the name of your kangaroo, Raju,' he said, everyone in the ward watching now. 'You can practise singing that to him. There's a song for your kookaburra too. It goes like this.' After singing the kookaburra song, John made a strange shrieking sound that made everyone laugh.

'We'll give your kookaburra a name too, and you can bring them both to school once you leave here,' Mya told Raju. 'And we'll practise their names and think of stories we can write using English words about where they live and what they eat.'

'Thank – you, Neek.'

'You're welcome.' Nick fixed his eyes back on Mya and when she looked over and caught him in mid-stare, he said, 'I … uh, was just admiring your dress. What's it called again?'

'A longyi.'

'Yeah, that. Can't remember you wearing one last time I was in Mae Sot.'

'No. There were reasons for that.'

'Yeah – course there were. It's beautiful. Lime green suits you. Your blouse is a beauty too.'

An improvement on what you've seen me wear in the past, she thought. But saying that might embarrass him, especially in the company of his brother, so aloud she just thanked him.

They watched Raju arrange his animals next to the laptops and chess set by his side.

'Leg's looking good,' John said. He pulled a couple of maggots out and dropped them in a jar, saying to Mya, 'You can tell him the maggots have done their job. They're fat and need replacing. But there's hardly anything for the replacements to eat. A couple more days, I reckon, and Raju'll be back in the classroom.'

Mya leaned close to Raju and repeated John's last sentence to him.

'Good, good,' Raju replied. This time only he said it.

* * *

On leaving the clinic with John and Nick, Mya felt there was a lot for them to talk about: their girlfriends, Bangkok, and how much longer John would be in Mae Sot before returning to his university studies in Australia. Plus she knew Nick would only be in Mae Sot for two days. He was due to meet his friend in Chiang Mai, so she wanted to spend as much time with him as possible.

She suggested the Casa Mia before John had a chance to, and in ten minutes they were there, seated at 'their' table. It had felt good sitting between the two of them in the AusAID ute, and again at the restaurant. Two Australian brothers she really liked and trusted: John smiling; Nick quiet but bright-eyed, appearing happy to be there too.

The brothers ordered stubbies, she a mango juice. They delayed ordering food. Their drinks came. They sampled them, no one saying anything. Finally, looking at Nick, Mya said, 'Talk.'

He smiled. 'What about?'

'How you are going to get back into Thailand.' They laughed. 'And you got back, didn't you?'

'Yeah. A bit easier this time around with the help of a visa.'

'I told you it would be.'

'I think I remember every word.'

'And you are a carpenter now in Tasmania and your girlfriend is still studying, yes?'

'I'm an apprentice carpenter, meaning I'm still training for another eighteen months to be one. And Annie's ... not around anymore. She turned Goth and is studying part-time at the university in Hobart.'

'Goth?'

'It's a style that ... emphasises darkness and dark tragic dress. Black clothes, gelled hair, black or dark red lips, heavy eyeliner, black or purple fingernail polish, ripped fishnet stockings, studs, rings – that sort of thing. Goth music's been around forever: bands like The Horrors, Love is Colder than Death, Shakespeare's Sister and singers like Zola Jesus, David Bowie and Marilyn Manson.'

'Lady Gaga too?'

Nick laughed. 'Same amount of make-up. But no, I don't think so. Anyway, not many Goths in Gretna, where we live. So ... Annie is with someone else now.'

'Oh. It is good that you are doing well at being a carpenter. I thought you might become one of those people who drop out of helicopters and save people.'

John: 'Search and rescue. Something he's had experience doing.'

Mya: 'I know. Fire, nightclub and river rescues his specialty.'

John: 'Hero material, my young brother.'

'Stop it,' Nick said, a pained scowl on his face.

John: 'Problem is his modesty. It can make you scream sometimes.'

'You can talk,' Nick countered. 'Your cross-border heroics didn't exactly fill the media. Just you, the mossies and that backpack medic bloke in the know.'

'Phoe Ni.'

'Yeah, him. Not even the walking ...' Nick checked himself. 'Not even Lina was certain what had happened until you got carted back to Mae Sot.'

John tilted towards his brother, reached out and ruffled his hair. 'Give us a kiss.'

Nick puckered and kissed the air between them, before lifting his stubby in a toast. 'To big brother modesty.' He took a large gulp.

'And to little brother cheekiness.' John return-toasted and drank.

Mya asked, 'So how was Bangkok, John?'

'Thought you might ask. Not a place I'd care to spend a lot of time in. But for a few days with a person who needed a complete break, it worked. Besides nursing qualifications, Lina has a degree in development economics, but would have traded it for a certificate in psychological survival techniques over there in the Middle East. Dealing with the huge number of war orphans was the worst of it.'

'So did riverboat trips and good restaurants help?'

'Yes to the boat trips, no to the restaurants. We ate at market food stalls mostly, and watched people and talked and slept and talked and slept and on the third day stopped doing all that long enough to … get intimate. Which I think was an indication that psychologically she'd survived her Syrian border experience.'

'Intimate?' Nick asked, eyeing Mya questioningly. 'Did you bring your dictionary?'

Mya gave him a mock-scornful look. 'I think you know what the word means.'

'Anyway,' John said, 'Time for a new address, again. Lina's changed her flight booking. We're flying back to Australia together in four days. I'll be heading back to Bangkok day after tomorrow.'

Of the questions that formed in her mind, one dominated. But she'd not ask it. She felt certain John would answer it in his own time before he left. Instead, she asked Nick, 'The same day you are going to Chiang Mai, Nick?'

Nick mentioned his plans to meet up with his friend Jake, but didn't go into detail. She sensed his hesitancy in talking about his friend, her fall and her last few nights with them at the Snake Skin. There was still that about Nick – his shyness. His self-confidence was nowhere near his brother's, though there was no doubting his compassion and courage. And it occurred to her again how much she would miss them. 'Did John tell you the Snake Skin has moved to Chiang Mai?'

'Yeah, but it's not a place we'll get within a bull's roar of after our last Snake Skin experience. Could stir up old wounds.'

She thought of Billy J, aware that Nick was thinking of him too. But she wouldn't mention his visit, not wishing to connect herself in others' eyes with him ever again. 'Let's look at the menu,' she suggested instead.

* * *

After school the next day, the three met again at Raju's bed, where Mya gave Raju drawing paper and coloured pencils. Together they cut out magazine pictures and labelled them with English words like 'house', 'tree', 'motor scooter', 'people' and more. She asked Raju to draw and label the open bamboo and thatch house he lived in at the refugee camp, the stick people he lived with, the passing motor scooters and overhanging trees. Raju did that, showing them at regular intervals what he'd done and listening closely to Mya's comments. And for doing so well, they took him to the Casa Mia.

Halfway through their meal, as Mya expected, John told Raju he would be returning to Australia the following day.

This time Raju didn't smile at John's Karen pronunciation, but just lowered his eyes, uttering, 'Oh.'

'But another western man named Matt, from America, will make sure you get to school and back each day.'

'Oh.'

They went to the river next, John and Nick alternating carrying Raju on their shoulders until they found an empty bench. They sat pressed together, watching the water, the sun setting in an orange haze, while John and Nick talked about their morning departures and future plans. At one point Nick mentioned he might cut his Chiang Mai visit short and return to Mae Sot for a couple of days before returning to Bangkok and Australia.

'I hope you do,' Mya said, her smile meant to be encouraging.

They were the last people to leave the walkway, their voices carrying far in the dusk's pink-grey stillness.

The following day Raju went missing.

35

Visiting Raju before school, Mya noticed his leg was gone, so she sat on his bed, thinking he was using the toilet. She picked up his camp drawing, with its creased and curled edges. She turned the drawing over. Two large stick people stood side by side. One was considerably smaller than the other, had long hair and was named 'Miss Mya'. The other was 'Mister John'. Above Mister John's head appeared to be a bird, but might have been a plane. Though where Raju would have seen one mystified her. Written in small Karen letters at the bottom was: *Good bye Mister John.*

She noticed a large lump under the sheet. She raised it and saw Raju's computers, chess set, Australian animals and crinkly bag. She walked down the ward asking people if they'd seen him leave. She asked a staff member to check the toilet. Raju wasn't there. She went to the office. Alarmed staff scoured the clinic grounds and checked the orphan dormitory. Two people reported seeing a young amputee on the track leading into the banana and mango groves at the back. From there, though his stump hadn't completely healed, he might have gone anywhere.

* * *

Immediately after school, Mya took a motorbike taxi to the medical clinic and checked Raju's bed. He hadn't returned. She walked through the nearby orphan dormitory. No Raju. She got another motorbike taxi back to her room intent on riding her bike through all of Mae Sot in search of him.

She didn't have to. He was sitting on the step outside the building's entryway waiting for her. Relieved, she paid the fare and went over and sat beside him. 'You okay?'

He nodded, watching the motorbike taxi until it disappeared around a bend. She waited, giving him time.

'Has Mister John gone?' he asked finally.

She checked her watch. 'Yes.'

'I didn't feel good so I tried to go to the river but I got lost.'

'Oh.'

'Somewhere I sat under a big tree.' He turned and looked into her eyes. 'Three monks came, Miss Mya. One could speak Karen. They took me to their monastery and gave me rice to eat and water to drink. I told them about why I am not living in the camp anymore and about Mister John and about the school and about you. After that they let me walk around their monastery, but I didn't go very far because ...'

He pointed to his stump.

'It hurt, did it?'

'A little – yes. Have you been to a monastery?'

'Monasteries are not for girls or women. But I once lived in a nunnery in Myanmar.'

'Was it good?'

'Yes.'

'Did it have a building made of stone with a big gold Buddha in it and smoking sticks and yellow flowers and whatever they call girl monks sitting with their hands together going *mmm*?'

'Chanting you mean?'

'I guess so.'

'Yes it did.'

'Did it have lots of trees and Buddha faces and animals made from stone like that baby elephant next to the eating place we go to?'

'Those stone faces and animals are called statues.'

'Ah. Did it have little rooms with little ladders where girl monks lived?'

'The little rooms are kutis and girl monks are called nuns.' Ever the teacher, she thought. 'Yes, the nunnery had all that … Tell me how you got back here.'

'The monk who could speak Karen got a bicycle.' He smiled, recalling. 'Not a very good one. And he took me to the school. From the school I know how to get here.'

Her relief was complete. 'I want you to remember that if you ever get lost again, you ask whoever is around to help you to do exactly the same thing. First to the school, then to here.'

'I will. Are there books at school about the Buddha?'

'Yes.' Actually, she was unsure whether they were suitable for beginning readers. But she knew where to buy some in town. 'Also, when we go back to the clinic, I'll show you where you can get information about the Buddha from your computer.'

'Good.'

'You've had a busy day. Are you hungry?'

'A little.'

'What about this? We ride my bicycle into town to get some books, then we go to the Casa Mia Restaurant, where Mister John took us a few days ago, and we eat. After that we return to the clinic.'

'Can I go to school tomorrow?'

'After what you've done today I think the clinic will let you out to do that. But you must come to school by motorbike taxi. Okay?'

'Yes!'

36

He'd left a note at the school: *Meet you at the Casa Mia at 6:30 – OK? My shout. Nick.*

He was at their table, which looked bigger without John or Raju, when she arrived. He got up, and for a moment was uncertain what to do next. Then he stepped towards her, saying, 'Please, I want to do this.' He wrapped his arms around her. Next to her ear, he said, 'Do you remember saying that in the mountains when you were about to leave me?'

'But I kissed your cheek. I did not squeeze the air out of you.'

He loosened his arms.

'But I remember, Nick. I remember.'

He let go. 'Right, well I'm happy you do remember and that we're here now instead of the mountains.'

They sat. The server came and handed them menus.

'How was Chiang Mai?'

His head lifted, his eyes grew bigger. 'Some surprises there, I can tell you.'

'Do.'

'You remember my friend Jake?'

'Sort of.'

'It's like he's aged twenty years since I saw him last. He's married. And he never told me until the three of us met up the first night.'

The server returned and took their order.

'So he brought his wife from Australia.'

'Yeah, he did. But she's Thai. Born and raised in Chiang Mai. He met her after he left here, what, about two and half years ago, I s'pose. Then just last year he returned to Chiang Mai and they got married. They live in outback Australia, a place called Broken Hill, where he's still working in a mine and she runs a small Thai cafe called The U2FORTHAI. Once a year, when he has holidays, like now, they shut up the cafe and fly to Chiang Mai.'

She kept him talking. 'How did he meet her?'

'She must have been a tour guide or something up there. Jake just said she was in customer services and that her English was really good, which it is.'

'So what did you do up there?'

'A lot, but not what you'd expect. I found some cheap accommodation and Jake and Arinya – that's her name – came by on scooters each morning and night. We went to an elephant park the first day, walked for half a day to a waterfall and back the second, and did a river cruise yesterday. At night we wandered around the night market and went to a place called the Discover Club.'

'Like the Snake Skin?'

It struck him that her past was an open topic between them, that she trusted him with it. 'Not even close. Only similarity – the beer was cold.'

She glanced around at a group of westerners arriving and sitting at the 'stress-reduction' table, sparking memories of her first visit here.

'Okay, my turn for questions. How's Raju?'

'Maggot therapy worked. He is back in the dormitory, at night anyway.' She talked at length about Raju's 'escape', his monastery visit and sudden enthusiasm for the Buddha, adding, 'I found a couple of books at his Burmese reading level, but he soon read them and now I am looking for more.'

'What about ones written in English?'

'Fine. Maybe even better. But I doubt I will be able to find any here.'

'With lots of pictures in them?'

She tilted her head. 'Of course. A picture can tell a thousand words.'

'Can it really?'

The tone of his voice, the exaggerated bug-eyed look on his face. She sensed – unusual for him – that he was teasing her. 'You did not know that?'

'No. You must have got it from your Tripitaka.'

'From my head.'

He leaned closer, elbows on the table, chin in his hands. 'I'm interested. What else is in your head?'

Flirting with her too. 'Maybe later I will tell you, if you deserve to hear.'

'Later, like at the river?'

She shrugged. 'For the memories maybe.'

He matched her smile, recalling that she'd last said that as Lady Gaga in the Snake Skin. Their meals came. She sampled her stir-fried fish, rating it vocally with a satisfied 'Mmmm.'

He kept his eyes on her, saying, 'I'm working on an idea about those Buddha books you're looking for. I reckon a stroll along the river walkway and some sit-down thinking time might be enough for me to offer up a solution.'

'Mmmm,' she uttered again, more ambiguously.

* * *

They got off the motorbike taxis, paid and walked.

'Day after tomorrow, when I get home,' Nick said, 'I'll have a talk to my mum. There are lots of Vietnamese in Australia, some even as far down as Tasmania. If the Buddha books you want can be bought anywhere in Australia, she'll soon find out where. They'll be in English though.'

'I will give you money.'

'No you won't. My shout. Donation to charity. I can claim it on my tax. Or at least that's what my mum will tell me to do. Just give me the school's postal address and … same email address?'

'Yes.'

'I'll let you know when the books are sent. Hopefully there'll be enough to keep Raju going until he's old enough to start shaving. Chin, neck and cheeks. Not his head.' Nice try at a joke, she thought, but it didn't draw the hint of a smile from her. 'Although,' he went on quickly, 'if he stays on a steady diet of Buddha books, his next home might be a monastery. I've seen boy monks here and in Chiang Mai.'

'Missing a leg and fingers?'

'No. But from what I've learned about Buddhism, missing body parts, or a trauma or two, aren't issues for those applying to enter a monastery.'

In the moonlight she listened for other people, but could only hear the river. She looked down at the dark water flowing by. 'I think … I would like a hug now,' she said, surprising herself.

'Oh … Okay.'

Seconds later she drew back, smiled into his face and took his hand in hers. What she felt was curiosity and strong affection for this boy who had shared more places and talk with her than any other male she'd ever known outside her family. Since the Snake Skin, she'd wondered if she'd ever be able to make love with someone like him, with a heart soft as mushy rice. And Nick was leaving the next day. She stopped and let her emotions lead her. 'I want to do this.' She raised herself up on her toes and wrapped an arm around his neck, felt his warmth against her breasts. She grazed his lips with hers and kissed his chin, his cheeks.

'I can remember when I thought kissing got a girl pregnant,' Nick muttered.

'Do you know what does now?'

Nick laughed. 'I think so.'

She pressed her lips to the side of his throat. 'I can feel your heartbeat.'

'Me too.'

She kissed him there. 'You once paid me,' she said, meeting his eyes.

'Yeah but it was worth it just to talk.'

'And further along from here I shouted at you to leave me alone.'

'Well I didn't really know what was—'

She kissed his lips softly, interrupting him. 'And minutes later I got stuck in the river and you came and helped me get to the other side. That night we slept together. Sort of.'

'You told me I snored.'

'And you told me I screamed.'

'I only heard you do it once. And it wasn't that loud. More a yelp than anything else.'

'So I am forgiven?'

'Yes.'

'Then can I ask you a question?'

'Yes.'

'What are you like at climbing through windows?'

He gave her a mystified look.

'I share a building with other people. If they see me take you into my room, they will gossip about me.' On her toes again, she placed her cheek against his.

For moments Nick looked like he could hardly believe his ears. 'Tonight you mean?'

'If you are not doing anything else – and want to.'

'I want to.'

'You were not comfortable with me once, at the Snake Skin.'

'I am now.'

'Okay. The window is big enough for you and it is not high.'

'Right.'

She lowered her arms, looped an arm around his and guided him back towards the road. 'Thing is, the bed is small. And I have to work tomorrow. So you will have to climb back out of the window early in the morning. Will that be alright?'

'Yes.'

* * *

Early in the night, she said to him, 'I sometimes wonder why you still want to be with me, you knowing what I was.'

He seemed unsure how to answer that, his eventual answer deflecting the question. 'I was scared that night at the Snake Skin. Scared I'd embarrass myself.'

'I know.'

'I'm not good at explaining things. But all I know is after you fell and ended up at the medical clinic, you filled up a big part of my brain. Your face, intelligence, what happened to you, and later us escaping into Myanmar. There are things I've done in the past, really stupid, embarrassing things that I wish didn't happen too. But in no way was I forced to do them.'

She held his hand.

'Anyway, there has never been a place or a time I didn't want to be with you.'

'The middle of the Moei River?'

'Especially there.'

'I have heard western men say "talk her up" or "sweet-talk her".'

'I've heard that too.'

'Well you have and I am happy we are like this now.'

Her 'could she?' question was answered. Even with the awkwardness, she could. And even with someone who first knew her as Lady Gaga. Heartened, she laughed when he said he hadn't come prepared, as he hadn't in the mountains that day. Food and water and a sleeping mat then. 'Pregnancy protection' this time. (He still found the word 'condom' hard to say.) Understandable. Like in the mountains, how could he have known he'd be spending the night with her? Thankfully her period was due in the next few days. After she mentioned that, she recalled the time she hadn't been so thankful, when she would have traded her period for sterility.

Middle of the night – candle still burning, incense stick smouldering – she thought of something else he'd said to her in the mountains, that he 'knew nothing about sex'. She mentioned this to him.

'I remember,' he replied, drawing closer. 'It still happens, weird words exiting my mouth before I can stop them. Sometimes weird is just normal for me.'

'Well I think you do know, and it might sound—' she hunted for the word '—strange, but so do I, now; the kind that is gentle and heartfelt … the touching.'

In the wee hours, aware she was awake, Nick said, 'We must be in our other lifetimes now,' referring again to their night in the mountains.

She laughed. 'Must be.'

He laughed too.

No dawn regrets, though there was a penalty to be paid. Not the fact that one snored while the other screamed in her nightmares. Neither of them slept deeply or long enough for that. The penalty was having to face up to the new day, realising that in all likelihood their second night together would be their last. Yet she took from the experience this: the night had felt like a test, an emotional one, and she'd passed.

'I'll email you when I get home,' he said, squeezing out the window into the dim dawn light. He dropped down into bushes and pushed his head back in. 'Promise.'

'Like Romeo,' she muttered.

'Pardon?'

'Nothing.' She stroked his cheek, kissed him quickly. And there stayed with her, of all possible thoughts, a passage:

Romeo: Lady, by yonder blessed moon I vow,
That tips with silver all these fruit-tree tops—

Juliet: O, swear not by the moon, the inconstant moon,
That monthly changes in her circled orb,
Lest that thy love prove likewise variable.[*]

'This time it's me who's leaving, and I don't want to.' He turned, looking for passers-by, before walking cautiously out to the road and disappearing.

'O, swear not by the moon, the inconstant moon...' There was that about great stories, Mya thought, her mind adrift, her emotions swirling after such a night. What happens in them can happen in real life, to anyone. And it was the skilled writer's insights and use of language that could make a relationship between two young people from two different backgrounds – what? Not awesome, but ... memorable.

The Buddha and Shakespeare. The Tripitaka and Romeo and Juliet. One day, probably when she was old and stooped and sitting on benches all day long like those two old men in Moulmein, she might review her diaries and poetry and spend time writing the story of Lady Gaga and Nan Pau and how they were transformed back into Mya Paw Wah, survivor, teacher, translator. She might even show it to her grandchildren one day, if ... She gave her head a wake-up-to-reality shake. Such a fine morning for fantasy. Juliet came from a rich, influential family. She could live out the extraordinary in her head

---

[*] *Romeo and Juliet*, Act 2, Scene 2, lines 111–115.

without ever having to get involved in the ordinary, like going off to work each morning.

Mya had half an hour before she had to leave. She went to her desk, took out her dictionary, pen and writing pad and composed a tanka.

> *First time in my mind,*
> *Hands to bellies, hips and thighs.*
> *Lips to lips, cheeks, breasts.*
> *'Sshh,' I say, sensing neighbours.*
> *We laugh and do not know why.*

It seemed a good place to stop – laughing. Hardly Shakespeare or the Buddha, but not Lady Gaga either. Somewhere in between. The Middle Way. Which was okay, as already her mind was diverting to the day ahead: translation, school kids, a routine that – though she was a little sore and sleepy – meant everything to her.

37

Two former political prisoners had arrived at the Burmese Political Prisoners' Office in the night with only what they wore and could carry in cloth bags lumped on their backs. With her pen in one hand, a strong black tea in the other, their words quickly dominated Mya's thoughts as she translated them for aid workers and journalists there to listen and take notes.

The first thing she noticed when she arrived at school in the afternoon was that Raju was absent and, according to staff, had been all day.

After school she went looking and found him sitting like before on the landing outside the entryway to her room. She sat down next to him, feeling every bit his guardian, and that frustrated her. She asked where he had been.

'The monastery, Miss Mya. It was really good. There are boys young as me there. They are called *dek wat*.' He scrunched his face up. 'But I don't know what that means.'

'Children of the monastery.'

'Oh. And they go to school there, and they do cleaning and they have to learn ten rules like not to help make babies, or drink drinks like whiskey, or kill or steal or lie or eat in the afternoon or night.' He stopped for a breath. 'Or wear hats or watches, or sleep on a soft bed or accept lots of money. And you don't have to be a boy monk forever. Just a short time if you want to. And you can go home for visits if you want to. But I guess not me.'

'So is that what you want to do, become a *dek wat*?'

He nodded his head slowly. 'Nobody is alone there. And *dek wat* share a room called a … I can't remember.'

'*Kuti*?'

'Yes, that.' His face dulled. He stared at the ground. 'But …'

She waited.

'Only one monk there can speak Burmese and a little Karen. So I have to learn how to speak Thai.'

'It takes a long time to learn a language.'

He leaned his head against her shoulder.

'Do you know that monks are not supposed to touch women,' she said, 'not even their own mothers?'

He sat up straight, as if practising for the future.

'But you're not a monk yet, are you?' She wrapped an arm around his back. In her mind the abbess: '*Detachment, Nan Pau. There's a need I think to constantly re-evaluate it …*' An idea came to her. 'There is a monastery in Myawadi,' she told Raju.

'Across the river?'

'Yes. But I don't know if you would be allowed to cross the bridge to get there.'

'Oh.'

'There is a word in English called *bargain* that means "deal" or "trade". People who speak English say, I will make you a—' she said the word in English again '—*bar-gain*. If you come to school every day for the next two weeks, I will make you a *bargain*.'

'What is it?'

'I will find out whether I can take you across the bridge to the monastery in Myawadi.'

'But women can't go into monasteries.'

'I know someone who can take you.'

'Does that monastery have boy monks?'

'Yes. I've seen them.'

'And trees and flowers and songbirds and *kutis* and a temple with candles and a great big golden Buddha?'

'I've only seen it from the outside, but monasteries are supposed to have all those things.'

'Okay. *Bar-kin.*'

* * *

MYAWADI.

It had become an unquestioned family ritual, their Friday night cooking and serving up of Mohinga on the balcony. And for Mya the best part was the cooking and being able to talk to her father on her own, hear about his week, though more often than not she was the one who, in answer to his questions, did most of the talking. Outside, Mohinga served and everybody seated, Uncle Zarni's customary exuberance took over.

This night, while cooking, she told her father about Raju skipping school and how he wanted to enter a monastery as a boy monk but that he, of course, could not speak Thai. She told him also she'd sought advice from people she knew in Mae Sot about how to get him over the Friendship Bridge. 'The problem is,' she continued, 'I can bring him over, but he will not be able to return to Mae Sot. Not unless I smuggle him back, or someone I know does.'

'If you get caught,' Nyan warned, 'you'll lose your border pass, so your work as well. I can take him into the monastery here. But before you bring him over, I should first visit the monastery, talk to the abbot and get his approval.'

'He will also need someone in Myawadi to be his guardian.'

'I suppose he will.'

'And a place to come to when he wants a break from the monastery, like on Saturdays and Sundays. And where he can get a little extra school instruction if he feels he needs it.'

He gave her a steady look. 'This amputee orphan re-settlement plan of yours, how long have you been working on it?'

'About two weeks.'

'And the idea.' He poked his skull with an index finger. 'How long has it been in there?'

'A while.'

He gave her a look she couldn't read, before saying, 'You're like your mother: forward-thinker, planner and organiser. She felt strong compassion for those wearing robes and holding empty bowls.'

'Did she?' Mya watched him.

He looked down, took an audible breath. 'Raju, huh?'

38

MAE SOT.

Nick's email came the day after she took Raju to Myawadi.

Hi Mya

First, theres no one here now to corect my spelling and if I use spell-chek it will take me fourever to write this. So good luck.

Second, theres a Buddhist Sosiety in Hobart I went to about a week ago. I bought seven begining English books about the Buddha. Even I can read them. Three have the same tital – The Story of Buddha – but use diferent words and look diferent on the inside. Cant remember the other fouer titals. Anyway, I posted them to your school yesterday.

Third, I'm living at home for awile becuse Im working on a building site in New Norfolk – about twenty minutes drive from home. Which leeds me to the big news item. Forth, how would you like to come to Tasmania? I no it sounds manic, but just read on.

Dad is in a servis club called Rotary. There are branchs everywere in the world. Rotary clubs rays money to help people anywere in the world who need help. Like theyve built water sistems for orfanages in Myanmar for the past twenty years. Since John first went to the Thai-Burma border Dad has been talking to people in lokal Rotary clubs about raysing money to support projeks in Mae Sot, like the Mae Tao medical clinic, and since John and I have been back and talked to him about the migrant school you teach at – that to.

The good news is it looks a goer. Goer mening it will hapen.

The Rotary clubs in New Norfolk and Hobart are planing to work together to rays money for the clinic and your school. Dad got mum to email the Rotary club contacts in Yangon to explane why the club would like you to come to Tasmania to talk about your school. They rekon youll be right to get a pasport and visa to come here. They've got your email and school adress. So get ready to hear from them AND from the New Norfolk Rotary club. Becuse you're a big part of there plan.

And this is the plan. 1/ John and Lina will come and talk to the clubs about the medical clinic and backpack medics. 2/ Then youll come when you have a school brake. All your flights will be aranged and payed for by the Rotary clubs here and you will stay with us. 3/ Mum will take you round to primary schools in the area. You can watch lesons and get school matearials and talk to kids about Myanmar if you want to. 4/ Dad and I will take you round to the diferent Rotary clubs on certin nights so you can talk about the migrant school and also the migrant Burmese organisasions in Mae Sot.

I now this is a big suprise for you. But everthing is going to be organised and payed for by Rotary Internasional. And the clinic and your migrant school should get project money for a long time. You just come, stay, look round and talk to people about your school. Plus therell be time for us to do things together. Yes?

Things are good here. Lots of work. I finish my aprentiseship in three months and will start erning more money after that.

Hows Raju going?

See you here.

Nick

She read the email twice, then walked down the road and back, returned to her room and read the email again. It had to be genuine. Who else could spell like Nick? She got out her dictionary, found the words 'hoax' and 'confirm' and used them in the next hour to write a reply.

The next day she got another email from Nick.

Mya –

Its no hoax. I confirm evrything.

I understand your fear. All I can say is that the famly will look after you. So no worries at all.

Good to here about Raju and that he can use the books on weekends in Myawadi. I rekon the Rotary clubs would like to hear about him to.

Dad said to me you and your principal will be geting leters soon from Rotary Internatsional in New Norfolk, Yangon and Bangkok. Theyll be full of informasion about dates, prosedures and people who will be helping you. Especialy with geting a visa.

See you soon.

Nick

In the next few days six letters arrived at the school. Three were addressed to Mya, the other three to the principal. They were the first letters Mya had ever received. She needed to use her dictionary for the word 'nominated'.

* * *

From the minutes before the massacre until she entered the nunnery, there had rarely been a day she hadn't felt fear. So she knew fear, knew its types and effects. The paralysing, sick-in-the-stomach fear from having to cross a minefield, being smuggled into Mae Sot, having to share time with an aggressive patron. Or the tight, nervous fear from travelling into the unknown to find her mother, to live in a cave.

Fear too about the unknown of Australia. About flying inside huge planes; landing in strange places; staying with strangers who might ask awkward questions; having to speak correct English to groups of Australians she shared nothing in common with but an interest in the Thai-Myanmar border region.

Yes, it would be good to be with Nick again. But so much better in a place she knew, with people she could predict and feel relaxed with.

Though she tried to calm herself with methods learned at the nunnery, anxiety continued to niggle away at her, especially when she was alone during the weeknights. After school one day, she made the decision to go see the principal. She confided her feelings and asked the principal if she would consider going to Australia in her place.

'I would, yes,' the principal answered. 'If I were considerably younger and if I had the sort of Australian connections you appear to have.'

She gave Mya a constrained smile. 'Sorry. But this is a small town, and the Casa Mia and river walkway are popular places.' She reassured Mya of the trip's value and that she, with her 'background and fluent English', was the right person to go. They talked of Mya getting an Australian tourist visa, the principal saying, 'School holidays in four weeks' time, so you'll need to get one quickly.' Then: 'And what about this, Mya? I haven't been to Bangkok in more years than I can remember. Why don't I go with you on the bus and train to Bangkok, just to make sure you get to the right airport? There are two you know.'

Part Four

39

TASMANIA.

From above, flat Melbourne had resembled flat Bangkok: a river winding through it, tall buildings giving way to small streets feeding into larger ones, vehicles moving ant-like along them. Further out, road-bordered warehouses and tracks of housing stretched towards the horizon. So, still nervously occupying a window seat in a different plane five hours later, that's what Mya expected to see as the plane descended through a valley corridor into Hobart Airport. But the land was near-empty, lumpy, a mixture of greens, greys and browns. It reminded her of the landscape around Mae Sot and Myawadi until they swept over a body of water she took to be ocean, with little wind-whipped waves like maggots crawling across its bright, sun-struck surface. On the edges a coastline of scattered houses and trees between gouged-out headlands and long curves of empty white sand.

So much variety down there that interest displaced her anxiety. But only briefly, anxiety returning again as they banked sharply and she followed the plane's shadow on the water moving so slowly she feared the plane might drop from the sky.

She willed herself to think of Nick, to use their night together, of him waiting for her down there, as a salve for her nerves.

They landed and as they approached the terminal an announcement came over the intercom: 'Welcome to Hobart Airport, the southernmost commercial airport in Australia. Those wishing to travel on to Antarctica, please check the departure board inside the terminal.'

Of those around her, only she didn't laugh.

'This afternoon we'll be departing by the front door only, the back one fell off over Bass Strait,' came a second announcement. More laughter. Then: 'Thank you for flying Virgin and putting up with the co-pilot's sick jokes. Hope to see you again soon.'

She looked out the window for Nick, but there was no one on the tarmac until other passengers began to descend a portable staircase, like that used in Mae Sot. Like Mae Sot's too, the small, single-runway airport, the walk to the baggage area inside.

But that's where the similarity ended.

She put on her daypack and wraparounds and left the plane, her nerves buzzing. The air outside felt lighter, looked clearer than even that around her retreat cave, but it was so much colder, and she had to lean into the wind. Nick had warned her, but how could she have understood weather she had never experienced before? The sweater the principal bought for her at Bangkok Airport was too light to keep the cold out. So she hugged herself, trying to warm her hands in her armpits, while following passengers rushing to get inside.

Once through the automatic doors, a brown and white dog tethered to the hand of a blue-uniformed man started sniffing her legs. It sat, nose pointed her way.

'Please stop for a moment, take off your daypack and place it in your hand,' the man with the dog instructed.

She did, and the man gave the dog something to munch, then told Mya to open her bag. Not even Friendship Bridge border police had asked her to do that. Passengers passed either side glancing at her as the man rummaged through her bag and took out the apple she'd bought at Melbourne Airport. 'Can you read English?' he asked.

'*Yes*.' Was that a tremor in her voice?

'There is a large sign outside warning passengers about bringing prohibited foods into the state. Apples are fruit. Fruit is prohibited.'

Barely in the airport and already in trouble with the authorities.

'What about your baggage? Any food?'

'I do not have any more food. I promise.' She was the last of the passengers now.

He gave her a smile she was grateful for. 'First time here?'

'Yes.'

He asked where she was from and she told him. 'I reckon if I ever get up to that part of the world I'll probably take as little notice of airport signs as you have here. Anyway, have a good stay in Tasmania.' He picked up the daypack, handed it to her and pointed in the direction of the baggage collection area.

She walked on, relieved, and rounded a corner and immediately heard a girl's voice shout, 'There she is!'

She made a little smile for the three flashed at her. Nick and a tall, older man with a soup-strainer for a moustache and wearing the longest trousers she'd ever seen (from boots to chest, two over-the-shoulder straps holding them up) stood either side of a woman with long, grey-black hair, wearing jeans and a thick blue-and-white checked shirt. In front of them, in jeans also and a grey sweater that hung down to her thighs, was a teenage girl holding a bouquet of yellow flowers. Obviously Ella, Nick's sister.

The girl approached and held out the flowers, her pretty face smooth except for a wrinkly scar on her right cheekbone. 'I'm Ella. Welcome to Tasmania, Mya. These are marigolds. We grow them in our garden and hothouse year round.'

'The colour of the sun. Thank you. They are beautiful.'

Nick's mother came up next, still smiling brightly, and wrapped her arms around Mya (she'd pictured Nick doing this), chorusing, 'Welcome, Mya. I'm Mother Alice. For a moment there we thought you'd missed the plane.'

Mya told her about the apple.

'Ah, right. Trying to bend the rules already, are you? (But she wasn't.) Just like the rest of my family. You're already fitting in well.'

Then came Nick. He touched her shoulder, and as she started to place an arm around his waist, he gave her a quick kiss on the cheek and stepped back. 'Good trip?' he asked. His look and formal manner were almost brotherly, like how Thant might have greeted her.

'Yes.'

'Did you sleep?'

'A little.'

Their night together in Mae Sot: 'Anyway, there has never been a place or a time I didn't want to be with you.' Not anymore, it seemed. There was nothing about Nick that indicated he was happy she was there. She thought quickly of something to say. 'I watched a movie on the airplane called *Red Dog*, which took place in Australia. But I think it must be a different part of Australia.'

'Yes, a very different part and far away,' Alice said. 'The Kimberleys, up in the far northwest of the mainland.'

Nick's father stepped forward and Mya prepared herself for another peck on the cheek. But he stopped in front of her and said, 'G'day.' She was comfortable with that. That was how characters in *Red Dog* greeted each other. 'I'm Ben,' he added in a slow drawl of a voice, different from the others.

'G'day,' she replied, gauging his reaction.

'You've been practisin'.'

She couldn't help smiling. 'I have.'

'I did too when I first came to this country. Pleased you're here.'

'Me too.' Though it was Nick's family, not Nick, who made her at least partially feel that way.

Ella collected her bag and soon they were inside Ben's dual cab ute, Ben driving, Alice next to him and Mya – flowers in her lap – pressed between Nick and Ella in the back, a tethered black and white dog staring in through the back windscreen. 'Got some border collie in her,' Nick said, seeing her eyeing the dog. 'Border collie, chihuahua cross I reckon.' Were his comments an indication he was warming towards her? 'Mum found her in a bad way on a road outside town a couple of months ago. No collar, so she must have been abandoned. We put a notice up at the pub, but got no response. So we named her Filthy, which she was, and have set about making her ours. Still young, still a bit mad. But she loves people. Harmless as a new-born, unless you're a fly ... which you're not.'

With the heater on, it was warming up.

'First time on a plane, Mya?' Alice asked.

Mya: 'Yes.'

Ben: 'Be the last time if you were me.'

Alice: 'Ignore him. How did it feel to you?'

Mya: 'I was a little nervous at first. But it was okay.'

They turned onto a wide, smooth road, passing empty land, distant warehouses then a cluster of buildings with huge signs over them: K&D Warehouse, Sleepy's, Harvey Norman, Allgoods, Anaconda and more. As strange to her as there being no oxen in nearby fields, no bicycles, food stalls or people walking along the side of the road.

Nick's phone buzzed with a text message. He read it, stuck his phone in his jacket pocket and stared straight ahead, hands back on his lap. Hardly the pose he'd struck when they were last together. Was he trying to provide her with a behaviour model? She had heard that western countries were very ... what was the word? From the word 'permit'. *Permissive*. That it wasn't unusual for permissive parents to allow their older children to sleep with their girlfriends or boyfriends in the family home. But maybe Nick's parents were not permissive. She would need time to determine that, and what their expectations were. Or maybe Nick would just straight out tell her once they got to his home. Or if he didn't, maybe she would ask him.

Up and over a rise they went and suddenly in front of them were masses of houses, a distant river, a humpbacked mountain range.

Alice pointed. 'Mount Wellington there. See it? Crouched like a lion, its rounded head propped over Hobart.'

Mya didn't see it, but answered, 'Yes,' anyway. Outside, so clean and glittery in the sun. Like Bangkok, so much metal and glass that made the world seem newer and shinier down here.

'Tasman Bridge,' Alice called out next, as they went over a bridge as big as Moul's but with no train tracks, just lines of trucks and big, shiny cars, and on elevated pathways either side, young people riding bicycles in skin-tight clothes with helmets on their heads.

'Derwent River down there.'

More sweeping turns and onto another wide, straight road with huge trucks dragging containers big as train cars. 'Middle of Hobart now,' Nick said to her. 'Less than an hour away from home.' His first words since describing Filthy the dog.

Traffic thinned and houses grew bigger close to a river that was slower and calmer and much, much wider than the Moei. Up through a valley they went, following the river, with houses giving way to yellow grass, bushy hillsides and a few skeletal trees, their branches like bleached bones. Soon orchards came into view, with fruit stalls by the side of the road. They all sold apples.

Talking stopped. It grew warmer. Mya felt a wave of weariness settle over her that she couldn't shake off. She told herself she would close her eyes for just a few seconds.

She woke to a dog barking, people opening car doors. 'Thought we'd lost you there for a while,' a woman said, sticking her head back in through the open door and looking at her.

Alice, her name was; the other names returned to her as she scooted out of the back seat.

Filthy, loose now, sniffed at her heels, reminding her of the airport dog.

'Don't let her worry you,' Ben said. 'Her breath is worse than her bite.'

Then Filthy started running in circles around them as they moved towards a big brick house with large rectangular windows. Panels of dark glass stood vertically atop an overhanging roof that ridged in the middle and sloped downwards like the straw hats of field workers back home. A wide veranda with potted plants and flowers and a cushioned basket – Filthy in it now – lined the front and garden side of the house.

Inside they went to a large, open room with a single grey rug, lounge chairs, what she took to be a fireplace, built-in cabinets and television on one side, a round table and chairs, a bar and a kitchen with a tiled floor on the other. Beyond all that, a hallway.

'I'll get the basics going in the wok,' Alice said, going to the kitchen and handing Ella a flower vase, 'if you can show Mya her room and get her settled.'

Ella took the flowers from Mya and put them in the vase, and Nick joined them, carrying Mya's bag down the hallway past bedrooms and bathrooms to the last two rooms. Ella pointed, 'Your room is there, and Nick's is there, just across from you.' Her eyes flicked between the two of them, as though calculating something, before she placed the flowers on a table just inside Mya's room.

Mya went in. 'It is beautiful … Awesome.' Certainly it would be the best room in the best house she had ever stayed in. Yet there was nothing in the room that didn't serve a purpose. The small table, a single bed, a cabinet with drawers, a closet with a large oval mirror inside the door. A curtain-drawn window by her bed, and on the opposite wall a large watercolour painting of a lake surrounded on three sides by white-trunked trees, rounded mountains in the background. She pointed to it. 'In Tasmania?'

'Lake King William, not far away,' Nick said. He dropped her pack on the bed and she opened it up, took out her Buddha and placed it on the table. From the Snake Skin to Tasmania, her way of clinging to something familiar in a world of strangeness.

'What about a look around outside when you're finished unpacking?' Nick asked.

'I can leave it until later if you would like to go now.' She noticed Ella's eyes were still in motion. 'Will you come too?' Mya asked her.

Ella hesitated, looking at Nick. 'I'd better stay and help Mum.'

'It's all hands in the engine room. Fire and food and a table to be set,' Alice announced, when they returned to the lounge area. 'Except for you two.' She handed Mya an apple. 'A replacement for the one taken at the airport.' She turned to Nick. 'Our guest looks in need of some orientation.'

'It's organised.'

'Good. On your way back, could you bring in the vegies you want for tonight?'

Outside they followed a path through a vegetable garden, Mya biting hungrily into the apple while Nick – still pensive and serious-faced – pointed to their choices, naming them: silverbeet, cucumber, lettuce, butternut pumpkin and broccoli; trenches of onions, carrots, and potatoes further along. All bordered by trellised beans and peas. He pulled a couple of carrots from the ground, brushing them off. 'Entree for the horses,' he told her. 'We'll do some more harvesting on the way back.'

They walked on past clothes-lines and another ute, Filthy running ahead, Nick scowling a little, like he was arguing with someone inside his head.

She searched for something to say. 'Your sister is pretty.'

'Sorry?'

She repeated herself.

'Yeah.'

'She seems to have recovered well from her burns.'

Turning her way and taking a step closer, he seemed at least partly with her again. 'Doctors worked some magic on her. A few patches to remember the day by, mostly in places people will never see unless she's wearing swimming gear – which she won't be for a while. Not like living up in Queensland here.' He took his hands from his pockets and pointed to fruit trees up ahead, chickens scratching away under them. 'Apple, apricot, nectarine, peach and plum. Finished for the season though. But mum's got a pantry full of jam, which I should warn you, she'll be insisting you try.'

She thought she knew what jam was. 'I will like it, I know.' She wondered when the conversation would get around to just them. 'Is John still in Queensland?'

'Yeah. He and Lina did the Rotary speaking circuit last month and must have ticked all the boxes. Rotary announced they'd be running a support project for the Mae Tao Clinic starting in a couple of months. I reckon you won't have to say too much to get Rotary to do the same for your school.' He pointed towards a small, flat-roofed wooden structure attached to a massive shed with a tractor and bales of hay inside. 'The "Honeymoon Cottage" Dad calls it. Where John and Lina slept when they were here. Did I tell you they got married?'

'No.'

'Sorry, I should've. Small, casual ceremony on the Sunshine Coast in Queensland. Besides us, only a few of Lina's friends were there. At one point, when they were exchanging the vows they'd written themselves, John pledged never to leave the toilet seat up, squeeze a tube of toothpaste in the middle, or cut his nails indoors. Had to laugh. I reckon Lina wrote that bit for him. Anyway, they had a starter honeymoon in a place called the Glasshouse Mountains, then came down here. Typical John. Has to be somewhere close to bush or mountains. Anyway, we might have a Skype session with them while you're here.'

'That would be good.'

'A lot to catch up on, huh? Like Raju for instance.' His phone buzzed again. He read the text; put the phone back in his jacket pocket.

They passed a few hens pecking the ground, lengths of timber and wire, a stable with two stalls, before going through a squeaky gate into a stony, yellow-grass paddock. As she talked about Raju, a few wary sheep (the first she'd ever seen outside of the internet) kept their eyes on Filthy before racing off. Opposite, two reddish-brown horses stretched their heads over the fencing wire, looking to Nick for handouts. He gave Mya a carrot, saying, 'Come on,' and seconds later they fed the carrots to the horses.

They walked on, the paddock dipping, the house slipping out of sight.

So quiet. So much space. Nick's family so warm and welcoming. Yet, in this new world everything was so different – much of it far beyond what she had imagined. Feeling tired, and confused by Nick's coolness, homesickness settled on Mya like a brick. She stopped and watched birds walk away from them and a lone crow – something she was familiar with – as it passed over them.

Nick kept silent. Something had obviously changed between them and she suspected now what it was. In a small, tight voice she said, 'Tell me again what your family know about me.'

He seemed surprised by the question, and thought a moment. 'What I told you in my email; what the Rotary Clubs know about you. That you're brilliant at English. That you got caught up in a protest massacre in Yangon. That your brother was killed and you had to escape in disguise. That you were arrested and forced to become a porter, and at one point crossed a minefield. That you spent almost two years in a nunnery after your mum died before becoming a primary teacher and translator.' He lowered his eyes, kicked a stone with his boot.

He'd missed a part, or two. 'And us?'

'A bit.'

'Lady Gaga?'

He looked down the paddock. 'John might have said something; I don't know.'

A hole opened up inside her. Mouth closed tight against all she felt like saying to him, she turned and headed back to the house. When he caught up and started to say something, she cut him off. 'A long day,' she said, as though her tiredness was the only problem.

40

If Nick's family knew about Lady Gaga, they didn't let on and it obviously made no difference to them. They stayed friendly and close, especially Alice who apologised for the 'second-rate rice and green chicken curry' she served up that night.

'No need to say sorry,' Mya told her. Certainly it was milder than the curries she ate back home, but also thicker, with so many new vegetables in it. She asked for seconds, and not just because it was her first meal since morning. They talked of food, and at one stage Ella asked Mya about her favourite dish. Hearing the answer, Alice booked Mya in to cook up Mohinga the next night once they'd returned from a New Norfolk primary school and a supermarket.

After watching television with the family, wood in the fireplace burn, sparks rising up the chimney, Mya excused herself before falling asleep and went to her room.

Morning seemed to come around in seconds. She waited until after seven-thirty, the time Nick went to work, Ella to school and Alice to morning teaching. Then she showered, dressed and went into the lounge room where Ben was sitting reading a book and sipping coffee. He greeted her, saying, 'You've got a choice. I can cook you up breakfast, though I should warn you, a few I've offered that service to in the past have declined fearing I might confuse the rat poison for the eggs and bacon. Or I can show you where everything is and you can cook yourself up something.'

'I like cooking.'

'A wise choice, especially around here. Don't want your stomach pumped out before your first school visit and speaking engagement tonight. I do make a safe coffee though. Interested?'

'Tea?'

He squinted and frowned. 'Tea?' His face brightened. 'Ah yes, I believe I've heard of it.' He shot a finger in the air. 'I reckon I know where we've got some. So I can do tea, unless of course you'd like to make it yourself.'

It felt good to do things for herself there, the stillness in the house almost cave-like, her thoughts wandering. She ate her scrambled eggs and quartered apple, sipped her tea. Her thoughts turned to her school laptop, which she'd brought with her, and the memory stick containing the two Powerpoint presentations she and her principal had spent so many hours preparing. She wanted to review the Rotary one, and it would help, she thought, if Ben could watch it with her and make suggestions. She asked, and by the time she had 'Mae Sot's Hsa Thoo Lei Burmese Migrant School: Where Results Replace Dreams' ready to go, Ben was sitting by her side.

'Mmm, yes,' Ben muttered, watching. Or, 'Great, your selling point here a crowded classroom, so the need for more of them.' Or, 'A useful photo. Shows there's plenty of room to grow outwards as well as upwards.' A series of approving grunts greeted the last half of the presentation. 'I prefer tractors to computers, so I'm probably not the best person to judge, but I reckon you've got the visuals right.' He got up and started to make a pot of coffee. 'Your audience might also be interested in hearing more about the history of the school, the reaction of the Thai community to it, the problems Burmese migrants face in Mae Sot. You right with all that?'

'I think so.' She asked if he would listen to her speech, and once she'd finished reading it, he looked at his watch. 'Good, good. Your speech and Powerpoint presentation answers everything I can think of in about forty minutes all up. Well within the stay-awake span of the more ancient-wooded ones who'll be there tonight.'

Two questions still nagged away at her though. Both had to do with Lady Gaga. She decided now was a good time to ask one of them. 'Do you think people will ask me any personal questions?'

'Hard to know. But anything outside your teaching and translating experiences in Mae Sot is not part of why you're in Tasmania. So if you don't like the question, answer it with a lie.'

She was close to asking the second question, when Ben said, 'I plan to toss this coffee in a thermos, jump on the tractor and head out to the old bloke's paddock. We call it that because I'm the only one who usually visits it. A few blue gums out there getting big enough to cast some shade. Good spot to relocate sheep, practise a speech or steady one's pre-Rotary presentation nerves. Plus I've got a second tractor seat that's not been used for a while. Why don't we brew up some tea as well, toss it in a second thermos and head out there?'

As it turned out, neither speech practice nor conscious effort at steadying her nerves occurred – though they did bounce and sway their way to the paddock Ben had in mind, with Filthy racing around until they got to a gate. They got off the tractor, went through the gate and Ben tied Filthy up.

'Interested in herding sheep?' Ben asked her, obviously enjoying the question.

'I have never done it before. But I will try.'

'Good. Let me know when you've had enough and we can settle in for a drink under those trees behind us.' They walked. He stopped beside a hollow log, looked into it and pointed to the 'resident blue-tongue lizard' inside. They continued on, Ben pointing high up into a dying tree. 'Wedge-tail eagle's nest there. See it? To be monitored and cherished. Not many of their owners about nowadays. Birds, trees, space. Can't help but feel whole out here, larger somehow.' He picked up a long stick, handed it to her, and through another gate and into a different paddock they went, sheep standing together at the far end eyeing them. It seemed in that hour of herding – really nothing more than running around, shouting and laughing – that the purpose was simply to move sheep from one corner of the paddock to another, stop, chat some more, then continue on with their so-called herding again. Ben pulled out a camera at one stage and snapped photos of her with her stick in the air running after sheep. 'We'll have the photos enlarged,' he told her. 'Use them to cover wall space in your Mae Sot classroom. Reckon it'll prompt a question or two from your students, like "What's that you're chasing?" Or "Why isn't it chasing you?"'

Back at the house, Alice was waiting for them with sandwiches on the dining table. An hour later Mya arrived at New Norfolk Primary School where a grade four teacher, Elise, introduced her to the students and provided a computer link-up to a whiteboard and a map of Asia and Australia. After showing the class where Thailand, Mae Sot and Myanmar were, Mya got out her memory stick, loaded the presentation for Tasmanian students, and showed them her school, classroom and what Thai students wore and did inside and outside school. Fifteen minutes all up. After which the students asked five questions: Are there tigers where you live? Are there crocodiles? What happens if a student doesn't wear their school uniform? Are you on Facebook? Do you like Tasmania?

It was difficult holding back a smile as she answered each question with a serious look and voice.

The rest of the afternoon, while Alice was with another class, Mya observed Elise teach a science lesson on bottle flutes: blowing into bottles to make musical notes. Students worked in groups of six, each student in the group with a different size bottle containing a different amount of water. After practising, each group performed a minimum fifteen second concert for the rest of the class and their guest teacher from Myanmar. There was as much laughter as music. After the class voted for the winning group, Elise pointed out that blowing makes air in the bottle vibrate, producing a note. The bigger the space between the water and the top of the bottle, the lower the musical note. The following week there would be another concert after the class made elastic-band guitars. The objective: to demonstrate that thinner elastic bands vibrate more quickly, so make higher notes than thicker bands. Elise was only a little older than Mya, but very skilled and so full of awesome ideas. After school finished for the day, Elise offered her a stack of materials for teaching maths and sciences to grade four students.

Going 'home' with the materials and a bag of ingredients for making Mohinga, Mya felt relaxed, content, accepted; Nick's coolness towards her was no longer at the forefront of her thoughts. And rather than worrying about her first Rotary presentation that night, she was now looking forward to it. After all, New Norfolk wasn't big. The male audience would most likely consist of the fathers, uncles, grandfathers or neighbours of the students who had played their bottles for her and asked her if there were any tigers where she came from, or if she liked Tasmania. No, there weren't any tigers. Yes, she liked Tasmania.

* * *

Alice measured out and passed the Mohinga ingredients Mya requested, while Ella boiled up the rice. Nick set the table then – picking a moment when Mya was on her own – moved closer to her than any time since she'd arrived and asked if he could talk to her outside after they ate.

So many 'Mmmms' after the family took their first Mohinga bites. But Mya noticed Nick's beer disappearing fast, and Alice's wine glass emptying, that everyone but Ben was soon reaching for the water jug. 'Maybe I put a little too much chilli in it,' she suggested.

Alice wouldn't hear of it. 'Absolutely not. It's lovely.' She drained the rest of her water glass, poured herself another one.

Ella's next high-pitched 'Mmmm' sounded somewhere between 'Good' and 'I'm not sure.'

Ben: 'Yeah, terrific. Might have more for breakfast.'

Nick's phone buzzed. He hopped up and moved away from the table, reading the screen. He texted a reply quickly and put the phone away. 'Don't remember eating this with you at the Casa Mia,' he said, sitting back down.

Another Gretna first: the first time in front of his family he'd acknowledged they'd actually spent time together in Mae Sot. 'Burmese food was not on the menu there.'

Nick's 'Well it should have been' seemed the most supportive comment he'd made since she arrived. She glanced over at him and met his eyes.

Twenty minutes later they sat together on the veranda, legs dangling over the side, eyes probing the darkness. Nick said, 'I'm sorry for the way I've been with you since you got here.'

She didn't know what else to say but, 'No worries.'

'Besides John getting married, I should have mentioned something else to you earlier. Do you remember me telling you about a girl named Annie, who I was close with, who turned Goth, and that we broke up?'

Feeling what was coming, a sense of relief moved through her. Annie, not Lady Gaga, was the issue. 'Yes.'

'We're back together.'

She nodded, keeping her eyes on the darkness. 'I am pleased you told me.' Though it would have been easier if she'd known before arriving in Tasmania. 'I hope this time it works out better for you.' In truth, at this moment, she didn't care much if it did or not. She recalled his brother at the Casa Mia one night telling her about his renewed relationship with the nurse, Lina. Fortunately, she and John had not gone beyond being friends. For her, Nick had become more. Time in the river, mountains and a night in her room together more.

'Thing is, Annie...'

The front door opened and Ben came out, 'Gotta move if we're going to get to Rotary on time. You coming, Nick?'

'You want me to?' Nick asked Mya.

Not particularly. 'Up to you. But you have seen the school. You know all about it. My talk I think will bore you.'

'Right. I'll see you tomorrow then.'

* * *

It was called The Bush Inn. It was beside a main road and was large and had white paint peeling off in places and seemed very old compared to the buildings she had seen in Hobart.

They entered through a side door and immediately encountered men sitting on stools beside a wooden bar, all of them drinking glasses of beer. Just like in that movie *Red Dog*. Everyone looked around, one or two with dazed expressions on their faces. She wondered if these were the men she would be giving the presentation to, until the man behind the bar pointed to an adjoining room, saying, 'In there.'

They went through into a large room filled with better-dressed men. A speaker's lectern stood in the opposite front corner, a table with a computer and screen next to it. Closer to her, a huge fireplace with metre-long cuts of wood blazed away. Viewing the rest of the room, Mya saw a long table and chairs at the back and in the middle of the room five rows of plastic chairs, ten chairs to a row.

A man approached, smiling. He greeted Ben, and Ben introduced him as Peter Roberts, 'president of the Derwent Valley Rotary Club'. Peter said how much everyone appreciated her 'travelling across half the world to come along and speak' to them, and, as the members had just concluded their meeting, they could get started right away with the presentation. Peter helped her get set up while Ben went to the back and placed information sheets on the table. The thirty or forty men milling about at the back picked up their copies and began to sit down and read. Ben returned and sat in the chair closest to the lectern.

As president, Peter introduced Mya to the members, spoke a few welcoming words then took a seat. Mya – her heart thumping away – positioned herself at the lectern and turned on the speaker's lamp, nerves worming their way into her stomach.

The lights dimmed. The room hushed.

She heard Ben in the first row say, 'Alice gave me a lesson last night on how to operate a computer mouse.' On the edge of her light, she saw him looking up at her. 'I could probably use some follow-up practice if you'd like someone to change the slides for you.'

That made her smile, and her nerves eased. 'Okay. When I nod my head you can press the mouse. On the right side.'

'Right side, right.' He carried his chair to the front table, sat, put a hand over the mouse and readied himself.

She took a few deep breaths, nodded to Ben and they got started. 'The first room of the Hsa Thoo Lei Burmese Migrant School was built nineteen years ago by Burmese migrant labour.' Nod. 'Now the school has six classrooms, but they are overcrowded and we need to find money to buy more computers and build at least three more classrooms and a workshop. We receive no government assistance. The families of our students are very poor and can pay no more than what is a few cents a day. So we depend on donor support.' Nod. 'Our students not only study classroom subjects, but practical subjects too, like advanced cooking—' nod '—computers—' nod '—bicycle, scooter and motorbike mechanics—' nod '—carpentry and ...'

Only once did Ben, in his efforts to keep up with the presentation, press the mouse wrongly. And after Peter got the slide show back on course and the comments ('A bit more instruction needed, love, before he'll be helping you launch any satellites.') and laughter died down, she got to the end of the presentation without further interruption.

The lights went on. Peter stood, looking at his watch. He thanked her and said, 'We've got ten minutes for questions.'

A few hands went up. Questions about her translating work, about opportunities available for migrants after leaving school, about further teacher training, the restrictions placed on her and Burmese refugees by the Thai and Myanmar governments. One hand at the back remained in the air.

'Yes?' she asked, anxious to quit the stand.

A big, red-faced man without much hair stood and held up his information sheet. 'In the brief here, the section about you and what you did before you started teaching, there seems to be a year missing between when you were a porter and when you went into a nunnery.'

Her heart flipped, thudded. She thought hard as she reached down for Ben's information sheet and pretended to read it. 'Ah … yes … That was a time I worked in customer services for a … entertainment business. Well, I would like to thank everyone for—'

'What specifically did you do in the job?'

Silence surrounded her. All the preparation and getting here, and it seemed the one mistake she'd made was not reading – or even being aware of – the information sheet until she and Ben got there. The growing silence felt like an indictment. 'I worked as a bar-girl.'

'As a bar-girl. Ah. You mean the kind that escorts gents upstairs?'

'Oversight on my part, Chris,' Ben said, hopping up. 'Let me fill in what's missing from the sheet. Our Mya, still branded a fugitive in Myanmar, was sold a second time to human traffickers and smuggled into Mae Sot, Thailand. She was then sold to a bar owner there and kept in virtual bondage doing the hard yakka for prisoner wages during the year you were referring to. You see, Chris, Mya was told that her mother would be imprisoned if she didn't do as she was told.' He looked around at Mya. 'Is that right?'

She was more stunned that Ben knew about Lady Gaga than by the shiny-headed man's comments. 'Yes.'

The man, Chris, sat down.

'There's more to the story,' Ben said, talking to everyone now. 'But I reckon you get the gist. Human trafficking, mostly in girls and women, is a thriving business in this world of ours. An updated version of slavery, it could be argued. Happening everywhere it seems, though more in poor countries with their vulnerable people and systemic corruption.' He sighed, as though sensing he may have said too much. 'Anyway, don't mean to sound all preachy and all, but, well …' He looked at Mya again, saying to her softly, 'You might want to ask if there are any more questions.'

She did.

No other hands went up.

Ten minutes later, driving out of New Norfolk on the empty, end-of-the-galaxy road, Ben asked. 'You okay?'

She indicated she was.

'Want to talk?'

She was curious about who told him: Nick or John? But she'd had her fill of talk for the night. 'No.'

* * *

Next morning Mya again waited until the cars left before she got up, readied herself and went into the living area. No Ben. So she made herself some eggs, ate, cleaned up, put on her sweater and went out into the cold air and sat on the veranda hugging her knees for warmth under the over-hanging roof. Mist lay in sheets over the land and moisture dripped down in front of her. Complete silence before boots clomped on the boards behind her.

'Breakfast?' Ben asked.

She turned to see him with a bucket in one hand, an egg between forefinger and thumb in the other. He showed her the egg. 'Got a dozen of these.' Filthy rolled onto her back next to him, legs in the air exposing her belly for a rub, and Ben obliged.

Mya told him she'd already eaten. She sniffed, her cold nose starting to run.

'Tea then?'

'Thank you.' Mya picked up a ball by her feet and threw it. In seconds the ball was back at her feet, Filthy ready for her to toss it again. She did.

Ben came back out, passed over her tea and a tissue, and sat down next to her, sipping coffee. 'You okay? Might mention that it's a habit of mine to ask that question whenever I see a glum face on the property.'

'Yes, okay … or maybe a little not okay.'

'Because of last night or tonight?'

'Both.'

He watched her. 'I omitted to say last night what a fine presentation you gave. Polished and professional. Can't remember ever witnessing a better one at a Rotary meeting.'

'It seemed alright, until … I think it was a mistake for me to come here. I think someone else should be giving the talks. I think I should go home early.'

He didn't answer immediately, taking time to absorb everything she said. 'If that's what you want. I reckon the Rotary clubs will still approve the migrant school proposal. But for what it's worth, I think you should speak at Brighton tonight and see what happens. Besides, I reckon this computer mouse business is a bit like drinking coffee. You don't particularly enjoy it at first, but after a while you become addicted. I've been priming myself for an improved performance tonight.'

Token smile as she gazed out, staying quiet.

'Back in the Dinosaur Age I had a university lecturer who used to occasionally shake his head and say, "Some ignorance is invincible." Strange what you remember from the deep past. Heard that word "invincible" before?'

'No.'

'Means too strong to be changed or defeated. That Chris bloke who questioned you last night will never get a posting in the diplomatic service. About as subtle as a kick in the shins. And he's got a few clones in the group as well who are no great Messiahs. Sometimes, in frustration, I feel like saying to them, "Talk like you have a brain." But there is this about Chris and his clones. They have big hearts, take a big interest in Rotary, rarely miss meetings and work hard. For sure, their view of things is not necessarily my view, but when decision time rolls around, there's about as much chance of them voting down a project as a sheep driving the school bus. I'll bet the house they'll approve the migrant school proposal.'

She nodded to indicate she'd heard that.

They sipped their drinks.

He tossed the ball, once, twice. 'You know, everybody carries something in them they don't want others to know about.'

'Secrets you mean?'

'Yep … You good for one?'

She kept her eyes on him, unsure what he meant.

'I'll take that look to mean you are. What I'm going to tell you, no one in Australia knows about. Only a few American blokes I served with in the Vietnam War do, and they're living close to comet distance away from here, if they're still living.'

'Maybe I'm not the one to tell.'

'I'll take the chance you are. Ever heard the term "R and R"?

'No.'

'Stands for rest and recreation. Something of a misnomer for the leave American soldiers fighting in the Vietnam War got to fly to Bangkok and seek out that city's cultural pursuits. Heard of Patpong?'

'Yes.'

'Then I don't have to explain to you what it's known for. Certainly not cultural pursuits. All up I had three lots of R and R there. Needed it. Doubt I could've kept my brain from unravelling – what there was of it. Anyway, the bar's name was "The Tiger Claw". Phailin was my bar-girl and companion every day I was there. Means "sapphire", I believe.'

'It does.'

'She ended up going back to her village before I left Vietnam. Paid off her family's debts, got married, had children, I was told. Like us all, tried to find some nobility in life, I s'pose.' He stared a moment. 'A good lady. Made a living. Took care of me, others, her parents; later on her own family.' He downed the last of his coffee. 'Good to find a place where you feel you belong, have a family to share all the good land with, a life quietly lived … Anyway, enough of this old geezer talk.' He got up. 'I'm going another coffee. Tea's at the front of the drink shelf now. Interested in more?'

Her face brightened a little. She handed over her mug. 'Thank you.'

Minutes later, re-charged mugs in their hands, she said, 'Can I ask you one thing about tonight?'

'I like answering questions. Makes me feel important.'

'The section that was missing in last night's information sheets, could it be filled in with, "Mya was a bar-girl in Mae Sot for a year before escaping"?' She'd not mention who helped her escape or how far into Myanmar they got together.

'I'll see to it.'

'Oh, and … maybe one more thing?'

'Yes, rest assured I'll perform my mouse duties better tonight.'

'I know you will. But I want to ask how you knew about me being smuggled into Thailand and having to work as a bar-girl.'

'Alice mentioned it.'

Another surprise. And the answer begged another question, before Ben answered it. 'I believe you've met John's wife, Lina. You might know she worked as an AusAid nurse in Mae Sot.'

'Yes.'

'Got the gift of the gab. A fine talker. Thing is, she really admires what you did in escaping back into Myanmar, and how you battled on and eventually returned to the area as a teacher. "Plucky" was the word she used, apparently, when she was talking about you. Know the word?'

'No.'

'It means spirited.'

'Like *khwan* in Thai.'

'Right … Anyway, we need to confirm your immediate future: Ouse District School this afternoon, Brighton Hotel tonight, yes?'

She gave a nod.

'Good.' He looked into the distance. 'Like living under a rock here; remote part of a little island at the end of the world … Love it.' He turned. 'So, we've got a couple of hours for tractor work and maybe some sheep relocation. Up for it?'

41

Once the presentation was ready to go and the men seated – having had more time than they needed to read their information sheets – Mya thanked the Brighton Rotary Club for inviting her to speak and, scanning the faces in front of her, asked if anyone had any questions before she got started. Heads turned, including Ben's, but no hands went up. So Mya got on with her talk.

Only one hand was raised after she finished and again asked for questions. She pointed and a thin-faced man with long white hair stood up holding a small pad. 'Reckon what you said and showed us tonight was what we needed to know about. Just wanted to say I saw a program the other night about some mainland professor bloke – got his name here cuz I knew you was comin' – name of Des Ball. Military expert, apparently, who's been advising rebels in the—' he read from the pad '—Karen National Liberation Army in their war against government forces. A one-sided affair it seems, with the Burmese army using advanced weapons and helicopter gunships bought to attack Karen villages. I'm amazed there're any o' those Karen people left in Myanmar. Can you tell us a bit more about the refugees who've been made homeless by the war? I mean, whatta they do for the rest of their lives?'

A question she had no problems with. 'The first thing I found out about Karen refugees is they have nothing. Their villages that connected them to a future, to just belonging, are gone. They will never again be who they were before they had to escape Myanmar. The second thing I have found out is, given help, refugees can adjust, can find a life to go on with. For example, I now have an adopted brother.' She told them the story of Raju, a Karen orphan, relocated and assisted by overseas aid to go to school, and how he was adopted by her family. That he was studying to become an English-speaking monk and, with his interest in practical things, would probably end up becoming a mechanic or builder later on.

When Mya reached down for her water glass, Ben gave the man the thumbs up. Mya wondered if the question had been pre-arranged.

Back in the ute and heading for home, Ben asked, 'So, what's the verdict? Leaving us early, or staying around a while longer?'

'We did alright back there, didn't we?'

'Uh huh.'

Minutes after arriving back home, Nick asked Mya outside again. They sat on the veranda, Mya warming her hands between her thighs waiting for him to talk. Finally, without turning, he said, 'I didn't quite finish what I was going to say to you about Annie last night. Thing is, she's got leukaemia. It's cancer of the blood. She had it before when she was a child. So it's treatable like before with chemotherapy: five sessions of it.' Now he looked at her. 'She's had three sessions already and wears a red beanie on her head now instead of hair. After work most nights I go to her place in New Norfolk ... When I was in Hpa-an and ... we were together, I just didn't think Annie and I—'

'Please,' she interrupted. 'Do not explain. I understand. She is sick. You feel strong affection for her. So you must be with her. It is right you should be.' She felt regret, for sure, but at least the mystery of his behaviour was solved. Her time in Tasmania would be easier, well, at least here at his family's house anyway. Her presence kept small, she was just a short-term visitor collecting teaching materials and ideas and speaking to old men about supporting her school. Simple. Uncomplicated. Nothing else to concern herself with.

The front door opened and Ella called out, 'Come in, come in! John and Lina are Skyping!'

For Mya, the timing could not have been better.

* * *

Their two faces on the screen, side-by-side, looking all big-eyed and eager.

'Yes!' John called out as Alice sat Mya in front of the computer. 'Confirmation she's survived the trip to Aussie, Tassie, Gretna. Home of footy and cricket. Land of the fair go, mates, punters, diggers and battlers; and one Texan-born dad, his ravishing wife and brilliant kids too. Food and accommodation passable, Mya? Transport adequate? Dad hasn't put you to work in the old bloke's paddock, has he? And what about the fossils-Rotarian? Using a cattle prod to keep them awake to hear what you've got to say, I bet.' He paused, but not long enough for her to say anything. 'And the school tour circuit? How's it going? Got a planeload of teaching materials by now, yes? And Mum's probably got you cooking, and—'

'When do I answer?' Mya interjected.

John laughed. 'Now.'

'Yes to everything, except maybe the cattle thing. And you need to add "awesome" to food and accommodation and transport.'

'As well as to your smile. Which I see the cold hasn't been able to chill … Anyway, good to hear things are as they should be.'

'How's Annie getting along, Nick?' Lina asked.

Standing behind Mya, Nick told Lina what he had told Mya outside, then added, 'I might get her out this weekend, take her somewhere for the day.'

'Sounds promising.'

'Yeah. Maybe Lake King William, take the double kayak and hopefully Mya too.'

John jumped in. 'So Ella, got your scholarship to go to uni yet?'

'No. But Dad said he'd build a couple of houses to earn the money for me to go.'

'When did I say that?'

Ella sighed and shook her head. 'The worry of course is his memory.' She couldn't hide a grin that Mya, worried for an instant, was thankful for.

'Still failing him, is it?'

'Especially when talk turns to money.'

'Sad. You reckon he can still remember a song or two?'

'A six-pack says I can,' Ben piped up.

'You've imported some proven talent there. But okay, a six-pack it is.' John left the screen for a moment then returned with a guitar.

Ella ran down the hallway and also fetched a guitar, which she handed to Ben, and small bundles of lyrics which she handed to everyone else. 'I better warn you,' Ella said to Mya. 'Coming up is a family performance of pre-us dinosaur songs that Dad and John just have to bet on. They alternate singing lines without the words in front of them. First one to stop or make a mistake before the song ends is the loser. We're the chorus, and our lyrics are marked in red. Don't worry. I'll guide you.'

'Right, great pretender. Your first choice and first line,' Ben said.

'One that reminds me of a place I never want to go back to – Dylan's "Knockin' on Heaven's Door ..."'

Lina: 'Were cars even invented when that was around?'

Alice: 'Barely ... Alright my team, deep breath. Ready your diaphragms. A-one, a-two, go.'

The two guitars picked up the melody, John sang in a baritone, and Ben followed in a growling bass, like an accelerating truck, and they alternated lines until Ella pointed at the chorus and said into Mya's ear, 'Now, four times in a row.'

First round of the chorus over, Mya glanced at the computer screen and the close faces either side of her, thinking, except for Alice, each had a heaven's door story to tell: from a protest march, fire, Vietnam War, snakebite, refugee camp, minefield and the Snake Skin. And here they all were singing together, and the unease she'd felt outside with Nick had vanished, replaced by a warmth in her belly that spread to her skin, and from her head to her toes.

Ella: 'Here, Mya. Here. Here.'

'Sorry.' They'd started a new song, Ella's sweet alto voice prominent, about a lonely man seeking company to help him make it through the night.

Four more songs followed, outbreaks of laughter and clapping between them, and still not one lapse from Ben or John.

'You been cutting classes and practising,' Ben said to John.

'So easy are these lyrics, Dad, I could be performing open-heart surgery and not miss a syllable.'

Ben: 'Not my open-heart surgery. Right, double the bet then.'

John: 'And re-double.'

Ben: 'Done. Crown Lager. A carton. Presented by the grovelling loser when next you're down here. Up for that?'

John yawned vocally. 'Does a slab get any easier to come by?'

'Not for me. What's your pick?' Ben said.

'Your choice.'

A minute passed and still they couldn't agree on who should choose.

'There's a song Nick taught me once,' Mya said quietly, not convinced it was her place to say anything. She sought Nick's help. 'Remember it?'

'Yeah I do. Rosanne Cash.'

'Modern era,' Lina interjected. 'Inside the forty-year rule. Not allowed.'

Alice looked questioningly at Mya. '"Take My Body"?'

Mya: 'Yes.'

Alice: 'How well do you know it?'

Mya: 'I bought an MP3 player and the song in Mae Sot. I used to sing it in my room there. I still do sometimes.'

Alice: 'Me too. Poetry in song. One of my all-time favourites.' She turned to Ella. 'You got the lyrics there?'

Ella found and passed them to her mother, Nick and Mya.

Alice: 'Right, listen up. New teams, new competition. All previous bets are off. The wager is now counter meals for the winners up at the hotel. Preferably this Sunday, Mother's Day, as I'm sure you're aware, John.'

John: 'Am I?'

Alice: 'You are. Now, you lose, don't worry about sending a card or flowers. Just put the money in my Mother's Day account. Lina, could you be judge?'

Lina: 'Certainly.'

Alice: 'Girls to go first, just to show the remaining no-hopers how important it is to feel what you sing. Ready? A-one, a-two.' Guitars, melody and first Alice, Ella, and Mya, and then Ben, John and Nick sang about the girl who viewed her body as an open door, that she didn't much need anymore.

Nine minutes later the judge consulted with herself for far longer than she needed to before declaring Alice, Mya and Ella the winners.

Hooting and applause from the winners, accusations of dirty tactics from their opposition before Ben called out, 'Finale, yes?'

John: 'Always. Ella, better chorus coach the newbie again.'

'Done.'

Mya got a script and Ella pointed to their lines. Seconds later Ben and John played and sang, while Alice's arm from one side, Ella's from the other, went around Mya's waist, and they swayed together to the Hunters and Collectors' 'Throw Your Arms Around Me'.

Ella: 'Now.' And the chorus took over.

And it seemed to Mya the song would never end, which was fine by her, with first John then Ben shouting between lyrics, 'Again the chorus!'

Finally, after ten minutes, the song ended in more applause and bows from everyone, as though they were the main act and had sung their final encore at a major music event.

'What'll we do when we're all rich and famous?' John shouted, looking exhilarated.

'Shear and crotch sheep, read, take in the lay of the land,' Ben answered. 'Leaving time for Dylan, Cash and Van Morrison of course.'

John shook his head. 'Modern capitalism is lost on you!'

Mya knew Burmese music, and of course that at the Snake Skin, but never music of this fun, house-filling sort: the guitars, singing, the laughter and banter.

The Skype call ended in more shouts and waves and praise for Gretna's new singing recruit. And Nick said quietly to Mya, 'So will you come with us on the weekend?'

An hour earlier she would have thought of an excuse not to. Now she felt – what? A sense of belonging, for sure. A willingness – no, more than that – a responsibility to play her part of Burmese visitor and supportive family friend. Still, if she was going to spend a day with Nick and Annie, there was one thing she felt she had to know. She asked the question.

His eyes – looking a little desperate – met hers. 'That was special. Not to be shared with anyone else.'

Before going to bed that night, Mya used the family computer to check for emails. None there. So she wrote an email addressed to both her father and principal, saying that the meetings and school visits were going well. That she had a 'plane load' of teaching materials to bring home. That she had been treated like royalty by her host family, but nonetheless was looking forward to returning home in another five days. She sent the email. Then, feeling an urge to say something more than just the expected to her principal, something personal, she wrote a second email just to her:

> Nick, the boy who I got to know well in Mae Sot and whose family I am staying with here, has a girlfriend who is being treated for cancer. He wants me to meet her tomorrow and go with them to a lake not far away. So I will. But I have this feeling now that I don't want to be attracted to a male ever again, that I don't want to feel anything more for them than just everyday affection. Have you ever felt that way?

An email was waiting for her the next morning:

> I was pleased to hear how well things are going there, at least with your presentations and school visits. I'll admit to having advance knowledge about your presentations. I'll save the details about that until you arrive in Bangkok, where I plan to meet you and help transport all those materials back. But I will quickly mention I've been contacted by the Rotary organisation and the news is very positive.
>
> As to your 2nd email and your wish never to be attracted to a male ever again, I feel that regularly after working all day, going home and seeing the house in a mess and my husband sharing jokes and drinks with the family next door. If

it weren't for motherhood ... Anyway, while on the topic, I should mention that a Karen Burmese – a male one – came into the school asking for you a couple of days ago. I told him where you were, what you were doing. His name is Phoe Ni – hopefully he is familiar to you. A handsome young man in a rugged, long-hair way. And by the way he conducted himself, an excellent candidate for everyday affection. At least in my view. See you in Bangkok on Wednesday.

Never, never any more than that, she whispered to herself; though it was good to hear Phoe Ni was back in Mae Sot. She looked forward to hearing about his latest backpack medic experiences, or at least those that didn't involve maggot therapy.

42

School visits and talks continued, the Rotary venues getting closer and closer to Hobart. Procedures stayed the same. Information sheets were distributed, branch presidents welcomed her and after her talk thanked her. Members applauded and questions were asked – though none about her Snake Skin past – before Ben took her home.

On the Saturday Alice and Ella took her into Hobart. They drove to the top of Mount Wellington, donned heavy coats and beanies, and walked to a freezing viewing platform and looked out over southern Tasmania. Alice treated the occasion as a photo-shoot for International Teacher Exchange Magazine, if there was such a thing.

Back down in the city, they parked in a tower full of cars, took an elevator down and walked past buskers and people wearing head-phones, carrying shopping bags, chatting or finger-tapping phones or tablets. They slowed and took in window displays, entered a huge, brightly-lit store, went up and down escalators eyeing off racks of clothing and handbags, navigated aisles of strong-smelling perfumes. In a section set aside for free make-up samples, Alice encouraged Ella to get 'a make-up makeover', and Ella said she would only if Mya did too. So the two sat together getting gloss on their eyelids, mascara brushed through lashes, blusher (rather than lightning bolts) on their cheeks, lipstick thick on lips. When Ella looked in a mirror held up by the sales assistant, she put on a glam pose and laughed. And Mya laughed too, but only a little, fearing being impolite. Looking both amused and embarrassed, Alice took quick phone snaps of the girls grinning cheek-to-cheek, before buying tubes of lipstick 'for my teaching friends' and leading the way back out.

Next stop Franklin Square to rid themselves of all the colour and polish.

That done, they continued on to the docks and the Salamanca outdoor market, wandering between stalls, sipping on smoothies, talking and people-watching.

As happy and relaxed as she had been on the Saturday, by Sunday morning Mya's feelings had changed. She, the visitor from another world, was about to meet the cancer-suffering girlfriend of a boy she had taken into her heart, slept with, had imagined sleeping with again in Tasmania, and whose family had installed her as one of their own.

Nick had stayed the night at Annie's family's place and in the morning, when they arrived, everyone went out to welcome them – Mya and Ben hanging back a little. After greetings and hugs, Annie – her face a thin wedge, gold studs either side of her small pinkish nose, blue eyes big as birds' eggs, red beanie a stark contrast to her pale skin – approached Mya, smiling warmly. 'Finally I'm meeting you.'

'Yes.' Feeling every bit as awkward as she had at the airport that first day, Mya extended her hand and Annie took it, moved close and kissed her cheek.

'I'm just going for the kayak,' Nick called out.

Ben: 'I'll give you a hand.'

Alice put a hand to the backs of Mya and Annie and moved them along towards the house, saying, 'I'll get the kettle on and you two can advise me on what to fill the picnic basket with.'

An hour later they were off for Lake King William and the high country, Annie in the middle handling CD responsibilities, the three of them accompanying the Hunters and Collectors in voices loud enough to wake up any roadside residents trying to sleep in. Then, as they began to climb and wind, Annie went still and quiet.

'Let me know, okay?' Nick said to her.

And the Hunters and Collectors sang on alone.

Grazing land gave way to towering, grey-trunked eucalypts.

Occasional log trucks and cars sped downhill on the other side.

'Okay?' Nick asked.

Annie nodded tightly, keeping her eyes on the road. Minutes later her face hardened; she took a series of long breaths – the cue for Nick to pull over and stop. No sooner had Mya let her out than Annie bent, grabbed her knees and vomited.

A log truck rumbled past, horn blaring.

While Mya rubbed Annie's back, Nick called out, 'Right. We'll turn around, head back to Meadowbank.'

'No, please.' Annie straightened. 'I want to go on. I'll be right in a minute.' She walked up the road, placed a tablet in her mouth, drank from her water bottle and returned.

They drove on, reaching the plateau and turning left onto a dirt road – Annie looking brighter. The Hunters and Collectors got a reboot, and Nick told stories about his brother riding into Lake King William, camping and fishing, then 'training to take on Cadel Evans by riding at Tour de France speed back down to Ouse'.

Half an hour later they arrived at the lake: an expanse of still waters covered in flakes of shimmering sunlight. To Mya it looked like an inland sea: huge, a seemingly endless shoreline, empty of people and boats and man-made structures. Far across the water, she could just make out tree-covered hills. They put on sweaters and unloaded the folding chairs, table and picnic basket, and stacked the wood and kindling beside a campfire site only metres from the water. The kayak came off the roof racks, the girls regarding it cautiously, Nick regarding the girls' reactions.

'You'll notice the kayak seats two,' he said, holding up a pair of rubber shoes. 'So who's the privileged first?'

Mya was quick to say, 'Not me.'

Annie gave him a grudging look, and his hands went up as though surrendering. 'If you want to, only if you want to,' he said. 'Occupying a seat going home doesn't depend on occupying one in the kayak.'

Annie bent over again – this time to roll up her trouser legs and take off her sandshoes. 'But not for long, okay?'

'You tell me when to turn back.'

Out they went, Nick paddling from the front, Annie still as stone in the back, Mya sitting on the shoreline in the retreat-like silence watching them.

Twenty minutes maybe before they arrived back, Nick jumping out to help Annie stand up and walk over rocks to the shoreline.

'Your turn,' Nick said to Mya.

It wasn't that she didn't want to go out. In different circumstances she wouldn't have hesitated. It was more to do with maintaining distance, of not matching Annie's closeness or time spent alone with Nick. It was their day, not hers. Besides, Nick looked full of energy, eager for a second, much longer tour. 'Will I still have my seat going home if I do not go?'

'Yeah, well … Not much competition around here for it, is there?' He didn't look disappointed though.

Nick paddled back out alone and the girls prepared the food – sandwiches, apples, muesli bars, cauliflower soup in three small thermoses, like those Mya had seen in the primary schools she'd visited. They glanced up occasionally to locate Nick going from small to tiny out on the lake. It was Annie who set the fire, cross-stacking the kindling over the wadded newspaper, the bigger bits on top. 'You do that well,' Mya commented.

'I've had a good teacher. Nick and I have been out here before. All seasons and never long without a fire.' She struck a match, lit the newspaper. They moved their chairs closer and sat to watch the fire catch and grow, listening to it spit and crackle. Annie looked out at Nick then turned to Mya, a half-smile under suddenly tired eyes. 'After I ditched Goth I let my hair grow. It got nearly as long as yours, halfway down my back.'

'How did you wear it?'

'Not in a braid. Never had the patience. Mostly, other than brushing, I did nothing with it. Just let it flow, or if it got in the way I used a hair band … Not many girls our age can say they've spent part of their youth bald.'

'No.'

'A novice nun, a cancer sufferer. Why else would you not have hair?'

'It'll grow back quickly once you finish treatment.'

Annie added wood to the fire then sat back down and looked out at Nick starting to grow again in the distance. 'I love it here on days like this ... My favourite spot now ... Can I tell you something in secret?' she asked.

Surprised, Mya didn't answer straight away. Secrets told to a stranger; the second time in three days. Secrets, along with her teaching materials and talks given to mostly silent old men, the legacy of her time in Tasmania it seemed. 'Yes, of course.'

'It's a serious something, so you might not want to hear it. But ... it's probably better that you do.'

Mya had a tiny suspicion, but buried it in the hope she was wrong.

43

MYAWADI.

Nine months later Mya got an email from Ella saying that Annie had died. Her funeral would be in New Norfolk in four days. It had only been a few weeks earlier that Annie had admitted to Nick she had lied to him about her condition: it wasn't a treatable leukaemia she was suffering from, but bone cancer that had spread to other parts of her body. Her parents knew, but no one else did until the truth became obvious.

Mya wrote back to Ella and Nick thanking them for telling her, saying how sorry she was, that though she'd only spent a weekend in Annie's company at the lake, at their home and the nearby hotel, she had liked her very much and got to feel very close to her. She would go to the pagoda in Myawadi and light a candle and say a prayer for her.

Mya went on to write that she hoped they could keep in contact, maybe even meet up again sometime, in Mae Sot, in Gretna, or somewhere in between.

Just why she felt so close to Annie, and the fact that her life had undergone a big change since she'd returned from Tasmania, Mya did not mention. The time was not right, though it might be one day.

Epilogue

A FEW YEARS LATER.

Saturday morning and Mya and Raju decided to escape the house. They walked down the road, the neighbourhood abuzz with activity, and stopped in at Uncle Zarni's workshop, strewn with gears and panels and engine parts, the smell of grease and motor oil in the air. Mya's husband and Uncle Zarni were talking while Nyan worked on the husband's scooter.

Mya told them she and Raju were going to the Moei River.

Phoe Ni turned from his conversation with her uncle. 'A running river, I've been told, is best for daydreams.'

'Time-proven,' Mya answered, without reminding him that she was the one who told him that. He knew.

As she and Raju started to leave, Phoe Ni said, 'Mother Suu has won.'

'The election, yes, I know, I know.'

In minutes they arrived. Mya sat on her favoured log and Raju, newly-shaven, sat beside her – the nicks in his skull reminding her of that day in Sule Pagoda when her own head was first shaved. Growing restless after a while, Raju hopped up and went down to the river's edge.

Soon her father passed, smiling over at her. He joined Raju and they talked before Raju spotted smugglers gathering further down-river. Interested, he moved towards them, leaving Nyan to ponder the river, as was his habit. Did he still see his missing years in all that water, flowing by yet always there? Years, Mya was convinced now, he wouldn't be sharing with anyone, ever. But that was okay. There was a part of her past she wouldn't be sharing either. Besides, in a few weeks' time there would be no shortage of family sharing.

She listened to the smugglers laughing and chatting to Raju and to a woman pounding laundry on river stones. And it struck her how rarely she'd seen a river smuggler looking tense or angry with life. Had they not been carrying something other than contraband, they could well have passed for river picnickers or workers on their way to a Thai plantation.

The inner-tube and its paddlers came and soon the smugglers were across the river and into Thailand doing what they did most every day of the year. If she were still here in an hour or two, she'd see and hear them again, returning with empty baskets on their backs.

She felt this place, those people, that river now as though absorbed in her bones.

If for some unexpected reason the migrant school ever closed and translation work dried up, she thought she would make an excellent smuggler. Little for her to learn considering how much border guard and smuggler contact she'd had, how much smuggling she'd witnessed first-hand.

'From Lady Gaga
To lady smuggler ...'

A good start for a poem, she thought. Necessarily a long one.

From behind came the clacking of sandals on rocks. Seconds later Phoe Ni kissed the top of her head and came around and knelt beside her, pressing an ear to her belly and listening intently. She expected him to say 'Like you swallowed a barrel' or 'Ripe to bursting, can't be long to go', as he often did lately when getting off his knees. With her, with other pregnant women she presumed, in his role as medic for nearby villages. Instead, with the back of his hand he stroked her cheek, his face growing a smile. 'I can hear the monkey in there.'

'You hear it, I feel it.'

'Happy here?'

Her eyes stayed on him. Still grease under his fingernails, bits of it coating his knuckles. Probably some on her cheek now as well. She told him that yes, she was happy, though she probably stretched the truth a little giving him what he wanted to hear. As she remembered Annie doing with Nick that time.

Certainly she was never unhappy here. Not for a moment. What was the English word she wanted? Ah, yes – 'equanimity'. Calm, contentment, an evenness of spirit and mind. Far beyond the workings of a Lady Gaga. But what she had strived for as Nan Pau – as herself.

Phoe Ni joined her father and the returning Raju by the river. The males in her life talked, most likely about the election or motor scooters, before her father drifted upriver for some more private time and Phoe Ni started back towards her.

She breathed in deeply, brushed strands of breeze-blown hair from her face. Not the place she'd planned to spend the rest of her life. And with the exception of her father, not the people she'd planned to spend her life with. But as she monitored the three of them – like she would her students – she thought how lucky she was. She could never want for more than this, ordinary things: good work, family, motherhood. A counter-thought asked: even with sore nipples, leaking breasts, middle of the night feedings and the washing out of nappies? Even when, in a couple of months, she'd have to balance teaching and translating responsibilities with raising her baby?

She placed her hands on her belly, one over the other. No worries, she thought. She'd overcome far greater challenges.

Acknowledgements

I'm indebted to Union Aid Abroad-APHEDA in Sydney, Australia, and to the staff at the Mae Tao Medical Clinic, the Karen News Mobile Media Team, the Backpack Medics' Office, the Social Action for Women Association (SAW) and the Association of Burmese Political Prisoners headquarters in Mae Sot, Thailand.

As Arthur Plotnik once said, 'You write to communicate to the hearts and minds of others what's burning inside, and we edit to let the fire show through the smoke.' Thank you, Linda Nix, for clearing away the smoke.

www.ingramcontent.com/pod-product-compliance
Lightning Source LLC
Chambersburg PA
CBHW050124030726
47505CB00007B/2026

* 9 7 8 1 9 2 2 1 9 8 2 8 0 *